Also by Kim Redford

Smokin' Hot Cowboys
A Cowboy Firefighter for Christmas
Blazing Hot Cowboy
A Very Cowboy Christmas
Hot for a Cowboy
Cowboy Firefighter Christmas Kiss

COWBOY FIREFIGHTER Heat

KIM REDFORD

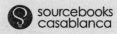

sourcebooks casablanca

Published by Sourcebooks Casablanca, an imprint of Sourcebooks
P.O. Box 4410, Naperville, Illinois 60567-4410
(630) 961-3900
sourcebooks.com

Printed and bound in the United States of America.
OPM 10 9 8 7 6 5 4 3 2 1

Chapter 1

FERN BRYANT ADJUSTED THE STRAPS OF HER BIG BLACK battered guitar case on her shoulders until it hung comfortably down her back. She grabbed the handle of her carryall and lifted it out of the rental car she'd picked up at the Dallas/Fort Worth airport.

She was back in pickup country—Wildcat Bluff County—along about midnight. She caught the sweet scent of roses in the air and saw a sliver of silver moon in the dark sky. It was a night obviously made for lovers. In her mind, she suddenly saw a tall cowboy stepping down from the cab of his truck. She could almost hear the click of his boot heels as he walked toward her, wanting what only she could give him. She quickly snapped the car door shut, dismissing the thought of that particular singing cowboy firefighter.

Tranquility reigned in Wildcat Hall Park, the famous North Texas historic dance hall and cowboy cabins, but not inside her. As co-owner of the Park with her sister, Ivy, she was glad to see it looked much like she'd left it months ago.

She'd met Bill and Ida Murphy on a genealogical site online. Once they'd figured out they were long-lost cousins, they'd shared their hopes and dreams. The Murphys had wanted to sell Wildcat Hall Park to a relative so they could retire and tour the West. She'd wanted to put down roots, build the honky-tonk's reputation, and nurture other musicians. It hadn't taken them long to come to an agreement.

She glanced around as she walked toward her cabin. Solar night-activated lights lined the path, while carriage lamps on poles under live oaks softly illuminated the area. Bill and Ida had built and decorated four rental cabins as well as a larger one that had been their home. They'd used recycled materials from deconstructed old houses and barns, as well as items from junk stores and reclaimed materials. The cabins had rusty corrugated tin for roofs, weathered barn wood for siding, and natural stone for entry stairs leading up to porches. All the windows and doors were repurposed, so they were different shapes, sizes, and colors.

Ivy had recently moved out of the big cabin to be with her fiancé, Slade, on Steele Trap Ranch II. That meant Fern could move right back into the place she'd lived before signing a contract to entertain on cruise ships. Gig complete, she was home, but she hadn't alerted anybody ahead of time. She wanted at least one night to unpack and unwind before...well, before she had to face the music of running out on her obligations and dumping the Park in her sister's lap, although that had turned out well in the end when true love came calling.

Home sweet home. The big cabin squatted on redbrick posts with a covered porch and crawl space underneath. A motion-sensor light came on over the crimson front door as she started up the stairs. The light was new. Ivy must have had it installed for security, which wasn't a bad idea. She felt a smile tug at the corners of her mouth when she saw two wooden rockers—one painted yellow and the other green. She'd spent many a happy hour in those chairs while she strummed her guitar.

Oddly enough, firefighter gear, as in a yellow reflective

vest, insulated gloves, and a black-and-yellow fire helmet, had been left in the seat of the green rocker. Had there been fire inside or outside the cabin? She glanced around, but she didn't smell smoke or see char damage. Maybe one of the volunteer cowboy firefighters of Wildcat Bluff Fire-Rescue had been there to inspect the buildings, but she couldn't imagine why any of them would leave behind equipment. Still, there was no way to know, so she'd just leave the gear alone in case somebody returned for it. In the morning, she'd check with the fire department and solve the mystery.

She set down her carryall, fished around in her purse, and came up with her house key dangling on a Wildcat Hall promotional steel ring. She cocked her head to one side as she listened to the Park. She was all about sound because she never knew when some little click or clack or bird trill might inspire her.

She heard rustles in the grass and wondered if one of the polydactyl cats that lived in the Park was hunting in the dark, but it could just as easily have been a raccoon, armadillo, or possum out foraging for food. She'd missed the cats, so she looked forward to seeing them now that she was back.

She took a deep breath as she slipped her key into the lock, then turned the knob, pushed open the door, and stepped inside. A night-light over the range cast soft glow over the warm patina of old wood from floor to wall to ceiling. Lemon yellow and sage green were the dominant colors used to brighten the open-floor-plan living room, dining room, and kitchen. Ceiling fans with wooden paddles lazily stirred the air scented by lavender and sage from dried bundles in a wicker basket on the kitchen counter. A touch of cowboy chic had been added here and there, like the longhorns with center-wrapped leather attached to the ceiling fan and vintage throw pillows in roping and riding cowboy designs accenting the leather sofa and armchair. A lamp in the shape of a cow with a green shade looked whimsical on a small table. A closed door led into a bedroom with a bath.

She walked over to the lamp, switched on the light, glanced around the room, and saw another oddity. A green mug had been left out on the yellow ceramic tile of the kitchen counter. The slight scent of coffee hung in the air. Maybe the place hadn't had a proper cleaning since Ivy moved out, or maybe a cowboy firefighter had spent a night here. Still, they didn't normally rent out this cabin, and the Settelmeyer family that managed every little bit of the Park was relentless in keeping everything in pristine shape. She didn't know what she'd have done without them when she'd first moved there, because they basically ran the place. But she wouldn't bother them with something like the firefighter gear or a single mug. She'd just wash, dry, and put up the mug after she'd had a chance to catch her breath.

She shrugged the guitar case off her back and set it in the seat of the chair. Her fingers itched to pluck a few strings, but it'd have to wait until tomorrow. She suddenly felt overwhelmingly tired. She'd dreamed of the Park, dreamed of relaxing into the comfort of familiarity. She'd loved being on the road, going places, seeing unusual things, meeting new people. Yet at this moment, she wanted nothing more than to get out of her clothes and get in bed in her own home. Even if the mattress was saggy and lumpy, needing replacement, it'd still feel good.

She set her carryall on a sofa cushion, zipped it open, and

pulled out an oversize crimson T-shirt emblazoned with an image of Wildcat Hall—almost as good as a teddy bear for comfort. She shucked off her sneakers, jeans, top, and underwear. She raised her arms straight over her head and gave her back a good stretch. She slipped on the T-shirt that fell to midthigh. For once, she didn't care about face, teeth, or anything resembling her usual nightly routine. She just wanted to be in her very own bed.

She turned off the lamp, found her way to the bedroom door by the light above the range like she used to do, and eased open the door. In such a small room, she knew just where the bed was, so she didn't need to bother with the lamp on the nightstand. She took a few steps forward, but she bumped into the mattress quicker than expected. That was odd. Maybe she was overly tired or she'd just forgotten the exact location in the months she'd been away. She started to toss back the comforter, but she touched sheets instead. She couldn't imagine the Settelmeyers leaving the bed unmade, too. Still, for the moment, she didn't really care.

Yawning, she lay down, slipped under the covers, and breathed a sigh of relief. And then she realized the mattress didn't feel the same. No lumps. Had Ivy replaced it? That'd be wonderful. She snuggled a little deeper. And she realized something else. Heat. The bed was way too warm. In fact, if she wasn't mistaken, and surely she was, there was a...

"About time you came home," a man said in a deep, melodic tone from the far side of the bed.

She screamed in shock, even as she recognized the unforgettable voice she'd tried so hard to forget. She leaped out of bed and switched on the nightstand lamp. "Craig Thorne! What are you doing in my bed?"

"I could ask the same of you." He sat up, the covers slowly, suggestively sliding down to his lap to reveal the chiseled planes of his bronzed, muscular chest. A slight smile tugged at the corners of his full lips, and his hazel eyes gleamed more jade than amber.

Now she understood why she'd found firefighter gear and a dirty mug. He was a cowboy firefighter...and he drank coffee. But what was he doing here? She sucked in her breath, ready to put him in his place, but instead she inhaled the scent of citrus and sage as it swirled outward from the heat of his body. That sight and scent sent her spiraling back in time to a hot and hungry place.

She traced him with her gaze but wished she could use her hands. She'd run her fingers through his thick chestnut hair, with just a touch of wave, that brushed his ridiculously broad shoulders. When she started to follow the dark line of hair down his bronze chest, she snapped her gaze back to his face. And those too-knowing eyes had turned too dark as they roamed her in return.

"How are you?" he said in a raspy voice.

"Fine. And you?"

"Better now."

She couldn't help but smile. He always knew exactly what to say, whether it was on stage or off.

"Are you here to stay?" he asked.

"I finished the gigs."

"Good ones?" He cocked his head to one side as if contemplating how it'd been for her.

"What's not to like about cruise ships?"

"Bet we've got better gigs at Wildcat Hall," he said.

"Yeah." She needed to get control of the situation, but

she was so distracted by the hot cowboy in her bed that she wasn't thinking straight. Still, it was Craig, and she couldn't go there again. He would try to corral her, like he'd attempted to do before she'd left for her dream job when he'd wanted her to stay. He'd offered marriage and babies, but there was plenty of time for a family later. She'd always wanted a gig on the high seas, and it'd been a once in a lifetime job. He hadn't understood. He'd made it an ultimatum—him or work. She wouldn't be fenced in, not when her sister could step in and run the Park for her. Besides, she'd always been a rolling stone.

"When are you leaving again?"

"I'm not."

He shook his head, scolding her with his gaze.

"I'm back. And I'm taking control of Wildcat Hall."

"Control, huh?" He gave her a little smile and cocked his head to one side as he contemplated her.

"Ivy is ready to get on with her life. Me, too." She didn't much like his smile. It looked cagey.

"Slade's a lucky guy."

"I'm happy for them." She needed to get their conversation back on track, so she could get him out of her bedroom. "Look, you're popular at the Hall. I still want you to play. It's just…there is no *us* anymore."

"You made that pretty clear when you left."

She nodded, feeling relieved he was agreeing with her. "I don't want to be rude, but I'd be more comfortable if you went home. I'm not even sure why you're here in the first place."

He leaned toward her, still with that smile on his face.

She froze in place, getting an uneasy feeling that life wasn't going to be quite as simple as she'd imagined when she was on the high seas.

"This is my home now."

"Ivy rented the cabin to you?"

"Not quite."

"What do you mean?" She shivered, suddenly chilled to the bone. She clasped her arms around her middle for warmth and comfort.

"I'm willing to share the bed with you. After all, it's only right."

She was more confused by the moment. "I appreciate the offer, but—"

"Fifty-one percent."

She felt color drain from her face. "You don't mean... Surely, you can't mean... my sister wouldn't do that to me."

"Ivy never had the same interest in the honky-tonk as you. Or me. It's lifeblood to us. And she has a new life with Slade on his ranch."

"Are you telling me straight out that Ivy sold you her percentage of the Park?"

"Yes."

"But she didn't discuss it with me or anything first." Fern felt incredibly betrayed by her sister.

"Guess it wasn't in the contract."

She shook her head, feeling a ringing in her ears that tried to blot out what she was hearing from him. "I suppose it's a done deal."

"Official and everything." He stopped, looking concerned about her. "It's okay. We worked fine together in the past. We can do it again."

"Forty-nine percent." She tried to wrap her mind around that agonizing fact. "You're in charge."

"We're partners."

She glanced around, suddenly seeing the bedroom in a different light. Masculine touches everywhere. "You live here now?"

"It's easier to oversee the Park on-site, instead of from my ranch."

"But—"

"Besides, we didn't expect you back. It made sense for me to take over something I love just as much as you love it."

"I always planned to come back. It was just…you, me, the gig of a lifetime. And I needed space."

"Space isn't what you needed." He slid toward her, arm muscles bulging as he reached out to her. "You needed us."

"I told you." She stepped back, putting more distance between them. "I'm loved on stage. Off stage, not so much."

"You got burned a few times. It happens to us all."

"It's more than that, and you know it. I give so much heart in my performances that I don't have enough left over to share…not the way you want to share life."

He placed a hand over his heart. "Mine is big enough for two."

She glanced away from the allure of him, shaking her head.

"Fern, just let me love you."

Chapter 2

HOT AS HELL. CRAIG THORNE STARED AT FERN AS IF SHE were the only oasis in a sea of endless sand. He tried not to appear as thirsty as he felt, but she was wearing nothing but an almost-see-through T-shirt, and he'd been without her for a long, agonizing time. He was trying to use reason on her, as well as himself, but he wasn't getting far. They spoke through music and all of the emotions it invoked deep in the soul. Words were tricky, easily misunderstood. Not music. It was a power all its own and a language all its own. But he couldn't use it now. He had to try to reason with her.

She was upset, and rightly so from her viewpoint. But he and Ivy had done the right thing. Wildcat Hall Park needed somebody taking the place to heart and building the venue where it could so easily go. With Fern gone, that left him. Besides, the Park was all he had left of her love. Some days, it was cold comfort. Other days, it was all that kept him putting one foot in front of the other.

He looked at her, standing there so stiff and straight with her long, ash-blond hair in disarray and her green eyes spitting fire. She was spoiling for a fight, but she was smart enough to know she couldn't win. It had all been over for her before it started. Still, she held the winning hand. How many nights had he lain in this very bed imagining her coming to him like she had tonight? Too many to count. It was why, at first, he couldn't believe she was actually sliding into his bed, snuggling under the covers, making those little satisfied sighs in the back of her throat that set him on fire. And now he was burning up just gazing at her.

He didn't know if he'd lucked out with her return or if her being here would be the final explosion that blasted apart what little was left between them. If he wasn't so obsessed with her, it'd be easier. He'd be able to think straighter. He'd be able to do what needed to be done without worrying about her. But that state of mind was never going to happen, so he might as well work with what he had right now and call it a blessing.

He didn't want to talk. He didn't even want to think. He wanted to draw her close and hold her, stroke her, smell her. She had silky skin and sleek muscles wrapped up in a package of long legs, curvy hips, and full breasts. She used to smell like oranges and lavender, a sweet-tart scent that made him want to nurture her and ravage her at the same time. But that was another world. He exhaled a sigh, lusting after what he'd lost.

As a rancher, he managed thousand-pound-plus beasts. As a firefighter, he contained out-of-control fires. As an entertainer, he sang for audiences till his voice gave out. If he couldn't get one woman to love him like he loved her, then he was a sorry excuse for a man. Come hell or high water, he was making a play for her. And this time, he'd do it right.

"I need to get this sorted out with my sister," Fern said.

"Nothing to sort out." He wanted to get out of bed, go to her, and wrap her in his arms, but he was stark naked—aroused, too—so it didn't seem like a good idea. Besides, he was already big to her petite, hulking over her, so he'd be setting off alarm bells that he wanted to keep quiet. Small women were particularly conscious of the physical power of men. If he wasn't careful, she might run.

"Ivy has some explaining to do at the least."

"Tomorrow ought to be soon enough." He patted the bed again, holding out little hope she'd actually join him.

"Are the other cabins empty? I need a place to sleep tonight."

"Full up." And he'd never been gladder for that fact. "It's too late to go anywhere else. You can stay here."

She glanced behind her, then back at him. "I guess I could take the sofa."

"Lumpy." He stroked the palm of his hand across the smooth sheet. "New bed here."

"I thought it felt new."

"Slade bought it for Ivy. They left it when they moved into his house."

"I kept thinking I'd get around to replacing the bed when I lived here, but I just never did get the time."

"It's comfy."

"No doubt. Still, I'll take the sofa, then find another place tomorrow." She turned and left the room.

He ran a hand through his hair in frustration, feeling it brush the top of his shoulders. What had he expected? He needed a head check if he really thought she'd just crawl right back into bed with him, even for a single night, but that was where he wanted her.

He threw off the covers and stalked over to the chair where he'd tossed his gray sweatpants. He pulled them up and tied the drawstring, but the pants still hung low on his narrow hips. He padded out to the living room on bare feet.

First thing he saw was her battered guitar case leaning against the back of the chair. If her vintage acoustic guitar was here, then she was well and truly back. He smiled, feeling a surge of pleasure at the remembered music that had brought them together. Maybe it could again.

"Still playing that sorry old Fender," he teased as he'd done so many times in the past, because they preferred different brands.

She placed a protective hand on the case, then glanced up at him with mischief in her green eyes. "I suppose you're still lugging around that battered old Martin."

He grinned, enjoying the fact that they'd fallen so easily back into their old sparring ways. "You don't walk out on Lady Luck, not when you're on a winning streak."

"Ever think how much better your luck onstage would be if you played something really fine with nice timbre?"

"You know good and well I've got that going for me," he said, chuckling. "Older is better 'cause there's nothing like the rich, warm tone of aged wood."

"Like my guitar?"

"Mine. And yours." He didn't mention the fact—although she knew it—that he played several guitars. He particularly liked his electric Fender when he played with his band. With the two of them, he preferred the sound of their favorite acoustic guitars.

"But I never share." She teased him back as she stroked her case up and down with long fingers. "Not when it comes to my instrument."

"But now you're sharing Wildcat Hall with me."

"Under duress." She looked away, smile fading, shoulders stiffening again.

He could've kicked himself for spoiling the mood. Still, she had to get used to the idea of them as a team again. "We've been partners. This is just a bigger stage."

"I simply can't wrap my mind around it." She plopped down on the sofa, leaning back her head and shutting her eyes.

"It'll come to you." He glanced down at the clothes she'd discarded in that sloppy way she had when she was really tired and down. He felt tenderness well up inside him like a big ball of sun rising in the morning.

"Not tonight, I think."

He reached down and picked up her jeans. He folded them and placed them on the seat of a kitchen chair. He neatly folded her T-shirt with the glittery image of a guitar and set it on top of the jeans.

"Leave it be," she said in a low voice. "I'll get my stuff together in the morning."

"You know I don't like messy." He picked up her bra and panties. White lace and smooth silk. Hot memories of their sweaty bodies twined together seared his mind at the sight. He couldn't resist stroking the fabric, feeling the softness catch under the roughness of his fingertips, calloused from long years of guitar work.

"Craig, don't play with my underwear." She sounded halfway between irritated and amused.

He'd take amused over irritated any day. He knew her voice. She was trying to resist teasing him but was losing the battle. "If you won't let me play with you, I'll just have to accept second best."

"That's more like third, four, or fifth best."

"A guy me like me can't be choosy."

She shook her head as the humor left her face. "A guy like you can have whatever he wants whenever he wants. And you know it."

"Not true." He crushed her underwear in his hand. Groupies were a fact of life for a musician, but it didn't mean he was available to them.

"Why don't we get some sleep?"

He let her change the subject. "I'd prefer you didn't sleep out here."

"I'm going to do it, so you might as well get used to the idea."

"I'll sleep in the chair."

"My guitar is sleeping in the chair."

"I don't want you alone out here."

"I've been alone a long time. Where I'm alone doesn't matter."

He felt her words strike him hard and deep. "I want you safe. If you're out here alone, I'll worry."

"Out there, I managed to stay safe."

"I worried about you every single day."

She lowered her head until her chin touched her chest, as if his words were a weight too heavy to bear. "I'm not your responsibility."

"I'm making it so."

She raised her face, looking at him with big green eyes. "I don't know how we're going to work together if you get possessive."

"I've always been possessive of you." He sat down beside her, resisting the impulse to take her hands in his own so they could be joined by more than words. "I've always worried about you." He put one hand on the back of the sofa, behind her head, and leaned toward her. He caught her unique scent—sweet and tart—and it went straight to his gut. "How could I do anything else?"

She sighed, shaking her head. "If you're trying to make me feel guilty, it's not going to work."

"I'm not. I'm simply stating facts." He stood up and walked away, unable to be so close without touching her. He carefully set her lingerie on top of her clothes, lingering a moment with his fingers on her panties, wanting so much more than that slight touch.

"Your facts. Not mine."

He turned back at her words, wanting to make them evaporate into thin air. "Okay. My facts."

She leaned forward, elbows on knees. "We might be able to do this if we keep it strictly professional. I don't want to fight."

"There's a lot of work to do if we're to meet your original goals." He backed way off the personal stuff. She wasn't ready for commitment. Not now. Not then. He'd known better than to give her an ultimatum before she'd left, but he hadn't been able to stifle his emotions, even though he knew she had commitment issues. He'd pushed too hard because he couldn't stand even the thought of being separated from her for a single moment. He wouldn't make that mistake again…not when he was on the edge of a second chance.

"I know it's a lot to accomplish."

"True. We added to the Hall's menu, and it's been a big success."

"That's great. Do you think we can do more in that area?"

"We can talk with Slade about it. We could possibly

offer more items from the Chuckwagon Café or more of his famous pies."

"Okay. Let's do it." She pushed her hair back from her face. "If we're going to come even close to the success of Greune Hall, we need to attract more musicians to our venue."

"We've already made inroads into it, but I admit we can do a lot better. Plus, we need more marketing and promotion to get the word out about Wildcat Hall."

"We can focus on its historic legacy and its current relevance. Right?"

"Yeah."

She leaned her head back against the sofa again. "I'm too tired for this right now. I can hardly think straight."

"Fern, you know I'd never hurt you, don't you?"

She raised her head, gave him a considering look, and then nodded in agreement.

He walked over, clasped her hands, and helped her stand. "We're going to bed. You hug your side, and I'll do the same on my side. We won't touch. We'll just share the bed."

She stared at him a long moment, as if considering all the pros and cons of his suggestion. Finally, she gave him a rueful smile. "I put the last of my energy into getting home…and getting into my very own bed."

"You've come a long way. You're tired. You need sleep. Everything will look different in the morning." He tugged her away from the sofa.

"You muddy my thinking, but…"

"Come on. I'm going to tuck you into bed."

He felt a vast sense of relief when she let him lead her into the bedroom. He fluffed the pillows, then watched as she lay down on her side and tucked her hands under her cheek, blond hair fanning across the pillow. He slowly pulled up the sheet, regretting his action every inch of the way.

She smiled tiredly at him, eyelids already droopy.

"You're home now." He covered her with the comforter. "Don't worry about anything. You're safe."

She exhaled softly as she closed her eyes, then she snapped them open and gave him a sharp stare. "Just so you know. I'm only indulging in a moment of weakness here. Tomorrow I'll be up to my usual strength."

"I don't doubt it a bit." He leaned over, pressed a soft kiss to her forehead, and turned out the light.

Chapter 3

FERN AWOKE ABRUPTLY TO THE FAST BEAT OF HER HEART. Something wasn't right. It was too quiet. She glanced around, but the room was dark except for a faint strip of light coming through slightly parted drapes on a single window. Not the ship. And then it hit her. She was back at Wildcat Hall Park. That was good. Yet something was bad. But what?

Reality returned full force, like a hard blow to her head and heart. Craig. He was now the majority owner of the Park. Unbelievable. Still, she'd have to believe it if her sister confirmed the sale. And she had a sinking sensation in the pit of her stomach that Ivy would do that very thing.

But where was Craig? Had she really slept in the same bed with him, even though she'd vowed never to go there again? He was less than the best for her state of everything—mind, heart, body, you name it. Well, maybe not music, but that was it. She reached out a hand and felt the empty side of the bed, affirming she was alone in the bedroom. Was he already up and around, at work? She hoped so. She didn't want to face him so soon after the shocking revelations of the previous night.

She was already vulnerable to him in so many ways, and the Park sale just upped that feeling. And that came on top of an overzealous fan who'd sent her white roses after every performance, whether he was on that cruise or not.

It'd been just a little too much and left her feeling uneasy. She needed to increase her sense of control to feel safe and secure. Work and being back in Wildcat Bluff County would surely do that for her.

On the tail end of that thought came the scent of freshly brewed coffee from the kitchen. She heard something that had to be a cup or plate clatter against the tile countertop. Oh yeah, Craig was still with her. She knew he just had to have his coffee first thing in the morning. And he knew she did as well. She sat up, snapped on the lamp, jerked down her T-shirt, pulled the covers up to her waist, and prepared for Craig's next move.

She took a deep breath when she heard a soft knock on the closed door. As she watched the door slowly open, she caught her breath in anticipation. Soon enough, Craig stood in the open doorway with a loaded tray in one hand. He smiled a little tentatively, as if not sure what to expect from her. No wonder. She realized she was holding her breath and slowly let it out.

"Morning." She decided to stake out her position as a calm, professional woman in control. It lasted about a split second...until he gave her a warm, loving look that tilted her world sideways. She took another deep breath to shore up her defenses.

"Thought you might need a little fortified sludge to help you wake up."

She closed her eyes against the sight and sound of him. He looked so good, with his tousled hair and sleepy bed-room eyes and his faded blue T-shirt stretched across his chiseled chest. It couldn't help but remind her of their other mornings together.

"How are you feeling?"

She checked to see what state she was in since he'd entered the room—somewhere between guilty and ecstatic. She needed to take charge of herself or she'd be skating on thin ice with him.

"That bad?" He set the small tray on the nightstand.

"I'm okay. How are you?"

"I feel good." And he gave her a long, slow perusal with half-closed eyes, as if contemplating joining her.

She reached for the coffee, grasped the mug handle, took a sip, and nodded in satisfaction. "Thanks. Texas pecan?"

"You know it."

"I missed this flavor."

"Is that why you came home?"

"Yeah. Coffee is the only lure in Wildcat Bluff County."

"Thought so." He smiled again. "I'll make it a point to stock the pantry with plenty of it."

"Good idea." She realized they were back to their easy, teasing banter in the bedroom.

"How do you want to go forward from here?" He turned serious, all humor gone from his gaze. "Do you want to talk with Ivy first?"

"I think that'd be a good idea."

"And then?"

"I don't know. I mean, I wasn't prepared to share the Park with you."

"That's your new reality."

She stared into the dark depths of her mug, holding it with both hands, since she suddenly needed the warmth. She had to get a grasp on not just her emotions but her life as well. She'd worked hard to get to this point. If it included

Craig, then so be it. She'd handled worse…or maybe it could be better, depending on how she approached her situation. She should be positive. He was doing everything possible to ease her into their new world. All she needed to do was help him…and maybe ease up on her need to control everyone and everything.

"I'm willing to share." He picked up his mug from the tray, then gestured around the room with his other hand.

"It's too small here."

"Bill and Ida shared this cabin."

"They were married."

He grinned, hot light shimmering in his eyes. "I'm not averse to marriage."

"Craig, be serious. There's a lot to figure out. Plus, there's a lot to do."

"Agreed." He took a sip of coffee. "And I'm damn serious."

She just shook her head, wondering how she was going to resist him and keep her mind on business. "I better get dressed."

"Not on my account."

She chuckled as she rolled her eyes at him. "You have a one-track mind."

"Only when you're around."

"You know we need to get on with our day." She held up a hand and counted on her fingertips. "I need to talk with Ivy. I need a place to stay. I need clothes. I need to go over what you've done with the Hall. And I need to make plans for Wild West Days. Labor Day is coming up fast."

"True. I stand ready to help you any way you need me. Whether you'd planned on it or not, we're in this together now."

She nodded as she considered her coffee a moment before she glanced up at him. "But no bedroom shenanigans."

"Not even a little bit?"

"We need to keep our relationship strictly professional."

"Fern, I don't know how you think that's possible after what we've meant to each other."

"That's in the past. You gave me an ultimatum. I made a choice. Let's leave it there." She only hoped she could stay true to those words, because his presence was having a powerful effect on her.

He shook his head, looking anywhere but at her. "What if it won't stay there?"

"We'll make it."

Finally, he turned hazel eyes back on her. "Not *we*. If that's the way you want it, you're on your own."

"Fine." She did her best to sound sure of that fact. "I've been on my own. I can handle it."

"Can you?"

"Yes." She shivered at the memory of that last time with him. She couldn't forget the power of it or how she'd lost complete control. "I'll do what needs to be done."

He took a sip of coffee, and then nodded his head. "Okay. We'll both do what needs to be done...for us and the Park."

"Okay." She drained the contents of her mug and set it on the tray. "First order of business today, I get up and get dressed." She glanced around and realized she'd left her carryall in the other room.

"Want me to bring your stuff in here?" he asked, as if reading her mind.

"I'd appreciate it. I only brought a change of clothes. I shipped the rest back, so it'll be here...well, whenever."

He set his mug beside hers on the tray, hesitated, and looked at her again. "We can make this work. I want to make it work. I just need your help."

"You've got it. And I really mean that. You know I love the Park and everything about it. We owe it to the heritage of the dance hall to put it on the map, so more than locals have the chance to enjoy it."

"I'm with you on this one."

"Good."

"I'll get your bag." He picked up the tray, turned, walked to the open doorway, then stopped and glanced back at her with a little smile on his full lips. "Let's make this fun."

She returned his smile, picking up his excitement about the Hall. She could do it. She wanted to do it. She just needed to let the past drift away. "Yes. If it's fun for us, it'll be fun for everyone."

"That's right." And he left the room.

She sighed in relief. Somehow or other, she'd make her Wildcat Hall dream come true because that was what was truly important—not her personal preferences.

When Craig brought back her carryall and set it on the end of the bed, he hesitated, as if reluctant to let go of something intimate that belonged to her. He clasped the handle, released it, and clasped it again before finally relinquishing it. He cleared his throat, then stepped back.

"Thanks."

"I'll wait for you in the other room."

"I can join you down at the Hall."

"You need to eat." He let his gaze trail down her T-shirt, then back to her face. "You lost weight."

She shrugged, not wanting their conversation to turn personal again.

"I'll scramble eggs."

"Toast is fine."

"Blackberry jam?"

"Perfect."

"More coffee?"

"Yes, thank you." She realized they'd become stilted with each other because neither knew where to go from here. She needed to get dressed, but he didn't want to leave her. He wanted to watch or help like the old days. She pointedly looked at her bag, hoping he'd get the message.

He cleared his throat again and took a step back. "Guess I'll go fix breakfast."

"I won't be long."

"Okay." He quietly shut the door behind him.

And she breathed a sigh of relief. She didn't want to hurt him. And she didn't want to get hurt. Everything about their partnership might not be as easy, but it was doable. She needed to talk with Ivy before she went any further with the situation. Maybe, by some chance of fate, she didn't own the Park with Craig.

She lifted her phone off the nightstand and hit speed dial.

"Fern, is that actually you? When are you ever up this early?" Ivy asked with wonder in her voice.

"Sister dear, believe it or not, I'm back in Wildcat Bluff."

"What? That's wonderful!"

"I didn't want to disturb anyone, so I came in late last night. And guess who I found in my bed."

"Craig Thorne."

"None other." As glad as she was to hear her sister's voice, she couldn't hide the irritation coming through her voice. "Please tell me you didn't sell your part of the Park to him."

"I can't tell you that."

"But, Ivy, why? This was our venture together. You're going to stay here now that you're engaged, so why couldn't you have held on till I got back?"

"Fern, you know I love you, but you can be flaky. I didn't know if you'd ever return."

"Flaky?"

"On occasion…well, maybe more than occasionally."

Fern snorted into the phone, chuckling at the truth of her sister's statement.

"Aren't you going to argue with me?"

"No. I can't. But Wildcat Bluff Park is dear to my heart… my biggest dream come true. You know it."

"I do. Still, you took off and left me holding the bag," Ivy said.

"I apologized over and over for it, but—"

"Why'd you do it?"

"I hadn't intended to leave you with the Hall, but the cruise gig was another dream come true. I couldn't pass it up. And Craig…well, he didn't want me to go. He wanted something else."

"He loves you."

"Maybe he did."

"Does."

"You know I've always been a rolling stone. I'm trying to settle down here because I love the Park and I want to build the venue."

"And Craig?"

"Why sell to him?"

"Besides you, he's the best person to own the Park. He loves Wildcat Hall like you do. He has the knowledge and skills to do what you planned to do. I don't. He was the best choice, since I wanted to move on with my life. And he's still the best choice, particularly since you're back."

"I don't know." Fern looked at the phone as she listened to Craig in the kitchen. "I feel vulnerable around him."

"I'm that way with Slade. But take my word for it, you can be vulnerable with some men and it only makes the relationship stronger."

"You're happy, and that's what counts."

"I want you to be happy, too. Craig used to make you happy."

"That's in the past."

"You can still work with him, can't you?"

"I'll have to, won't I?"

"Music. That's the way to go with him."

"And the Hall." Fern stood up, accepting the reality of her situation. "I love you, but you've put me in a difficult position."

"If you'll give Craig a chance—"

"I plan for us to be professional and do what's best for the Park."

"That's a good place to start," Ivy said.

"I hope so. I'm anxious to see you."

"Same here."

"But Craig's in the kitchen."

"And?" Ivy sounded more than a little interested in that fact.

"I need to get dressed, so we can go down to the Hall and get to work."

"So he was there last night?"

"Yes."

"And?"

"Nothing."

"Okay. I won't pry...at least not yet."

"Thanks."

"I love you. I'm so glad you're here. Come see me...or I'll come see you. I've missed you so much."

"I'm glad to be back, too. And you know I love you."

"Call me."

"Will do." And Fern cut the connection. Ivy had really done it. Even with the best of intentions on her sister's part, it was a shock. And yet, she was still co-owner of the Park. She could put her plans into action with Craig's help because, above all else, she trusted him.

She zipped open her bag. First things first.

"Breakfast's ready," Craig called.

And she felt a little thrill, despite everything, to be with him again.

Chapter 4

CRAIG SAT ACROSS FROM FERN AT THE DINING TABLE and watched her eat as if she wasn't completely committed to the act. Even so, it felt just right. He'd feared they'd never get here again, but here they were at last. And still… could a rolling-stone cowgirl and a stay-put cowboy make it work?

Love and laughter were two sides of the same coin. They spelled happiness. If she couldn't love for now, she could laugh. Music was the way to her heart and happiness. If he could take her there, she might truly come back to him.

"Do you want something else to eat?" At least he hadn't burned the toast like he'd heard Slade had burned the cookies in this very room.

"It's fine. Thank you." She picked up her mug of coffee and smiled at him over the rim.

"Maybe you'll like the cookies at the Hall, too."

"Who made them?" She cocked her head with interest.

"Alicia."

"What would the Park do without the Settelmeyers?"

"Offhand, I'd say it'd all fall apart. They've been here, generation after generation, from the beginning of the dance hall."

She nodded in agreement. "They really saved me when I arrived here not knowing nearly enough."

"They did the same thing for Ivy."

"Bless their hearts. I look forward to working with them again." She hesitated, staring at her coffee. "I bet they can set me up in one of the other cabins."

He felt his heart sink. She wasn't going to live with him. He might as well accept it. "One more night and a cabin will open up."

"Really?" She looked at him with pleasure sparkling in her green eyes.

"Yep." He felt his heart sink a little lower. "I'll move over there."

"No, I won't have it." She set down her mug. "You're already living here. I need to create a new home anyway, and a small place will suit me fine."

He might as well not fight her. "Okay."

"Which one is it?"

"The cabin next door." He felt somewhat lighter that she'd be near him.

"So close?"

"It's best. I can keep watch on you that way." Once he heard his words, he cringed at how they'd sound to her. She'd already said she was fine on her own. "I mean, that way it'll be easier to work together."

"True."

"If you don't want to live in the Park, I bet Ruby would find room for you at Twin Oaks."

"That'd be fun." She turned a pleased smile on him. "I love her B and B."

"Everybody does." Happy was the ticket. For her. For him, too. They both deserved to be happy. It hit him hard, that knowledge. He hadn't been completely happy since she'd left. Now that she was back, it was time to grasp happiness and run with it. He squared his shoulders in anticipation of carrying that ball to the finish line for a big win.

"But I want to be here at the Park near you...so we can make plans and put them into action."

"Good." Life was definitely looking up. She wanted to be close to him, even if only to take care of the place. It was enough—for now.

She spread jam on a wedge of toast, then took a bite.

"Hungrier now?"

"Yes. Maybe all the uncertainty has been getting to me."

"It can knock you off your feet."

"Guess so." She ate another piece, glancing reflectively at the front door. "About Wild West Days."

"Hedy, Bert, Morning Glory, and Ruby are already planning it, as usual."

"I suppose Eden and Jack will livestream events over KWCB. They've done wonders with the ranch radio station since she got back. I've been keeping up while I was gone."

"Yeah. They turned the Wildcat Den around in a short time."

"That's what I want us to do with the Hall."

"We're already headed that way."

"I want more."

"Me, too." He wished she'd say that about him.

"But to get back to Wild West Days." She rubbed long fingers, calloused from playing a guitar, around the lip of her mug.

He wanted those fingers on his body, tracing him all over like she'd once done. He ached for it.

"Craig?"

"What?" He shook his head, jerking his thoughts back to the present moment.

"Wild West Days. I agreed to help with the music, but I don't know much about the event."

"We get a lot of tourists in Old Town looking for a taste of the Old West like they do in Tombstone, Arizona."

"I've been to Tombstone. It's great."

"We're wall-to-wall folks during Wild West Days, since it's the last big event of summer. Folks like to see our reenactment of the shoot-out between the Hellions and the Ruffians for control of the town."

"Sounds like the shoot-out at the OK Corral in Tombstone."

"It's similar. Sometimes those old-time outlaws fought the law. Sometimes they fought each other for turf."

"Where does the shoot-out take place?"

"Lone Star Saloon."

"And that's where we're to provide music?"

"Right. Old Town hasn't changed much since the 1880s. The Lone Star Saloon still serves the same function—food, drink, dance hall."

"But it's competition for Wildcat Hall, isn't it?"

"It could be, but it's not due to its location. The Lone Star is in town, while the Hall is out here on the old cattle-drive trail."

"Still, they are both dance halls."

"We have the cowboy cabins, the outdoor garden with picnic tables, and a lot more space."

"I just don't want there to be a venue conflict of interest."

"Don't worry. There'll be plenty of people for both places."

"Okay. I'm convinced we're in good shape here."

"Locals get involved by dressing up and playing parts. If

you didn't know, dance hall darlings in their fancy dresses and white pinafores turned the tide. You'd look good all dolled up like that."

She laughed, eyes crinkling at the corners. "And you'd look even better dressed as a gambler with aces up his sleeve."

"We'd make quite the saloon team." He joined her laughter, feeling as if they were finally getting off on the right foot. Work—that was definitely the right way to go. Plus, Wild West Days was a good cause that benefited the entire county, so he was happy to support it. And it was fun...and it'd be even more fun with Fern.

"I'm supposed to sing at the Lone Star."

"Me, too."

She set down her wedge of toast, looking to one side. "I know. We were going to play together."

"We can still do it. Why not? You're back. I'm available."

"Like before?" She glanced at him with an uneasy expression in her green eyes.

"We always made beautiful music together. You don't really think that's changed, do you?"

"No." She toyed with her piece of toast. "I guess we could practice some numbers at Wildcat Hall."

"I'm ready anytime you are."

"But the Lone Star isn't our priority."

"Guess not...at least not yet."

"I'm ready to get into managing the Hall."

"Remember, you have a working partner now."

She tossed her toast onto her plate and stood up, turning her back to him. "I had it all to myself before I left."

"I know." He stood up, too. "If we're going to butt heads over who's in charge here, then let's get it over with."

She walked to the front door and pulled it open. She crossed her arms and leaned against the doorjamb as she looked toward the dance hall.

"I'm serious." He walked over and stopped by her side. He saw what she saw. At the end of summer, the Park was a beautiful blend of colorful flowers, trimmed bushes, and leafy green trees. A mockingbird was singing its heart out in a series of spirited melodies.

"I know, but I'm not sure I know how to share." She let out a breath as she stepped outside.

He followed her. "You can make this easy, or you can make it hard."

"Compromise?"

"I'm all about compromise, but I don't think we need it."

"No?"

"Let's just work together as a team, like we did before you left."

"But I was in charge of the Park then." She picked up the firefighter gear, set it to one side, plopped down in the rocker, and tapped her foot to a tune in her head.

"Not of the music. That was teamwork."

"True. Oh, I don't know." She abruptly stood up.

"First, let's get this out in the open."

"What?"

"I always knew you were a wild thing, but I don't think I completely understood what that meant until you were gone." He moved closer to her as he caught the special scent that was so much a part of her that it spun him right back in time to those fragrance-filled nights in the woods. "Wild things can't be caught and held, or they'll make a break for freedom sooner or later. It's their nature."

"I just wanted the cruise gig."

"And I just wanted to hold you here any way I could do it…but now I know something else."

"Craig—"

"If you let a wild thing run free, she'll eventually come back to hearth, home…and love."

"Love?"

"Yeah." He held out his hand, palm up. "Maybe your body has been gone, but your heart has always been here in Wildcat Hall Park. And my heart has always been with you."

She glanced up at him with misty green eyes, then clasped his fingers.

"Let's make music together."

"That's when we're truly alive and in each other's world…in our own world."

"Partners?"

"Yes." She squeezed his hand. "But I'll always be a wild thing."

"I wouldn't have you any other way." He raised her hand and gently kissed her fingertips.

Chapter 5

"Do you want to see the Hall now?" Craig asked. "That's where we made our best music together."

"Inspiration will do that for an artist." Fern smiled as she headed down the stairs with him on her heels. She felt happy as she walked the path that wove in and out around the cabins with the sweet scent of roses and the trills of birdsong filling the air. She glanced at the cowboy cabin that would be hers tomorrow, as always appreciative of the creativity and love that had gone into its construction. Overall, the building was the color of soft, weathered gray from the tin roof to barn wood walls, but it was brightened with a shiny red door and two rockers on the porch painted a matching crimson. She could hardly wait to move in there.

Home. She was really back home. And she was glad to be here. After all her years of roaming, she felt as if she was finally at the point of being willing to put down roots...with Craig still here to share Wildcat Hall and music with her.

Happiness filled her as she reached the honky-tonk. She loved the look of horizontal wood slats painted white with a western false front that had a steeply pitched tin roof with side flaps for open-air dancing. The double front doors and tall windows allowed plenty of circulation back in the day, so they had screens with black-painted slats, while a side door led to the huge outdoor garden. A parking lot in front had been changed to cement years ago, so that it now accommodated gas-powered vehicles instead of grass-fed horses with buggies.

She stopped in front, simply enjoying the sight.

"Like what you see?" Craig asked.

"I missed it here."

"And you were missed by everyone." He gestured around the Park. "I meandered quite a bit before I came back, too."

"How is your ranch near Sure-Shot?"

"Horses will always be in my blood, but music is my first love."

"Can the ranch get along without you?"

"It's not that far away, and good help lives there full-time."

"Beautiful out that way."

"Yep." He smiled at her, shrugging slightly. "Guess I'll always be a singing cowboy."

"Quite a long and respectable heritage."

"Thanks. We're doing our best to keep the tradition alive…just like you. We need our singing cowgirls, too."

She returned his smile, leaning toward him, lured by the warmth in his hazel eyes.

"Want to go inside? I brought the key."

"Yes. I'm more than ready."

After he unlocked the doors, she walked into the front bar and flipped on the overhead lights. For her, this room was the heart and soul of Wildcat Hall. It had a long wooden bar with a black cast-iron foot rail, a pressed tin ceiling accented by ceiling fans with schoolhouse lights, and floor-to-ceiling windows in front. A big red professional-size fire extinguisher lay on its side, as if ready for use, across one end of the wooden bar. She relished the cozy, old-fashioned ambience that had nurtured folks since 1884, well over a hundred years.

The decor was minimal. Rusty metal beer advertisement signs had been tacked around the walls, along with sepia-toned photographs of cowboys on horseback and country music legends. A framed Lone Star State flag hung in back of the bar while a rack of deer antlers loomed above the front doors. A flat-screen monitor above the bar was the only contemporary touch, but it could mostly be ignored if it wasn't turned on. Hand-hewn, scarred wood tables with high-back chairs filled the area.

"We haven't changed a thing," Craig said. "It's just the way you left it in here."

"What about the dance hall?"

"Check for yourself."

She quickly walked into a short hall, then turned and moved through an open doorway into the center of the big room with rows of long, narrow, hand-made wood tables with matching benches placed on each side of the dance floor in front of a wall of screened windows. Natural light filtered inside, throwing shadows across the rough wood floor.

She glanced from the stage to the other end of the dance floor at the long bar that served munchies, coffee, sarsaparilla, beer, and wine. Two open windows allowed bartenders to serve customers on the dance hall side and on the front bar side at the same time. She liked the practical set up, just like she liked everything else about the Hall.

It didn't make as big a statement as fancy honky-tonks like Billy Bob's Texas in the Fort Worth stockyards with 127,000 square feet of boot-scooting space or the famous Longhorn Ballroom in Dallas with 20,000 square feet. But Wildcat Hall was plenty spacious with 4,000 square feet inside and room for more in the garden with picnic tables outside. She just wished the Hall had the tourist draw of those two famous places, but a major destination attraction and music venue could be built with the right promotion and entertainment from up-and-coming as well as established artists.

She was drawn to the recessed, raised stage with its hand-painted backdrop of crimson curtains trimmed with gold pulled open to reveal a pastoral scene of cowboys herding longhorns. She glanced up at the high ceiling with exposed wood rafters that held black ceiling fans, hanging light bulbs, sprinkler system, and a row of stage lights. She'd played under those lights many a time with Craig.

"Remember?" he asked, stopping by her side.

"It's a small stage, but a good one."

"Do you want to play this weekend?"

"Us?"

"Yes."

"What about your band?" she asked.

"We'd bring you on for a set, not the entire time."

"I haven't practiced with y'all in so long."

"How about just the two of us? I'd play bass."

She walked over to the stage, shivering inside, and stood still, letting the memories of performing there with Craig wash over her. It was such an intimate act, playing together…anticipating each other, harmonizing with each other, leading, following, joining…about as close to sex without the actual act as they could manage.

"Are you getting cold feet?" He walked over and sat down on the edge of the stage, looking up at her with seemingly endless patience.

"I just…maybe I don't need to perform. It's plenty to do making plans, setting schedules, reaching out to bands."

"Fern, stop it. You're a performer. You can't live without it any more than I can. Anyway, you've got fans in the area that are just waiting for you to return. You don't want to disappoint them, do you?"

She plopped down beside him so she didn't have to look into the reality of his eyes. The stage felt cool and comfortable, even inviting. She glanced up at the lights. At night, they'd be hot and brilliant, showcasing her fret work as she played her guitar and sang her heart out, while she evoked emotions with words and melodies that spoke to the deepest desires, loves, and pains that people might not be able to reach otherwise. It was a calling.

She did feel as if she owed it to folks to give them the gift that was her single blessing in this life. Everyone had their own gift, but hers was meant to ease the pain of others, nurture their happiness, elevate their lives. Could she say no even if she wanted to run away from the commitment? Maybe that was why she always moved on when things got too close, too intimate, and too emotional because she already felt so on edge, so giving, so connected to others. When she'd told Craig she'd needed space, she'd really meant it. And of course, there'd been the once-in-a-lifetime gig on the high seas that had lured her away, too. *Wild thing*, as he called her, was a good way to put it.

And yet, here she was, back in Wildcat Hall, sitting on the stage with Craig as if she'd never been gone.

She stood abruptly. She wouldn't let anyone down this time. Wildcat Bluff's tight-knit community depended on her skills and her love of not just the Park but the entire special county. She'd give her all for the dance hall and Wild West Days.

She walked into the center of the honky-tonk and

twirled around and around, revving up her energy, her spirits, her determination.

In a moment, she felt Craig take her hand and twirl her around, and then he led her into a slow dance, humming a Willie Nelson's tune.

As they moved as one across the dance hall, she knew why he'd picked that particular, heart-wrenching song. In it, Willie laments that he saved an angel flying too close to the ground with love, but that he'll let her go if she needs to fly away because that is the true giving nature of love. Craig was telling her with the song that if she couldn't stay, he'd let her go…healed by love.

She tightened her hands around his neck, pulling him closer, feeling his hands on her back tighten until they were moving body-to-body across the dance floor with no other accompaniment than the rich tone of his voice as he changed from humming to words, beguiling her into not flying away.

She understood only too well that he wouldn't clip her wings. Instead, he would lift her up with both hands until she was strong enough to fly free. But would she? He didn't know. Neither did she.

For now, she wanted nothing more than to be in his arms, dancing to the beat of their hearts and the sound of his voice.

"It doesn't get any better than this," he finally said, breaking off the song and stopping the dance.

She leaned back so she could see his face. He looked like the song—in love and at peace.

"I'll always have this memory. I can live a long time on it."

"We'll make more…music and memories." She went up on tiptoes and placed a soft kiss, almost a secret whisper, on his too-full, too-sensitive lips.

Chapter 6

"THAT'S IT, VARMINTS!" A DEEP VOICE COMMANDED AS several booted feet hit the wood floor of the main bar, followed by the slamming of the front door. "Come out with your hands up or eat lead." Those ringing words were followed by the ratchet of a shotgun.

Craig gave a loud sigh as he stepped back from Fern, shaking his head at the lousy timing of what could only be the Settelmeyer family. They must've seen lights on in the Hall and come to investigate.

Fern clutched his arm, looking alarmed at the intrusion.

"It's okay." He patted her hand in reassurance before he looked toward the bar. "Claude, it's me!"

"Craig, what are you doing out and about so early?" Claude called back.

"Come here. I've got a surprise for you."

"Better be a good one. We're trying to stay on schedule here."

Fern chuckled, squeezing Craig's arm. "Heaven help anybody who gets them off schedule."

"Looks like that's going to be us today."

"Oh my."

After more boot stomping, a family of three tall, muscular, blond, blue-eyed folks stepped inside, looking put out. They were identically dressed in crimson long-sleeve T-shirts with the Wildcat Hall logo emblazoned on the front, Wranglers, and black cowboy boots. They were a good-looking family.

Claude and Lana appeared to be in their fifties, while Alicia looked about thirty or so. They radiated strength and competence with a no-nonsense attitude.

"We're already ten minutes off schedule." Lana put her hands on her hips along with a frown on her face. "Craig, what are you doing back here on the dance floor?"

"I brought him." Fern stepped forward into the light of a window with a smile on her face.

"Good grief! Is that really you?" Lana put a hand to her chest as a grin spread across her face.

"Fern!" Alicia shrieked, ran forward, and threw her arms around Fern, crushing her in a big bear hug. "When did you get back?"

"Last night."

Lana hugged Fern next, patting her on the back before she moved aside to look at her closely. "You lost weight. We'd best get busy putting some meat back on your bones."

"Why didn't you let us know ahead of time, so we could've made you comfortable?" Claude asked as he broke open the shotgun, removed the two cartridges, and dropped them in a pocket.

"We could've met you at the airport," Lana said.

"I didn't want to be a bother." Fern gave them a warm smile. "I just picked up a rental and headed on up here."

"Where did you spend the night?" Alicia glanced at Craig, raising an eyebrow in obvious interest.

"She woke me from a sound sleep."

"I stayed with him last night," Fern said, "but I need my own place now. I'd like to move into one of the other cabins."

"I guess you know about…the change in ownership." Lana glanced from Fern to Craig, then back again.

"Yes. I talked with Ivy this morning."

"Are you okay with it?" Claude asked. "We want to be supportive, but if you've got a burr under your saddle about it, best let us know now."

"If you're not happy about the situation and we run into trouble, we might never get everything done in time for Wild West Days." Lana turned intent blue eyes on Fern.

"Lots of folks depend on us about this time of the year." Alicia rubbed her hands together as if there was so much more to do.

"Folks depend on y'all all year long," Craig said.

"True enough," Claude agreed. "But in particular for this event."

"I guess it was a shock to find out your sister sold her share of the Park to Craig," Lana said.

"She's been a real trooper about it." Craig decided he'd better set everything straight before gossip got out that they were in a big fight over Wildcat Hall Park.

"We have the same goals," Fern said, following up on his opening into their relationship. "And Craig loves the Hall as much as I do, so we've agreed to work together."

"Hallelujah." Lana put her hands on her hips. "So, that's in place. All to the good. Now what do you need from us?"

"Time's a wasting." Claude glanced around the room, then back at Craig. "Were you looking to change something in here?"

"No thanks. We were just discussing how we were going to move forward with the Hall." Craig was glad they hadn't seen the slow dance, or they'd have taken a completely different spin on the situation.

"That's right," Fern quickly said.

"She wants that cabin next to mine," Craig said. "Aren't those folks checking out tomorrow?"

"Today." Alicia looked from Craig to Fern. "Are you sure you want it? I mean, Craig's got the big cabin and—"

"No," Fern said. "I want my own place."

"Okay," Lana replied. "We'll get it cleaned up and ready for you by late this afternoon."

"Is four about right?" Alicia asked.

"Four is good." Fern smiled at the group. "I need to pick up some clothes and supplies in town, so that works perfectly for me."

"Don't bother with supplies," Lana said. "We'll stock it with everything you need to get started out right."

"Thanks. That's a big relief."

"Food, too," Alicia added. "Some of our own specialties will get you back in shape in no time."

"That'd be great," Craig said. "Don't tell anybody I told you, but y'all are the best cooks in Wildcat Bluff next to Slade Steele and his family."

"Thank you." Lana smiled warmly at him. "We do our best."

"Looks like all's right as rain." Claude glanced at the watch on his wrist. "We'd best get back to work. We're twenty-three minutes off schedule."

Alicia gave Fern another quick hug. "We're so glad you're back. Now things can really move forward with the Park."

"Thanks. I'm glad to be back," Fern said. "Let's catch up later."

Alicia gave her a wink. "I can't wait to hear all the news."

As the Settelmeyers headed back the way they'd come, Craig looked at Fern. "Fine family. What would we do without them?"

"I can't imagine. And I'm so glad I'll have my own cabin tonight."

"Can't say I feel the same, but I do understand. I want you to be happy." He returned her smile. He glanced around the dance hall, feeling a lift of his spirits. Maybe life wasn't perfect, but it was way better since she'd returned to the Park...and him.

"I guess we ought to get on with our day. Where do you want to start?"

He glanced around again. "Nothing we need to do back here. Let's go up front and look at the schedule."

"Okay."

"Later, you'll want to settle into your cabin, so let's get as far as we can right now." He followed her, watching the sway of her hips in her tight jeans and feeling the same want and need as always, only now the lust—and the love—was fired by the overwhelming knowledge that he had to get it right this time.

And around and around in his head went the same litany that he'd lived with for months. He needed her, but he didn't want to need her. He wanted her, but he didn't want to want her. He loved her, but he didn't want to love her. Why couldn't another easier woman do? And he always came back to the same answer that another woman wouldn't be Fern Bryant...and his heart wanted what his heart wanted, and that was a singer named Fern.

He stepped into the front bar right behind her. He wouldn't waste a single moment of time. If there was any way to her heart, it was through music and the dance hall. He needed to get that right, too. He felt a lot of pressure, but at the same time he felt relaxed, like the calm before going into a battle that must be won at all costs.

She sat down on a stool, then swiveled and smiled at him.

He felt her smile all the way to his gut, and that's when he knew he would win somehow...for both of them.

"It's going to be so much fun making plans, coming up with agendas, leveraging everything we have here."

He didn't say anything as he sat down on a stool beside her, thinking about how to make it all fun when it felt like a battle.

"Isn't it?"

He took her hand and stroked across her soft palm, feeling their connection as something that would endure through the ages. "We'll make whatever we do together fun and anything else your heart desires."

She clasped his hand, joining them as one.

"And when we're done—" He never finished because the front doors were thrown open and crashed into the walls on either side.

"Fern! I couldn't wait to see you," Ivy cried out as she rushed into the bar like a whirlwind, pulling a wheeled suitcase and setting it near a front table.

"That's right." Slade Steele quietly shut the front doors, then set two sacks of food with the Chuckwagon Café logo on the table near the suitcase. "She was hell-bent on getting here fast."

Fern leaped off the stool and ran to meet her sister in the middle of the room.

Craig watched as the sisters embraced with tears of happiness in their eyes. He felt a little tug at his heart, as if he'd lost Fern just as he'd found her. But then he glanced at Slade. The big blond-haired, blue-eyed cowboy looked about like Craig felt, as if he too might lose the love of his life to the longer, stronger love of sisters. But he also knew they wouldn't come between Fern and Ivy for the world, because they belonged together, too.

"I hope I'm not interrupting anything," Ivy said as she stepped back, glancing at Craig.

"No." Fern chuckled as she reached up and brushed back a strand of her sister's thick, russet hair. "The Settelmeyers just left."

"You didn't disrupt their schedule, did you?"

Fern laughed again. "I'm afraid so, but I bet they get back on it pretty quick."

"I hope so. I was three days early putting up Christmas decorations, and you know what?"

"I can kind of guess."

"They took them down, waited three days, and put them back up."

Fern laughed harder, and everyone joined her. "That sounds about right. But you've got to admit, their system works."

"I'm certainly not one to mess with success."

"Me either," Fern said. "They're getting one of the cabins ready for me to move into this afternoon."

Ivy glanced at Craig with a raised eyebrow.

He just shrugged and shook his head, letting her know it was out of his control.

Ivy smiled at her sister. "So, did Craig kick you out for snoring so loudly?"

"Something like that." Fern returned the smile. "I'm just used to my own space."

"I bet Craig was doing the snoring." Slade nodded in understanding to his friend.

"We brought you welcome presents." Ivy quickly pulled the conversation out of the ditch.

"Really?" Fern clapped her hands together. "What?"

"Food from the Chuckwagon Café." Slade pointed at the sacks. "Figured you could use some good vittles."

"Oh yes, I'm starved for Chuckwagon food."

"I knew you'd send most of your clothes, so I packed you a suitcase full of mine, since we're the same size," Ivy said. "If it doesn't suit, you can always go shopping at Gene's Shoe Hospital or Morning's Glory."

Fern hugged her sister again. "It'll all be great. And it'll save me time. That's really important about now."

"How so?" Slade asked.

"We're gearing up to do more with the Hall."

"That's great!" Ivy said. "We made progress, but not nearly enough."

"Thank you again for stepping in for me." Fern took her sister's hands and squeezed them.

"Thanks to you for getting me here." Ivy glanced at Slade. "It's the best thing that ever happened to me."

Slade gave her a big grin. "Best thing that ever happened to me, too."

Craig felt their happiness wash over him like a big warm blanket—one he wanted for his very own with Fern in the center of soft fleece. If Ivy and Slade could do it, surely he and Fern could do it as well.

"Look, we won't keep you," Ivy said. "We're on our way to pick up some feed for the ranch."

Fern chuckled, giving her sister a big grin. "Now that's something I never expected to hear you say."

"Feed?" Ivy laughed, too. "But this is special feed for a very special bull."

"Fernando?" Fern glanced at Craig. "I heard on the news

about him making his way home for Christmas after cattle rustlers nabbed him."

"Everybody heard about him," Slade said. "I didn't think we'd ever see that Angus again, but my niece, Storm, never gave up hope he'd be here by Christmas."

"Fernando was definitely Wildcat Bluff's Christmas miracle," Ivy added.

Fern glanced around the group. "I'm sorry I missed the cattle drive and Fernando's triumphant return home."

"It was really special," Ivy said. "But you're back in time to celebrate Wild West Days."

"You'll need to help us make plans." Slade nodded to punctuate his words. "The Lone Star Saloon is important to the event, but so is Wildcat Hall."

"I'm ready to do whatever I can to help," Fern said.

"We're starting to make plans here." Craig glanced around the group. "Count us in on anything that needs doing in town."

"Good." Slade grasped Ivy's hand. "We'd better be on our way. Fernando may be tolerant if his special feed is late, but Storm's another matter."

Craig chuckled. "Go ahead and get going. Nobody wants to be on the wrong side of that little girl."

"Sure the truth of it," Slade replied, laughing. "Why don't y'all come out to the ranch, so Fern can meet Fernando?"

"I'd love to," Fern said. "He's quite the celebrity."

"Give us a call and we'll set it up." Ivy gave Fern a quick kiss on her cheek. "We'll have a nice sisterly visit later on. If you need anything, just holler."

"Thanks."

Craig watched the couple leave, then glanced at Fern.

"It'll be fun to have you both in Wildcat Bluff at the same time."

She turned a happy smile on him. "Yeah."

"Want to see what they brought you?"

"Hungry?"

"I smell something mighty good." He clasped her hand, squeezed, and kissed the tip of her nose. "Let's start the day off right."

"I thought we already did with the dance."

"That was just the beginning."

Chapter 7

FERN STOOD STILL A MOMENT, LOOKING AT THE CLOSED front doors. *She felt it.* Love between Ivy and Slade was like a living, breathing, towering blaze. And it hadn't consumed them. Instead, as a couple, they were stronger…now a powerful force to be reckoned with. She'd never seen her sister so content, so happy, so relaxed. She couldn't quite understand it. She'd always felt as if she were losing part of herself instead of gaining a supportive partner in a relationship… except with Craig.

She envied her sister in a way she never had before this moment. Maybe she'd been moving too fast through life, never daring to look back at anything that might be gaining on her, to appreciate what was before her eyes. Could she learn to grasp the present with both hands?

She glanced at Craig, who sat at the table patiently waiting for her. He gave her a slight smile, as if he knew she was pondering more than the taste of Chuckwagon goodies and was encouraging her to move forward in life. That's why she'd come home. She was ready.

She sat down across from him with a smile. "Please tell me those sacks hold barbeque and all the trimmings."

"I resisted tearing into them to find out."

"Sure smells like the best barbeque in the state." She opened one sack and pulled out two plastic dinner containers with two small bags of plasticware. She set one of each in front of him and took the others for her.

He ripped open the last sack and withdrew two small containers. He popped them open. "Best of all worlds. Slade's award-winning pecan pie." He pulled out two drinks and pushed one over to her. "Bet it's sweet tea."

"Yum." She took a sip, nodded in agreement, and opened the top of her container. "Looks like barbeque brisket sandwich with potato salad, coleslaw, and fried okra."

"Dig in." Craig took a big bite of his sandwich, then watched her with a happy light in his gaze.

She followed his example, closing her eyes in ecstasy at the taste of tender, savory meat slathered in the café's special barbeque sauce.

"Good?"

"Oh yeah." She licked her lips, moaning in deep appreciation.

"If you keep making those sounds, I'll be over this table and licking you for dessert."

"Did I make a mess?" She patted her mouth with her napkin, even as she saw he was teasing but ready to put his words into action. "What about Slade's pie?" she teased back.

"You're a whole lot sweeter."

"Not tart?"

"Not even close."

"I bet I could be—"

"A tart?" He grinned, revealing white teeth against tan skin.

"That's not what—"

"I wouldn't complain."

She rolled her eyes at him before picking up her fork and putting potato salad into her mouth so she wouldn't be tempted to pursue his line of thought. Truth of the matter, he was tempting her in lots of ways she'd vowed to put behind her. And yet, this was Craig with that old, familiar tug at her senses.

"I pushed, didn't I?"

She nodded, taking another bite of barbeque, but it didn't taste quite as good as before his words.

"You know what you do to me." He sipped tea. "Can't I tease you at all?"

"It's not that."

"If we can't tease or enjoy each other, how are we going to get through this partnership?"

"It's just—"

"No, it's not just you or me. It's Wildcat Hall. It's Wild West Days. It's all the people who depend on what only we can do for them."

She set down her sandwich. "You're right. But still—"

"There are no buts here. We either do it right or we don't do it."

"But how?"

"We play music. Isn't it the best way to communicate with each other?"

"That's the way we speak to the world."

"And to each other?" he asked.

"Yes."

"Let's get guitars. The stage is empty."

"Don't we need to make other plans first?"

"The schedule is pretty well set up until Wild West Days. That's only a month away."

"What if I want to add talent between now and then?" she asked.

"If you can do it and want to do it, that's fine with me. We can work around our schedule to a certain extent. You know how it is."

"Yeah."

"I left a couple of acoustic guitars in the equipment cabinet in the dance hall. Let's go for them." He stood up.

She hesitated only a moment, and then she joined him. She needed the world of music, where she could lose herself in the comforting strains of songs she knew and even just the touch of guitar strings underneath her fingertips. She abruptly ached with the need to reach out to the comfort and familiarity of her greatest love.

As they walked into the dance hall, she clicked her fingers in time to the beat of his footsteps, leather against wood, a muted sound that resonated upward into the high ceiling with excellent acoustics. She felt excitement build as she walked toward the stage. Yes, Craig was right. This was where she belonged, where she could make a difference in life. He belonged right here with her. And a thought struck her.

"Am I taking my life too seriously?"

"You've been pretty serious since you got back."

"I used to laugh more."

"We both did."

"And tease."

"That, too."

She stopped in the middle of the Hall and turned around in a circle, looking and thinking of audiences. And as if from far, far away, she could almost hear the sound of fiddle, mandolin, and banjo, making the toe-tapping music that resounded down over the years to permeate the honky-tonk and resonate with the present. She could also almost see the long skirts on women as they swirled in colorful arches on the dance floor and the red suspenders holding up dark trousers on men who held big glasses of beer or sarsaparilla. And from outside in the garden, she thought she heard the high-pitched laughter of happy children playing together.

"What is it?" Craig glanced around as if he was missing something important that she was seeing.

"I wonder. Maybe I'm not appreciative enough of all the people who come here to share community through music while they get away from the trials and tribulations of everyday life. They bring love to this dance floor for me, you, other performers. And each other."

"That's so true."

"I'm grateful for all their love and support. Where would I—or any performer—be without it?"

"There'd be no dance halls without them."

"But we'd all still find a place to gather, wouldn't we?"

"That's true, too. Like I said earlier, you've been missed by our local folks, no doubt about it. Are you up to going onstage this weekend?"

She turned toward him and cocked her head to the side, considering everything she'd experienced in the short time she'd been back. Now was the time to let light, love, laughter enter...and hold on to them because they were what was truly important in a world of shifting sands.

"Let's get those guitars." And she held out her hand to him.

Chapter 8

As Fern sat down on the edge of the stage, light from the row of windows filtered onto the dance floor, highlighting the scuffs and scratches from so many years of use by generations of Wildcat Bluff residents that spread across the narrow wood slats. She doubted there'd been much change in all these years except for the overhead lighting and a sprinkler system designed to stop a fire that could quickly get out of hand with so much dry wood.

She felt a deep connection with all those people who came before her. She wanted to leave her mark here, too. Not in the wood, but in the air. Music bridged the gaps in life, cementing generations together as if no time passed between them. She wanted to leave her contribution here. Would she? She hoped so. But it was still too soon to tell.

"Here you go." Craig handed her an acoustic guitar and sat down beside her with a similar one.

She looked at what he'd given her and shook her head in dismay. "Where'd you get these?"

"I think they came with the Hall."

"They look rough." She rubbed fingertips across the wood that was gouged and scarred, with the varnish worn down to the wood near the sound hole.

"Guess that's why they were left here."

"Well loved by somebody at some point." She crossed her legs and positioned the waist of the guitar against her thigh. She rested her right elbow on the edge and wrapped the fingers of her left hand around the fingerboard.

He sat down, crossed an ankle over one knee, and rested the guitar on his leg as he plucked a few strings. "Steel. Guess they wanted a bright and brassy sound."

"And guess they weren't beginners or these would be nylon strings."

"Yeah. Easier on the fingers."

"Still, I like the mellow sound of nylon."

"Give me steel any day."

She strummed downward with the fingertips of her right hand. "Ow. That hurts my ears." She chuckled, shaking her head. "This one's sadly out of tune."

"Bet mine's the same." He joined her laughter as he made another discordant sound.

"What can we expect? Guitars go out of tune so easily. After that plane ride, mine will need some serious adjustment."

"At least we can fix these." He pulled his cell phone out of his pocket and hit the tuning app. While he watched the meter on the screen, he twisted the tuning pegs until his guitar slowly came into tune.

"Much better." She smiled as she followed his example, but she couldn't get her guitar to adjust correctly.

"What's the problem?"

"Not sure."

"Let me take a look." He turned his guitar and set it so the strings rested against his crossed knee, then held out his hand.

She could tell what was going on just as well he could, but she handed it to him anyway. If he wanted to help, she appreciated it. She enjoyed the entire process of sitting on the stage with guitars in hand, easing their way back into music together.

"Sad to say it." He shook his head as he examined the guitar. "But this one's had its day."

"Neck?"

"Yeah. Look. Here's the problem." He held up the guitar and sighted down the long neck. "It's bent."

"Isn't there a screw to put it back in alignment?"

"Not on this model." He handed it back to her. "Might as well throw it away."

"That's a shame, but it's what you get with cheap."

"Back in the day, cheap was cheap. Nowadays, cheap gets you a pretty good guitar."

"And one that has an adjustable screw in the neck."

"You bet."

She set the guitar aside and cocked her head to one side. "Looks like you're the guitarist of the hour."

He grinned, nodding. "Just what I always wanted to be."

"Don't get cocky," she teased. "I could take that guitar away from you."

"As if you need it...not with that voice of yours."

She smiled, enjoying his compliment as he hit a few bars in a minor key, always her favorite. And with as little as that, her entire world broke open as Craig went into Willie Nelson's "Crazy," written in 1961 and made famous by Patsy Cline's sultry voice.

He looked at her with a slight smile as he played only for her, saying with music which could sometimes come so hard with words, telling her that he was crazy for loving her, crazy for feeling so blue, but he wasn't going to stop anytime soon because she was his world.

Nothing he'd said so far could have touched her like his music. She joined him, letting her soprano soar over his bass as they blended together, rising, falling, rising again. She felt her entire body react—hearing the music, feeling the music, doing the music—as she leaned toward him. And he turned to her, fingers flying over the strings as they edged closer and closer until they were joined as one in music and soul.

And she knew what she'd been missing...maybe her entire life. Giving. Accepting. Connecting. She let her voice soar in clear, pure notes to the rafters above as she opened her heart and let love flow into her, because it came from him in wave after wave, like a living, breathing elemental force so strong that there was no denying its power.

Finally, he let the song fade softly away and leaned toward, her, smiling sadly but hopefully. "I love you."

She kissed him on the lips, so full of the emotion he'd instilled in her that she couldn't speak—she could only feel a love that was like the blazing passion of the song they'd created together.

"That's how I feel," he said. "That's how I'll always feel."

She smiled, feeling so much stronger than she had in a very long while. "I want to change that song. Maybe another of Willie's, where he talks about nothing being better than making music with his friends."

"Nothing's better than making music with my love." Craig set his guitar against the stage, then turned and cradled her face with his hands. "Are you going to tell me to stop?"

"If you dare to even think about stopping, I'll tell you to keep going."

He slowly lowered his head, then pressed a soft kiss to

each corner of her mouth before gently taking her plump bottom lip between his teeth and sucking it into his mouth.

She'd forgotten—or had she?—how the slightest touch from him could make her feel as if she were soaring on an undulating melody that took her higher and higher until there was only the music...and the two of them.

She wound her hands around his neck, thrusting her fingers into his thick, shoulder-length hair, as she kissed him in return, nibbling his lips, nipping at him, licking him. She needed to taste him, feel him, delve into him, so she thrust into his mouth just as he picked her up and set her on his lap. Now she was surrounded by his heat, his strength, his desire. And she shivered in response.

He raised his head to look at her, keeping his hands around her hips. "You can't be cold. Not in here. Not in August."

"It's you. And you know it." She put her hands flat on his chest, feeling the hard contours of his muscles, the fast beat of his heart, the quickened pace of his breath.

He tightened his hands, then slid them slowly—so very slowly—upward, as if to give her time to reject him if she needed to be free, until he reached the lower curve of her breasts. He stopped, his breath coming quicker.

She traced down his chest until she reached his hands, those talented hands with the rough fingertips that she knew so well, and then gently but determinedly moved them up and over her breasts.

He squeezed gently. "You're sure?"

"I stopped being sure the moment I saw you again."

He rubbed thumbs across the tips, until they hardened into taut peaks, and she couldn't hold back the groan that rasped from her lips.

With that sound, he slipped his hands under her bottom, lifted her, and spread her legs to straddle him on the edge of the stage.

She nestled into him, feeling his hard, hot bulge press against the most intimate part of her, separated by nothing more than the thin fabric of their jeans. She grasped his shoulders and pulled him tightly to her as he put one hand around her back and the other around her hips, holding her steady as he rocked against her, letting her feel his need, building her desire, joining them closer and closer.

She kissed him, softly, moist, urgently, on his lips, his cheeks, eyes, then to his ears, where she traced the intricate whirls with the tip of her tongue. She felt him shiver at her touch, so she returned to his mouth and delved deep, tasting him, toying with him, taking him with her to their own special place until he broke the kiss.

"Fern," he rasped. "I need to ask again. Do you want this? If not, we need to stop now. I can't take much more and hold on to my control."

"I don't want you in control."

"No problem. You've got me exactly where you want me."

She pushed back and looked deep into his eyes, knowing she wasn't as sure as she sounded, but she wanted to try and see if she could go there again...to a place where they could reconnect and find a deeper pleasure in each other, as they were now. "Let's go back to your cabin."

"Why don't we make it *our* cabin," he said.

As she started to respond, she heard the front door slam open. She jerked back from Craig, looking toward the bar.

"Fern Bryant!" a voice called out. "Heard you were back. Where are you?"

COWBOY FIREFIGHTER HEAT 63

She jumped to her feet, pushing hair back from her face while feeling as if she'd been caught in an indiscreet act.

"Why the hell didn't I lock the front door?" Craig growled, glaring in that direction. "Can't we get any peace and quiet around here?"

She looked toward the entry, where a woman in a power wheelchair and with thick silver hair in a long plait, who was wearing a blue shirt, Wranglers, and black boots, zipped toward them. She was followed by a tall, slim woman with curly ginger hair wearing a crimson blouse and a long swirling skirt with rhinestone-studded cowgirl boots and a dozen or so long necklaces.

Fern clapped her hands in delight at the sight of two of her favorite folks from Wildcat Bluff. "Hedy Murray and Morning Glory!"

"And just how long were you going to take to let us know you were back in town?" Morning Glory asked as she gave Fern a big hug, then stepped back and looked her over. "You lost weight. On purpose or were you wasting away for that big hunk over there?"

"Leave her at least a secret or two, can't you?" Hedy held out her arms to Fern.

After Fern gave her other friend a tight hug, too, she stepped back and took a deep breath, feeling love bubble up inside her. "I've been gone too long, haven't I?"

"Too long!" Hedy scoffed. "Never should've left in the first place."

"She may have just needed space to find herself," Morning Glory said.

"In case you didn't notice, we left the sixties some time

back." Hedy gave her BFF a roll of her eyes with a teasing grin on her face.

"Some truths are eternal," Morning Glory said, giving a slightly superior sniff. "Anyway, the sixties will live on forever."

"At least so long as hippies like you survive," Fern said.

"I plan to live forever." Morning Glory gave Fern a wink with an eye sporting bright-blue eye shadow.

"See that you do," Fern said. "We need you."

"That's the truth of it," Craig said. "The county couldn't manage without you two...particularly Hedy masterminding Wildcat Bluff Fire-Rescue."

"I couldn't do it without all our fine volunteer cowboy and cowgirl first responders." Hedy gestured toward him. "They're the backbone of our community."

"Speaking of which," Morning Glory said, "we're here on a mission."

Craig groaned, glancing at Fern. "You know what that means."

She grinned, nodding. "They might be in need of volunteer services."

"Wild West Days has hit a snag," Hedy said.

"When has it ever gone completely snagless?" Craig asked.

"Never," Morning Glory replied. "But once we heard Fern was back in town, we figured the two of you could help us out."

"How?" Fern wondered if she was ready to be thrust back into the heart of the county so quickly after her return. Then again, these tireless powerhouses could overrun the stiffest objections, so she doubted she stood a chance of resisting them, even if she wanted to.

"Out with it." Craig grinned around at the group. "MG, this had better be good, or—"

"Don't complain before you've even heard our suggestion," Hedy said.

"Suggestion?" Craig laughed, shaking his head. "When have you two ever suggested anything? Generals giving orders is more like it."

Morning Glory put a hand over her heart as she glanced at Hedy. "I'm deeply wounded that he'd even suggest such a thing to lovely ladies like us. Aren't you?"

"Not in the least," Hedy said. "I just want to know where they stuck my stars."

"I could make you some," Morning Glory gave Fern a mischievous little smile.

"Ash might have put them in his kitty bed, thinking, as the fire station cat, he's the general," Fern said.

"Well, that's the truth of it," Hedy agreed. "Nothing gets by him."

"And that's just what he'll wear around his neck for Wild West Days," Morning Glory said. "He'll look good in stars."

"He looks good in everything he wears for the holidays." Hedy gave them all a self-satisfied smile. "But there's no use trying to get us off point by talking about the handsome Ash."

"Wouldn't dream of it," Craig said.

"What do you have in mind?" Fern glanced from one friend to the other. "I'm not sure how much I can help."

"It's right up your alley," Morning Glory said.

"Here's the deal." Hedy tossed her plait over one shoulder. "Bert Two was supposed to work with the high school drama department to spearhead the reenactment of the shoot-out between the Hellions and Ruffians for control of Wildcat Bluff during Wild West Days."

"Right," Craig said. "And it sort of combines with music events at the Lone Star Saloon, doesn't it?"

"That's where we're going to play, isn't it?" Fern felt confused by all the events that she'd never participated in before.

"Yep." Hedy nodded in agreement.

"Bottom line," Morning Glory said, "Bert Two broke his foot when his four-wheeler turned over while he was chasing down a bull."

"Not Fernando, I hope." Craig appeared concerned at the news.

"As if Storm would let him endanger her beloved bull," Hedy said. "No, it was a bull on Bert's ranch. The bull's fine, of course. Anyway, we're trying to keep Bert Two off his feet till he has a chance to get a little healing under his belt."

"How's that going?" Craig asked, smiling.

"About like you can imagine," Hedy said. "Bert is about to tie his son to his bed to keep him down."

"He'll heal," Morning Glory glanced at her friend, then back up. "But he needs time to recover."

"Right," Hedy agreed. "And as if that wasn't bad enough, funding was cut for the fine arts department by the state, so we basically don't have a drama department."

"That's bad," Fern said, feeling a terrible loss at the news. "Music, too?"

"Not gone yet." Morning Glory played with her necklaces in agitation. "We're scrambling to put together something, but it'll take a while, and kids are already in school again."

"What can we do to help?" Fern asked. "Students need fine arts to develop creative skills for later in life."

"You don't need to tell us," Hedy said. "But that's not where we need you right now."

"We're a month out from Wild West Days." Morning Glory glanced around the group. "Not much time for a change in leadership, but lots of stuff is already in place."

"I hope you're not suggesting that Fern take over," Craig said. "She's just back in town and—"

"Wouldn't dream of it," Hedy said, interrupting him. "We want the two of you to chair Wild West Days to make it the biggest, most successful event ever known in this town."

"We're running Wildcat Hall here. That's plenty, isn't it?" he asked.

"We need both of you on this," Morning Glory said. "As you well know, it's a big fund-raiser for Wildcat Bluff Fire-Rescue…and it helps all the merchants in town."

Hedy turned sharp brown eyes on Fern. "What do you say? Are you in, or are you out?"

Fern glanced at Craig and shrugged her shoulders. "How can we let down the entire county?"

He groaned, glanced down at the guitars, then back at her. "If you think you can do it, I'm with you. But it's a big bite out of the next month."

"I know." She looked at her friends. "I guess you can count us in, but we'll need all the up-to-date information on the events."

"You've got it." Morning Glory gave her a big grin and a bigger hug. "I knew we could count on you."

"Right," Hedy said. "Ivy says you've got the show-biz touch and that's what we need here."

"I don't know about that, but I'll give it my best." Fern felt as if she'd been hit with nothing but shocks since she got back to town.

"Craig can help you with the particulars," Morning Glory said. "He's been at this rodeo a time or two."

"I have at that," Craig said. "But I've never chaired it."

"Just round 'em up and head 'em in the right direction." Hedy chuckled with a mischievous glint in her eyes. "We'll do all the rest."

"Famous last words." Craig clasped Fern's hand as he glanced at her. "Was it calmer on the high seas?"

"One thing you can say about Wildcat Bluff County"— she grinned at the group as she squeezed his fingers— "there's never a dull moment."

Chapter 9

LATER THAT AFTERNOON, CRAIG CARRIED IVY'S SUIT-case, along with Fern's carryall, toward her new cabin. Fern wore her guitar on her back and held what was left of their lunch in a crushed sack. He walked as slowly as possible, regretting every single step that took them closer to her place. He had no appreciation whatsoever for birdsong, rose blooms, or the sultry, sweet-scented air of late summer.

They'd come so close, so very close, to where he wanted them to go…and then, once more, it'd all skittered out of his control to land somewhere totally unexpected and unwanted that took Fern's attention away from him. If he couldn't even keep her in his cabin, how did he expect to keep her in his life?

He felt frustrated even as he did what needed to be done. She had to have her own space. He got that. He just didn't want to get it. Music was the key, but now they'd been put in charge of Wild West Days. It was about as far away as they could get from where he wanted to go. At least they'd gotten a little closer to music in planning entertainment for the Lone Star Saloon.

Anyway, how did you lose funding for an import-ant program in a school? Short-sighted or cash-strapped administrators, he guessed. Bottom line, it meant another fund-raiser coming up in the near future. That was okay by him. It was about the only way for a small county community to take care of its residents when individuals—and in this case, a school district—ran into financial trouble due to big medical or other unforeseen bills. They'd pull together like they always did to support their own folks.

He couldn't complain about helping out with Wild West Days, although it was bound to slow down his pursuit of Fern. He'd step up to the plate to help others like he always did when they were in need or trouble. Maybe it was the first-responder instinct in him or simply a man who understood that sometimes folks just needed a little extra help to get over a hurdle. Even so, he trudged up to Fern's cowboy cabin with a heavy heart.

The Settelmeyers had prepared the crimson cabin, so named because of its accent color. It had red window frames and a shiny red door to brighten the overall appearance, and squatted on vintage redbrick posts about two feet in diameter, with brick posts holding up the front corners of the porch, leaving a crawl space underneath.

He followed Fern up the stairs, appreciating her even more than the well-done rock work and hand-carved wood railing. She stepped onto the porch and moved past two comfy rockers—both painted bright red.

"Ready for the unveiling?" She turned to him with a smile and dangled the key before his eyes.

"Anytime you are." He forced the words past reluctant lips, wishing they could go back down the stairs, over to the big cabin, and finish what they'd started in the honky-tonk.

She pushed open the front door and disappeared inside.

He followed her into an open-floor-plan room enclosed in the warm patina of old wood from floor to wall to ceiling, including a small kitchen with turquoise laminate countertops and pine cabinets adjacent to the living area and bathroom. On either end of the room, stairs led up to sleeping lofts with queen beds. Every bit of space was carefully designed for maximum use, since the cabin was so small.

He set the two cases beside a plush chair covered in roping-and-riding cowboy fabric near an end table that held a lamp in the shape of a cowboy on horseback with a turquoise lampshade. A coffee table that was hand-carved from rich, smooth, red cedar nestled in front of a brown leather love seat. A large barn-wood-framed photograph of a barrel-racing cowgirl took up much of the wall behind the sofa.

"What do you think?" He glanced around the room, trying to see it through her eyes and hoping it didn't look as small to her as it did to him.

"It's great. These cabins are so charming, the way they're built and the way they're decorated." She set her guitar in the chair before she walked into the kitchen and set the Chuckwagon sack on the countertop.

"Good." He heard the overhead fan on the center-exposed beam squeak slightly with each turn of the blades. He looked up, wondering if the sound would bother her.

"Yeah. I noticed it right away. I'll ask the Settelmeyers to see what they can do to stop that sound. It'll get more annoying the longer I'm here."

"You could turn it off till they do. AC is on, so you'll stay cool."

"Right. But heat rises to those lofts, so it's best if I leave it on…at least till it bugs me too much."

"You're so sensitive to sound I doubt it'll take long for that noise to get on your nerves. I'm sure they'll come right out if you call them."

"I know, but I'd rather not bother them so soon after they fixed up the place for me. They keep such a tight schedule."

He nodded, glancing around again to see if there was anything to do to make her more comfortable. "Which loft do you want?"

"I'll use the one that looks out over the front of the Park."

"Pretty view. If you want, I'll take your bags up there."

"Bathroom's down here, so I better keep my carryall with my personal items there."

"I bet the Settelmeyers stocked the bath as well as the kitchen."

She grinned, clapping her hands together. "Do you think they remembered which brands I like from when I lived here before?"

He chuckled, gesturing toward the bath. "Go check. I won't be a bit surprised if that's what they put in there for you. We're talking the Settelmeyers, and they never forget anything."

"They're amazing, that's for sure."

After she disappeared into the bathroom, he walked over to the kitchen. He opened the cookie jar in the shape of a purple cow, saw cowboy cookies, and nodded in satisfaction.

"Craig," she called as she headed toward him. "Just like you said, they remembered everything. They're making it so easy to move in here."

"Fresh cookies."

"Perfect." She opened the fridge door and peeked inside. "Look! Lots of little glass containers of food they prepared for me or got at the Chuckwagon."

"You're all set now." He peered over her shoulder. "Looks good."

"What do you bet they knew we'd been chosen to chair Wild West Days before we did?"

"I wouldn't take that bet." He laughed at the thought. "They appear to know everything before anybody else."

"Right. And they wanted to make sure I didn't waste any time on everyday stuff when I needed to get my head in our new game."

"That'd be my guess, too."

"I bet MG and Hedy let them know."

"Yep." He looked around again, realizing he didn't have much reason to stay in her cabin, and he didn't want to wear out his welcome so soon. "Let me run Ivy's suitcase upstairs, then I'll get out of your hair."

"What?" She looked at him, green eyes widening in surprise. "You're leaving?"

"I figured you'd want a little time to get unpacked and do whatever you want to do to make this more your home."

She stepped in close to him, put her hands on his shoulders, went up on her tiptoes, and placed a soft kiss on his lips. "I said I wanted my own place, but I didn't say I wanted to be alone."

He took a deep breath but didn't move as he watched her step back, smiling at him with that old light in her eyes. Was she teasing him? Was she being sincere? Was she inviting him upstairs? Maybe she wanted him to make the first move, but he was reluctant to do it because the last thing he wanted was to drive her away. Maybe what they'd shared in the Hall had simply been the result of playing emotional music together. Maybe he ought to just throw caution to the wind and take her in his arms until she begged him to finish what they'd started earlier.

As he moved to do just that, she whirled around and stepped outside. He followed, deciding he didn't understand her at all. He guessed he never had, but he had about five minutes to figure her out, or he felt as if he was going to lose her all over again.

"Let's go upstairs." He stopped beside her where she looked out over the Park, as if seeing it for the first time. Maybe he just needed to push her into what was right for both of them.

"What?"

"Let me prove to you that we can do this."

She wrapped her arms around her waist. "It's so intense between us. I think I need tender, but we're so fiery we never get there."

"I can do tender." He stepped closer, letting her feel his nearness, letting her sense his true intentions, letting her remember how he'd always supported her.

She didn't look at him, but she reached out and touched his arm...tentative at first, then more firmly as she stroked down his forearm until she clasped his hand and held on, breathing shallowly as if controlling great emotion.

"I'm here for you." He gently threaded their fingers together, giving her space and time and control. "I've always been here for you. I always will be."

"We don't have time for me...or us." She leaned into him, shivering even in the heat of the summer.

He took the weight of her body—he wanted her to understand she could lean on him in all ways, not just physically. And he, finally, began to understand what she needed from him. Sex wasn't going to do it. At least, not yet. Too many men offered it to her and too many men wanted it from her. She needed gentleness. She needed love. She needed to be nurtured, just as she nurtured so many through her music. His heart hurt for her. She didn't know what she needed because she'd given so much for so long. She didn't even know to ask for it or how to reach for it. But he did. Finally, he knew how to understand and help her... and maybe himself at the same time.

He would set aside his own hopes and desires to give her what she needed, not what she thought she wanted from him. In time, perhaps her needs and desires would merge into a great love that would heal her bruised and battered heart. He would be there, always there, to share her unfettered love or once more let her go out into the world alone.

He cleared his throat, decision made. "We ought to get right on making plans for Wild West Days."

"Oh." She glanced up at him, appearing surprised as she stepped back and dropped his hand.

"And not just that event, but we need to make sure we have everything under control for the Lone Star Saloon."

"And Wildcat Hall."

"Guess I kind of forgot we had so much to do now."

"Me, too." She glanced back into the cabin. "Do you suppose Hedy sent us that list of times and events for Wild West Days yet?"

"MG won't let her forget."

"We could check my laptop."

"Good idea." He smiled at her, feeling his heart beat a little faster as he realized they'd be together for the next month at least. It felt good.

"And we need to pull up the Hall's schedule."

"Right." He followed her back into the cabin. "Do you

feel like singing this weekend? It'd make a lot of folks happy to see you again."

She stopped in front of the kitchen sink and then whirled around to look at him. "You're right. I need to get back on the horse before I completely lose my nerve."

"You might feel a little stage fright, but you'll never lose your nerve—not with a guitar in your hands."

She smiled, nodding in agreement. "Okay. Let's announce on Wildcat Hall's website that we'll be performing Friday and Saturday nights."

"We?"

"Do you really think I'd go onstage here without you?"

"You've been singing without me."

"But that's because I didn't have you with me."

"And now that you do?"

"We'll knock their socks off."

"Just what I had in mind." He chuckled, so glad to see the old high-confidence Fern back that he could've given her a big kiss, but he restrained that impulse. In time, he'd go there again, but for now they'd focus on the one thing that always drew them close—plucking a few strings on their guitars and blending their voices in harmony.

Chapter 10

FRIDAY NIGHT, FERN STOOD UNDER THE HOT, BRIGHT lights of Wildcat Hall. She was back on her maybe-forever stage. She was glad Craig had checked the sprinkler system and the fire extinguishers to make sure they were all in good working order. With so many folks congregated in one area, they weren't about to take chances with the possibility of fire.

She'd travel like other performers from time to time, but she realized now that home would always beckon to her... like it did this time. And Craig. He stood to her left, backing her up on bass guitar, being there for her. Would he go with her, or would he stay? Was he rooted to Wildcat Bluff, or could he carry the roots with him? Could she?

She glanced at him, shimmering in all black like the legendary Man in Black who'd left his mark on country music forever and a day. Craig mostly chose songs that lifted spirits, found lost love, and nurtured the faint of heart. She was right there with him, listening as he brought their world of music to vibrant life before a honky-tonk of avid listeners.

From above, a rotating multicolor light show splashed across him, bouncing off the black lacquer of his electric guitar, turning the lone star on the alligator hatband of his black hat to silver glitter and emphasizing the high cheekbones of his handsome face. She smiled at him, couldn't help it, and caught his eye. They shared the moment, just the two of them in a crowded room. Yes, they made a complete circle, nothing more needed than the single glance of connection that they were in the right place at the right time with the right people.

On cue, she gave a quick nod, stepping back to give him center stage for an impressive riff, his quick fingers moving across the guitar strings. Folks sat on benches, clustered in groups, or line danced to a local western swing band while Craig Thorne played and sang his heart out.

He was accompanied by his band of cowboys playing fiddle, mandolin, banjo, guitar, accordion, and trap set. She tapped her toe as she listened, enjoying playing with them again, as their music brought people out onto the dance floor to a slow dance that was made for new lovers to connect and forever couples to reconnect.

Craig glanced at her, then stepped back so she could take center stage again. She hit the opening bars with her guitar, and then launched into Dolly Parton's legendary "Jolene" that begged a woman who had it all to please not take her man. Fern really didn't like this song much because she'd been put in that position a time or two by women who thought all she had to do was crook her little finger to come away with their man. She never did and she never would, but she understood the fear. She glanced at Craig. She wasn't the only one with admirers, and she might beg, too, if another woman had the power to take him away. And with that thought, she understood that she couldn't bear to lose him—not for any reason.

At the agreed upon time, she saw Morning Glory move up near the stage. She wore a blouse and long skirt of crimson and gold, and long chains dangled around her neck. She gave her friend a nod to let her know they'd take a break soon for the announcement. Beyond MG, DJs Wildcat Jack and Eden Rafferty, along with video and sound specialists Nathan Halford and Ken Kendrick, clustered in preparation for KWCB, the Wildcat Den, livestreaming from the Hall. She glanced at Craig, then stepped back again to let the band take over in an instrumental number that would lead into the announcement.

They'd been busy the last few days with Ivy updating the Wild West Days website while she and Craig contacted shoot-out reenactors, stores, and vendors. All was quickly coming together because Wild West Days was a yearly event and folks knew what to do and when to do it. She was the new kid on the block, so she'd been staying up late studying everything Hedy had sent her, so she could catch up to everyone else. It'd also given her a good excuse to stay in her cabin when everything in her had wanted to be next door with Craig, but he hadn't come knocking on her door, and she hadn't gone to him. She supposed it was for the best, but still she had that deep burn that wasn't going away anytime soon. And so she'd focused on work.

They'd come up with a promotion for Wild West Days at the dance hall tonight that featured her and the fact that she'd also be performing with Craig at the Lone Star Saloon during the big event. She had a couple of other local bands she knew were good that she wanted to add to the roster of the Hall and the saloon. She'd get to them in the next few days, as soon as she carved out some time to contact them. For now, she needed to keep her focus on her enthusiastic audience and the upcoming announcement.

As the music died away, she signaled, and the lights turned down on the stage and up on the audience. For the first time, she could see the happy—and in some cases sweaty—faces looking up expectantly as they stopped dancing and waited for their next entertainment.

She gestured toward Morning Glory, who stepped up on the stage with a big grin. As she handed MG a mic, Eden, in a crimson snap shirt, tight Wranglers, and red cowgirl boots, and Wildcat Jack, wearing his trademark fringed leather jacket despite the heat, joined them onstage. Nathan and Ken, both dressed in Wildcat Den T-shirts, jeans, and sneakers, moved into position on the floor and started live-streaming to the radio station's large audience.

"Folks, we won't keep you long from your boot-scooting fun," Morning Glory called to the crowd. "We just want to share our big kickoff to Wild West Days by announcing that our very own Fern Bryant is back in town and will be performing with our beloved Craig Thorne at the Lone Star Saloon."

A loud roar of approval went up from the crowd, along with a lot of boot stomping and catcalls.

"That's right, folks." Morning Glory raised her arms outward to encompass the honky-tonk. "Come Labor Day weekend, you'll be getting the best of both worlds right here at Wildcat Hall and in town at the Lone Star Saloon. So don't be a stranger." She stepped back and handed the mic to Eden.

"Aren't they the best?" Eden gestured toward the band. "You'll be seeing Fern Bryant and Craig Thorne perform together again, by special request from all y'all in Wildcat Bluff County. So come on out and join us." She turned and handed the mic to Wildcat Jack.

"That's right, all you cowboys and the cowgirls who love

'em for whatever wild and crazy reason, we're gearing up big-time for our annual Wild West Days," Jack said with a wink. "And we invite every last one of you to join us for all the fun."

Applause followed Jack's words, as he did a little soft-shoe shuffle back and forth on the stage.

"You know it. You love it," Jack called out. "Let's hear it for the biggest, baddest, bestest Wild West Days to ever grace our beautiful county."

Fern couldn't keep from grinning as Jack received another wild response from the audience. He really knew how to rev 'em up and reel 'em in. She appreciated an expert entertainer of his quality.

"So y'all come on out and enjoy all the fun."

She was still grinning when her breath caught in her throat and all humor fled at a sight she thought she'd left behind on the cruise lines. It was no apparition, although she tried to make it into an unreality. A tall man who moved like a hunter on the prowl stepped to the front of the crowd. He stared at her—and no one else—with a particular hungry gaze that cut straight through her. He wore his shock of silver hair a little long, a little tussled, and it contrasted with tanned skin stretched tightly across sleek muscles emphasized by a lapis silk T-shirt and ripped, faded blue jeans. *Powerful*, that was the only word for him. Simon Winter—if that was his real name.

She felt a little dizzy and Jack's voice faded away as Simon sighted her as if focusing to get her exactly in the center of his crosshairs. She wanted to disappear. She wished she'd never agreed to perform here tonight and put her name out there. Most of all, she wished she'd never crossed paths with this supremely confident man.

She instinctively eased toward Craig, feeling a need for his protection. She stopped, frozen in place by a chilling thought. Would Simon view Craig as an obstacle to his goal? That could be dangerous. Then again, maybe Simon had simply been in the area and decided to stop by, although that possibility seemed remote.

She needed to do something to defuse the situation. She raised her chin and stared into Simon's cold gray eyes. He smiled at her response, just the faintest movement of his too-perfect lips. He had her complete attention now, so he stepped forward and carefully placed a huge bouquet of perfect white roses—at least two dozen—in transparent green plastic wrap on the stage. She didn't trust this gift one bit, just as she hadn't trusted this man from the first. When she glanced up, Simon was gone, as if he'd never been there.

She stepped back from the front of the stage. Not what she was supposed to be doing, so she felt Craig turn his focus on her. From the corner of her eye, she caught his puzzled stare. She simply shook her head, trying to reassure him but not knowing how to do it.

"How pretty." Morning Glory picked up the flowers and held them out to Fern. "You obviously have an admirer."

Fern shivered with deep cold because she knew that Simon was much more than an admirer. Somehow or other, he represented danger. Craig must have picked up on her dismay because he moved closer to her. At his nearness, she started to come back to her senses. She heard Eden and Jack continue their spiel about Wild West Days as MG held out the flowers.

"Don't you want them?" Morning Glory asked with eyebrows quirking upward.

"Please." She finally found her voice. "You keep them."

"She needs her hands to play." Craig quickly covered for her, moving even closer.

When she felt his body heat, she breathed a little easier. She wasn't alone—not here, not now. She was back in Wildcat Bluff with her friends and sister. All was well. She repeated the words over and over for reassurance but also to hold any other thoughts at bay.

"Okay." Morning Glory gave Fern a puzzled look even as she cradled the roses to her chest, then she turned back toward Eden and Jack.

Fern felt hot then cold at the thought of sharp rose thorns. Most would have been clipped from the long, green stems, but any inadvertently left could puncture vulnerable skin, causing pain.

"Are you okay?" Craig whispered as he slipped his guitar to the side away from her, so he could move even closer. "Do you need to leave?"

She swallowed hard, feeling the dryness of her throat, the tightness in her chest. She wasn't at all sure she could continue to sing. Simon showing up here in her safe place had definitely spooked her.

"That's it. We're getting you out of here," Craig said. "Something happened and I want to know what, but first, we go."

She reached for his arm, connected with heat, and felt his muscles bunch as if readying for battle. She tried to smile and reassure him, but her face felt rigid along with the rest of her body. She glanced at MG, who was giving her another concerned look.

Morning Glory turned away, caught Eden's eye, and

gestured that something was amiss and they needed to finish up.

Eden took the mic from Jack, giving him a shrug before she looked out over the audience. "And so, folks, that's just a reminder of all the fun to be had during Wild West Days. You don't want to miss the recreation of the shoot-out between the Ruffians and the Hellions for control of Wildcat Bluff, so be sure and join us for that exciting event. Just to remind you, live ammunition certainly won't be used, but you'll think you've stepped into the middle of the battle with all the noise and smoke."

"That's right," Wildcat Jack said as he leaned close to the mic. "We want you to be sure and join us for that and every other event during Wild West Days."

"Thank you for your time. And now let us return you to the music of Wildcat Hall so you can dance the night away." Eden turned off the mic as Nathan and Ken stopped livestreaming.

Morning Glory eased close to Fern. "What happened? Can we do anything?"

"I'm okay," Fern managed to say.

"No, she's not." Craig signaled for the band to start a lively tune. When music once more filled the honky-tonk, he put an arm around Fern's shoulders. "I'm getting her out of here."

"What can we do to help?" Eden asked while keeping a smile on her face for the audience.

"Distraction. We'll help keep the audience busy toe-tapping after y'all leave." Jack grabbed the mic from Eden. "Use the side door off the back of the stage. We'll take it from here."

"You sure?" Craig asked.

"Piece of cake. Now get." Jack gave them a big grin.

Craig set their guitars on stands, then leaned down to the keyboard player. "She's sick. I'm taking her home. Jack's great with a crowd and great with the stories, so he'll keep things lively in between songs while you handle the music."

Fern watched the player nod in agreement, feeling like she was acting like an amateur. She wanted to pull herself together, but she wanted more than anything to get off the stage and out of the light. And take Craig with her.

When the stage door shut behind Fern, she took a deep breath of the sweet-scented and warm summer air. She felt a vast sense of relief to be offstage, but she wanted them out of the open and the dark.

"Can you talk about it now?" Craig squeezed her shoulders, tugging her closer to him.

"Please, just take me home."

"Yours or mine?"

"Your cabin. I don't want to sleep alone tonight."

Chapter 11

WHEN CRAIG CLOSED THE FRONT DOOR BEHIND HER, Fern made sure it was locked tight before she walked into the kitchen. She slid a chair out from under the table, carried it back to the door, and tucked the edge under the knob. Only then did she feel like she could draw a deep breath.

And still she watched the door as she slowly backed away from it, waiting to make sure it didn't magically pop open and Simon leap inside. Why was she reacting so strongly to him? He'd never been improper. And yet he'd frightened her. When she felt the back of her legs hit the sofa, she sat down abruptly—maybe too abruptly because she started to shake, and once started, it spread like wildfire until her teeth chattered in her head.

"Fern, what the hell?" Craig sounded terrified for her, looking around to find what she saw that so frightened her.

She clasped her arms around her waist, shivering harder and harder, as if everything she'd been holding back for months was coming out all at once in a giant geyser of emotion.

He strode from the room, then quickly returned carrying a quilt. He sat down beside her, pulled her onto his lap, wrapped the soft fabric around her, and enclosed her in a tight embrace.

And still she shivered, despite the warmth and the safety of his arms. All the while, she tried to pull back from the abyss, telling herself that she was overreacting. So a fan followed her to hear her sing in a new venue. It wasn't unusual. Groupies were nothing new to performers. Still, Simon simply did not belong in a honky-tonk, and she didn't want him anywhere near Wildcat Hall…or Wildcat Bluff County. And yet the roses were proof of his presence.

"Fern, talk to me. Let me help you." Craig rocked her back and forth like he would comfort a crying baby.

She shivered harder, feeling vulnerable being so emotionally exposed to him when she wanted to appear in control. Maybe she'd been onstage so much that she no longer knew how to share, or even feel, real emotions…even if she'd wanted to, which she didn't. Feelings were dangerous. Shared feelings were even more dangerous. And here she was in a full-blown panic attack cradled in Craig's arms, so what could be more dangerous? That thought brought her up short. Simon Winter—he could very well be more dangerous. And her shivering stopped, as if something deep inside her body knew she couldn't afford to be vulnerable any longer. She wasn't the only one at stake here.

"Can you tell me what's bothering you?" Craig asked in a gentle voice that was meant to soothe.

"The roses."

He grew still. "Roses? I don't understand. How could they scare you? And don't think for a minute I don't recognize what you're going through. It happened onstage…after the roses and—"

"The man."

"What man?"

"He brought the roses."

"There was so much going on between the band and the

announcement that I didn't notice him." Craig tugged her closer, as if he could protect her from the unknown man who frightened her.

"Think back. He didn't fit."

"What do you mean?"

"Wrong clothes. Loafers instead of boots. Slick looking."

"Wait a minute. Silver hair?" he asked.

"Yes."

"I got a glimpse, but I didn't think anything about it. Just another fan. The Hall was full of them tonight."

"He's not just another fan," she said.

"What do you mean?"

"He was on several cruises. He watched me perform. He sent me white roses."

She felt Craig's body tense around her.

"He wasn't on every cruise, but white roses arrived after every performance and let me know I was on his mind."

"That's not good."

"One night…my last night, the roses came with a bottle of champagne and two crystal glasses."

"What did he want?"

"He included a note inviting me to dinner."

"Yeah, sure. Dinner." Craig hugged her hard against him. "Why do people think entertainers are easy, as if we're there for their complete pleasure? I get it, too."

"I know you do."

"How did you handle it?"

"Fortunately, it was my last night, and I declined with a note, explaining that I wasn't available and would be leaving the cruise line."

"Did you hear anything else?"

"No. Not until tonight." She shivered again and snuggled against Craig. "I thought it was all over, just a cruise infatuation."

"And now?"

"I'm uneasy that he found me and followed me here."

"I think it's a very bad thing. It borders on stalking, if it isn't outright stalker behavior."

"I don't know about that, but it was a surprise to see him in my world, as if he'd somehow invaded it."

"We won't take any chances. I'll alert Sheriff Calhoun," he said.

"Let's don't take it that far yet. Simon could've—"

"Simon? That sounds like you know him a lot better than you let on. Tell me the truth. Did you do more with him than accept roses and champagne?"

"What!" She leaped out of his lap, struggling with the quilt, and glared down at him. "Are you suggesting I had some sort of flagrant affair with him on the cruises so he followed me here?"

"It's been known to happen."

"If that's what you think, then I'm going back to my cabin. No way am I spending the night here."

"I'm sorry." He stood up, holding out his hands to either side. "I got jealous. I'm scared for you. This type of thing can get out of hand and if—"

"I rejected him from the get-go. Besides, there's just something about him that I don't trust—will never trust."

"Okay. I'm sorry, but I had to hear the words from you. The sheriff will ask you the same thing."

"Oh." She felt her shoulders slump as she deflated like a tire losing air. "Of course, that's what folks will think."

"Not all people."

"But they'll wonder. Just like you."

"I never doubted you, but I had to put it out there."

She pulled the quilt up over her shoulders and wrapped her arms around her waist. "What if he tells people around here that we're..."

"Lovers?"

"Yes."

"Do you think he will?"

"I have no idea." She paced across the room, then turned back. "As you can imagine, I have no idea who this man is and what he's capable of doing or saying or sending or anything."

"Okay. We won't take chances. And another thing—no matter what he tries to pull, he's in Wildcat Bluff County now. He's the outsider, and he'll be treated as such."

"Do you mean folks won't believe him?" she asked.

"We've got a pretty good radar for slick operators, so nobody will be taken in by him."

"Still, we don't need problems, not with Wild West Days coming up."

"True. I ought to contact the sheriff right now."

"Wait. What if we're wrong? What if Simon was simply passing through, caught my name in the news, and decided to stop by and give me roses again? It's possible, isn't it?"

"Yes. But not likely. We're off the beaten path here."

"Let's wait." She tightened the quilt, feeling a little bit calmer as they talked out the situation. Maybe she really had overreacted at the sight of those silly white roses. Simon didn't have to be a stalker.

"I'm not inclined to wait. How long?"

"If he doesn't show again and I receive no more roses, then I'd say he was just passing through and moved on to his final destination someplace else."

"Okay. But I'd feel better if we contacted Sheriff Calhoun to be on the safe side."

"I don't want to look like I'm overreacting, and I particularly don't want that image at just the time I reappear to put my life back together here," she said.

"Nobody would think that of you. They'd think you're smart to be cautious. It helps no one if you take chances."

"I won't take a chance."

"You sure won't, not if I have anything to say about it." He walked over to her and held out his arms. "I'm sorry if—"

"It's okay." She let him enclose her again, feeling grateful for his heat, his strength, his concern.

"I know you won't want the restrictions, but please don't go out alone anymore."

"I'm back in Wildcat Bluff. I'll be okay here."

"Humor me, will you?" He tilted her face up with the tip of one finger, so he could look into her eyes. "If anything happened to you, I'd never forgive myself…or recover."

She nodded, smiling slightly. "I truly think I overreacted to a fan, but to tell you the truth, I'd feel better not going out by myself at night."

"Good. That's the way we handle it till we're through Wild West Days."

"We probably won't see him again."

"Maybe not. But one white rose or sight of that guy, and I'm calling Sheriff Calhoun."

"Okay. I won't disagree with that plan."

"Another thing." He pressed a soft kiss to the tip of her nose. "You either sleep here, or I sleep in your cabin. There's no way I'll leave you alone at night no matter how much security we have in the Park."

She hesitated, thinking how she'd barely moved into her new cabin and she'd been enjoying it...except for missing Craig.

"No compromise on this one."

She could see the determination in his eyes. And she knew he was right. Neither of them should take a chance. They'd be stronger together—and she'd sleep much better.

"My cabin or yours?"

"Yours is bigger."

He smiled, appearing pleased with her choice. "I can take the sofa."

"Maybe the Settelmeyers could bring in an inflatable or rollaway bed for me to use out here."

He groaned, shaking his head. "That's going to be about as comfortable as the sofa. Are you sure we can't share the bed?"

She didn't want to give in too easily, but she didn't want to be separated from Craig, not anymore.

"Can't we?"

She smiled and traced his full lips with a fingertip. "If you promise not to snore and stay on your side of the bed, I don't see why we can't share that nice, new, comfy bed."

He flicked out his tongue to touch her fingertip. "I see you're going to make that requirement hard to handle, but I'll manage it. I won't do anything to drive you from this cabin."

"I'm not sure you could right now."

"Good." He tucked her head against his chest and stroked down her back with his large hands.

She could feel the strong, steady beat of his heart. He comforted her in so many different ways. She was grateful he was here for her when she truly needed him. She'd like to show him her appreciation and what he meant to her. And there was one perfect way to do it. She rose up on her tiptoes and placed a soft, hot kiss against his mouth. When he stiffened against her, she raised her head and looked at him in surprise.

"Craig?" she said just as the doorbell filled the cabin with a discordant sound. She jerked back, swiveling to look at the door. "Are you expecting anyone?"

"No." He stalked over, pulled aside the chair, and jerked open the door.

"Here you go!" Morning Glory thrust the bouquet of roses toward Fern. "You weren't feeling well, so I knew these would perk you right up."

"MG, you'd better come inside." Craig stepped back to make room for her.

"Poor dear, how are you feeling?" Morning Glory sashayed into the cabin, then held out the roses again.

Fern took one look at them and felt nauseated all over again. She quickly sat down on the sofa, pulling the quilt up around her middle.

Craig grabbed the roses, tossed them outside, and slammed shut the door.

Morning Glory looked from one to the other in shock. "Was it something I said?"

"Something you brought inside." He gestured toward the sofa. "Why don't you have a seat? As long as you're here, you might as well be the first to know."

"Oh dear." Morning Glory gave a big sigh, sat down

beside Fern, took her hand, and squeezed in sympathy. "Don't tell me you caught a summer cold. They can be so pesky. I have just the thing to help you down at the store."

Craig sat in the chair. "The roses."

"Yes?" Morning Glory asked. "Lovely. But there appears to be an issue with them."

"Did you see the guy who brought them?"

"Absolutely," Morning Glory said. "Silver-haired dude with a fine physique. He might not be my cup of tea, but I doubt he gets turned down very often."

"He may be a stalker," Craig said.

"Oh no!" Morning Glory put a hand over her heart as she turned to Fern. "In Wildcat Bluff?"

"He came to a few of my concerts on the cruises." Fern felt her heart beat faster at just the thought of it now. "And he always sent white roses."

"But we aren't sure," Craig said. "We don't like the coincidence, that's all."

Morning Glory nodded in agreement. "It can happen. I've had a little of that action over the years, groupies."

Fern gave her friend a long look, brought up short by that revelation. What was Morning Glory's story? Did anybody know? She was a flower child of the sixties, but what did that really mean? By now, the time period was mysterious history, unless still embodied by someone like MG who could never be tamed by society. She'd always be someone who went her own way. And it was a good thing because everyone benefited from her knowledge, expertise, and support.

Craig cleared his throat, giving MG a considering look that reflected Fern's internal interest.

"Reminds me of that eighties Police song," Morning Glory said with a faraway look in her eyes as if remembering something from her own past.

"Yeah," Craig replied. "Sting's 'Every Breath You Take' turned out to be a real stalker of a song."

"Times change. It was a big hit back then," Morning Glory said. "Nowadays, it's a cautionary tale."

"I'm definitely feeling cautious." Fern wrapped the quilt tighter around her body.

"That's smart," Morning Glory said. "In my experience, they usually lose interest in time if they don't get what they want."

Craig hummed a few bars of the Rolling Stones' "You Can't Always Get What You Want."

"But sometimes you get what you need." Fern added the refrain in her rich soprano.

"Exactly," Morning Glory replied. "We'll get what we need, but if this guy turns out to be a stalker, he won't get what he wants."

"That'd be ideal," Fern said.

"Now, what are you going to do about the situation, if anything?" Morning Glory fiddled with her long necklaces, obviously considering possible scenarios. "Sheriff Calhoun?"

"If the guy shows up again, that's exactly where we're going," Craig said with finality in his voice.

"I want to wait until there's definite proof that I have a stalker before bringing in the authorities." Fern leaned toward MG to make her point.

"Understandable." Morning Glory patted her hand. "Still, I want to tell Hedy, so she can be on the lookout if the guy turns up. Do you know his name?"

"Simon Winter," Fern said. "Real name or not, I have no idea."

"Okay. I'll share this news with Hedy but no one else. For now." Morning Glory stood up. "But, Fern, just in case, don't go anywhere alone."

"Right," Craig agreed, standing. "And she's living here now."

"Perfect." Morning Glory headed for the door, stopped, and looked back. "Tonight was a big success, despite your early departure. Fern, everyone loves you, and they're so glad you're back in Wildcat Bluff."

"Let's just hope somebody doesn't love me too much," Fern said with all sincerity.

Craig nodded in agreement.

"Don't see me out." Morning Glory opened the front door. "I'll get rid of the roses. Sorry I brought them here, but I'm glad I got the news. We'll take it from here. Nobody messes around with our folks." And she was out the door in swirl of long skirts, jangling necklaces, and determined energy.

"Are you okay?" Craig looked down at Fern.

"Actually, I'm a lot better. I'd forgotten how fiercely protective MG and Hedy are about our community."

"You're safe here. Never doubt it." He walked over to the door, checked outside, then shut and locked the door.

She rose to her feet and held out her hand. "Come on. I've had more than enough of this evening. Let's go to bed."

Chapter 12

CRAIG HAD FERN IN BED WITH HIM. HE HAD HER NES-
tled against him. He had her wearing nothing more than
a Wildcat Hall T-shirt. He took a deep, shaky breath. She
totally encompassed him from her sweet-tart scent and
silky-soft hair to her satiny-smooth skin. He sighed out
loud. What was the pot of gold at the end of his personal
neon rainbow just a few days ago was now a nightmare setting him on the edge of wildness.

Control—he had to stay in control so as not to spook
her any more than she already had been this night. Yet how
could he do it when his weakening will was rapidly losing
the battle against his blazing body? He'd made a promise
to himself to take it slow and easy with her, but he hadn't
counted on a knife thrust abruptly into their private
world…and her fragile psyche.

She needed comfort as well as reassurance. But was sex
the best way to go about it? No doubt they both wanted
it—and needed it to reconnect in the deepest, most spiritual way possible. But would it cause more harm than
good? Maybe he was overthinking the entire situation
when he simply needed to let the strongest part of him
override any reservations he had about going forward
tonight.

"What are you thinking?" She nudged him with her
foot, tracing down his calf with her soft toes.

He groaned, knowing that if he answered her truthfully, she'd be out of bed so fast she'd simply be a blur of movement.

"That bad?" She grew completely still. "It's about Simon, isn't it?"

"I wish you wouldn't use his name. It feels like that gives him too much power in your life."

She turned silent, as if thinking about his words. "You're right. It's just that… I don't know… He can't have that much power, can he?"

"Not if we don't let him."

"It's all about power, not attraction, isn't it?"

"I'd guess it's one motivating the other." He didn't want to go down this path, but if it helped her better understand her situation, he'd go there.

"It's not really me, is it? It's his attraction, then his need to control the object of his desire. Is that right?"

Craig could feel her soft breath against his bare chest, the strong beat of her heart, the warmth of her body curled against him. He pressed her closer with his arm around her shoulders, seeking to comfort but not really knowing how to do it best. If she needed words, that was what he would give her. In the back of his mind, a song began to develop…about how to be there for your love when she needed you bad.

"Right?"

"I'd guess it's different for every man or woman. In this case, he saw you, wanted you, and went after you. I don't think it's all that complicated an issue."

"You've dealt with it, too."

"Women can be aggressive. Nowadays more so than in the past…maybe there are fewer social restrictions." He hesitated, thinking about what he wanted to cautiously say next. "We're professional entertainers. Fantasy is our stock in trade. Sometimes folks want more than we're here to give them."

Fern placed her hand on his chest and followed the swirls of hair with fingertips slightly rough from playing guitar.

He went rigid all over, hardening from a need that went way beyond the physical into the mystical. They were bound in a way she didn't understand yet. He had to give her time while being there for her. When she rubbed her thumbnail gently across his nipple, he groaned and put his hand over hers to still her. He could only take so much torment, no matter how pleasurable.

"I want to hear about these aggressive women. Names. I'll make sure they never bother you again." She rose on one arm and kissed him softly, gently on his lips. "But first I'll make sure you forget they ever existed in your world."

He tried to resist her. He really did try. And yet, she tasted him with her tongue and nibbled him with her teeth, demanding, coaxing, persuading. He wasn't made of stone—although he was beginning to feel like it.

"I don't hear names yet." She chuckled deep in her throat as she teased him with her lips and her words.

"No names. You're wiping my memory clean." He heated up all over as she placed soft, warm kisses across his face, nibbling on his earlobes until she moved farther down to linger on the vulnerable indentation at the base of his throat. She stroked there with the tip of her tongue, playing with him, raising the heat between them until he was riding the leading curl of a powerful wave of passion. She had to be feeling the strong beat of his heart and know just how much she was affecting him.

She lifted her head and looked at him in the soft light of the lamp on the nightstand. "No memory of them at all?"

"Not a single one."

She smiled with a light in her pale green eyes that said everything about her intentions with him this night.

He finally gave in. Who was he to deny her or himself? They both needed the closeness, the pleasure, the ability to forget the outside world. Here, it was only the two of them. No audience to please. No stalker to avoid. No plans to make. They only needed to make each other happy... and at the moment, that seemed the greatest calling in the universe.

He pushed long fingers into her thick hair and cradled her head in both hands, leaning over to place a soft kiss on softer lips. She let him linger a moment, then she pushed him back against the pillow, as if needing the control after her recent experience. He relaxed on his back, letting her take charge, but then, he'd have given her anything her heart desired at that moment.

He just wished he weren't wearing sweatpants. He wanted them naked, so he could feel skin against skin as they both grew hot and slick with sweat. He kissed her, delving deep into her sweet-tasting mouth as he slid his hands up the back of her thighs, rucking up her T-shirt until he reached her enticing curves. He stroked there, molding her shape as he felt a mounting need to be deep inside her. He continued upward, stroking across her back, feeling her skin heat up with every touch of his hands, and the kiss between them grew ever hotter as they reached fever pitch.

She raised her head and looked at him, eyes dark with need. "I'm on the edge and about to tip over."

"I won't let you fall."

"You're sure?"

"I promise to be slow and tender." He spread his hands, moving them to her sides until he could nestle his fingers under the curves of her breasts.

She caught her breath, hesitated as if making a decision, and then rose slightly to give him further access.

He gently cupped her full breasts, rubbing the tips with his thumbs until the hard nubs told him of her mounting desire. She shivered all over and moved restlessly against him. He was relentless in building her passion, stoking their flames higher and higher with his hands and mouth and body. And she was moaning and undulating until he was about to go over the edge with her. He'd yearned for her so long that nothing could have held him back now, not when she was with him all the way.

She raised her head again, giving him a soft smile, and kissed the tip of his nose. "I'm not sure if slow and tender will be enough tonight."

"I'll give you whatever you want. You set the pace. I'll follow."

She stared back with a mischievous glint in her eyes. "You'll follow for how long?"

He chuckled. "As long as possible."

She rolled over, kicked the covers off, bent one knee, and held out her arms. "Let's see what we can make possible."

As he sat up and reached for her, he stopped, raised his head, and looked toward the open bedroom door.

"What is it?" she asked, glancing in that direction, too.

"Do you smell smoke?"

"Oh no, surely not."

"Maybe not." He couldn't believe the bad luck, but he couldn't take a chance, not with tinder-ready recycled wood on all the cabins.

"I don't smell anything."

"I'll just take a quick look outside. Stay here."

"Not on your life. If there's trouble, I'll be right by your side."

He hesitated, looking down at her. He could see she meant she'd stand beside him. And it was more than just this moment, when there was possible danger to what they both held dear.

"I'm serious."

"I know." And still he hesitated, even with seconds to stop a fire. "You'll be by my side?"

"I've got your back." And she gave him a straight-up look that carried a lifetime of commitment.

"If I asked you to marry me this very moment, would you say yes?" The minute the words were out of his mouth, he knew he shouldn't have uttered them, but he'd also felt it was the right thing, in that moment, to do.

She glanced away from him, shuttering her emotions. "How did we get from fire to marriage?"

"Commitment." He slipped off his side of bed, jerked on a T-shirt, pulled on sneakers without lacing them, and walked around the bed. He picked up his cell phone from the nightstand and slipped it into his pocket.

"You ask that right now, while at the same time you're leaping out of bed and leaving me all hot and bothered?"

He grinned, chuckling at the idea. "Yeah. Guess my timing leaves something to be desired."

"Glad you agree." She smiled, shaking her head. "Let's go see about this imaginary fire of yours. Cowboy firefighters—I guess you're always on call."

"Always. You just never know."

"And it's a good thing for everyone."

He walked into the main room and glanced around the area. He didn't see anything worrisome or hear suspicious activity, but he could definitely smell smoke stronger out here. He jerked open the door under the kitchen sink and pulled out two heavy-duty fire extinguishers as well as two metal flashlights before he walked over to the front door.

"I can smell smoke out here." She joined him at the front door. "What should we do?"

"Check it out." He handed her a can and a flashlight while evaluating what she wore. She'd put on sneakers, so her feet were okay, but if they had a fire on their hands, she'd definitely need to put on more clothes and go someplace safe.

"Should we call Hedy or someone?"

"Not yet. It could be somebody burning a brush pile."

"At night?"

"They could've left a smoldering stump. If the wind came up, it might've stirred up the embers and spread smoke."

"In other words, this smoke doesn't necessarily have anything to do with the Park."

"Right." He slung the canister by its strap over one shoulder and punched on his flashlight. "But I wouldn't count on it."

"I'm not." She picked up a can by its strap, settled it over one shoulder, and grabbed a flashlight. "Let's go."

He opened the door and got hit in the face with a wall of smoke and the stench of something burning as he stepped outside.

"Guess a smoldering stump is out of the question." She followed him, shutting the door behind them.

"Yeah." Nothing more to be said. "Don't leave the porch. I'll check the crawl space."

"Craig." She coughed on the smoke, then held up a hand to cover her nose and mouth.

He stopped on the first step and glanced back. She looked more like an apparition than a real woman with white smoke illuminated by the porch light swirling around her. For just a moment, he wondered if he'd imagined her coming back and moving into the cabin with him. He'd wanted it for so long that maybe… He scoffed at the notion. He needed to get his head in the game and fight a fire, not grapple with ghosts.

"Don't take chances. We can call backup."

"I'll be careful." And he bounded down the stairs with light from his flashlight leading the way.

He quickly walked away from the cabin to get a bigger picture of what was going on in the area. He left the smoke pretty quickly, so he looked back and zeroed in on the crawlspace underneath the porch. Smoke billowed out from under there, where it'd be easy to set a fire, but he didn't see red flames, so hopefully it'd be fairly easy to contain.

But why would somebody do it? And who'd do it? He felt the hairs on the back of his neck rise, an indicator that he was being watched…maybe from nearby. He dropped into a crouch to make a smaller target while he glanced up the stairs to where Fern stood in the glow of the porch light. He felt his heart sink. Maybe she was the target. Not him. Not the cabin. Smoke would send them running outside to check on a fire or to get better air.

"Fern, go back inside and shut the door," he called, hoping she'd obey him but not counting on it.

"What?" She took several steps forward and looked down at him over the railing.

Of course, she'd done the exact opposite of what he wanted her to do. Frustrated, he looked at the fire, then up at her. She came first, always. He bounded up the stairs, opened the door, and urged her inside.

"What is it?"

"I'll tell you in a minute. Just stay here. Give me that can. I think I can contain the blaze myself. It's more smoke than fire."

"Don't you need help?"

"Please, stay in here where it's safe."

She gave him a brisk nod, then handed over her canister. "If you're not back in five minutes, I'm coming after you."

"Okay."

He slammed the door behind him, raced back down the stairs, and crouched down near the heart of the smoke. He pulled a pin, aimed the nozzle, and sprayed the area. He emptied the first can, then backed it up with the second. After he was satisfied the blaze was out, he used the bottom of a can to drag out the smoking, burning material. A bunch of oily rags. It looked as if somebody had intended to smoke them out of the cabin but not burn it down. Why?

There'd been a fire under one of the small cabins last

Christmas, but it hadn't done much damage and the culprits had been caught. Surely this didn't have anything to do with that incident. He glanced around again, but even with the smoke clearing, he couldn't see anyone or anything out of the ordinary. But he was on alert now. Too much was at stake to let this go.

He pulled out his phone to alert Hedy at the fire station and Sheriff Calhoun at the police station. If somebody thought they were easy marks, they were going to learn you didn't mess with the folks of Wildcat Bluff County.

Chapter 13

"THERE'S SOMETHING YOU'RE NOT TELLING ME." FERN sat down beside Craig on the sofa after she'd changed into an Aqua Cruise promo tee, cutoffs, and flip-flops. She didn't sit too close because there was a distance between them that hadn't been there before the fire. Something had changed in him and she didn't know what. Maybe he was worried about her...about himself...about the Park. She figured he had good reason.

"Slade is coming over to take samples. Sheriff Calhoun is coming to check out the site. I doubt they'll find much more than burnt rags."

"That's not what's bothering you." She felt chilled even though the AC was struggling to overcome the heat outside.

"It is and it isn't."

"What do you mean?"

"Somebody wanted us out there."

"Why?"

"That's the question, isn't it?"

She felt even colder and rubbed up and down her arms to get warmer. "Did you see something or someone?"

"No." He sighed and leaned back against the sofa. "But I felt watched, as if somebody was waiting to see our reaction."

"Anybody could've guessed we'd go outside to get fresh air, so what was there to see?"

"Another good question."

"Maybe the sheriff can figure it out."

"It's possible, but I don't think we should count on it."

"Why not?" She leaned back against the sofa, too, and he put an arm around her shoulders and drew her into his warmth. It felt good. Maybe everything was still okay. She hardly knew which end was up anymore.

"He's a busy man. We don't have much for him to go on."

"Surely they'll find something."

"Like I said, we can't count on it. Anyway, Wildcat Hall Park is the target, or we're the targets."

"You mean we're the ones best suited to figure out what's going on," she said.

"Yeah."

"But we don't know anything, either."

"Not yet." He picked up her hand and pressed a soft kiss to the palm. "I'm sorry about all this drama. I know you came back for calm sanity and—"

"And you." She wrapped her fingers around his hand, squeezing lightly as she realized her words were absolutely true.

"Me?"

"I don't know why I thought I could live without you."

He clasped her hand in both of his and held on tightly. "But you can live without me. We both know it."

"What if I say I choose to live with you, not without you?" She knew his words had been true at one time. Now, she doubted it. She needed him. She wanted him. She longed for him.

"Nothing would make me happier, but tonight's thrown you off balance. And no wonder. I doubt you can be sure of what you're saying till we're through this mess."

She sighed, feeling like they were on a seesaw and she was dizzy from it all. And yet, there was Craig, just as strong and steady as he had always been for her. She was the one who was changing from moment to moment.

"Do you know what I mean?" He pushed for an answer, looking down at her with concern in his gaze.

"Yes. It's a mess. And I'm concerned my past has come back to haunt us."

"Do you think the fire is about you?"

"It didn't happen until I was back here and on the Hall's stage."

"That man?"

"Maybe."

"If he's a stalker and he's hunting you, he'd—"

"Want to know where I was sleeping, wouldn't he?"

Craig squeezed her hand, then raised it to his lips and pressed a kiss to each fingertip in turn.

"And if he set that smoky fire, then now he knows." She felt chilled at her own words and snuggled closer to Craig.

He pulled her tightly against him. "You know I'd never let anything happen to you."

"And I'd never endanger you or the Park."

"If you think you're going to leave to protect us, then think again." He sat up and looked into her eyes.

"It might be best. If he's behind this trouble, then he'll follow me."

"And what if he catches you…alone out there?"

She shivered and folded her arms across her stomach. "I could go to ground someplace."

"Oh, Fern, you're breaking my heart." He picked her up and set her on his lap, cradling her, stroking her, kissing her.

"I'm serious. I think I need to pack my two bags, pick up my guitar, and go. Anywhere. It doesn't matter, just so long as everyone here is safe."

"You're not going anywhere."

"And Ivy. She's here now. What if this mess spills over onto her?"

"Slade and Wildcat Bluff will keep her safe."

"You can take care of the Park. Ivy could help, if you need it."

"I'm telling you in all seriousness that I'm not letting you go anywhere. If I have to, I'll tie you to the bed and keep you there till we get the goods on this man, if it's him causing the trouble, and put him away or run him out of the county."

She felt deeply touched by his words. She'd constructed her world to depend on no one else, and that had worked fine until she'd run into trouble. A stalker who went to the effort of setting a fire was putting thoughts into actions. It was scary. And here was Craig, riding to her rescue and bringing the entire county with him. But was it fair to endanger them?

"I can almost see the thoughts whirling around in your mind. If they involve leaving me, forget it."

"Wild West Days is right around the corner. No one here needs trouble or distractions. If I left now, I could come back after the events are over. Y'all can do everything without me."

"Yes, we could do it. We've done it without you for years."

"See? It'll work."

"No, it won't."

"Why not?" She stirred against him, getting ready to pick

up and leave. She absolutely could not even contemplate endangering the entire community with her problem.

He wrapped her tighter in his arms. "I love you. You love me. We'll see this through together…and Wildcat Bluff will back our play."

She wanted it. She wanted it all. She wanted to never leave his arms again. But she was built of sterner stuff. "It's just too dangerous with me here."

"It's even more dangerous for you out there alone." He sighed into her hair, stroking up and down her arm with one hand. "Fern, will you just once bend a little? Will you just once let me, and all those who love you, step up and take care of you? You're strong, yes. But we're not lightweights either."

"Am I really that rigid?" Could he possibly be right? She backed just little bit off her position, trying to understand his viewpoint.

"No." He pressed another kiss to her hair. "You're a musician. You're always fluid, changing, evolving all the time."

"Thanks. That's a relief."

"But you're like a mama mountain lion. You'll protect those you love to the very end, even if it means sacrificing yourself."

"No, really, I just—"

"Yes, really. But this time you're not alone. You can't be. If anything happened to you, we'd all be wounded."

She turned quiet, feeling the fast beat of her heart, as if she were already deep into fight-or-flight territory.

"Do you understand now? You have to stay and let us work as a team to stop this attack on our territory by an outsider."

"Well, when you put it that way, I guess—"

"No guess. Stay."

She exhaled on a long breath, feeling all the fight against him go out of her. If he was right—and after his explanation, she now had no reason to believe he wasn't—she needed to stay and defend her turf. Anything else would be turning tail and running from a struggle for all she held dear. She couldn't let a stranger, if it turned out to be Simon who'd set the fire, hurt her or anyone else.

"Are you with me?"

"Yes. I'll stay."

He sighed and slumped back against the sofa, taking her with him. "If you'd said anything else, I'd have tied you to that bed."

"Do I have to change my mind to get you to tie me to your bed?"

He chuckled, shaking his head. "All you have to do is say the word."

"Is that a promise?"

"Yeah. And it comes with a ring."

"Didn't I ask for rope, not ring?"

"You get both, and anything else your heart desires."

She sat up and looked at him, smiling in the little coy way she knew he'd recognize from other amorous times. "What I desire right now is just a few steps away in the next room."

He grinned, eyes lighting up. "I can make it that far, but no farther."

"That's plenty far."

He stood up and held out his hand, still grinning at her.

She clasped his hand, giving him a big smile in return as

she stood up, moving into the warmth of his embrace. But she stopped when she heard voices and other noises outside near the stairs.

"Oh no!" Craig swiveled to look in that direction. "I forgot Slade and the sheriff were coming over to check the fire site."

"Lousy timing." She didn't know when she'd been more frustrated in a situation. Every time they got close to the bed, something interrupted them.

"Guess we'd better go help them."

"But once they're gone…"

"Right." He opened the front door.

She stepped out into the hot, muggy air that was a little cooler than during the day but still plenty warm. A floodlight had been set up below, so there was a lot of light on the crawl space under the stairs.

"Fern!" Ivy called as she hurried up the steps to the porch. "Are you okay?"

"I'm fine. We caught the fire in time."

"Hey, Ivy," Craig said. "You didn't need to come, too."

"If it involves my sister, it involves me." Ivy clasped Fern's hand and gave a squeeze. "Come on. Let's check out the cabin for any problems."

"I don't think there's structural damage, but it's best to look now, with good light," Craig said, following them down the stairs.

"Fern, good to see you. Sorry it isn't under better circumstances." Slade Steele stood up, holding an evidence collection bag in one hand. He wore a T-shirt that revealed a barbwire tattoo around his bulging right bicep and a rope tattoo around his left.

"Thanks for coming," Fern said. "I regret you had to get called out here so late."

"No problem. Glad to help out." Slade gave her a quick nod.

"Sheriff, we appreciate you getting here so soon. I hope we aren't wasting your time." Fern smiled at their local law officer, always pleased at his care for their county.

"I'm sorry you had a problem out here." Sheriff Calhoun walked over to her. He wore a tan police uniform with a holstered revolver on one hip, black cowboy boots, and a beige Stetson. He doffed his hat, returning her smile.

"We're sorry, too." Fern glanced at the burned mess under her porch.

"Craig gave me the details over the phone," Sheriff Calhoun said. "Is there anything you'd like to add to his assessment of the situation?"

"Bottom line, we smelled smoke, came out here, and found smoldering rags."

Sheriff Calhoun nodded. "I understand there could be a possible stalker involved here."

"Maybe." Fern stalled, not wanting to accuse without proof. "I don't know for sure, but there was an incident at the Hall earlier tonight."

"Fern!" Ivy gasped in dismay. "You didn't call me about that?"

"It doesn't necessarily mean anything. A fan from the cruises was there and gave me roses."

"He's given her roses before," Craig added in a serious tone as he put an arm around Fern's waist.

"It happens." Fern shrugged, still trying to defuse everyone's alarm before it got out of hand. "I don't want that incident to escalate into an indictment of the fan."

"We don't want that either," Sheriff Calhoun said, "but we also don't want you in danger."

"Okay." Fern focused on the sheriff. "What do you suggest we do at this point?"

"There's not much I can do officially until we catch this man in the act or he leaves incriminating evidence."

"I doubt he did that," Slade said, "but there might be a clue in what I collected here."

"I'll have patrols check the Park more frequently." Sheriff Calhoun glanced around the group. "But you'll need to up your own surveillance and stay alert. Fern, you shouldn't be out alone at night."

"I'll see to that," Craig said, tugging her closer.

"I agree." Fern felt touched by their concern. And safer for it. "I'm hoping he's gone and this was just some sort of prank that got out of hand."

"That's what we all hope," Ivy replied, "but you must be extra careful now."

Slade gave Fern a thoughtful look. "If you don't think it's safe here at the Park, you can stay at my place on Steele Trap Ranch. Ivy and I are at Steele Trap II, so you could use it."

"Thanks." Fern glanced at Craig, wondering what he'd think of the idea.

"Appreciate it." He tightened his hold on her. "But she's staying here in my cabin, where I can keep her safe."

"Good," Slade agreed. "Still, in case you decide you'd be safer out of the Park, keep my offer in mind."

"That's very generous," Fern said. "We definitely appreciate it."

Ivy smiled at her sister. "Above all else, even if it puts a glitch in Wild West Days, we want you both safe."

"Right," Slade said.

"We'll be okay and we won't let this affect our plans." Fern spoke with a conviction she didn't feel at the moment, but she wanted the others to have confidence in her decision to stay here and move forward with upcoming events.

"Sounds like the best we can do for tonight." Sheriff Calhoun put his hat back on his head. "We'll get out of your hair now, so you can get some sleep."

Ivy gave Fern a quick hug, then snagged Slade's hand as the three started down the path away from the cabin.

"Thanks for coming over," Fern called before she glanced at Craig, thinking that sleep was the last thing on her mind.

"Do you believe we should chance going to bed again?" Craig asked, humor lacing his voice.

"At the rate we're going, it'll probably catch on fire."

He chuckled, giving her a sidelong look. "Oh, I definitely think we left something turned on there."

She joined his laughter. "Guess we better go put out that blaze."

Chapter 14

"I DON'T KNOW ABOUT YOU," CRAIG SAID AS HE SHUT AND locked the door behind them, "but I need a glass of Slade's muscadine wine."

"You get the wine. I'll get the glasses." Fern headed for the kitchen cabinets. "Is everything in the same place?"

"Pretty much. I don't think Ivy changed anything, and I sure haven't." He plucked a bottle of wine out of the fridge and opened it, then grabbed a can of mixed nuts and poured them into a bowl.

As fast as he was, she still beat him to the sofa and plopped down on the cushions. She slipped off her flip-flops, tucked her feet under her, and looked up at him with an expectant expression.

"I'm right behind you." He set down the bowl, poured two glasses of wine, and handed her one.

"Toast." She held up her glass.

He sat down close to her—so close he could feel the heat of their touching thighs. He tipped his glass against hers, setting off a silvery ring.

"What are we celebrating?" She smiled at him over the rim of her glass while she tilted her head to one side as if getting a different view of him.

"Like what you see?"

"Best view in the Park."

He chuckled, shaking his head. "I have the best view right in front of me."

She smiled, feeling so happy just to be with him.

"Let's drink to surviving this very long night."

"No."

"No?"

"Let's drink to our very long future," she said.

At those words, he heated up. He nodded in agreement as he took a sip, watching her do the same over the rim of his glass. He tasted another of Slade's amazingly good wines. He hoped his friend would find a way to market it soon, because the world deserved this very special brew.

"Oh, that's good." She looked at the wine, then at him. "Slade is a fine man. And he deserves a woman as fine as my sister."

"I couldn't agree more." Craig took another sip. "But tonight is about us. At least, I hope it finally is."

"Do you think the cabins are safe now?"

"I can't say for sure, but I figure whoever did what they did got what they wanted tonight and left."

"I suppose we need more security," she said.

"We've resisted putting up security cameras in the Park to protect the privacy of guests, but this may be the end of that."

"You're probably right, but let's wait on it. I hate giving up the privacy if it isn't completely necessary."

"At least let's install cameras in the Hall's parking lot."

"Okay. That suits me." She sipped her wine thoughtfully. "I just want things to get back to normal so we can make music and plan Wild West Days in peace."

"I'd like nothing better."

"Think it'll happen?"

"I think we need to make it happen."

"Yeah."

"If we don't control our lives, somebody else will try to fill the void. And they just might accomplish it." He sincerely meant every one of those words, because he'd seen it happen with excellent musicians who'd lost their way when somebody took control of their talent. He had no intention of letting that happen to Fern or himself.

She set down her wine and turned to face him. "You think he's out there, waiting and watching. Don't you?"

"I don't want to alarm you, but…"

"That's what you believe."

"It's a distinct possibility." Craig turned his glass around in his hands, gazing at it thoughtfully. "Nothing else makes much sense."

"If so, I brought it down on us."

"No. Never think that. It's all on him…nothing on you."

"But still—"

"No. Besides, he can't win. He may think he can, but he can't. Not in Wildcat Bluff County. He's out of his league here."

"If I stay, it'll be trouble."

"No. If he tries to cause trouble for you, he'll wish he never set foot in this county."

"I could still go. There's time."

"We already settled that idea. You're going nowhere unless it's with me." He watched as she eyed the front door. "It's beginning to look like I may need to make a run out to the ranch and pick up a rope."

She glanced back at him, chuckling. "Not tonight you won't. I have other plans for you."

He grinned as he set down his glass. "And what plans are those?"

"Let's start with your T-shirt."

"My tee?" He felt completely confused. He'd been thinking about the bed while she was thinking about clothes. Made no sense, but he probably wasn't hitting on all cylinders at the moment anyway.

"Yeah." She grinned, appearing predatory as she looked him up and down. "Why don't you stand and take it off for me?"

Now it was his turn to grin, feeling decidedly predatory himself. "You want me to strip for you?"

"If it were winter and you were cold and wearing lots of layers—maybe four or five—it'd be more interesting, but since it's summer and you're not wearing much, I'm willing to go with what I've got."

"Thanks, I think," he said, laughing as he stood up. If she wanted to play games, he was more than willing to play with her. It'd been way too long since he'd had fun, particularly in a bed...and even more particularly, with Fern.

She sat up straight and leaned back against the sofa. "Strip for me, cowboy. I want to see that six-pack on display."

He laughed even harder. "You are in a mood, aren't you?"

"Let's just say I'm feeling a little bit ornery after a real rough evening."

"In that case, I guess you deserve whatever you want."

"No guesses about it." She put a fingertip to her lips, parted them, and stroked the nail with the tip of her tongue.

He felt heat race through him like he was standing next to a blazing inferno. "You know you're playing with fire, don't you?"

"Really? It's hard to tell with you wearing so many clothes."

At those words, he got even hotter…and harder.

"You can strip slow or fast. I'm not particular about the pace, but I'm getting a wee bit impatient for you to start."

"Are you?" He tried to keep the grin off his face. He tried to look serious. He even tried to look sexy. All for her. But she was right about the impatience. He wanted them in bed. And he wanted it now. Yet he was determined to give her every little thing she wanted, even if it was a clumsy strip on his part.

"Yeah." She looked him up and down again, as if reevaluating all his assets.

"Still like what you see?"

"Impossible to say, seeing as how slow you are off the mark."

He chuckled, unable to stay serious in the face of her big tease. "Okay. I'll give you what you want if you'll give me what I want later."

She lost her serious face as she gave in to a grin. "Let's see what you've got first, cowboy firefighter."

"You're not willing to commit to a pig in a poke?"

"If what you've got is what I think you've got, I'm more than ready for a ride."

That was it. He couldn't take any more. He grasped the bottom of his T-shirt, jerked it up over his head, and tossed it to the floor. He put his hands on his narrow hips, where his sweatpants hung low. He stood there, letting her look at what he'd spent a lifetime building as he roped cattle and rode horses. Yeah, he had plenty of muscle, but it was because he needed it to handle a ranch. With her looking at him like he was all the eye candy she'd ever want or need, he was glad for those hard workdays because he wanted her to have exactly what set her heart ablaze. And at the moment, his body was it…and he'd gladly let her have her way with it.

She stood up, walked over, and placed the palms of her hands on his chest, spreading her fingers apart as she lightly massaged, then moved lower until she reached his navel and tucked a fingertip into the indentation.

He inhaled on a groan, wanting to crush her to him but staying still so she was in control. When she stroked lower to cup him through the fabric of his pants, he broke out in a sweat from the heat she was generating in him.

"Do you need help with the strip?" She tucked her thumbs under the waistband of his pants.

"At this point, I'll take any help you're willing to give me." He heard his voice go low with a gravel edge that would work well with the song that was growing by leaps and bounds in his head.

"I'm not sure that'd be fair." She stepped back to arm's length, letting her hands linger on him before dropping them to her sides. "It's your strip."

"Maybe I'm too easy."

"Easy is good." She gave him a mischievous look with her luminous green eyes. "I like easy a lot."

"Me, too." He decided two could play her game—and should if they stood any chance of prolonging it.

"More, please."

He kicked off his shoes. "There you go."

"Not fair, although you do have sexy toes."

He chuckled at those words. "Thanks. I think."

"Pants?"

He put his hands on his hips and looked her over, lingering here and there to stoke her interest. "What've you got under your T-shirt?"

She grinned, glancing downward, then back at him. "What do you think?"

"Something interesting, I'd bet."

"Could be."

"How about stripping off your T-shirt and letting me see?"

"Think you're up to it?"

"I'm definitely up."

"You're so bad." She laughed, even as she shared a hot look with him.

"Only as bad as you want."

"Do you think I don't need this tee anymore?"

"Far as I'm concerned, you never need it in this cabin."

"In that case, maybe it is a little warm in here."

"Hot, more like it."

She grasped the bottom edge of her tee and slowly, ever so slowly, raised it to reveal the low-riding, frayed-edge cut-offs that showcased the indentation of her bellybutton. She kept raising the T-shirt to show more and more of her toned stomach until the fabric bunched under her breasts.

He swallowed hard, not sure how much more he could take of her too-slow strip for him. And then she upped the ante by pulling her T-shirt completely off and tossing it on top of his tee. She wore a white bra that revealed rosy tips under the delicate lace. He took a deep breath as he marveled at her beauty and what it did to him.

"Is this what you wanted to see?"

"You're on your way to getting there."

"Slow or fast?"

He just smiled as he tucked his fingers under her bra straps and slowly pulled them down her arms until her breasts were completely exposed to him. He cupped the soft, round mounds and felt something in him give—he'd been holding back, not sure if he should surrender to the force that connected them until this very moment—and he knew there was no turning back.

She reached up, twined her hands around his neck, and tugged his face toward her. He slid his hands around her back and undid her bra even as he pressed his lips to her mouth. She was soft and warm and utterly captivating as their kiss grew hotter and more urgent until she was tugging at his hair, pressing her breasts to his chest, urging him onward like she had in the old days. Old days. What if he… No, he wouldn't go there, wouldn't even think it, or he might back out now for fear of losing her all over again. They could do this. They could move out of the past into the present.

She lifted her head, cupped his face with both hands, and gave him a look of deepest love. "Let's go to bed. I can't wait any longer."

"Are you sure?"

"I'm not sure about anything except I won't let fear keep me from loving you." She stepped back, letting her bra fall to the floor, and held out a hand to him.

When he clasped her fingers, he felt her tremble but not from cold. He led her into the bedroom, where light from a lamp on the nightstand lent a soft yellow glow to the area. He closed and locked the door behind them to make sure they weren't disturbed in any way.

She shucked off her cutoffs and settled into the center of the bed, beckoning him with a slow, almost shy smile.

He sat down on the bed and pulled off his sweatpants before he opened the drawer in the nightstand, took out condom packets, and set them on top. He glanced over his shoulder, where she watched him with a question in her eyes.

"Just so you know, these have been here waiting for your return."

"No other women?"

"Never. You're all I could ever want." He hesitated, but he had to clear the air between them. "Men?"

"None. You were all I could think about while I was gone."

"Good." He felt a vast sense of relief, knowing there had been plenty of guys bird-dogging her. She'd had her chances, but she'd turned them down—just like he'd rejected offers in the Hall.

He slid toward her, pulling the sheet over them for a touch of privacy. And then nothing else mattered as she tugged him to her and he buried his face between her breasts just as he spread her legs and nestled between them. Finally, he'd come home to where he'd always longed to be.

"Don't hold back," she whispered, stroking long fingers through his hair, down to his shoulders, to tightly clutch him.

With that release, he kissed her breasts, using his tongue, his lips, his breath till she writhed up against him, her heat enveloping him as she raised her legs and he placed them over his shoulders.

"Too quick?" He didn't think he could hold back, but still he didn't want to rush her.

"Now. I can't wait."

He pushed into her, as gentle as possible because she was hot, tight, wet, and it'd been so long for her, as well as for him. But desire quickly overtook them until he was loving her as he'd wanted to do every single moment of every single day since she'd left him, and she was responding as if her hunger for him grew greater with every thrust. He was taking them higher and higher until they took flight to the highest peak of passion, and their world swirled into a red-hot blaze that consumed the past and ignited the future of endless love together.

Chapter 15

FERN HAD ONE THING ON HER MIND OVER THE NEXT several days—at least when she wasn't working in Wildcat Hall or making plans for Wild West Days—Craig Thorne. Not only was he physically with her most of her days and nights, but he was in her thoughts, her emotions, her spirit as well. And then there was the bed. Every time they came together, the experience grew more intense, heightening their pleasure in each other.

"You're miles away," Craig said. "What are you thinking about?"

She glanced at her watch, noticing it was about noon. They'd been working quite a while and making good progress. She tapped her fingertip against the timeline printout on a table near the Hall's front bar and then gave him a mischievous smile. "You, of course."

He chuckled, giving her a hot look. "Want to take that thought back to the cabin?"

"Yeah...but maybe we'd better be responsible for a little bit longer."

He nodded, appearing reluctant, then glanced down at the printout. "How many cancellations do we have now?"

"Two bands. One vendor," she said. "At this late date, I wonder why."

"I'd guess scheduling conflicts for the bands."

"Maybe they got a better offer at a bigger venue." She shifted in her chair, feeling the pressure of making Wild West Days a winner.

"Could be." He shrugged. "You know how it is."

"Yeah."

"What about inviting those Sure-Shot musicians that put together a band over the summer?"

"Aren't they teenagers?" she asked.

"Right. High school seniors."

"That's not a bad idea. They're from your neck of the woods. Have you heard them play?"

"Yes. They're pretty good. And everybody needs a place to start," he said.

"True enough."

"Another thing. They'll bring in parents, grandparents, cousins, neighbors. They'll all want to see their hometown band perform here."

"Like folks at ball games."

"Right."

"I like the idea," she said.

"They've got a good fiddler. And they're putting their own spin on classic western swing from greats like Bob Wills, Hank Thompson, Spade Cooley, and others. They're even going back to old-timey songs with lyrics like 'she'll be coming 'round the mountain when she comes' as a way of connecting to their heritage." He hummed a few bars of the song as he tapped his toe.

"Now that's interesting. Plus, those are simpler songs and easier for audiences to join in a singalong."

"They're a smart group, I think."

"Sounds like it."

"Anyway, you know as well as I do you're going to give them a chance."

"True. Bless their hearts, they're starting down a long road if they get where they're planning to go."

He squeezed her hand, lingering a moment. "Remember, that's part of what you want to do at the Hall."

"Support musicians."

"And this is a good way to do it."

She glanced down at the list, then back up. "Thanks for the reminder. I'm getting so deep into our event that I'm not seeing the forest for the trees."

"Happens to the best of us."

"I just had an idea. Do you think we could make room for a special stage for local up-and-coming musicians?"

"That's a great idea."

"It's kind of a late start, but with cutbacks in our local school for the arts, this could showcase talent that needs to be nurtured by our country community." She highlighted a section of the printout. "Could we make it work?"

"Great idea. I don't care what it takes, we *should* make it work." He glanced around the room, as if contemplating expansion. "Wild West Days already supports artisans with their handcrafted wares, so why not enlarge support for all our musicians, not just the youngsters?"

"Is there enough local talent?"

"Maybe not bands, but what about the individuals who sing in churches, at potluck dinner benefits, at sports games, or—"

She leaned toward him, feeling excitement well up in her. "Yes, this is exactly what I'd hoped to accomplish when I acquired the Hall, but I was thinking too small, wasn't I?"

"I doubt you ever think too small, but this definitely enlarges the scope of what you envisioned from the start."

"Almost everyone in the county creates something, whether it's cedar furniture, oil paintings, stainless steel knives, or music, while they're also ranchers or tradespeople or builders or firefighters."

"We do tend to be creative around here."

"And we need people and events to nurture it."

"You'll get no argument from me," he said.

"Okay. If this is what we plan to do, how do we go about setting it in motion?"

"Do you really need to ask?"

She smiled, knowing just where he was going. "Morning Glory and Hedy."

"Let's go to Bert and Bert Two for even more help."

"That's right. I heard Bert Two won the Fernando sighting benefit last Christmas and donated his winnings to our high school, to help fund the arts shortfall."

"Right. They'd get the word out."

"We'd need to organize it," she said thoughtfully. "If we made this a special stage or spotlight on locals throughout the weekend, Ivy could add it to our Wildcat Bluff website with a form to fill out. That'd save time."

"MG and Hedy would still let the community know about it."

"Some folks won't go online, so we'd need to leave forms at Adelia's Delights and Morning's Glory."

"They'd be happy to help, I'm sure."

She sighed as she glanced over their to-do list. "But is there time to add this at the last minute?"

"It's our idea, so it's our choice."

"But the time?"

"I'm willing to work extra hours to get it done. What about you?"

She didn't have to think long. She was here to nurture musicians of all ages and experiences. "Wild West Days only comes once a year. If we miss this opportunity, we'll have to wait until the next Labor Day weekend."

"We can set up events at the Hall on other occasions."

"And I want to do that, but this is a really big showcase for local talent."

"Tell you what." He leaned toward her. "Why don't we go to Sure-Shot later and catch this band's act? I need to check on the ranch, too. Let's do both."

"When do they play? And where?"

"Weekend evenings and Sunday afternoons at the town gazebo."

"They must have a following," she said.

"Yes. Plus, it's free entertainment for folks after a hard day's work on the ranches."

"Okay. I'd like to hear them. And see your ranch. But we play Friday and Saturday nights at the Hall."

"How about this Sunday?"

"If we can take time away from our plans, I'm all in."

"We'll make it work. We might even catch a movie afterward at the Sure-Shot Drive-In."

"I'd heard Bert and Bert Two had it up and running again. How's it doing?"

"Great. It's open on weekends and hosts other events during daylight hours."

"I've been meaning to go see it, so this is a good excuse."

He grinned at her, raising an eyebrow. "Do you want to park in the back row of the Passion Pit?"

She laughed, patting his arm. "So all of this is really about getting me into the back seat of your pickup?"

"Yeah."

"Bed not good enough for you?"

"I just want to experience what it must've been like back in the fifties and sixties when necking in the back seat was as good as it got."

"I think we can improve on it."

"I'm willing to let you show me."

"No doubt." She leaned into him, feeling his solid warmth, as she glanced from her marked-up paperwork on the table to the scarred wood of the long bar to the beams of the high ceiling. It just didn't get much better than this in life. She hadn't heard any more from Simon, and she hoped he was long gone, but she still felt a little uneasy that he might have stayed in the area.

As if Craig picked up on her thoughts, he covered her hand with his large strong one. "I'm glad the Settelmeyers installed surveillance cameras and more lights in the parking lot. Do you feel safer now?"

"It should help. Still, he could park out on Wildcat Road and walk into the Park."

"I know that only too well." Craig squeezed her hand. "Are you sure we shouldn't go ahead and install cameras on the cabins?"

"Let's wait and see. As far as we know, he hasn't been back, so I'm hoping the roses were sort of a farewell gift."

"I hope so, too."

"We need to come up with a place for the local band

stage." She desperately wanted to ditch their talk about Simon, so she hoped Craig took the bait.

"The Lone Star is already booked solid except for those two cancellations."

"That's not enough time for what we want."

"I know."

"We could fill one of those spots with your Sure-Shot band and put them on the other stage as well."

"Sounds good." He drummed his fingertips on the table, then stopped and looked at her. "What about the Chuckwagon Café?"

"Folks will be coming in and out, talking while they eat, and—"

"Not inside. Outside. You know the café is at the end of the Old Town block of stores, so there's a little garden with three or four picnic tables out there."

"That's perfect." She smiled, feeling as if things were finally coming together in a great way. "We could schedule so as not to interfere with other events, but this way shoppers and folks just walking down the street or even those who came especially to hear them could park nearby."

"It'd bring more business to the Chuckwagon, too."

"Do you think Slade and his family would agree?"

"They're big backers of Wild West Days, so I'm sure they'd come onboard to support local musicians."

"Good. This means we need to contact Slade about the café and Ivy about the website." She leaned back in her chair, trying to think of anything that needed doing at the moment.

"First, we'd better run it by Hedy and Morning Glory."

"Plus Bert and Bert Two."

"Right."

She picked up her marker and fiddled with it a moment. "We're really going to do this, aren't we?"

He chuckled, glancing over at her. "If we're not, let's back out before we get everybody in two towns excited about it."

"It feels good, like we're doing the right thing."

"I know. It's what we do in Wildcat Bluff County."

"Right. We help others."

"And the entire community."

She glanced over at him, feeling mischievous. "Help others. That means you're going to participate in the cowboy firefighter dunk for charity event, aren't you?"

"No. Absolutely not. It's a lousy idea. There are plenty of other ways to—"

"You're not averse to getting wet, are you?"

"I'm averse to a long line of cowgirls just itching to dunk every cowboy they know…for good measure if nothing else."

"But it's for charity."

"Nope."

She walked her fingertips up his forearm to his elbow, to his shoulder. "Pretty please?" she asked in a soft, high-pitched tone.

"No."

"With sugar on it?"

"Fern, I'm a grown man. Baby talk is not going to work on me."

She leaned in closer, letting her breast rub up against his arm, feeling their body heat rise and merge. "You sure?"

"I'm the cochair. I have more important things to do during Wild West Days. Besides, there are plenty of cowboy firefighters who'll take part in it to raise funds for the station."

She walked her fingers back down his arm and moved in even closer. "But there are none of your caliber."

Finally, he chuckled, grasped her hand, and kissed the tip of her smallest finger on her left hand. "You think you've got me wrapped around your little finger, don't you?"

"Don't I?"

He gave a long sigh. "You're determined to get me soaking wet in front of the whole county, aren't you?"

"A little eye candy could do it a whole lot of good."

"That Sydney Steele. First, she comes up with the cowboy firefighter charity calendar and has to rope a dozen cowboys to get them to hold still long enough for a photo shoot."

"Smart cowgirl."

"And now she comes up with a charity cowboy firefighter dunk."

"She'll probably take photos for the next calendar."

"You think?" He appeared startled, then horrified at the idea.

"You might plan your clothes with that in mind."

"I didn't say I was going to do it."

"Isn't Sydney kind of like MG and Hedy? Doesn't she always get what she wants in this county?"

He leaned back in his chair, in the pose of a long-suffering male. "Yeah, she sure does."

"I rest my case."

"One thing."

"What?"

"If I survive Wild West Days, I may have to hang up my spurs."

"Oh no. Just let me polish them for you and you'll be

good to go." She gave him a little hint of a smile to let him know she could handle that job and plenty more for him.

As they were sharing a look that promised more heat later, she heard Ivy's ringtone. Brought back to reality, she grabbed her phone.

"We're at Steele Trap II," Ivy said in a concerned voice.

"What's wrong?" She gripped the phone, feeling her heart speed up.

"It's Fernando." Ivy lowered her voice.

"Uh…is he sick?"

"What's going on?" Craig leaned toward Fern, appearing puzzled.

She shrugged at him, trying to understand why Ivy would call her about the famous Angus bull.

"If you don't mind and have the time…" Ivy said.

"Of course we have time for you. What's going on?" She shook her head at Craig, trying to convey that she was clueless.

"Please just get over here as quickly as you can. I'll let Storm explain the situation. Please bring Craig and your guitars." And she was gone.

Fern looked at Craig. "They need us at Steele Trap II."

Chapter 16

FERN WATCHED THE NORTH TEXAS COUNTRYSIDE, turned from spring wet and green and cool to summer dry and brown and hot, while Craig floor-boarded the gas pedal of his dark blue pickup as they drove down Wildcat Road. They were silent, surrounded by the high whine of tires burning up pavement in their rush to help.

When he abruptly wheeled off the road, she glanced up at the cut-out, black-painted steel sign that read STEELE TRAP II as they hurtled under it. They rattled across the metal pipe cattle guard and headed up a narrow lane that led to a single-story ranch house constructed of natural rock and cedar trim with double front doors and big picture windows. Several pickups in various colors and sizes were parked haphazardly in front of it.

But that's not what drew Fern's attention most. She glanced to the left, at an ornamental pond that reflected the brilliant blue and fluffy white clouds above with green lily pads dotting here and there. In the center of the water stood a big black Angus bull—easily two thousand pounds of solid muscle—with his head held low in dejection, instead of high in pride.

On the edge of the pond stood an eight-year-old girl with a mane of wild ginger hair wearing turquoise cowgirl boots, faded, ripped jeans, and an aqua, rhinestone-studded T-shirt. She held a metal bucket in both hands out toward the bull, but he ignored it. Ivy and the Steele clan clustered around her. Lula Mae led the family that consisted of her daughter, Maybelline, grandchildren Sydney and Slade, and granddaughter, Storm. They all wore jeans, shirts, boots, and hats.

"Looks like Storm is trying to lure Fernando out of the pond," Craig said. "But what's he doing there? His pasture is on the first Steele Trap Ranch since he was Storm's last Christmas gift."

"I don't know," Fern said. "And why do they need our guitars?"

"Guess we're about to find out."

Ivy looked up, saw them, and gestured to park on the side of the road.

Craig stopped the truck across from the pond, then jumped out and picked up their guitars from the back seat while Fern stepped down onto dry, crackly grass. When she walked around the front of the pickup, he held out her guitar. She slipped it out of its case, then returned the case to the pickup while Craig did the same thing.

"Fern!" Storm set down her bucket and sprinted across the road, holding out her arms.

Fern caught her with one arm, squeezed her tight, and then looked into bright hazel eyes.

"I'm so glad you're here!" Storm gave Fern the once-over followed by a big frown. "Still, you shouldn't have left us. We need you in Wildcat Bluff."

"I'm here now."

"You better not go away again."

"I'm not planning on it." She glanced up at Craig and saw him smile.

Ivy walked over with Slade by her side and gave Fern a quick hug. "Thanks for coming."

"Of course. What's going on?"

Ivy glanced down at Storm. "Why don't you explain the situation to my sister?"

Storm stretched up as tall as she could get and took a deep breath. "Fernando has…had…a friend on the Lazy Q."

"That's the ranch next to ours the Tarleton family out of East Texas bought not too long ago," Slade said.

"Daisy Sue lived there till yesterday." Storm's bottom lip trembled as if she was doing her best not to cry.

"Daisy Sue?" Fern asked, still confused by the situation.

"She lived on the other side of the fence from Fernando. It's all that separated them," Storm said.

"She's a fine Angus cow." Slade reached down and put an arm around his niece's shoulders, tugging her small frame against his muscular bulk. "We kept finding the metal gate between the two pastures open."

"Fernando is the smartest bull in the whole wide world," Storm said with pride. "Gates are nothing for him to open."

"Do you think he's been visiting her?" Fern cocked her head in question to Slade and received a nod in response.

"We figure after dark." Storm looked over her shoulder at Fernando, then back again.

"True," Slade agreed. "What we think happened is that once Fernando found her gone, he spent last night walking down here. That pond used to be his favorite spot."

"He's a sensitive bull with a sensitive soul," Storm said in a hushed, reverent tone.

"She thinks he came to his old watering hole to soothe his soul's loss," Ivy said.

"Right." Storm stroked Fern's guitar. "And he likes music."

Fern looked at the pond with Fernando standing belly deep in water. "I've never played for a bull before today."

"He loves your voice. And guitar." Storm smiled at Fern. "Uncle Slade downloaded your recordings to my phone, and I play them for Fernando. It always soothes him when he's feeling cantankerous."

"I know animals, as well as plants, respond well to music, but how will this help Daisy Sue?" Fern asked.

"It won't help find her," Slade said. "We're working on it."

"We'll get her back. And soon." Storm straightened her small shoulders. "She's Fernando's lady love...and she loves him. There might even be a baby on the way."

"Most likely," Slade said. "He's a popular fellow."

"True," Storm said matter-of-factly. "Now that he's a cow bull instead of an AI bull, he's in demand. But Daisy Sue is his love."

"Looks like somebody is going to get another free top-of-the-line calf out of Fernando," Craig said.

"Yeah. But he's stayed on the ranch since escaping the rustlers and getting safely home." Slade looked in the direction of the Lazy Q. "The new owners have been mostly absent, so things have rocked along pretty much as usual till now. We heard a daughter of the family named Belle Tarleton is on her way to make this her permanent home. You've probably heard of Lulubelle & You."

"I own clothes from that western line." Fern glanced down at her jeans. "I'm not wearing any of it now, but I love the designs."

"She's the owner," Slade said.

"That's a surprise. Why would she move here?" Fern asked. "I'd think she'd live near her big-city office."

"Nobody knows," Slade said.

"If she's got Daisy Sue someplace," Storm said, "then we make her give Fernando's love back to him."

"We're looking into it right now," Slade said. "Daisy Sue may already be on Tarleton family land in East Texas."

"Is that far away?" Storm stomped her foot in impatience.

"Not so far that she can't be returned to this ranch." Slade stroked Storm's narrow shoulder with his big hand in comfort.

"Good." Storm looked up at Fern. "Would you and Craig sing and play for Fernando? I think it'll lift his spirits...and maybe get him to eat again."

"I'm happy to sing for him." Fern was touched by the request and hoped it would help the downcast bull.

"Me, too," Craig said.

"Thanks." Slade clasped Storm's hand and caught Ivy's with his other. "Come on. Let's all get back to Fernando."

Fern hesitated, watching them walk away. "Isn't that a wonderful family? Imagine everyone turning out to help Storm with her grief and worry."

"That's Wildcat Bluff for you."

"True enough. I hadn't thought about playing music for a lonely bull when I returned, but it's just what the folks of this county would do." She clasped his hand, smiled up at him, then followed the others down to the pond.

Sydney strode over to them, looking like a grown-up version of her daughter. She gave Fern a quick hug. "Good to see you. Thanks so much for coming out. Storm is really worried about Fernando. He isn't acting normal, particularly since he left the ranch and walked down here without her."

"He's always waiting for her first thing in the morning." Slade took off his cowboy hat and pushed long fingers through his thick blond hair.

Lula Mae and Maybelline, beloved cooks at the Chuckwagon Café, gave Fern hugs and big smiles before they stepped back to clear a path down to the pond through dry grass.

"Any news on the missing cow?" Craig asked. "Have you heard from this Belle Tarleton?"

"No," Slade said. "Looks like our message has to go through a lot of folks before it gets to her, and who knows where she is or if she'll respond at all?"

"What about the foreman on the Lazy Q?" Fern asked.

"He's being cagey," Sydney said. "Basically, he's telling us to mind our own business, but he says Daisy Sue is okay."

"Guess there's not much more you can do for now, is there?" Craig asked.

"Once we reach the top dog, we ought to get answers," Slade said. "Till then, best we can do is help Storm and Fernando."

"Bert and Bert Two are friends with the Tarleton family, so we'll probably go to them next and see if they can get some information about Daisy Sue for us," Slade said.

"Good idea," Craig replied.

On the edge of the pond, Storm picked up her bucket of oats and rattled it. "Please, come on. Let's get this show on the road."

Fern gave everyone a smile before she walked over to the pond with Craig beside her. She adjusted her guitar strap, strummed a few chords, then leaned toward Craig.

"Follow my lead," she whispered. "I know the perfect song for Fernando."

"You got it."

And she hit the first notes of "The Lonely Bull," a big instrumental hit from the sixties by Herb Alpert and the Tijuana Brass. She hummed the original sizzling trumpet part, and Craig added more depth to the number with his guitar.

As she played and hummed, she watched Fernando to gauge his reaction. He tentatively raised his head, gave her a curious look with his big luminous eyes, and a peaceful calm radiated out from him. She could almost see a smile settle across his face as he raised his head and sniffed the air in her direction.

She glanced at Storm, who was holding out the bucket of feed and crooning in time with the music.

Craig added his deeper voice to hers as they looped the song, adding their own variations to keep it going, since the music was obviously having a soothing effect on their own lonely bull.

As they played, Fernando stretched out his neck toward Storm's bucket and sniffed the air. She shook the oats in time with the music like a tambourine, luring him to the sound and smell of his favorite food.

Finally, he stepped forward, powerful muscles sending out concentric waves from his massive body as he slowly, gracefully moved through the water. When he reached Storm, he didn't go for the oats. Instead, he lowered his massive head and gently bumped her small chest until she set down the bucket and wrapped her thin arms around his neck. He blew air out his nose in a deep sigh and laid his head on her shoulder for a long hug.

Fern kept the music going, but tears filled her eyes as she

watched the little girl and the big bull comfort each other. She glanced up at Craig. He was watching her with a smile on his lips. She got it. Love came in all forms under the rainbow…and it was the most precious gift of all.

Storm turned her head and looked at Fern and Craig. "Fernando needs a distraction while we're waiting to get Daisy Sue back."

Fern stopped humming but continued softly playing her guitar. "What do you have in mind?"

"Y'all are in charge of Wild West Days, aren't you?"

"Yes," Craig said.

"Fernando's online fans have been asking to see him." Storm frowned in concentration. "I didn't want to take him off the ranch, but now I think it'd be good for him to get away for a bit."

Fern glanced over at Sydney and Slade to get their reactions. Both looked surprised but nodded in agreement.

"I don't see why not if he's in a controlled environment," Craig said.

"We could surely find a place for him in Old Town." Fern didn't want to disappoint Storm, and the big bull would be an added attraction.

"We could sell Fernando T-shirts and stuff." Storm's hazel eyes glinted with excitement.

Slade chuckled, shaking his head. "She's always the budding entrepreneur."

"We can use the proceeds for his special feed," Storm said. "We can even share with Daisy Sue when she gets back."

"Can you set up a corral or something to hold him for viewers, in case he gets upset or takes it in his mind to wander?" Craig looked at Sydney.

"We've got time, so I imagine we can come up with something if that's what we decide to do," Sydney said. "You know, it took a little time, but Storm worked magic with Fernando until he came to trust her...and he tamed her wildness a little bit, too."

"Yeah." Slade glanced at his sister. "They were both pretty wild till they formed a friendship, but then wildness is a little on the standard side for Steele women."

Sydney chuckled, nodding in agreement as she turned toward her daughter. "Storm, why don't you see if you can lure Fernando up to the barn with that bucket of oats? I'd feel better if he was safely confined in his old place."

Storm patted Fernando on the head. "Come on, we've got plans to make if we're going to wow folks at Wild West Days."

Chapter 17

By Sunday, Craig decided they were making good progress on Wild West Days. Everybody was on board with what they'd dubbed the Wildcat Bluff Musicians stage near the Chuckwagon Café. They were getting forms filled out at the stores and on the website. Things were moving fast. It was time for a break, and they needed to get out of the Park to do it. And so they were on Wildcat Road, headed out of town.

Fern looked good, but she had natural style and pizazz no matter what she wore, so that was a given. Today she'd thrown on a pair of her sister's Wranglers, a red shirt with white snaps and white piping, along with a pair of red cowgirl boots. He wore his usual jeans with a big brass rodeo buckle, shiny black boots, and a blue-striped, pearl-snap shirt. All in all, they made a fine-looking pair that appeared to belong together much like they did onstage. That was another thing good about the day—they were together. They were in love. And nothing was going to keep them apart, not even a stranger with white roses who, fortunately, hadn't been heard from or seen in the area since that night, so Craig was cautiously optimistic on that front.

Today he wanted nothing more than to have fun with Fern. And they both deserved it, even needed it. If he could get away with it, he'd make their outing a date, almost like a first date to get reacquainted with each other and what made them tick beyond entertainment. As important as music was to both of them, and although that was at the heart of what brought them together and kept them together, music wasn't everything. They ought to mesh the rest of their lives, or eventually their relationship might fray like a ragged rope coming apart. And he had no intention of letting that happening to them, so it meant a fun day in Sure-Shot.

Fern was humming to the radio, seemingly as content as he felt, when he turned west onto Highway 82. He watched as the fence lines that stretched along both sides of the road changed from barbwire to white pipe or four-slat wood enclosures, announcing they'd moved from cattle country to horse country. One ranch after another flashed by, announcing their names—from whimsical to practical—in black sheet metal cutouts or burned into wood arches that towered over entryways.

Thoroughbred horses with rich chestnut coats in a variety of shades grazed in some pastures, while in others, brown-and-white painted ponies sought shelter from the sun under the spreading limbs of live oaks and tall elms. Crimson barns and metal corrals—along with houses ranging from single-story, redbrick, fifties ranch style to cream-colored stone, two-story contemporaries—nestled well back from the road for privacy.

Soon he turned south at a sign with western-style letters that read SURE AS SHOOTIN' YOU'RE IN SURE-SHOT! under the black-and-white silhouette of a smoking Colt .45 revolver.

Fern chuckled as she pointed at the announcement. "I'd forgotten that fun sign. Annie Oakley is still alive and well in Sure-Shot."

"Yeah." He joined her laughter, feeling lighthearted heading into his hometown. "The founders probably knew her or at least heard of her. I mean, back in the day, who wouldn't know about the famous sharpshooter and exhibition shooter known as Little Miss Sure Shot on the Wild West show circuit?"

"I bet somebody knew her." Fern cast him a thoughtful look. "If you name an entire town after someone, then you probably know them pretty well."

"Maybe they just admired her."

"Could be. But I like the idea that she'd been through here a time or two…maybe even spent a night or more with a special gentleman."

Craig chuckled, reached over, and squeezed Fern's hand. "You're a romantic at heart, aren't you?"

"I just kind of identify with her. Entertainers live in their own fantasy worlds, so reality is rare and it's what's special to us. Maybe Annie found that down-to-earth, once-in-a-lifetime love here with a rancher, but then fame and fortune lured her from reality back into her fantasy world."

"But he never forgot her."

"And she never forgot him." Fern cocked her head to one side, glancing at Craig from the corners of her eyes. "Today…their great love lives on in the name of a small Texas town named Sure-Shot."

"Never to be forgotten."

"Exactly." She appeared sort of wistful as she watched the western town come closer. "I want our Annie Oakley story to be real, even if it is fantasy."

"It's real for us now. Far as I know, nobody remembers how Sure-Shot got its name anymore beyond a tribute to the famous lady."

"That makes our story just as good as any other."

"Better." He felt her story touch his heart, adding even more to the song about her that was gaining strength in his head all the time. "Maybe I'd better change the name of my family ranch."

She glanced over at him and shook her head. "Tradition is important. Best not mess with it."

"We could always start a new tradition."

"Aren't we doing that at Wildcat Hall?"

"Yes. Still, I'm thinking about rancher tradition of protecting and working with land and animals."

"That's important, too. But you know as well as I do that you can't just go around changing brands and ranch names and all. It's not done."

He felt his heart fill even more with her—every little bit of her—at those kind words for his family heritage. "Okay. We'll leave it be…for now."

And then they were in Sure-Shot as he drove down the asphalt two-lane road that turned into Main Street. The small town still nestled at what had once been the vital intersection of an old cattle drive trail that ran north to south and the railway line that crossed east to west.

Sure-Shot looked similar to the set of an Old West film. Old Town in Wildcat Bluff was built of brick and stone, while Sure-Shot had a classic wooden false-front commercial district. A line of single-story businesses connected by a boardwalk, covered porticos, and tall facade parapets extending above the roofs were individually painted in green, blue, and yellow with white trim. Small clapboard houses with wide front porches and fancy double-wides fanned out around the downtown area.

Once upon a time, Sure-Shot had catered to cowboys

on their cattle drives from Texas to Kansas and back again. Lively dance halls and noisy saloons, along with the mercantile, café, blacksmith shop, livery stable, bathhouse, bank, and freight depot had all done a brisk business, just like the same types of stores had in Wildcat Bluff.

As always, Craig felt as if he'd stepped back in time. A few pickups and Jeeps were parked in front of the businesses, but a couple of saddle horses with their reins wrapped around the hitching post in front of the Bluebonnet Café swished their tails at flies. He had no doubt their riders wore hats, boots, and spurs while they waited for takeout or sat down for an early supper inside the café. Life around here had its own tempo. It might not be fast, but it was steady.

He neared an open area created by two buildings being lost to a fire years ago. For a long time, it had been a stubble of dry grass in winter and a colorful swathe of wildflowers in spring that ranged from orange Indian paintbrush to bright bluebonnets to crimson clover. In the last year, enterprising folks had added a white Victorian style gazebo with landscaped gardens of native plants and wildflowers in the center of the two town lots.

On the other side rose the old gas station with the same tall, flat, wooden false front as the other structures. It had been repurposed to serve a new clientele. "Sure-Shot Beauty Station" emblazoned in a western-style typeface, in bright turquoise against a white background, replaced the original green-and-white Sinclair logo. Instead of double bay front doors, the entire front was now glass, so passersby could see the goings-on inside and customers could watch the goings-on outside. Mirrors dominated the interior walls, and a row of turquoise chairs sat facing them from a few feet away.

"Looks like folks are gathering for the band's concert," Fern said.

"Guess it's time to park and join them."

"Don't they appear happy to be here?" She pointed at the women dressed in tight jeans, short cutoffs, flirty skirts, and bright tops, while the men wore Wranglers, colorful western shirts or T-shirts, and boots. Everyone wore a hat or cap to protect their faces from the hot sun beating down overhead. They were mostly in family groups, from babies to grannies. And they all carried chairs of various types.

"Sure do." He glanced at folks setting up in haphazard rows on the manicured lawn around the gazebo, while he looked for a place to park among all the pickups. He continued down the street until he found an empty place across from the beauty station. He quickly parked and turned to Fern.

"I'm excited to be here," she said. "It's like getting back to our roots before we became professionals."

"Hope you like the band." He pulled two bottles of water out of the cooler and handed her one. "No way to get around the afternoon heat, so let's stay hydrated."

"Right. Texas in August." She chuckled, amusement filling her eyes. "It just means I'll glow and—"

"I'll sweat, because Southern ladies wouldn't think of doing anything more than glow no matter how hot they get."

She laughed harder. "So true. At least, no guy would ever say anything else."

"Right. I wasn't raised in a barn."

"Not even close." She leaned across and placed a soft kiss on his lips. "But I might not mind meeting you up in a hayloft."

He grinned, feeling a burst of sheer happiness just to be with her. "I've got a hayloft on the ranch."

"Is it available?"

"If it's not, it can be."

"Maybe that's something to put on our to-do list."

"Before or after Wild West Days?" No way was he was losing out on an opportunity like this one. He needed to get it nailed down fast.

"Let's catch your hayloft at the first opportunity."

"I'm with you on that one." He'd make sure it was before the big event. There was fresh hay from July in the loft, all ready for winter. He could toss several quilts on top of it and they'd be good to go. He was almost losing interest in the concert. If they left right now, they could go straight to the ranch and fulfill that fantasy.

"Too bad we can't go now," she said thoughtfully.

"Yeah." Maybe the concert wouldn't last too long, but he didn't have much hope of that idea. He'd just have to put the hayloft on a back burner till he could get her there and make up for lost time.

He got out, opened the back door, pulled out two folding chairs in their cloth cylinders, and looped them by their straps over one shoulder. By the time he walked around to her side of the truck, she was already standing on the ground, smiling at him. He clasped her hand and felt an instant blaze that had nothing to do with the ninety-five degree heat.

They walked hand in hand across the street to tread on the soft, closely-trimmed grass on their way to the gazebo. Several people called to him, recognizing him from living there and from entertaining at the Hall. He greeted them in return, smiling as he kept moving with Fern until they

COWBOY FIREFIGHTER HEAT 153

reached a spot to one side but with a good view of the open-sided gazebo.

He set up their chairs, side by side, so they'd be close together, then waited for her to sit down. When they both were seated and had placed their bottles of water in cup-holders, he sighed in contentment. It was good to be home, good to be with Fern, and good to be waiting to hear an up-and-coming band.

"How does it feel to be on this side of the stage?" she asked, leaning toward him.

"Good. How about you?"

"Odd…but good, too."

"The band is setting up. How do you like their look?" He gestured with his head toward the group, which had a singer, lead guitar, bass guitar, fiddle, Dobro, and drums. They wore black cowboy boots, blue jeans, and black T-shirts with "Red River Wranglers" emblazoned in crimson Old West type across the front.

"Simple is smart. And I like the band name, too."

"It's a good place to start."

"Yeah." She reached over and squeezed his hand as her smile reached from her lips to her eyes.

"We're in a good place, too."

As she nodded in agreement, Elsie—owner of the Bluebonnet Café—sashayed up to the front of the gazebo. She wore cat-eye, rhinestone eyeglasses and her bright red hair in a curly ponytail. She'd squeezed her long-limbed, athletic body into a turquoise tunic worn with hot-pink tights and purple cowgirl boots. She wrapped a long-fingered hand around the mic on a tall stand while the audience grew quiet in anticipation.

"Welcome to another Sunday afternoon at the Summer Music of Sure-Shot!" Elsie called out as she gestured toward the group in front of her.

She was met with wild applause and whistles as folks reacted to the coming performance.

"That's right," Elsie said. "You've got a good reason to be excited because our very own Red River Wranglers from right here in Sure-Shot, Texas, are about to set your toes tapping with their western swing favorites. Let's hear it for them!"

Elsie pointed toward the band, then stepped back and let them take over with an upbeat rendition of "San Antonio Rose."

Craig listened while keeping an eye on Fern to get her reaction. The band was getting better every time he heard them. He'd be proud to have them play in Wildcat Bluff during Wild West Days.

When the Red River Wranglers finished that number and launched into another, Fern leaned over to Craig, smiling and nodding as she kept rhythm with her fingertips on the arm of her chair.

He leaned toward her. "You like?"

"Let's book them. And not just for Wild West Days."

"Really?"

"They're just what I want to nurture at the Hall."

"Let's do it."

After a few more numbers, Elsie took the mic and looked out over the crowd until her gaze came to rest on Fern and Craig. She nodded at them, smiling.

"Folks," Elsie said. "We've got a special treat for you at this Summer Music of Sure-Shot. We have with us none other than Fern Bryant and Craig Thorne from Wildcat

Hall. Fern is just back from entertaining on luxury cruises on the high seas. And Craig is our hometown boy made good. Please give them a warm welcome and persuade them to take the stage just for us this lovely afternoon."

Fern turned to Craig, eyes wide in surprise.

He just shrugged and stood up, knowing she would follow him. They couldn't turn down such a request or a chance to promote Wild West Days. Besides, he owed the folks of this town for their continual support all his life.

When he held out his hand, Fern took it and stood up beside him. Applause came quick and loud, following them up to the gazebo.

"Thank you so much," Elsie said with a big grin. "I can't tell you how much we appreciate you performing for us."

The guitar player slipped the strap of his guitar over his head and held his instrument out to Craig. "I'm Renegade. At least that's what they call me. I'd be honored if you'd use my guitar."

"Thanks." As Craig shifted the strap across his own shoulders, he leaned down toward the boy. "You've got a fine band here. We want you to play at Wildcat Hall when you turn eighteen."

"We're already there…just this summer." Renegade grinned, excitement shimmering in his widened eyes.

"Good. We'll talk later." Craig turned back toward the audience.

Fern plucked the mic from its stand, then glanced at Craig and whispered, "You Are My Sunshine." He nodded, knowing she'd picked the perfect song for a family outing on a Sunday afternoon in the park.

And then she was singing while he was harmonizing

and accompanying them on the borrowed guitar. Soon they were deep into their fantasy world, where nothing existed except the two of them and their music carrying everyone with them into happiness.

After a bit, Fern beckoned for the audience to sing along. "Hey, folks. You know this song. Please join us."

He quickly glanced back at Elsie and the band. "Step right on up here and let's see what we can really do with this number."

"An honor," Renegade said as he moved up beside Craig, grinning all the while as he leaned toward the mic while Elsie and the other band members joined them.

Craig felt the thrill of a perfect performance as the uplifted voices of the audience joined their song to fill the park with joyful sound on a sunshiny day in August.

Chapter 18

AFTER SHARING THREE SONGS WITH ELSIE, THE RED River Wranglers, and the audience, Fern felt a deep sense of satisfaction. This was why she'd come home. She could nurture not only musicians but communities as well. Sometimes she just thought too small. What if they brought the original Sure-Shot honky-tonk back to life? Bert and Bert Two had already revived the drive-in. The Sinclair filling station had been repurposed to meet contemporary needs. Obviously, the area was growing, instead of shrinking like so many places. And it was Craig's hometown.

She grew excited at the idea. As soon as they left the stage, she'd ask him if he knew whether or not the original dance hall structure still stood intact or if it'd burned or been bulldozed years ago. She thought they might be able to manage Wildcat Hall as well as Sure-Shot Hall, sharing bands, food, drink, promotion, resources, so there was less overall work. Maybe the Settelmeyers would even agree to get involved, but then again, maybe not, since they were pretty devoted to the Hall.

Yet she didn't need to nail down facts and figures right now. She couldn't, anyway, because she didn't have enough information to even make a guess as to the feasibility of another honky-tonk in the area. Still, it revved up her energy and gave her a burst of creative direction. Besides, wouldn't it simply be fun?

With a smile, she glanced over at Craig just as he completed a complicated riff on the borrowed guitar…and saw his face freeze in a guarded expression. He flicked his gaze toward her before he quickly handed the guitar back to Renegade, then focused forward again.

Something about Craig's reaction struck deep in her heart. She didn't want to look, but she slowly swiveled her gaze back to the front. And she froze, too. Simon was there, as if appearing out of nowhere.

He gently, carefully laid a bundle of green-wrapped, long-stemmed white roses on the floor of the gazebo, at her feet. He looked as well put together as ever, so he'd been sleeping just fine, wherever he'd been staying. And now he was back. He gave her a hint of a smile, then turned and walked to the side of the gazebo and disappeared from view.

She felt her breath catch in her throat and a chill race up her spine. How had he even known where she was if he hadn't been following her? And the roses? No one knew ahead of time that she'd be on the stage. Had he been stalking her all this time, roses at the ready?

When Craig grasped her hand, she squeezed in acknowledgment that everything they'd hoped to be true had just been proven false.

He quickly returned the guitar to Renegade, with a nod for the band to take over again. As music filled the air, he tugged Fern to the back of the gazebo.

"How lovely!" Elsie cried out, snatching up the roses and carrying them to Fern.

She shrank back, not wanting to touch the flowers. "Please, you keep them. They'll look beautiful in the Bluebonnet Café."

"Really?" Elsie put a hand over her heart, grinning big. "Are you sure? I mean, I'd love to have them, but they're such an expensive gift and—"

"Trust me," Fern said. "I want you and the residents of Sure-Shot to enjoy them."

"I understand." Elsie gave her a conspiratorial nod with a toss of her head that sent her ponytail swishing from side to side. "You've received so many flowers from admirers that you're willing to share. You're so generous."

"If you're happy with the roses, then I'm happy for you." Fern held on to Craig's hand, wanting to disappear from sight. "By the way, have you seen the man who left those roses around here before today?"

Elsie gave a quick shake of her head. "No. And I'd have remembered a good-looking man like him. Besides, he'd stand out among our cowboys. Do you know him?"

"Not really." She desperately wanted to get off stage and out of sight in case Simon lurked somewhere nearby, watching and waiting to get her reaction to the roses or setting her up to get something from her that she couldn't yet fathom.

"Elsie, thanks for inviting us to perform today." Craig edged toward the stairs, taking Fern with him.

"Thank you both. It's been our pleasure, believe you me." Elsie gave a huge smile to them both.

"You'll still be doing some catering at Wild West Days, won't you?" Craig asked.

"Wouldn't miss it."

"We'll be in touch," he said.

"Just let me know what you need, when you need it."

"We will. And thank you," Fern said.

"You're welcome here anytime." Elsie beamed at them. "Now don't be a stranger."

Craig quickly led Fern away from the gazebo and toward his dark blue pickup with bright chrome trim. She kept her gaze straight ahead, not about to encounter Simon's watchful eyes if he was out there just waiting for her to notice him. She didn't feel safe again until she was in the front seat of Craig's pickup and he was beside her.

"Guess that tells us what we needed to know." He glanced over at her.

"But we didn't want to know."

"How are you?"

"I'm okay." She took several deep breaths. "Really. It was just such a surprise, particularly in Sure-Shot."

"I hate to say it, but it looks like you've got a serious stalker." He checked his side mirror before he looked out all the windows.

"Is he there?"

"Don't know." He glanced back at her. "We don't know what he drives."

"A fancy sedan?"

"Not a chance. He won't want to stand out in pickup country."

"Where's he getting the roses?"

"If he's smart, and I figure he is or he's done this before, he won't leave a trail, so he's shopping and living out of town. He could even be ordering the roses online with overnight delivery, so he keeps fresh ones on hand."

"I hate to think any of that, but you're right." She felt the chill go deeper. "Do you think I'm not the first woman he's stalked?"

"No way to know, but he does appear to have a system in place."

"I don't want to believe others were subjected to his attentions. He could be making it up as he goes along."

"Right," Craig replied. "We'll contact the sheriff. He might be able to come up with some answers."

"Okay."

He turned to face her and clasped her hand. "You're not in this alone. I won't let anything happen to you."

"There's still my first option."

"No way in hell." He squeezed her fingers, let go, and put his hand on the leather-wrapped steering wheel. "And no way am I taking you to the drive-in. It's too easy for him to follow us there, and we'd be too exposed in that environment. Plus, we might endanger others."

She exhaled on a sharp breath in irritation, regretting this sudden curtailment of her life. "Danger? What would he use, roses?"

Craig threw her a stern look, then started the engine. "We don't know how far he's willing to take his obsession."

She put a hand over her heart, as if already struck by some unknown force. "Violence? You think he could get—"

"We're going to the ranch. It's the safest place I can think to take you right now."

She didn't say anything as he turned the pickup and head back the way they'd come. She was stuck on the idea that Simon might want to hurt her. She just couldn't wrap her head around that fact, and yet there were stories out there—real-life stories—of obsessions gone bad. She had to take the situation even more seriously than when she'd believed he'd left the county.

Craig gunned the engine, and Sure-Shot went by in a flash, startling folks and horses in front of the Bluebonnet Café.

"We can't let him frighten us." She tried to sound calmer and more collected than she felt.

"I'm not in the least frightened," Craig said through gritted teeth. "I'm furious some guy thinks he can come into Wildcat Bluff County and stalk you...or any other woman here, either."

"But you just said you thought he was dangerous."

"No. I didn't want to chance putting others in a potentially dangerous situation."

"I don't understand the difference."

"Fern, you ought to know by now, even if you are from the city, that every man and most women in this county are armed and ready for trouble."

"You mean like Hedy, MG, Ruby—"

"Bert, Bert Two. You could name names all day. There's no point. Out here in the country, danger is around us all the time. Poisonous snakes. Coyote packs. Poachers. Cattle rustlers. We'd be fools if we didn't know how to protect ourselves and what belongs to us."

"I guess 911 isn't a lot of help out here."

"Sheriff Calhoun is a good man, but it's a big county. And seconds can make the difference in life and death."

"I don't want to even consider this might come to anything that serious."

"Me either...but we're going to err on the side of caution. Okay?" He glanced over at her for emphasis before he turned onto Highway 82 going west toward Gainesville.

"Yes, of course."

"Good."

She didn't say anymore while he drove and she furiously tried to think of ways to get out of the situation. How had her life suddenly spiraled out of control? No, she wouldn't think that way. She couldn't accept that fate. She would accept that she had a problem, but it wouldn't stop her from going forward with her life. She'd take precautions now. Others around her would do the same thing. And they'd all be fine.

For now, her main concern needed to be Wild West Days. They just had to get through it without any overt incidents, particularly dangerous ones. Roses she could handle. She'd just throw them away. If he lurked at venues, she could handle that, too. She'd just ignore him. In time, he was bound to realize that she'd never return his interest, so he'd give up and go away. She only hoped it was sooner than later.

"Place is probably a mess." Craig broke into her thoughts. "I haven't been there much lately."

She glanced up in time to see him turn off the highway and drive under an arched and polished cedar sign that read THORNE HORSE RANCH. As he headed up the winding gravel road, he passed horses in black, gray, and roan colors that grazed in several pastures with ponds sparkling blue in the late-afternoon sunlight. They raised their heads and looked up, swishing long tails as they watched the pickup pass them by.

"Hope you like the place. Folks left the running of it to me after they moved down to South Padre Island for sun and surf."

"How come you didn't bring me here before?"

He drummed fingertips on the steering wheel. "You were a city girl. I didn't think you'd much like it."

"You were trying to impress me by not showing me your ranch?"

"Yeah. Something like that."

"Did you think I wouldn't like horses or critters?"

"I didn't want to take a chance. And by the time I figured out you actually liked country living, you were up and gone."

"You do realize that's pretty convoluted thinking, don't you?"

"Could we set it down to the fact that I took one look at you and my brains scrambled?"

She chuckled, feeling decidedly better now that they were off the main highway and onto private property with lots of protective fences. And then, when she was with Craig, she always felt better.

"Listen, we'll be alone up at the house and grounds, surrounded by a stout fence. The foreman and ranch hands are in their own compound farther out on the ranch, near the barns and pastures."

"Okay."

"That's all you've got to say?"

"I'm with you, so I'm okay with whatever I get."

He chuckled, glanced over at her, and shook his head. "That's pretty compliant for you."

She laughed, too. "I know, but at the moment, I just want to be someplace I feel perfectly safe, so I can relax."

He grinned, eyes lighting up with an inner fire. "I might have a few ideas on relaxation techniques."

"Only a few?"

"Push comes to shove, I bet I could come up with as many as you like."

"I might like a lot."

"You've got it."

"Thanks." She reached over and squeezed his forearm. "I needed to laugh a bit."

"He's not going to get us down, and he's not going to make us cower in a corner."

"Right."

"We just need to regroup now that we know he's still in the area."

"And come up with an action plan of our own."

"Yeah."

He drove up a rise where a sturdy chain-link fence enclosed a two-story house with a peaked roof, as well as a white gazebo adorned with lacy gingerbread and a swimming pool with sparkling blue water. He hit a button on the remote control on the sun visor above his head, and the double gates slowly swung open. He drove inside, pressed the remote again, and the gates closed behind them.

She looked ahead at a charming turn-of-the-twentieth-century farmhouse that was painted bright white with Victorian gingerbread gracing the eaves and a wide wraparound porch that contained a long oak swing with a high back that hung from the ceiling by chains on one end. Two wooden rockers with plush, blue-and-pink floral cushions appeared perfect for guests to sit and visit a spell. The polished oak front door with a frosted, etched glass inset and brass hardware set off the entry to perfection.

"I'm so happy to be here. Thank you for sharing your home with me." She was charmed by the house...and Craig Thorne.

He stopped, then turned to face her. "I've wanted to bring you here from the first. I just thought it might not be fancy enough for you."

"Fancy?" She leaned over and pressed a quick kiss to his lips. "Warm and cozy suit me so much better."

"And ranch life?"

"I think I could learn to love it, but…"

"Wildcat Bluff Park."

"And our music."

"Don't you think we can have it all?"

She looked around, feeling the serenity and peacefulness of the ranch point her toward a wider world of possibilities.

"You'll never be content to be in one place all the time," he said. "And the cabin will get too confining after a while."

She smiled, considering his words. "If I feel a need to run, I could always take off for the ranch."

He returned her smile. "Out-of-town gigs are a possibility, too."

She nodded in agreement. "I had an idea while singing today."

"Yeah?"

"I guess I sort of fell in love with Sure-Shot. It's cozy, just like your farmhouse."

"Down-home folks like it here."

"There must have been a dance hall, or more than one, in Sure-Shot back in its heyday, like our Wildcat Hall."

He started to grin, chuckling under his breath. "I know just where you're going with this idea."

She grinned back at him. "You like?"

"I love."

"Perfect. Is it still standing?"

"Not sure. Maybe one or two might have survived the years. If so, they'd be out of town, on the old cattle drive trail like Wildcat Hall. I doubt they'd be in very good shape, and they'd probably be overgrown with trees, vines, weeds."

"Phooey. That doesn't sound so good."

"Anything in town is already preserved and in use. Still, when we get time, we could check old maps and plats for locations."

"I know we don't need anything else on our plates right now, but still...it might be fun."

"And it could make a viable business, as well. Folks are getting out of the cities and looking for a comfy home at the end of the road. They'll want entertainment and a taste of the past."

"Plus, it'd be another venue for entertainers."

"Maybe it could serve more than one function." He looked thoughtful. "Education. Arts. Crafts. Music. It could all be in the western tradition."

"If we can't get funding reinstated for Wildcat Bluff's school, maybe we just need to establish a private venue that serves the entire county."

"You know what you're doing, don't you?"

"What?"

"You're talking yourself right out of leaving Wildcat Bluff County ever again."

She rolled her eyes at him, realizing he was stating the truth. "Let's get out of this pickup before I come up with any more bright ideas."

"It's a good one...just like you. A keeper." He opened his door. "Come on, let's go inside and get comfortable."

"Is that where I get to hear all about your ideas for

relaxation?" She picked up her purse that had the essentials in it, but not nearly enough for an overnighter. She shrugged, realizing she cared a lot more about safety than looks or comfort.

He stepped outside, then glanced back at her. "That's where I'll demonstrate my relaxation techniques."

And she was out the door.

Chapter 19

FERN LINGERED ON THE FRONT PORCH AS CRAIG inserted a key in the lock. She caught the scent of old-fashioned lilacs and glanced around to find the big pale-purple blooms in a border along one side of the house, which were so appropriate to the lovely setting. His pioneer ancestors had probably planted the flowers to remind them of their old Kentucky home, as the classic song went. She treasured the deep connection to land and home that had sustained the Thorne family for generations.

When he opened the door and waited for her to enter first, she felt as if she'd been given another great gift besides his love. She'd come to this county to nurture others, and here she'd found nurturance—perhaps even for herself—in abundance. She'd fallen hard for Wildcat Hall Park. Now she was continuing that fall right into the waiting arms of Thorne Horse Ranch.

As she stepped inside, he flicked a switch that turned on lights in an overhead fan that whirled to distribute cool air-conditioned air. She took in the living room décor that perfectly fit the age of the house. Two chairs with blue-and-pink floral upholstery stood sentinel on either side of the redbrick fireplace. A lapis-blue sofa and a cherrywood coffee table with a silk floral arrangement in a porcelain bowl looked too feminine for Craig, so she suspected his mother must have added pieces or refinished original items.

Pale blue-and-pink floral wallpaper added more color to the pretty room.

"I doubt you expected to see me live in a place that looks like a ladies' tearoom." Craig chuckled as he gestured around the area.

She smiled and squeezed his hand. "It looks cozy. I can see sitting by the fire in winter and reading a good book."

"You can change anything you want."

"Oh, Craig, let's not even go there. This is lovely." She put a hand on his broad chest, rose on her tiptoes, and kissed his cheek. "This is perfect for a hundred-year-old house."

"Yeah. But it's kind of fussy, too."

"I bet you have a den or someplace where you like to hang out."

"Kitchen." He caught her hand. "Come on."

She gasped in surprise as she entered a large room with a wall of tinted glass that extended across the back of the house. French doors led outside, onto the wide porch where white wicker furniture with forest-green cushions and a white cast-iron table with matching chairs beckoned her to lounge and watch colts frolic across the bucolic acres of pasture. And even closer, an infinity pool urged her to throw off her cares and lose herself in the cool water on a hot summer day.

"Like?"

"Oh yes!" She whirled around, grinning in happiness. "I'm totally captivated with the outdoors, but let me look in here."

"Be my guest." He pointed at the stainless steel appliances. "I took out walls between the smaller rooms to make one great room back here."

"I like the space."

"I needed something besides small rooms and flowery stuff."

"It's perfect for you." He'd utilized an open floor plan with the kitchen on one end with a bar and barstools separating a large family room on the other side. She liked the big brown leather furniture in the den that also contained a large hand-carved cedar desk with a laptop, keyboard, and papers on top, as well as a flat-screen monitor on the wall above it all. She set her purse down on top of the bar, then ran her fingers across the smooth, utilitarian stainless steel.

"Thanks." He put his hands around her waist and tugged her back against his chest. "Think you could be happy here?"

She covered his hands with her own smaller ones, feeling his heat, his solidness, his love. "Yes."

"Good. I can't imagine living in this house without you now."

"And I can't imagine leaving you here alone."

"We're together here." He turned her in his arms and lowered his head to kiss her.

She reached up and grasped his shoulders, wanting nothing more than to be close to him—as close as humanly possible. As she pressed her lips to his mouth, she heard a text buzz on the cell phone in her purse. She stopped, puzzled, and glanced over there.

"Are you expecting a text or call?"

"No. Folks know we're in Sure-Shot today."

"Forget it then."

"Okay." Yet the texts kept coming and coming, demanding more and more of her attention. "Maybe it's the Settelmeyers."

He sighed. "I guess it could be an emergency with the Hall or Wild West Days."

"But they're not trying to reach you."

"If it's important, I'm probably next on their list."

"Yeah. Let's wait and see." She sighed in relief when the phone stopped annoying her…but then it started up again. More text alerts.

"Guess you better check and get it over with, then we can go back to what's important today."

"Hold that thought." She patted his chest as she stepped back. "Your relaxation techniques are on my mind."

"Keep them there."

She turned to the bar, picked up her purse, pulled out her phone, and checked her messages. Chills hit her. She felt weak in the knees. She abruptly jerked out a stool and sat down.

"What is it?"

She held out her phone so he could see the messages.

With a frown on his face, Craig started scrolling and reading aloud. "Did you enjoy the roses? I'm thinking of you stroking their soft petals while you inhale their scent and think of me. Are you? Right now? Why don't you answer me? You looked beautiful today. Sunlight becomes you. Were you as happy to see me as I was to see you? Yes, I know. I felt as if our hearts beat in unison. We need to meet soon. I can't wait much longer to hold you. Text me a time and place. You know I'll be there because nothing can keep me from our love."

"Don't read any more." She put her face in her hands, so she couldn't even see her phone. "I can't stand it."

Craig turned off her cell and slammed it down on top of

the bar. "Okay. This has gone way beyond rational behavior. He's a stalker on the prowl now."

"He's delusional."

"Did you talk with him at all on the cruises?"

"Never." She wrapped her arms around her waist, feeling as if her world had just slipped out from under her.

"Let me handle this." Craig gave her a warm hug, then pulled his cell out of his pocket. "It's best if you don't use that phone again or at least not until you change the number."

"I'll never touch it again. It's too dirty for me now."

"We'll get you a new one."

"But how could Simon have my number?"

"Don't use his name."

"Okay. I forgot. I don't want to give him any more power."

"We're using our phones for Wildcat Hall and Wild West Days. He could have found your number that way or another. It's not like we have much privacy in our lives anymore."

"True." She felt colder by the moment. "I'm going outside in the heat."

"Good idea. Let's go." He unlocked the french doors, then gestured for her to go before him.

She stepped into the summer heat and immediately felt better. She quickly walked across the porch, down the steps, and out into the sun. She needed those golden rays to penetrate her skin and warm clear to her bones. She sat down on a chaise near the pool, taking a deep breath to calm her emotions. She couldn't let Simon scare her, but his texts read as if he was contacting somebody he knew well, but that wasn't her. Roses, that's all. Nothing but roses in all this time, until suddenly it was like a dam burst—and he revealed his true self…one she couldn't possibly understand or want to know.

Craig walked up, talking on his phone. "Sheriff, I hate to tell you, but Fern's situation escalated this afternoon." He sat down beside her, hitting the speakerphone button so she could listen to the conversation.

"Can't say I'm surprised, but I'm sorry to hear it," Sheriff Calhoun said. "Do you need me or a deputy right now?"

"No. We're at my ranch, so she's safe."

"Excellent. I'm listening, so give me details."

"We gave an impromptu performance at the gazebo in Sure-Shot this afternoon. He showed up and left flowers."

"Like before?"

"Yes…except how did he know she was in Sure-Shot?"

"Bird-dogging," Sheriff Calhoun said. "It wouldn't be hard to do around here. Did you get a look at his vehicle?"

"No. We were onstage, before a crowd. He just slipped away. We came straight to the ranch."

"But that's not all," Sheriff Calhoun said, "or you wouldn't be calling me. What else did he do?"

"He got her phone number and sent a series of disturbing texts."

"Stay where you are. I'm sending a deputy right over to pick up her cell. We may be able to get something from tower pings, but I want those messages off her phone right now."

"I'll meet your deputy at the gate and give him the phone."

"Good. In the meantime, I don't need to tell you to be careful and stay safe."

"I'm on it, but we need to get back to Wildcat Hall tomorrow," Craig said.

"Fern should be okay if she isn't left alone."

"Right."

"Another thing. As much as I hate to say it, there's not a lot we can do until he makes an overt move. Still, folks in the county will be on alert, along with my deputies."

"Thanks. We can't ask for more."

"Call if there's anything else." And Sheriff Calhoun was gone.

Craig put his phone back in his pocket. "You heard it. What do you think?"

"I think I'm really glad I'm sitting in the sun or I'd be shivering all over."

"Come here." He took her in his arms and held her close.

"Thank you." She felt better so close to him. "I just need to get my feet under me, then I'll be okay."

"It's not your fault."

"But it seems like it. I mean, it's me he's after."

"I told you before that it's all on him. You're an entertainer, and you deserve respect for what you give to your audience."

"Yes, I know."

"And nobody—absolutely nobody—gets more than you're willing to give."

"I needed to hear those words."

"I'll repeat them as often as necessary till we get this guy and he gets what he deserves."

She nodded in agreement as she stayed still, soaking up heat from Craig and the sun as she stared out over the pastures with green grass and trees under a beautiful blue sky. She heard crows caw overhead, then they wheeled on wide wings and floated down into the spreading limbs of a hundred-year-old post oak tree. She envied the birds their freedom. She wanted it. She would get it back just as soon as they caught Simon and put him in his place. As those calming thoughts spread through her, she felt better, more herself again.

"Deputy ought to be here anytime. I'll take your phone down to the gate. You just stay here."

She clutched his arm a moment, then felt foolish at her anxiety. She'd never been afraid before to be alone. She wouldn't start now. "Thanks. I'm happy to wait here where I'm comfortable."

"Good." He stood up and walked back into the house.

Alone, she took stock of her surroundings. She wasn't about to let a stranger dictate her life from a distance. She was in the wonderful world of a terrific man who'd promised her happiness. Who was she to turn down paradise?

Now that she'd warmed up, she felt hot. She was definitely overdressed for an August afternoon beside a shimmering pool of water. From hot to cold, that's what she wanted now.

She reached down and tugged off one boot, then the other, followed by her socks. She wriggled her toes, liking the peach polish she'd chosen for her toenails. Still, she was too hot. She jerked her shirttail out of her jeans, jerked open all the pearl snaps, and tossed her shirt aside. Much better. Still, her jeans were too hot and tight. She stood up and shucked them down her legs until she could kick them to one side. Nothing left but peach lace bra and thong. She could feel a little breeze against her bare skin. Even better. And yet, the water looked almost cold...and plenty inviting. Maybe just a quick dip before Craig got back.

She sat down on the edge of the pool, slipped her feet into the lovely coolness, and moaned in pleasure. Maybe just a few laps. And that'd be best with no constriction at all.

She unhooked her bra, slipped it off, and turned to toss it toward her other clothes. She stopped in midmotion at the sight of Craig grinning as he stood there looking down at her with enough heat to rival the sun. She grinned back and held up her bra by a single strap dangling from one fingertip.

He plucked the bra from her finger, tossed it over his shoulder, and sat down on a nearby chaise. He watched her watching him as he took off his shirt, boots, and finally jeans. Nothing left but his briefs. And her thong.

She raised her hips, slipped off her thong, and tossed it at his feet. He grinned even bigger as he picked it up and draped it over the edge of the chaise. And that's where he hung his briefs before he walked over to the deep end of the pool and made a perfect dive into the depths with his perfect body.

When he came up for air, tossing his shiny hair back from his face, he started for her. She pushed into the water with both hands and swam toward him. When she met him in the middle, they stopped face-to-face and lowered their feet to the smooth bottom. And smiled at each other.

He reached out, dripping water from his arms, and cupped her cheeks with both palms before he lowered his face and placed a soft kiss on her lips. From there, he trailed rough fingertips down her throat to the upper slopes of her breasts, then he used his thumbs to coax the tips into hard peaks.

She felt the hotness of his skin through the coolness of the water, urging her along the path he blazed as he moved lower and lower, teasing and tormenting until he clasped her bottom with both hands, pulled her upward, and entered her just as she wrapped her legs around his waist.

He carried her to the edge of the pool, where she sat as he moved inside her, harder and faster and hotter, splashing water over the edge and into the air as he stoked their blaze higher and higher. She clung to his broad shoulders, feeling the sun hot on her shoulders, the water cool on her legs, and Craig as the center of her universe.

And she wanted more...so much more—riding him, kissing him, completing him until they reached the peak of passion together and water arched overhead in a sparkling rainbow of endless possibilities.

Chapter 20

SEVERAL DAYS LATER, CRAIG WAS DOING HIS BEST TO keep things under control, but he felt as if he was on the edge of losing ground even as he continued to push forward with Wild West Days. He glanced around the pocket park beside the Chuckwagon Café, with its closely trimmed grass and wildflower garden in one corner. Fern was inside discussing menus with Slade, Sydney, and the rest of the Steele family. They'd need extra of everything for the big upcoming event, since folks would want to get inside, not only for the great meals but to get out of the Labor Day weekend heat. Foot traffic in the stores would be high because everybody would crave the AC indoors, as well as shopping for gifts and mementos.

With that in mind, he walked over to Main Street, imagining how it would look without parked or moving vehicles. The town would close both ends of the street to through traffic so vendors could set up tents and trailers to showcase their handcrafted wares and offer food and drink. No way to tell just how hot it'd be in a couple of weeks. They could hope for the low nineties, but they could just as easily get high nineties. Five degrees either way would make a big difference in it feeling acceptably hot or hot as hell. He was hoping for low nineties, but he wasn't counting on it. If he was making a wish about the weather, it'd be for a dip into the eighties, but that wouldn't stand a chance of happening unless they got rain, which would present its own set of problems. He was in a wait-and-see mode.

No matter the final temperature, it'd still be hot, so iced drinks, ice cream, and all sorts of cold delights, particularly easy on-a-stick treats, would be highly prized by everyone. Elsie's Bluebonnet Café's offerings would also bring a big crowd to her trailer because it just didn't get any better than her burger and fries, or Indian tacos and fry bread drizzled with honey.

There wasn't anything to be done on the street till the night before Wild West Days, so he walked back to the pocket park. He put his hands on his hips as he examined the area. He needed to get a small bandstand set up against this side of the Chuckwagon. Bert Two did some fine woodworking, so he'd be the guy to ask about making it, particularly since he was now getting around pretty well with a medical boot supporting his broken foot. They could fit another picnic table into the park, and that'd make five tables that could handle anywhere from eight to ten folks each. It wasn't enough seating for a big crowd, but most people would be standing for the entertainment, eating, drinking, and listening. Many would bring their own folding chairs and fan out from the bandstand. He was glad it'd make a great venue for local talent.

As he was considering the size they'd need the bandstand to be, he felt that itching on the back of his neck that alerted him to possible trouble. He whipped his head around to look at the street. A dusty, rusty pickup with faded green paint idled on the street across from the Chuckwagon. A man wearing a blue ball cap pulled low on his face and oversize dark sunglasses obscuring his eyes focused in that direction. As if he felt Craig watching him, he turned his head, aiming those glasses that looked like insect eyes at the pocket park, then he eased forward, leaving a cloud of smoke from the oil-burning engine in his wake.

Craig tried to get the license number, but the plate was covered in mud, so he could only watch until the truck was out of sight. But not out of mind. The stalker. Yes? No? Maybe? The chill left in the wake of the sighting was a pretty good indicator of the needle pointing toward positive, but he had no proof, and that was what he needed to stop the torment aimed at Fern.

There'd been no more roses or texts since Sure-Shot and the ranch, but that didn't mean the man wasn't still out there, watching and waiting for his next opportunity to reach Fern. It wasn't easy for him now. She carried a new cell phone for safety, and she had a new number. She was also never alone. But harder didn't mean impossible…and that pickup was just the type of camouflage necessary for a stalker to disappear into the tapestry of Wildcat Bluff County.

He wasn't going to tell her about the sighting or call the sheriff. No point in worrying either of them about something they couldn't do a thing about at the moment. But at some point, it would all come to a head. He didn't know when or where, but he had to be ready to react instantly if and when the time came to keep her safe.

For now, he'd go about his business of setting up Wild West Days with Fern's input all the way. It'd be upon them before he knew it, and he wanted all the events to go smoothly. Of course, it was a given that there'd be glitches here and there, but folks were used to adjusting to unforeseen incidents, so even those would turn out okay in the end.

It was time to pick up Fern, so he stepped up on the boardwalk and headed that way. As he reached the door to the Chuckwagon, it burst open and three tall, muscular cowboys almost mowed him down getting out of there.

"Trey, Kent, Shane, what's up?" Craig asked, stepping back to make room for them. They were all dressed about like him in hats, shirts, jeans, and boots.

"That Sydney!" Trey Duval jerked his cowboy hat off his head, revealing thick dark hair, and slapped his hat against his thigh as if knocking off dust. "Once she gets something in her head, there's no getting it out."

Craig took another step back. "She's not collecting volunteers again, is she?"

"Oh yes, she most certainly is doing that exact thing," Kent Duval said with a dimpled grimace. "You'd better watch out."

"Right," Shane Taggart said, rolling his hazel eyes. "You're not out of the woods any more than the rest of us."

And the door burst open again. This time the tall, strawberry-blond cowgirl under discussion, wearing a Chuckwagon T-Shirt, ripped jeans, and flip-flops, stalked out. She cocked her head and gave all four cowboys a sharp-eyed look.

"I'm just here to pick up Fern." Craig backpedaled to the edge of the boardwalk.

"Glad you showed up." Sydney settled her hands on her narrow horsewoman's hips. "As the cochair of Wild West Days, remind these guys why they're volunteering for the firefighter dunking booth."

All three cowboys swiveled their heads toward Craig and gave him steely-eyed looks.

He was caught between a rock and a hard place. Did he get on Sydney's bad side or betray his cowboy brethren? On the other hand, he was cochair, and he had a responsibility to the event.

"Craig, this is not a multiple choice question," Sydney said, putting iron in her voice. "Need I remind you that Wildcat Bluff Fire-Rescue is one hundred percent volunteer and one hundred percent self-funded? There is only one correct answer."

"I'm not sure if I can make the dunking booth either." He held up his hands as if the matter were out of his control. "I'm cochair, and I'm performing at the Lone Star. My days and nights are full."

Sydney shook her head as if at a recalcitrant mount. "Okay, firefighters, I'm going to pull out the big guns now. I've already talked with the ladies—Misty, Lauren, Eden— and they're sure you'll want to step up and do your duty to your county. And Dune, being my fiancé and all, was only too happy to volunteer to help us."

Craig sort of doubted it, but on the other hand, all those cowgirls could get cowboys to change their minds about most anything, particularly when love was added to the mix.

"Fern just said she thought you'd be happy to make time for the dunking booth, too." Sydney smiled, eyes lighting up with mischief.

"Yeah, we did discuss it." He felt a sinking sensation in the pit of his stomach as he glanced at his friends. They had the same look on their faces that he felt in his gut. Once the womenfolk got behind an idea, you might as well grin and bear it, because you loved them and wanted them to be happy. The trouble was that sometimes happy to them wasn't happy to you. And still you did it…for them. Only for them.

"You're not going to snap photos and make a calendar out of it, are you?" Kent asked.

"Yeah," Trey said. "We haven't lived that one down yet."

"We're still getting ladies coming to town looking for the fire station," Shane added. "I mean, what do they think we do there? We're volunteers. We've got ranches to run. We don't live there."

"For some reason, they think we're corralled at the station just waiting for them to arrive and take their pick." Trey slammed his hat back on his head.

"That calendar's a menace," Kent said. "No doubt about it."

"If any one of you were still on the market, you'd be singing a different tune." Sydney laughed as she glanced around the group.

"I had no idea posing as Mr. September would garner so much interest in me," Craig said thoughtfully.

"Better not let Fern hear you say that." Sydney gave him a sharp look. "Anyway, I figure she put an end to any outside interest."

"Right," Craig quickly agreed.

"Y'all should be glad that calendar is such a big hit, instead of running for the hills every time you think I might have a camera with me. Dune made a great Mr. December in the last calendar."

"We don't need another calendar," Trey said. "There are plenty of other ways to fund-raise that don't involve us getting ogled by hungry women."

Sydney grinned as she looked from one cowboy to

another. "Now, where's your sense of adventure…or to be more exact, where's your sense of letting others have an adventure?"

"We don't want to even go there," Kent said. "We're trying to maintain some dignity for the county here."

"I do believe dignity is highly overrated in this day and age. Sex sells. Get over it." Sydney cocked her head to one side, as if considering possibilities. "I've got it. *Wet and Wild Cowboy Firefighters*. Am I good or am I good? This calendar is going to be an even bigger hit."

All four cowboys groaned in unison.

"You'll be happy you volunteered when those sales numbers come rolling into the station…and money along with them."

"Think we could get a new rig?" Craig asked hopefully, trying to at least get something fun out of the trouble.

"Right," Trey replied. "It could almost make the whole ordeal worth it."

"Ask Hedy. She'll make the final decision." Sydney opened the door behind her, letting out the tantalizing scent of barbeque. "Thanks again for being so generous with your time…and bodies. We do love our volunteers in Wildcat Bluff." And she disappeared inside, letting the door shut firmly behind her.

Craig glanced at his buddies. "We were never going to get out of it, were we?"

"Not unless we left Texas and missed Wild West Days." Kent looked toward the street as if he was considering heading out.

"At least the dunking can last only so long," Shane said.

"I hate to mention it," Trey added, "but there could be a

really long line of cowgirls just waiting for the opportunity to dunk us."

"Payback?" Kent asked.

"Let's don't go down that road. It's just trouble." Craig held up his hands as if to ward off impending doom.

"Right," Kent agreed. "There's not a heartbreaker among us."

Craig watched every one of them look as if they were moving back in time and counting numbers. He had a feeling that line of women might stretch from Wildcat Bluff to Sure-Shot. In any case, the line stood a good possibility of being a lot longer than the organizers would likely anticipate.

"Anyway," Shane said, "it'll be a hot day, so it won't be so bad to cool off in the water."

"Good point." Craig nodded at his friends in encouragement. They all knew it was going to be bad, but they were just going to have to man up and take it. After all, it was for a good cause. At least, that's what they'd just have to keep telling themselves till they got through Wild West Days.

"Yeah, good point," Trey said, agreeing. "Right now we've got stuff to do."

"Someplace where Sydney can't find us," Kent added.

"You might rethink opening that door to the café." Shane slapped his friend on the shoulder. "See you later."

Craig watched his friends take off down the boardwalk, long legs power-walking away from the Chuckwagon.

He wished he could go with them.

Chapter 21

FERN WAVED GOODBYE TO HER FRIENDS IN THE Chuckwagon Café, then pushed on the front door with one hand to go out just as Craig pulled the door open from outside. She fell into his strong arms, chuckling at the delightful surprise. When she glanced up at his face, she discovered he looked leery about what awaited him inside. She wasn't too surprised, because she'd overheard the conversation Sydney had with three of their cowboy firefighters. She understood their reluctance about the calendar, but it really was a worthy cause.

"Did Sydney work out the details with you cowboys for her dunking and calendar?" She smiled, wanting him to see the humor in the situation.

"Don't even go there." He shut the door as if to provide a protective barrier. "No point in fighting it. Once Granny Duval gets to cooking in her kitchen, the whole county is gonna eat whatever she serves up and they better like it."

"They usually do like it, don't they?" Fern chuckled as she nodded in agreement, adjusting the strap of her purse on her shoulder. "Anyway, steel magnolias have a way of getting what they want."

"Right. Add her granddaughter Sydney to the mix and you better just step back, so you don't get trampled on their race to the finish line. And don't even get me started on MG and Hedy." Craig tried to sound perturbed, but there was too much humor and admiration in his eyes to back it up.

"I take it your friends headed out to find the nearest border to cross and left you to face Granny alone."

"I'm cochair." He pulled Fern a little tighter to him. "I've got to say Wild West Days is shaping up to be a little on the interesting side."

"You think?" She chuckled as she patted his chest in reassurance, feeling the strong muscles react to her touch just as she was getting hotter by the moment, even after cooling off in the AC of the café.

"Yeah. I hate to ask, but do you know what else they have planned for the firefighters?"

"Don't worry. I'll keep you safe."

"There is no safety around here, not when the womenfolk get out their pens and honey-do lists," he said, chuckling.

She joined his laughter, then she stepped back, straightened her crimson Wildcat Hall T-shirt over her Wranglers, and hooked her hand around the crook of his arm. "Come on. You're all volunteered and everything."

"It's 'everything' that's got me concerned right now."

"Let's take a walk."

"Why?" He sounded suspicious. "Is there something in the café you don't want me to see?"

"I'm happy for you to go right in there and talk with Granny and Sydney…if you're up for more volunteer work."

"I'll take the walk."

"I want to go to Morning's Glory." She laughed as she tugged him down the boardwalk, enjoying the sheer pleasure of being with him in Wildcat Bluff. Just like the good

old days. She heard sparrows chirping, chittering, and fuss-
ing in the eaves of the buildings as they laid claim to their
personal lairs. She felt as if she were doing the same thing—
laying claim to her personal cowboy firefighter. Instead of
chirps, she'd break into song to construct the strongest of
sound fences. And she'd join Craig inside it.

"Now? I thought we were going to the Lone Star to
make plans."

"We were, but MG came by the Chuckwagon and told
me she wants to show us something she found at her store."

"Can't it wait?"

"I guess it could, but we're fast running out of time
before Wild West Days to do anything except that event."

"Far as I'm concerned, anything else can wait."

"We're talking MG here. She was sort of insistent."

He stopped and looked at her. "More volunteer stuff?"

"She heard about our interest in the old buildings near
Sure-Shot."

"Can't keep anything a secret around here."

"It's not a secret."

"Did you tell her?" he asked.

"I might have mentioned it to Hedy."

"That's like announcing it to the entire county."

"I thought it might cut down on research time if somebody remembered something that'd help us."

He sighed. "It's just that we're short of time right now."

"I didn't expect an answer so soon. I simply thought I'd
get the process started for later."

"Let's get it over with and then go to the saloon."

"She probably doesn't have much to show us anyway."

She led the way to MG's store where MORNING'S GLORY

was painted in purple and green using a sixties' fancy font on a front display window. She opened the door and stepped inside with Craig right behind her.

"Y'all made it!" Morning Glory called from the back of her store, then hurried toward them in a flurry of bright color—long, full, rustling skirts and long, dangling, clanging necklaces. Somehow, she never looked a moment past her glory days as a flower child of the sixties.

"Your news intrigued me enough to bring Craig over to see what you found for us," Fern said.

Morning Glory enveloped her in a big hug and a cloud of patchouli special blend perfume.

As Fern stepped back, she glanced around the store, noticing the open arch that led into Adelia's Delights next door. She appreciated the tie-dyed fabric wallpaper, old oak floors buffed to a waxy sheen, and decorative pressed-tin ceiling. MG had filled the store with wood shelves containing colorful glass jars in all shapes and sizes that held perfumes, bath salts, lotions, and all manner of beauty supplies. Several sections were devoted to individual artisan creations, such as hand-carved wooden animals like wildcats, buffalo, horses, and cattle, as well as beautiful, colorful original quilts. One wall displayed delicate watercolors in gold frames depicting local scenes of the Cross Timbers.

"Good thing you told Hedy, who told me," Morning Glory said. "She'd come over from next door, but I'm watching her store for her right now."

"I bet she's all involved with Wild West Day plans," Craig said. "I think she said she'd be coordinating with the sheriff's department to make sure everything is ready for extra EMT, fire, and security."

"That's it exactly. We don't want any slipups with so many people depending on us for safety." Morning Glory clasped her hands together over her heart, bracelets jingling on her wrists. "Anyway, I'm just so excited to share what I found in the old archives."

"What archives?" Fern asked.

"Well, I guess you wouldn't exactly call them archives, but that's the way I think of them."

"What do you mean?" Craig sounded impatient and glanced around the store as if wanting to be on his way.

"When I bought this place, I found a bunch of disintegrating cardboard boxes in the storage room. They'd been stacked and shoved out of the way behind newer boxes and file cabinets."

"Really? That's interesting." Fern was intrigued by the idea of so much resource material about the county.

"I think so, too. Anyway, it was a bunch of different stuff, like old newspapers, assorted business papers, yellowed telegrams, tintypes, and faded photographs. Those pictures of downtown are really interesting. I need to get them scanned and preserved for everyone."

"I'd like to see them," Fern said.

"All in good time." Morning Glory gave her a big smile. "I'm still sorting through everything."

"And there's something in your archives to help us?" Craig asked.

"Well, wouldn't you just know that pack rat of a former owner would squirrel away some old plats of the town and surrounding areas. And wouldn't you just know that all these years later, they'd be just what we needed for research."

"You're kidding." Fern could hardly believe her ears. "I figured we'd be going to the county courthouse."

"That's always an iffy proposition, what with fires over the years." Morning Glory flicked a hand in dismissal at the idea.

"Yeah," Craig said. "But who knows what's still standing out on the prairie."

"That's not our concern…not at the moment." Morning Glory whirled around and headed deeper into the store. "Come over to this counter."

Fern followed with Craig right behind her. She looked over MG's shoulder at several faded, cracked, yellowed papers on top of a glass countertop.

"There you go." Morning Glory flicked a hand toward the papers.

Craig leaned closer. "Are you saying this is…"

"Sure-Shot and environs."

Fern looked closer, realizing it was hard to tell much from the lines and notes on the paper. "This is what you wanted to show me?"

"Yes. And you can thank me later." Morning Glory grabbed several sheets of regular typing paper. She thrust them toward Fern. "I made copies."

"I can read a plat." Craig took the pages, then quickly examined them.

"Excellent." Morning Glory smiled at him. "That's all I have for you right now, but it's enough to get you started on your journey. And remember, time's a wasting. Every moment you delay means structures still standing will most likely deteriorate even more."

"Go?" Fern asked, feeling surprised at MG's suggestion. "You mean, right now?"

"Yes, of course." Morning Glory pointed toward the front door.

"We're chairing Wild West Days. That has to come first." Fern glanced up at Craig for confirmation.

"Right," he said. "We hadn't planned on following up on Fern's idea until our big event is over."

"Wild West Days isn't going anywhere," Morning Glory said. "But another gully washer or wild wind, and you could lose whatever is waiting to be found out there so you can preserve it for posterity."

"But…" Fern started to say, then stopped at the determined look on MG's face.

"Thanks." Craig rolled up the papers. "We appreciate your help."

"No need for thanks just yet." Morning Glory gave them each a brusque nod. "Just get out there and get the goods."

"Right." Fern put a hand on Craig's arm to let him know it was time to get out while the getting was good. MG was on a crusade, so their best bet was to simply not get in her way.

Morning Glory walked with them to the front door, opened it, and gave them a big grin and a thumbs-up.

Fern gave a little wave, tugged Craig out onto the boardwalk, and headed toward the Chuckwagon, where they were parked in front.

"You're not thinking about going on this wild-goose chase right now, are you?" he asked.

"Bet she's watching us. Let's just get in your truck and head toward Sure-Shot." She grabbed the rolled up paper from him.

"I don't care if she is watching us. We can't just take off

and waste time on something that doesn't need to be done till later."

"I know. But we don't want to hurt her feelings."

"That's true." He unlocked his truck and opened the door. "She's more sensitive than she lets on. And your idea seems to mean a lot to her."

Fern stepped up on the runner, sat down on the leather seat, and placed her purse on the floorboard.

He closed her door, walked around the front end, and joined her inside. "We still haven't been to the Lone Star."

"Let's do it later. For now, let's just go."

"Where?" He started the engine and pulled onto Main Street.

She hesitated a moment, considering the copied plats, considering their workload, considering just a bit of escape. "Sure-Shot. Why not?"

"What do you mean 'why not'? There are lots reasons to stay in town versus leaving it."

She held up the plats. "I think things are pretty much under control here. I'm curious, aren't you?"

"Yes. But I'm not sure I'm curious enough to drive to Sure-Shot and tromp across overgrown pastures."

"When we check the plats, I bet all the structures were built near railroad tracks or old roads."

"Winter would be a better time to look, when things aren't so overgrown."

"We're wearing boots. And jeans."

"You're really serious, aren't you?" he said.

"It's kind of like a treasure hunt."

"A bunch of rotted wood is not my idea of treasure."

"You're just grumpy because it's not your idea."

"If I'm grumpy, and I'm not saying I am, it's because I'm about to get caught up in another problem."

"You said it was a good idea."

"That was several days ago. Now we're a lot closer to Wild West Days."

"Guess you're right." She looked down at the roll of plats, feeling let down in a way she hadn't expected. He was right. She should be practical. They already had too much to do. And Simon was still out there, as far as she knew, although there'd been nothing more from him. Maybe he had given up and gone away for good.

"Do you really want to do this now?" Craig spoke in a quiet, gentle voice, glancing over at her with concern in his eyes.

"It's okay."

"No, it's not. You're disappointed."

"Really, it is okay. Let's just go back to Wildcat Hall. I'm being silly about wanting to tackle something new and intriguing that could lead to even more interesting and exciting things. Now is not the time. You're right."

He groaned but didn't say another word. He just headed his pickup toward Sure-Shot.

Chapter 22

"THANKS." FERN LEANED OVER, SQUEEZED CRAIG'S shoulder, and then moved around in her seat until she was more comfortable. "Maybe I just needed to get away from all the pressure."

"It's been nonstop since you got back."

"I hadn't realized it'd built up. That must be why I jumped at the chance when MG offered a reason to get out of town that had nothing to do with work."

"Makes sense." He glanced over, as if evaluating her, then looked back at the road. "I also think you'd really like to find something we could use."

"I know it's an outside chance, but I want to know right now, not tomorrow or next week or next month. I feel this driving force to find another dance hall if one still exists."

"I don't want to disillusion you, but structures built of the old growth pine will decay in ten to sixty years."

"Really?"

"Yeah."

"But we're looking for hundred-year-old-plus buildings."

"Those won't be pine."

"Why would anyone build with it?"

"Cheap. It's probably all they could afford at the time. Plus, cow towns didn't usually have long shelf lives, because the trails kept moving west. Quick and cheap was the order of the day, so tents and knocked-together pine buildings suited folks just fine."

"That's why you didn't seem in any rush to get out here."

"We could still get lucky. If we do, we're looking at a building made of hardwood because that wood will last over two hundred years."

"Hardwood?"

"Oak. Cherry. Hickory. Elm. That type of tree."

"And it's more expensive."

"Yesterday and today, too."

"Maybe it'll be a log cabin, so they could've just cut down hardwood trees on the spot and built it cheap but good."

"That's a possibility."

"We're probably on a wild-goose chase." She tapped the roll of papers on her knee thoughtfully.

"It could be unless we decide to make more of our afternoon."

"What do you mean?"

"Why don't I stop at the Easy In & Out. I need to fill up with gas before we hit the highway. You could pick up bottles of water, snacks."

"Picnic! What a great idea."

"It won't be the same caliber as the Chuckwagon or the Bluebonnet, but we can make it fun. I have a couple of blankets and towels on the back seat. I always carry them in case of a grass fire that I need to knock out, but we can make good use of them for ourselves."

"I love the idea." She squeezed his shoulder again. "Thanks. I really needed to take this afternoon away from town."

"And I needed this time with you."

"Me, too…with you."

She leaned back in the seat, content to watch him drive to the edge of town and pull up to a pump at the convenience, gas, and bait store.

He glanced over at her. "If you don't want to move, I can pick up stuff inside."

She chuckled, shaking her head. "I want to be lazy, but not quite that lazy."

"You don't have a lazy bone in your body, but if you want to sit this one out, it's okay with me."

"Not on your life." She grabbed her purse from the floorboard, opened the door, and cast a quick glance over her shoulder. "And this picnic is on me."

He grinned. "I'd never argue with a woman on a mission."

"Smart man."

She quickly crossed the parking lot, hit the sidewalk near the entry, and walked past a freezer with bags of ice, a newspaper stand, and a live bait container. As the automatic doors slid open, she saw a notice announcing hunting and fishing licenses for sale. Once inside, the big open area looked a lot like most convenience stores with bright florescent overhead lights, back wall of refrigerated drinks, fresh coffee dispensers, and a center console for fast food and payment. It had everything a busy traveler could want to enhance their trip.

She made a quick stop in the bathroom, came out, and was on her way to the food dispenser when she saw a ball cap display. Cowboys tended to wear colorful caps when they weren't wearing hats. And she could use something to keep the sun off her face. She quickly looked through the display, knowing Craig must be waiting on her by now.

Nothing…nothing…nothing   suited   until…   She

stopped with a pleased smile on her face. She plucked two matching red caps with black Old West type that read WILD WEST DAYS on the first line, then HELLIONS VS RUFFIANS SHOOT-OUT on the second line. The caps were a perfect way to promote the event.

She plopped one on top of the other and snugged them both down on her head. She picked up four bottles of water and headed for the food counter. She set the water on the counter in front of the cashier, then pointed to chicken strips, potato wedges, okra pieces, and two fried apple pies. When they were selected and wrapped up, she paid for the food and the caps, picked up the sacks, and headed outside.

She saw Craig right away, since he'd pulled up in front. He leaned casually back against the passenger door, one ankle casually crossed over the other, looking like a hunk and a half, with his broad shoulders, narrow hips, and long legs. All cowboy. All man. All hers.

A little half smile on his lips let her know he was watching her watching him...and liking it.

She walked right up to him, holding the sacks against her chest, with a smile on her face that said it all. She wanted him right then and there, in the parking lot of the Easy In & Out. And he knew it.

"What've you got for me?"

"What do you want?"

"There's only one thing that'll satisfy me." And he looked her up and down with enough heat in his gaze to turn the asphalt beneath their feet into soft, sticky goo.

She felt that heat turn her insides into molten lava, but she rallied to get through the moment till they could be alone. "Will a new cap stave off your hunger?"

"No…but it'll tide me over till we get to the good stuff." He gave her a little bit more of a smile to let her know he knew she was changing the subject but he was letting her get away with it.

"They're good promotion, and they'll keep the sun off us." She realized she was trying to sell the caps when they both obviously wanted something that had nothing to do with her purchases.

He plucked the caps off her head, then pulled out a knife, snapped it open, cut off the tags, and stuffed them with his knife back into the pocket of his jeans. He tugged a cap onto his head, covering up his thick hair, and then gently placed the other one on her.

"Do you like?" Now she wanted his approval for her choice, making her only too aware of just how far down the lane she'd gone in needing him.

"Yeah. They're great. Thanks. But I like you best." He lifted the sacks from her arms and set them on the floorboard of his truck. "Let's get out of here."

She was more than ready and quickly sat down in his pickup, inhaling leather, testosterone, and his unique scent. It was a heady combination…and she hoped the cap helped to hold in place what was left of her unraveling wits.

He pulled out and headed west on 82, a divided highway with a wide swatch of green grass between double lanes.

Inside the enclosed cab, she caught the rich aroma of fried food just begging to be eaten right away.

"Smells good." He glanced down at the sacks, then back at the road. "It'll get cold if we don't eat it soon."

"I was thinking the same thing."

"Let's make this fun." He pointed up ahead. "There's still

one of those little roadside parks left over from the fifties. I doubt anybody uses it much anymore, but the state maintains it anyway. Want to stop there?"

"Sounds like fun. And it goes perfectly with a picnic."

"Okay. You got it. Doubt if we'll get too much traffic going by there."

Up ahead, she saw a curve off the road in front of a cement table with attached benches under the shading limbs of an old elm tree. A big drum rested in a container near it for trash. The old-time park looked to be an idyllic setting for a warm summer afternoon.

Craig pulled in front of the table and stopped the truck, shielding the area with the bulk of his pickup from the road. He turned to look at her with a smile. "You get the food. I'll get the blankets and my guitar."

"Always the music." She returned his smile, knowing they never went anywhere without an instrument because you just never knew when inspiration might strike, particularly in a beautiful setting. Plus, life simply wouldn't be natural or right without music.

When he got out of the truck and opened the door to the back seat, she picked up the sacks of food and stepped down to the packed dirt around the table of cement, pitted and scarred from years of use and weather. She brushed off a few dried leaves from the top, then arranged her sacks on the cleared area.

"Here you go." He set his guitar in its case on top of the table, along with towels, before he draped blankets across the bench closest to the pasture.

"Thanks." She spread out the towels to use as place mats, then opened the sacks and set food and water on top.

"It smells even better outdoors."

"And I'm so hungry." She sat down on the bench, opening the packets of napkins and plasticware before putting a set on his side.

He joined her, turning his cap around backward before he leaned over to kiss her cheek. "You were so right to get us out of town."

"Just remember how right I can be in future."

"If I don't, I'm sure you'll remind me."

"No doubt."

And those were their last words as they dug into the food, listening to a vehicle pass by now and then, but mostly enjoying a mockingbird's medley in the treetop above as the pretty blue bird watched them to see if they might throw away something worth investigating to eat.

When they were almost done, Fern tossed several fries to one side and watched in delight as the bird flew down, grabbed a fry, and flew away with the prize.

"Didn't your mama ever tell you not to feed wild things? If you do, they'll never leave."

She cocked her head as she looked at him with a smile on her lips and mischief in her eyes. She picked up her last fry and held it out to him.

He took it in his mouth and slowly chewed as he watched her, nodding in agreement that her assessment of him was true.

"If you want your wild thing to never leave, it's best to feed them something that'll keep them coming back for more." And she reached up, rubbing her thumb across his lips to remove a speck of potato.

He licked her thumb before sucking it into his mouth while he watched her with eyes turning dark with desire.

"Still hungry?" She gently tugged her thumb from between

his lips even though she didn't want to do it. She wanted to continue that and so much more with him. But regretfully, now was not the time or place.

"Always...for you."

As if he understood, he turned away, zipped open the case, slipped out his guitar, and swiveled his legs over the side of the bench. He crossed his leg at the ankle over his knee and plucked a few strings. He glanced at her, raising an eyebrow.

She swiveled so her legs were outside the table, too, and she faced the tall grass and wildflowers in the pasture behind them. She caught the scent of high summer, from the dusty grass to the blooming flowers, and the sound of buzzing bees to chirping birds. She leaned back against the edge of the table and gave a sigh of contentment.

"I wonder"—he played a riff that turned from major to minor key—"if we really need any more than what we have right this moment?"

She sang a few notes that wove up and down and around his music, answering his question with her voice as they created something new, fresh, and unimagined until this very moment of perfect togetherness. They leaned toward each other, excitement building between them, as their music soared above, beyond, and ahead of anything they'd experienced before this time.

"Wait." Craig abruptly stopped, pulled his phone out of his pocket, and turned on the recorder. "We don't want to lose our song."

"We won't." She smiled, leaned toward him, and kissed his lips. "And to answer your question, we are at the heart of all we need...and all we'll ever need. Everything else is simply icing on the cake."

Chapter 23

AFTER THEY'D MADE THEIR RECORDING WITH SEVERAL variations of their new song, Craig set his guitar back in his truck, along with the blankets, towels, and trash. He picked up the plats from where Fern had left them on the dashboard and walked back to her. She was still enjoying the aftermath of food, music, and relaxation, so he regretted having to disturb her, but if they were going to search for her lost dance hall, they'd better get started before it was too late in the day.

"I know Sure-Shot and its environs pretty well, so I think I'll recognize locations on the plats." He sat down beside her and spread out the copies on top of the table so he could get a better look at them.

"Let me know if I can be of help, but I doubt I know this area well enough to be of much benefit." She glanced at the papers, then turned her attention back to a red-tailed hawk wheeling above the pasture.

"Thanks for the offer, but I've got it." He studied the plats, one after the other, setting in his mind the locations of early buildings.

"It's just so beautiful here." She pointed toward the hunting hawk.

"I know. North Texas is the best of all worlds. We'll go back to the ranch soon, so you can enjoy the wide-open spaces at your leisure."

"I'd like that a lot."

"If these buildings aren't connected to the town, they'll be on private property."

"Does that mean we won't be able to see them?"

"I think we can get to most because they're near the old roads and railroad tracks. We might have to wade through tall grass, but we should be able to get close enough to tell if a structure is still there."

"Sounds workable."

"It is."

"I almost hate to leave here because it's so pretty and peaceful. And it's special to me now."

"We can always come back another time," he said.

"Let's do. This picnic area harkens back to an earlier time when life wasn't so hectic and frantic."

"When we get on the other side of Wild West Days, things will settle down and you can dig into your new life."

"I want that. I really do." She reached over and squeezed his fingers.

"You'll get there." He clasped her hand, running his thumb over her palm, feeling her softness and warmness go straight to his heart.

"Guess we better be on our way." She raised his hand, pressed a soft kiss to his fingers, and stood up. "I'm ready for my afternoon adventure."

"Let's get to it."

When Fern was seated shotgun, he settled inside, pulled onto the highway, and headed toward Sure-Shot. His mind whirled with the possibilities that lay ahead, but he didn't think they were going to find what she had in mind. If the structure still stood, he figured the owner would have investigated its viability long before now and locals would know about it. On the other hand, they were in the Cross Timbers, so if it was located in dense undergrowth, folks could have missed it for many a year.

When they neared Sure-Shot, he pulled off on a rutted road that paralleled what had once been a narrow gauge, north-south railroad line that had connected communities that were no longer in existence, not even as ghost towns, since their pine construction had rotted long ago. He didn't figure they'd find much because the railroad ties would have been salvaged at some point for their hardwood. Still, he followed the road to what would have been close to the right location. Knee-high grass filled the area, but he didn't see any structures.

He stopped the pickup. "If a building was still standing, you'd see it from here. It wouldn't have been a dance hall anyway. Most likely it was a farmhouse."

"Just think, once upon a time a husband and wife raised children and animals and crops here. They'd have laughed and loved and probably sung songs at the end of a long workday. But now the house that held all those memories is gone."

"Yet their descendants probably live around here. They'd still be raising kids and horses and maybe singing in the gazebo at Sure-Shot."

She smiled at him. "I like that idea. Life continues no matter what gets thrown at us."

"And we build bigger, stronger houses that will withstand the seasons…and storms that always come with them."

"I was disappointed at first, but now I'm not. We're just seeing the progression of life."

"And we'll probably set it to music."

She chuckled, nodding at him. "No doubt."

"Don't lose hope yet. We still might get lucky."

He backed out and hit the highway again, watching for traffic and trouble. Out here, all was blessedly peaceful, so he drove to the next turnoff, followed the dusty road—not much more than a couple of rutted tracks in the grass—to another of the plat locations. The area had been brush-hogged, so it was easy to see that there was not a standing structure anywhere in the area.

"Do you want to get out and look around?" He glanced over at her. "We might find an old foundation or something."

"No point." She shook her head, looking regretful. "I've brought us on a wild-goose chase, haven't I?"

"No. It's interesting. Farmhouses out here, I'd guess. I think if there'd been a dance hall, it would have been near the town instead of on the plains. And I also think we'd have heard about it before now."

"I bet you're right."

"Let's try at least another one just to test my theory. It's not too far away."

"Okay."

He returned to the highway, then turned north and drove along a rutted field that paralleled the road, sending dust and debris flying around them. He stopped, looked at the area, and shook his head.

"There was once a building here?" She lowered her window to get a better view, but there was nothing but horses grazing in pastures as far as the eye could see.

"That's what the plat shows, but it's long gone now." He

could smell dust and horse and hay carried on the breeze coming in through her open window.

"What we need are stone structures."

"That would help a lot." He picked up the plats again, thinking there was one in a location that seemed familiar. He checked it again. "This one is closer to Sure-Shot. Why don't we try it?"

"Okay. I'm willing to see another location before we head home." She raised her window, cutting off the clear view. "Today's been wonderful even though we're not finding any buildings. It was just a wild thought anyway."

"But a good one."

He returned to the highway, watching for a little-used dirt road that meandered its way onto the east side of Sure-Shot, where horse pastures stretched up to the town. After he'd gone several miles, he stopped again, picked up the plat he wanted to look at more closely, studied it a moment, and laughed out loud.

"What is it?" Fern glanced at him in concern.

"There's this crazy little triangle of property I bought recently, sight unseen. It was too small to do much with, and the land had been through several family member's hands after the owner died years ago, so they put it up for sale. Nobody was bidding on it, so I picked it up."

"Why did you want it?"

"It connected my ranch to the town, so I thought it might come in handy someday. Plus, I like to expand Thorne Ranch whenever I get the opportunity, which isn't often since families hold on to their land."

"Are you telling me there's a building on your new property?"

"Looks like it, if the construction was originally sound, but we can't expect it to still be standing."

"What kind of building?"

"Don't know."

"Well, let's go check it out."

He started back down the road that had turned into little more than washboard ruts that bounced the truck with every turn of the wheels. Pretty soon that played out into nothing but a tall stand of horse-belly-high grass. He stopped there, feeling puzzled. Far as he could tell, his new land started somewhere around here, but there was no road, no fence, no gate. What he saw instead was a thick section of old growth vegetation that reared up out of nowhere.

The Cross Timbers once stretched from Kansas to Central Texas, cutting a wide swath between East Texas and West Texas. Each side of the plains was densely bordered by sturdy post oak, flowering cedar elm, hard-as-nails bois d'arc, blossoming dogwood, Virginia creeper, and thorny blackberry.

The area had originally been part of the Comanche empire that had stretched from Central Kansas to Mexico. In the old days, there had been a brush fire every year and the tree line that made up the border of the Cross Timbers would grow back too dense to penetrate. Comanche warriors had used the prairie between the two tree lines as a secret passage, so enemies couldn't see or attack them.

Lots of folks in Wildcat Bluff County were descendants of the Comanche and still protected thousands of those acres, but they kept the wildfires under control, so the thicket line didn't grow back as dense. But this section didn't grow north-south. It grew east-west. And no way, no how did it belong here.

"What is it?" Fern sounded concerned at his silence.

"You know about the Cross Timbers, don't you?"

"Yes. We're in the center of it, aren't we?"

"Pretty much." He pointed at the thicket line. "That's out of place."

"What do you mean?"

"Look at it. Hundred-year-old-plus post oaks do not grow in a circle, or semicircle from what I can see from here, with a pretty dogwood tree set in between each trunk. It's not natural. Dogwoods grow well in the shade, but eighty years is about their limit…unless the soil is enriched in some way so the trees last longer."

"Maybe the trees aren't that old."

"They're old, all right. And they're entwined with black-berry vines that would shred most anything trying to get through on foot or hoof."

"What are you saying?"

"At some point way back in time, a grove was planted here…looks like to keep somebody in or somebody out."

"That's a chilling thought."

"You know it. And why right here near Sure-Shot in the middle of ranchland? It makes no sense."

"And you own it."

"Yeah." He felt a sinking sensation in the pit of his stomach. He didn't like mysteries. He liked cold, hard facts. And he particularly didn't like something strange and unusual on his property. It'd require investigation. And he didn't have time for any more problems in his life.

"What should we do? Maybe MG knows what this section was used for back in the day."

"I doubt it. I bet her memory doesn't extend that far."

"Wildcat Jack?"

"Maybe. But we probably need one of the last surviving elders. They'd know if anybody still remembers why this is here, but it doesn't mean they'd tell us. If it has a dark history, which I suspect is possible, then they might want that knowledge lost in time."

"You're saying they might not trust us younger ones to handle the truth of Wildcat Bluff County?"

"That, yes…or they'll think that some secrets are meant to stay secret."

"To protect the innocent?"

"Or not so innocent but still family." He hated to say those words, but facts were facts and he had a feeling he didn't want these facts.

"This could turn into an ugly mess, couldn't it?"

"Yeah. But we don't know anything yet. It's all speculation on our part."

"We don't want to stir up anything before Wild West Days."

"That's sure the truth," he said wholeheartedly.

"And still…"

"I've got an ax with me."

"For firefighting?"

"You never know, so it's wise to be prepared for anything."

"Right."

"I think I can hack my way through the blackberry vines between that post oak and that dogwood." He pointed at the largest gap he could see that would allow entry.

"Is it wide enough?"

"If I can't get through, you can probably squeeze in there and see what's on the other side."

"It's probably just more thick growth."

"Smaller understory trees and lots of vines are all it could be, because there won't be enough sunlight getting through under the oaks for something bigger."

"We could wait and just let this be till after Wild West Days."

"What?" He glanced over to see if she really meant it, because there was no way he could wait to see what was on the other side of that thick growth.

She smiled at him, appearing mischievous.

"Right." He chuckled as he opened his door. "You can't wait any more than I can."

"So true."

"Let's try not to get scratched up." He stepped down and opened his back door. "I've got a couple of sturdy firefighter jackets back here that ought to protect our upper bodies."

"Good."

When she walked around to his side of the truck, he tossed her a jacket, then slipped into the other one. He fastened it up the front, slipped his ax out of its protective sheath, and was ready to go.

"Just in case, you ought to take this." He held out a big, heavy metal flashlight.

"We're going to get really warm." She rolled up the sleeves of the too-big jacket, then glanced at the sun lowering in the west. "Hottest time of the day."

"We can give up now and go home where it's nice and cool."

She just rolled her eyes as she took the flashlight, then tromped off through the tall grass.

"Watch out for snakes," he called as he caught up with her.

"Thanks…as if I could see one in this mess."

"If you don't step on one, it'll usually get out of your way."

"That's also good to know." She tossed him a look that meant they were both on their own when it came to the local snake population.

He chuckled, knowing she was right. There just wasn't much you could do about snakes, spiders, or other creepy-crawlers except hope for the best.

When he came to the vegetation line, he pulled leather gloves out of his pocket and tugged them onto his hands. He hefted the ax in one hand, checking its weight, then glanced at her.

"You'd better stay well back when I get to chopping at the blackberries. There's no telling what's living in there. Could be a lot of little stuff that'll swarm out, or bigger things like possums, skunks, squirrels."

"You don't have to tell me twice. I'm backing up right now."

"Good."

When he made the first downward cut, the loud thud echoing through the area, several crows flew up, cawed loudly in protest, and swept away. After that, all went still and silent. He set to work, chopping long strands of green Virginia creeper that brought forth a swarm of flies when he pulled it loose. He hacked through the thick base of poison ivy, hoping he didn't get infected when he jerked it out and tossed it aside. He kept hacking and chopping until finally he created an opening so he could see there was a clearing on the other side, but the twisted and thorny branches of a bois d'arc were in his way.

"Fern, we can get in there."

"Great."

"But I've got to get us past this bois d'arc."

"Do you need help?"

"I don't want you anywhere near it. If we got scratched or stuck, the spot could get infected or burn for days. It's the last tree you want to see when you're fighting a fire because you know you're going to get hurt by it. I hate them."

"Is there no other way in?"

"I've come this far, so I'm going on through."

He started on the bois d'arc, hacking out the deadwood first, then moving on to the live limbs. He tossed away debris, working as quickly as possible until he'd made a tunnel through the thorny, twisted, dangerous mess.

And then he stepped through to the other side.

Chapter 24

FERN WATCHED UNEASILY AS CRAIG DISAPPEARED FROM sight. She wanted to run after him, but she decided to be practical, so she stayed in place just in case he needed her to take him something or go for help.

"Fern, get in here! You're not going to believe it."

"I'll be right there."

That was all the encouragement she needed to carefully slip through the opening and step into a glade that was mostly shadow, because only dappled sunlight reached through the green, leaf-laden trees to the bare ground below.

When she stopped beside Craig, he put an arm around her shoulders and nestled her close to him. She needed his warmth and presence, because she felt chilled even on the hot summer day.

"Why is that structure here?" he asked.

"I'm not sure." And she wasn't.

She felt as if she'd stepped back in time to another era captured in the perfection of a small Victorian building with gingerbread trim around the peaked roof and a railing around the front porch with a crawl space underneath. It even had a fancy bell tower. After a hundred years or so, it still looked beautiful. Of course, the white paint had faded or eroded to almost nothing except bare wood, and pieces of gingerbread hung haphazardly from the eaves, but overall it looked remarkably well preserved for its age.

"Looks like we found your hardwood structure," Craig said. "That building was well put together with the finest of material for the era."

"But what was it used for? It's certainly no dance hall since it's too small and too fancy. And it doesn't look like a farmhouse either."

"No idea." He gestured around the area. "What I find even stranger is that these trees were planted in a perfect circle around it. Next to white oaks, post oaks are the hardest, longest-lasting oak in existence. And dogwoods have deep spiritual meaning to many people."

"Long spiritual life?" She shrugged her shoulders. "I don't know, but it looks as if that building, this glade, these trees carry a special message sent to us over a hundred years ago."

"But what? And why isn't there a record of it?"

"Maybe there was at one time, but it might have been lost as time and people moved onward."

"Still, you'd think word of it would have passed down through the generations at least as a legend."

"I agree. It's definitely a mystery."

"And it's one on my property." He tugged her closer. "Now that I look back, the sale appears odd. Nobody snatched up this property. It's as if buyers couldn't see it any more than we could see inside this glade."

"If we had all the facts, there are probably simple explanations for everything surrounding our mystery...as well as the mystery itself," she said thoughtfully.

"You're right. I'm probably overthinking the whole thing anyway."

"I admit it's strange."

"Let's take a closer look."

As they got nearer, things didn't look quite as pristine as they had from a distance. In fact, the front door had been boarded over in a way that could only have been fast and rough. It was a sharp contrast to the meticulous gingerbread work on the eaves. Blackberry vines twined up the railings and across the floor of the porch, creating a thorny barrier.

"Something happened here," Craig said in a low tone. "Whoever nailed those boards up used hardwood that would last a long, long time."

"And it has done exactly that, hasn't it?"

"Yes." He clasped her hand, entwined their fingers, and led her to the north side of the house.

She felt a little more chilled all the time, as if they shouldn't be here, as if they were disturbing a long-buried secret.

"One window and it's boarded up, too." He squeezed her fingers while gripping his ax in his other hand. "I like this less all the time."

"Me, too." She moved closer to him.

"Let's check the back." He turned the corner and stopped completely still and took a deep, ragged breath that sounded loud in the quietness of the glade.

"What is it?"

He raised the ax and used it to point toward the lower half of the building, where dark stains tarnished the wood and stroked upward toward a brick chimney that was blackened with soot and partially crumbled to the ground.

"What am I looking at?" She felt his right hand tremble slightly as she held more tightly to him.

"Fire." He dropped her hand and reached palm out, as if to hold back the flames. "Long ago. It must have started in the fireplace or the chimney. The smoke would have been tremendous and more problem than the fire…at first. No back door. There's only one, small, high window on this side and probably the same on the other side."

"This isn't a home. Maybe nobody was here at the time."

"But if there was a blaze in the fireplace, then…"

"Volunteer firefighters. Whoever was in there was saved by firefighters."

"They didn't have the resources we have today, but still folks probably got out in time."

"And they didn't want to use the building anymore, so they boarded it up." She didn't really believe their scenario any more than he did, but it comforted them for the moment, so she let it stand.

"Still, it's odd. They could've repaired the structure."

"We don't know what it was used for, so maybe they just moved into Sure-Shot to be closer to resources and people."

"Maybe." He turned back. "Let's go inside."

"Is it structurally sound?"

"We'll see." He took off in a long-legged stride as if he could still rescue whoever'd been trapped in there with a rampaging fire.

She understood his impulse. He was a first responder at heart. When the need arose, he'd always put his life on the line for others. Only this time, he was a hundred years too late…and she knew he would still grieve if there had been loss of life on land that was now his responsibility.

She watched as he edged up the stairs leading to the front door. She could tell he was being careful, as he tried one step after another, to make certain the wood wasn't rotten or termite eaten as he trampled down blackberry vines.

When he reached the door, he glanced back at her, gave a quick nod, then hefted the ax, swung, and embedded it into one of the boards.

As far as she could tell, it didn't look as if the solid wood gave much under the impact. Maybe they wouldn't get inside today—and maybe she didn't really want to see what was in there anyway.

Still, he was strong, and he wasn't giving up. After several deep cuts on the boards, he changed tactics and used the flat of the ax to pry up one long nail after another until finally the boards gave way and he tossed them over the railing onto the ground.

Now she could see the door. It had been a pretty thing, probably hand-carved with lots of fancy designs that went with the rest of the building…except it had no doorknob or latch or anything except a round hole where the hardware must have been at one time. She didn't think that looked good, not if you'd been trapped inside.

"Do you want to join me or wait to learn what I see inside?" He pointed toward the stairs and porch. "If you come up, step where I stepped and you'll be okay."

"Wait for me. I'll join you." Even if she dreaded what they might find, she was not so weak of heart that she would let him go in there alone. She knew firefighters frequently saw troubling things nobody else had to see, but she still wanted to be by Craig's side in times of trouble as well as happiness.

He pushed on the door, but it resisted until he put a shoulder against it, shoving hard. Finally, it squeaked under protest and slowly edged open to let in the light of day.

She carefully ascended the stairs, then cautiously walked across the porch. For a brief time, she stood with him, not moving a muscle, as they gazed into each other's eyes, prolonging the moment before they discovered something inside that might change their lives or even their view of the world forever.

"Ready?" He spoke in a low tone, as if not to disturb the house or the glade. He held out his hand, palm up.

"Yes." She also kept her voice soft, almost reverent, as she handed him the flashlight.

He switched it on and stepped into the house, illuminating a single room with wide sweeps of the flashlight.

She followed, sneezing at the odor of dust, decay, and smoke. The building had been shut up for so long that all the old scents were still trapped inside. After that, she took shallow breaths as she followed—the squeak of old floorboards loud in the stillness.

He cast the arc of light slowly and carefully around the room.

It wasn't a big room. It wasn't even a fancy room. It was utilitarian. Wooden walls. Wooden ceiling. Wooden floors. And wooden benches that had seats and backs made of single boards with circular saw marks. Most were overturned on their sides. A single, straight-backed chair with charred rungs lay crumpled near the fireplace where the floor was scorched and blackened from the fire.

And hats. It'd been winter. To one side of the fireplace, three round felt hats still hung on the rows of pegs that had been pounded into the wood for that purpose. All the other hats were on the floor near the fireplace in various stages of decay from completely burned to partially burned to twisted and crumpled and stomped on.

"They used the hats to put out the fire." Craig broke the

silence in a deep, sad voice as he aimed light at the hats. "It was a good idea."

"Yes. But was it in time?"

"I don't know. Smoke would have been their biggest danger."

She walked closer. "All the hats are small."

"I know."

She took a deep, ragged breath, almost unable to contain the emotion that flooded her as he turned his light on a single book, splayed open on its back with broken spine and charred pages.

"Schoolhouse," he said, voice breaking on the word.

"Children. They got out in time. They escaped the fire. I know they did—surely they did." Yet tears filled her eyes at the sight of the small hats and what they meant to those who might have been trapped inside a burning building.

"It would explain the trees."

"They put a sacred memory to rest, didn't they?"

"And now we've disturbed it," he said.

"Yes."

"We don't know what happened here other than there was a fire. And they fought it the best way they knew how. And it probably worked because the entire building didn't go up in flames."

"That's true."

"But they wouldn't have trusted their children here anymore," he said.

"No, of course not."

"They would have taken them to town for their educations."

"Yes. That's right." Still she felt forlorn at the loss, even if it was a hundred years in the past.

He walked over and clasped her hand. "There's nothing more we can do here today. Let's go to the ranch."

"I'd like that." She walked to the door with him, then glanced back. "There was fire here, yes. But there was great love here, too. That's what I want to remember."

"I'm sure that's exactly the remembrance they wanted to leave in this grove."

"And they did it well." She stepped outside, taking a deep breath of fresh air.

He closed the door behind them. "I'll come back and nail this door shut later. I'll also push back some of the vines so the entry point is less noticeable."

"Good."

"I don't want the place disturbed until we know exactly what happened here."

"Will we be able to find out?"

"Somebody will know. It might take a bit of asking around...and we can't follow up until after Wild West Days."

"It's waited a hundred years. I'm sure it can wait a little longer...if we're ever meant to know the truth."

Chapter 25

CLOUDS SCUDDED ACROSS THE SKY, BLOCKING SUN-light as Craig drove toward the Thorne Horse Ranch. Fern sat quietly beside him, reflecting his somber mood. Lack of bright light suited them after their schoolhouse discovery.

"Life's not always fair," he said thoughtfully, breaking their silence.

"I know. It's just…children." She held her new red ball cap in her hands, turning it around and around thoughtfully. They hadn't felt like wearing them after their discovery since they simply seemed too frivolous. Another time, they could enjoy them again.

"Sometimes it's least fair to them because they're so vulnerable. We do our best and still…"

"Tragedy strikes."

"Yeah." He gripped the steering wheel harder. "But sometimes we get miracles. I suspect maybe all or at least some of those kids got out alive."

"Do you really think so?"

"Yes. I've seen the destructive power of fire up close and what devastation it can leave in its wake. That structure is still very much intact."

"What about the deadly power of smoke inhalation?"

"I know…believe me, I know. Yet everything I've experienced fighting fires and what I saw in that schoolhouse tells me at least some of those children lived to ripe old ages and left descendants."

"That's what I want to believe."

"Then that's what we'll believe…until we learn different."

"Okay." She leaned her head back against the seat and closed her eyes as if to block out the memory of the one-room schoolhouse.

He felt the same way. He was more than ready to let the past stay in the past. They had plenty in the present that required their attention, and they needed to focus on that for now. Later, they'd figure out what happened in the Sure-Shot community that led to the creation of a beautiful memorial grove.

When he saw the entry to the ranch up ahead, he felt an uptick in his heartbeat. Good news—he wouldn't have to think about fires there. All was safe and secure. He just needed to drive up to the house, park his truck, take Fern inside, and hold her in his arms until they had a chance to let love renew their spirits.

All of a sudden, she sat up straight and leaned forward. "Maybe I just have fire and smoke on my mind, but are the cowboys burning brush on your ranch?" She pointed toward the horizon.

He felt his gut clench as he followed her line of sight. She wasn't wrong. There was a dark-red smudge where none had any reason to be.

"Craig? Please tell me I'm wrong." She set the cap down on the floorboard near her purse.

"I wish I could, but you're right. That is all wrong."

He gunned the engine and tore down the highway,

hoping against hope that what he thought he saw he didn't see, but the closer he got to the ranch, the higher the smoke rose into the sky. Fire on Thorne Horse Ranch, no doubt about it.

"Fern, would you call Hedy? She's probably at the fire station. We need a rig at the ranch. It looks like there's a blaze near or at the horse barn."

"Oh no." Fern snatched her cell phone out of her purse. "I'm so sorry. Surely it's not—"

"I don't want to take any chances. It'll take time for a rig to get here. In the meantime, I have firefighting gear in the pickup and more in the shop."

"But what could've happened?" She hit a programmed number, then clicked speaker phone so he could join the conversation.

"Anything."

"Wildcat Bluff Fire-Rescue," Hedy answered in a no-nonsense voice.

"Hedy, this is Fern. I'm with Craig. We're headed to his ranch. We see smoke near his horse barn. He wants a rig."

"Is one enough?"

"We won't know till we get there," Craig said.

"I'll send Slade and Sydney with a booster, but I'll alert Kent and Trey to be on standby. Keep us posted."

"Will do." Fern clicked off and put her phone back in her purse.

"Okay." Craig glanced over at her. "I'll take you to the house and leave you there, where you'll be safe, then I'll—"

"There's no time to lose and you know it. We go straight to the barn. Are cowboys up there? Are horses in the barn or the corral?"

"Don't know." He hit the brakes as he turned off under the Thorne Horse Ranch sign, crossed a cattle guard, and barreled up the road toward the barns. "This late in the day, cowboys ought to be out in the pastures, but it's about time they headed home."

"I'm not trained to fight fires, but I can point a fire extinguisher or do whatever else needs doing."

"Thanks. I may need your help."

"You've got it."

"For now, reach over the back seat and snag those jackets. We need them again. And there's a pair of fire-resistant pants I can slip over my jeans."

"One good thing." She glanced at him. "There aren't any kids involved in this fire."

"Yeah...but what about innocent horses?"

"I hoped the barn was empty."

"Maybe it is, but don't count on it."

She leaned over the seat, then tugged the jackets and pants into her lap. She shrugged into a jacket and rolled up the sleeves.

He passed the road leading to the house and continued toward the barns and outbuildings on a rise to the east. He could see the fire was eating at the horse barn, but no cowboys were in sight, which meant they were out in the pastures. They'd have seen the smoke and would be making their way back as quickly as possible. He knew there was no point in trying to contact them, since they had no phone reception out there. He could only hope they arrived soon, along with Slade and Sydney.

For the moment, he and Fern were the first and only line of defense. He wouldn't be able to put out the fire, so the best he could do was try and contain it. If sparks hit the hay rolls stacked nearby, the dry grass would go up in flames and spread to other structures. And if he didn't get that fire under control, it would blaze a trail impossibly fast up to the house. At that point, there wouldn't be much of the ranch left except the land. And that was totally unacceptable.

When he neared the horse barn, he groaned at the sight of fire licking up the south wall as it sent black smoke spiraling high into the sky. He hit the brakes, not about to get close enough to endanger the truck in case they needed it for a fast exit. He hated to even think about the expensive ranch equipment in the nearby shop or the cow barn or... He stopped his thoughts. He had to focus and focus fast or risk losing it all.

"What do you want me to do?" Fern clenched her hands in her lap but looked ready to leap in any direction he named for her.

"Two canisters are in back. If you'll get those, I'll pull more out of the shop and meet you at the barn." He took the jacket and pants from her. "But whatever you do, don't put your life in danger. Nothing is worth losing you."

She leaned toward him and pressed a quick kiss to his lips. "Same to you. I'm not about to lose you now."

He opened the door, stepped out, and heard the sound of horses kicking the doors of their stalls and neighing in agitation. He froze in horror for just a second before he changed his plans.

"Fern, get the blankets and towels." He quickly pulled on the pants, jerked on the jacket, and slipped on the gloves. He needed headgear, so he opened the back door, grabbed his hard hat, and slapped it on his head. His cowboy boots would do to protect his feet and ankles, so he was as ready as he was going to get.

"What?" She looked at him in confusion for just a second before she glanced toward the barn, obviously hearing the horses. That galvanized her. She leaped out, jerked open the back door, grabbed the blankets and towels, then ran around to him.

"I still need you to bring the cans."

"You can't go into that burning barn."

"I won't leave the horses. The structure isn't fully engulfed, so there's still time." He took the blankets and towels from her.

"Please, no...if anything—"

"Go get the cans. I want you to stand guard outside, so if anyone arrives you can send them in to help. If it looks like I'm going to get trapped in there, try to spray me an exit through the flames."

"Oh, Craig, this makes me sick."

He pressed a quick kiss to her lips, then took off running. Not that he could outrun a fire, but if he could get through the open double barn doors before the blaze spread to the interior, he could win this one. He hoped.

He skidded to a stop just inside the barn. He could smell hay, feed, and leather above the rising stench of smoke. And he could hear the horses. He ran down the center aisle, checking each stall as he went, thanking his lucky stars every time he found an empty one.

In the center, he found Sheba, a wild-eyed buckskin mare, kicking and neighing in a desperate attempt to escape the coming fire. He didn't want to do it, but he left her there. He had to know how many horses were located in which stalls in case the smoke got so thick it cut down visibility. If he could do it, no animal would be left behind. Across from the mare, a sorrel gelding named Winston put his head over the door to his stall and nickered for help.

He wanted to stop and reassure both horses, but he continued to the end of the barn, checking inside each stall in case a mount was down and couldn't be seen otherwise. He was relieved to find only the two horses. He could handle that small a number, but at the same time, he heard the roar of the fire getting closer and the stench of smoke getting stronger. He was losing visibility due to the thickening air and was having trouble catching his breath. He could drop to his knees and get better oxygen, but the horses couldn't do it…not if they were to get out of the barn. He had almost no time left to bring them out alive.

He draped the two towels around his neck and dropped the blankets to the floor. He ran back to Winston, grabbed his halter with one hand, and opened the door with the other. He led the horse out of the stall, not taking the time to cover his eyes and hoping it wasn't a mistake. As he passed Sheba, she neighed and kicked the door, determined not to be left behind in the burning barn.

He coughed as he headed out, leading Winston, lowering his head to get more oxygen and better vision, but it didn't help much to relieve the growing problem. Winston shied, nickered, and bumped his shoulder with his nose, but the horse remained fairly calm all the way to the entrance. Once outside, Winston threw up his head, prancing sideways, wanting to escape, but Craig stayed in control as he led the horse away from the barn and to a nearby corral where he opened the gate and shooed Winston inside.

"Craig! Are you okay?" Fern ran up to him, carrying a canister in each arm. "Is that the only horse?"

"No. I'm going back for one more."

"You can't. Look at the fire."

He glanced around. From outside, it looked even worse than from inside. Flames were spreading fast, licking toward the barn entry.

"Hedy called me. The rig will be here soon. Please wait."

"Can't. I won't leave Sheba in there to die...not while I have breath in my body."

"Okay. I understand. But I'll stay near the entrance with the cans." Fern followed him until she stopped at a safe distance.

He ran back into the barn. Smoke was thick now. Flames were licking around the entry. Sheba was frantic, neighing as she tried to kick her way out of the stall. No way would he lose her, but the barn was already a lost cause. All the hay, feed, and wood would feed the flames like throwing gasoline on the building.

He bent low to get more oxygen as he held the towels over his nose. Visibility was so limited he couldn't depend on eyesight any longer. Instead, he ran a hand down the row of stalls, feeling the wood, counting doors as he made his way to Sheba. She was wild by the time he reached her. He wasn't sure if he could control her, so he reached up and let her smell his hand. That seemed to help a little, because she recognized him. He stroked up her nose, feeling her shiver in fear, but he had no time to do more for her. They had to get out and get out now.

He unlatched the door to her stall but didn't open it as he grasped her halter with one hand while he wrapped the towels around her eyes with the other. And all the while, his eyes were burning, tears streaming from them as he struggled to get enough oxygen to stay on his feet.

He eased open the gate as he backed up slowly, hoping to keep her calm enough so she didn't knock him down. She jerked up her head, almost pulling the halter out of his hands, but he hung on and headed back the way he'd come. Now he could see light at the entry, but it was cold comfort because it was the bright orange-red of a raging fire.

And in that instant, he heard the shrill siren of a Wildcat Bluff Fire-Rescue booster with a 250-gallon water tank getting closer and closer.

Chapter 26

IN DESPAIR, FERN SPRAYED THE LAST CHEMICAL OUT OF her second canister on the burning boards around the barn's entry, even as she knew it couldn't stop the fire from closing off Craig's exit, but it was all she had left to save him…until she heard the booster's siren.

She whirled around, hope springing alive in her heart. She'd never been so glad to see a sight in her life as the bright red rig with siren wailing rocket up the road toward her. If anybody could save Craig, it was the volunteer firefighters of Wildcat Bluff.

She hurried to one side, breathing hard and fast, as if she took in enough oxygen, she could somehow get it to Craig through her own lungs—she knew he had to be only moments away from falling unconscious beside his beloved horse. And she couldn't stand the thought.

When the booster stopped in a cloud of dust near the front of the barn, Slade and Sydney—dressed in protective, yellow firefighter turnout gear—leaped out and ran to Fern.

She pointed toward the barn's entrance. "He's in there, trying to get Sheba out."

"How long?" Slade demanded, blue eyes flashing determination.

"Too long."

"I'll get Craig," Slade said. "You two pump and roll."

"I don't know how." Fern felt horrible that she didn't

know enough to help save Craig or the barn. When this was over, she was going to train as a volunteer firefighter.

"I'll show you." Sydney grabbed her arm and tugged her toward the back of the booster.

"No." She dug in her heels. "I don't care if the barn burns. I just need to see that he's safe and in my arms."

"Right." Slade exchanged an understanding look with his sister. "Sydney, start without me. Fern, you come with me."

Slade grabbed an SCBA tank with compressed air in a backpack that he slipped on and adjusted over his shoulders. He let the face mask dangle in front as he headed for the barn.

Fern kept up with him, feeling more alarmed by the moment because Craig still hadn't come out.

"Stay back here." Slade stopped and gave her a hard look. "I'll bring him out. And the horse, too, if I can."

"Thank you. Stay safe."

"Always." He gave her a nod before he pulled on the face mask. He took long, purposeful strides to the barn, where he passed through the burning entrance into the darkness beyond and disappeared from sight.

She clenched her fists, shivering all over as she waited... and waited...and waited. Everything intensified around her, as if she were straining all her senses to pick up Craig's heartbeat which she couldn't possibly do. Instead, she heard Sydney stretch out the hose from the pumper, crows caw to each other in the pasture, the horse rub against the gate inside the corral, and above and beyond all the normal sounds came the hissing, crackling, roaring of the raging fire.

And finally—after what seemed like an aeon—Slade emerged from the inferno, slowly but surely leading a blindfolded buckskin that threw up her head, sidling, shying, trying to break free so she could run away, but he held her firmly with two hands as he brought her away from the fire.

Fern felt her breath catch in her throat. Sheba was alive, but where was Craig? Had Slade been too late to save him, so he'd brought out the only living entity in the barn? Tears burned her eyes. She had no reason to hang back now. If Craig was still in there, she was going to bring him out herself, no matter what it took to do it.

She launched her body toward the barn, but Slade jerked down his face mask before he caught her with one arm and held her back.

"Fern, I've got him!"

She was so focused on the blaze that at first she didn't understand what he was saying to her. "Here?"

"Check the horse's back," Slade said. "Craig couldn't walk, so..."

She didn't hear anything else he had to say as she ran around him. Craig lay facedown across the back of Sheba, but he was so very, very still that she felt her heartbeat thud hard in her throat from anxiety.

"He's alive," Slade said. "Come on. Help me." He walked the buckskin over to the corral, removed her blindfold, and led her through the gate. He gently lifted Craig from the horse's back, carried him out of the gate, closed it behind them, and carefully laid Craig on the ground.

She knelt beside him, brushing sweat-wet hair back from his soot-encrusted face. He blinked, looking up at her in confusion. And then her tears came, running down her cheeks in relief that he was still with her.

"Fern, let me help him. Get back," Sydney called.

She glanced up to see Sydney barreling toward her with a bright red, soft-sided emergency case with an oxygen tank and mask inside slung by a strap over one shoulder. She also carried a bottle of water.

Fern moved back slightly to make room, but she still kept a hand on Craig's shoulder.

Sydney quickly covered Craig's nose and mouth with a mask. "Let's keep him on oxygen till he comes around. As soon as he can do it, get him to sip water. He's dehydrated from the heat." She held out the water.

Fern gladly took it, anxious to help Craig any way she could to help him quickly recover. "His lungs?"

"Don't know yet." Sydney stood up. "Watch him. If you see his condition worsen, call me over. For now, Slade and I need to contain the fire."

"Do you want me to ask Hedy for backup?"

Sydney glanced up and assessed the situation. "No. We can handle this fire with the booster, but the barn's a lost cause."

"That's okay." She rubbed Craig's chest, then looked at the two horses. "We got what's important out of it."

"Right." Sydney stood up.

"You're okay." Fern smiled at Craig as he opened his eyes. "You're fine. The horses are fine. We're all fine."

He appeared as if he wanted to speak, but she shook her head to remind him to remain calm and still so he could recover.

"In a little bit, if you feel up to it, I'll help you sit and you can sip water. For now, please just relax and breathe the oxygen."

He gave her a slight nod, then glanced toward the barn.

"I regret to tell you, but it looks like a total loss."

He looked toward the ranch house.

"Sydney says they can contain the fire, so the only building you'll lose is the barn. I know it's not good, but it's not the worst it could be."

He nodded again, then closed his eyes, taking deep breaths.

She rubbed his chest with the palm of her hand. "Please...please don't ever do that to me again. I can't tell you how scared I was when you didn't come out of there."

He slowly sat up, leaned back against the white wood slates of the fence, and pulled down the mask. He jerked off his gloves, then raised a hand and rubbed the tears from under her eyes.

She grasped his hand and pressed a soft kiss to the palm.

"Sorry I worried you," he finally rasped as he cupped her face with long fingers, smiling at her.

"I know, but oh my..." She couldn't speak for a moment as emotion welled up in her. "You did save the horses. I'm proud of you."

"My concern," he started to say, then stopped and massaged his throat.

"Oh, I forgot." She cracked the bottle of water and held it out to him.

He took several small sips, then swallowed. "My concern is...I might not be able to sing at Wild West Days."

"Oh, Craig, don't give it another thought."

"But—"

"You're alive and well. That's all that matters."

"I can still play...my guitar." He sipped more water.

"Yes, you can, but please don't think about it now."

"Okay." He smiled as he looked at the rig. "Is that all they could spare me?"

She chuckled, realizing he had to be feeling pretty much himself if he was going to give the firefighters a hard time about sending nothing but the booster. "That's all you asked for and you know it."

"Yeah. I can still rib them later, can't I?"

"I suppose they'll even expect it."

She glanced over her shoulder. "It looks like they're getting the blaze under control. Will they have enough water in the rig?"

"Sure." He sipped more water. "I knew we wouldn't need the tanker. That's best for a really big job."

"Your barn looks like a really big job to me."

"I know, but they're containing it. In a minute, I'll get up and help them."

She put a hand on his chest again. "No. We're either going to the emergency room in town or putting you straight to bed."

He grinned, raising an eyebrow. "I opt for going straight to bed."

She just shook her head at him. "Sleep is what I had in mind."

"It's not on mine."

"Really. How are you feeling?"

"Better all the time." He put the mask to his face, took several deep breaths, and then glanced at the barn. "I admit it was close, but I knew the booster was on its way. It's just that the fire was faster."

"Aren't they always?"

"Seems that way."

She turned back to watch Slade and Sydney laying down a line of water defense that appeared to be bringing the fire completely under control. As if they'd heard her thoughts, Sydney jogged over while Slade continued his water bombardment.

"We're about done," Sydney said.

"Looks like you're doing good. I think I can help now." Craig made as if to get up.

"No you don't. It's pretty much contained." Sydney glanced over her shoulder, then back again. "Slade's finishing up. And don't worry about later. We're both staying the night to make sure that fire doesn't break loose again."

"The cowboys will be back soon, so they could keep an eye out."

"You know better." Sydney gave him a dismissive look. "We have the equipment and know-how. We're not leaving till it cools off."

"Thanks." Fern patted Craig's chest again. "Do you think I should run him to Wildcat Bluff to the clinic?"

Sydney cocked her head to the side, considering Craig. "How do you feel?"

"I inhaled some smoke, but I'm okay."

"Are you sure?" Fern asked.

"I'm an EMT. I'd know, and I'd go if I thought there was a real need for it."

"If you're not going to the clinic, take the EMT kit to the house with you," Sydney said. "If you feel a need, you can keep track of your blood pressure and stay on oxygen till you're back to normal."

"Will do." Craig rubbed his chest. "Right now, I feel like a horse kicked me."

"Maybe one of them did and you didn't notice." Sydney chuckled at her own joke to lighten the moment as she replaced the oxygen tank and mask in its bag, then handed it to Fern.

Fern appreciated her attempt at humor, so she laughed, too.

"By morning, I'll probably be sore all over," Craig said. "But I don't care. I saved two horses and that's what counts."

"It sure does," Sydney agreed. "Looks like Slade's ready to pack it in. Let me go help him."

Fern watched her walk away, more grateful than ever for their volunteer firefighters.

"If I'm not going to the clinic and they won't let me help here, why don't we go to bed?"

"I can see you're going to be trouble now that the trouble is past." She slipped the strap of the bag over her shoulder.

"I'll definitely need some TLC."

"Come on." She stood up. "Let's get you home, get you a shower, and get you comfortable."

"I like the shower part. I think I'll need a lot of help."

She laughed, shaking her head. "I bet you do."

"And you'll be willing to help?"

"Let me help you up." She held out her hand. "We can negotiate how much more help you need later."

"I'm pretty good at negotiations." He used the fence to leverage upward before he took her hand. He stood still for a long moment as he looked at what was left of the barn. "What a loss."

"But not as big a loss as it could have been."

"True enough."

"Do you think you can you walk to your truck?"

"Think so." He took a few unsteady steps, straightened his back, and walked to the booster.

Slade finished rolling up the hose, then glanced at Craig. "Looks like you're going to make it."

"Yeah. Thanks to you. And Sydney."

"Anytime."

"I owe you a round of drinks at Wildcat Hall."

"I'll be happy to accept them." Slade gave him the once-over. "Are you sure you don't need the clinic?"

"I'll be okay. If not, I'll go there in the morning. Right now I just want to go home."

"If you need anything, we'll be down here."

"I'll call my foreman and let him know what's going on. He and the cowboys should be getting close enough to be in cell range."

"Don't worry about it. Save your throat. I'll bring them up to speed when they get here. And I'll call Sheriff Calhoun. I suspect he'll want to take a look and ask us to collect samples."

"Do you know what started the fire?" Sydney asked.

"No idea," Craig said. "We weren't here. And I haven't been in any position to check it out."

"He's still not." Fern squeezed Craig's hand. "He's going straight home to rest."

"Good idea," Sydney replied. "We'll take over."

"Thanks," Craig said. "I'll be on top of things tomorrow, but for tonight, y'all know where to find me."

"Thanks again," Fern said. "Both of you come see us at the Hall soon and we'll treat you right."

"I'm looking forward to it." Sydney reached inside the rig, pulled out the EMT bag, and handed it to Fern. "Keep an eye on him."

"Thanks. You know I will." Fern walked with Craig to his truck, feeling exhausted from the ordeal. She wanted nothing more than to get in bed and sleep for a week.

"I can drive." Craig glanced at her, obviously seeing if she'd object.

"Are you sure?"

"It's just up the hill. Get in and let's get."

She did exactly that, but she watched him carefully as he eased into the front seat and drove away from the fire site. He seemed to be okay, but she would definitely keep close watch till morning.

He drove up to the gate leading to ranch house, then he hit the opener above his head and the gate started slowly to swing open.

She gasped. "Stop."

"What is it?"

"Look!" She pointed at the dozen white roses wrapped in green cellophane attached with a big white ribbon to the gate.

Chapter 27

"I'M SO SORRY." FERN SLUMPED IN HER SEAT, HOLDING both the EMT kit and the oxygen bag in her lap, as she stared at the roses in horror. "It's my fault. Barn…you… horses…all are my fault. I never dreamed he would escalate this far. I didn't even know he knew about you and the ranch. I'll pay to replace the barn, of course. But the time, the effort, the worry I can't correct."

"Fern, please stop it."

"I was right. If I'd left the first moment he appeared in the Hall, this would never have happened to you. I should've gone. I will go. It's the only way to deal with a person who is not in their right mind."

"It's not your fault. I don't blame you."

"I'll leave. I'll go tonight." She turned toward him, feeling even sicker at the sight of soot smeared across his face from the oxygen mask. He needed to be cared for now, not put under even more duress.

"No, you won't."

"You'd better take me straight back to the cabins. You can be checked out at the clinic."

"Fern, please, stop eating at yourself like this."

"I'll pack a bag. Ivy can drive me to the airport in Dallas. I'll go so far he'll never find me."

Craig took a deep, ragged breath, then coughed several times.

"Please, let me go."

"Fern, we can either let this tear us apart or we can use it to draw us closer together."

She caught her breath at his words, spoken in a raspy tone due to the smoke inhalation but delivered to her with so much sincerity that they stopped the whirl of her mind.

"It's your choice." He glanced at the roses, then back at her with absolute determination in his eyes. "You can run, but if you do, I'll go with you. There is no way I'll leave you anywhere in this world defenseless against that man."

She was trying to be strong. She was trying to be practical. She was trying to save all she held dear. And yet, everything kept turning to dust in her hands. How had it come to putting Craig's ranch on the line? Horses could have died. Cowboys could have been trapped in there. Every building could have gone up in smoke. Fortunately, they'd seen the fire before it was too late. But what about next time? She felt terrified and furious at the same time. Even worse, she felt vulnerable...and trapped in a no-win situation. If she couldn't run, what could she do to stay safe and keep those she loved safe?

"You're overthinking the situation," Craig said quietly in his rough voice. "Two choices. We go or we stay. And I do mean *we*."

She wanted to touch him, but she resisted the impulse. If she felt his warmth, his love, his tenderness, she'd start to cry, and if she started, she wasn't sure she could stop. It'd just been too much, too long, and she'd been so shaken by her near loss of him. Then again, maybe it was that simple. *Her near loss of him.*

She took a deep breath, feeling righteous anger well up in

her. How dare some stranger think he could come into her life and not only threaten but actively try to destroy those who loved her and whom she loved? She wouldn't have it. And she wouldn't let the stalker defeat her…not while she had breath left in her body.

"We—and I do mean *we*—stand and fight right here in Wildcat Bluff County." She reached over and squeezed Craig's hand to make her point.

"That's exactly what I wanted to hear."

"But not tonight. You need to rest."

"Tonight. We don't have a moment to lose." He pulled out his phone, hit speed dial and speakerphone.

"Sheriff Calhoun here."

"Guess you heard about the fire at my ranch," Craig said.

"I'm on my way right now."

"It was the stalker. He left white roses on the gate leading up to the ranch house."

"Don't touch the flowers. We might get lucky if he left prints."

"Doubt we'll be that lucky, but we can try," Craig said.

"Either the guy isn't in the system or he's using an alias," Sheriff Calhoun said. "I checked for him by name."

"I'm not surprised." Fern leaned toward the phone. "Everything about him has been suspicious from the first."

"It's gone too far," Sheriff Calhoun said. "We can't predict what this stalker will do next, so we have to be a step ahead of him."

"I'll leave cowboys on guard duty at the ranch 24/7."

"What about the Park?" Fern asked.

"I bet the Settelmeyers will mount a round-the-clock watch," Craig said. "We couldn't have better watchdogs."

"You're right," Sheriff Calhoun said. "Once they hear about this fire, they'll be armed at all times. I wouldn't want to be that stalker if he runs into them."

"I wouldn't, either," Fern said. "We just need to keep everything stable until after Wild West Days."

"We're working on it," Sheriff Calhoun said. "I already have deputies pulling extra duty. I'll step it up in town. Out there, well—"

"That's okay," Craig cut in. "We're on alert now, so there won't be a repeat out here."

"Good," Sheriff Calhoun said. "Craig, how are you feeling? Shouldn't you be up at the house in bed?"

"That's what I keep telling him." She gave Craig a little gentle rebuke of a smile.

"That's where we were headed when we saw the roses." Craig returned her smile with a slight nod, as if thinking about what they would do in bed if not for all the interruptions and trouble.

"Get on up there," Sheriff Calhoun said. "We'll gather what evidence we can get at the barn and take the roses on the fence. When you're feeling up to it, just stop by the office and make a statement."

"Are you sure you don't want to interview us tonight?" Craig asked.

"There's no need to put you through any more right now," Sheriff Calhoun said. "Shut the gate behind you and we'll do the rest."

"Thanks. That's exactly what we'll do." Fern felt much better now that the sheriff was on the job and she could take Craig up to the house.

"We'll see you tomorrow," Craig said.

"Take care." And Sheriff Calhoun clicked off.

"I still think I ought to go down and help." Craig coughed several times.

"They've got it under control." She patted the containers on her lap. "We need to get you in the house. You still need oxygen. And I want to check your blood pressure."

"I'm okay...or well enough. I don't want that guy to win on any front."

"He won't win, not in the long run. Tonight we need to regroup and plan how we go on from here."

"Guess you're right."

"I'm not alone in wanting you at home. That's EMT orders from Sydney, too."

He chuckled, nodding in agreement. He drove through the open gates, then shut them behind his pickup.

Finally, she felt a little safer as he eased up the rise to the front of the house. It'd be dark soon, and she wanted to be safely indoors before it was hard to see outside.

"I'm going to park in front," he said. "It'd be the quickest exit."

"Do you think he's done something in the house?" She felt her breath catch in her throat at the idea of the stalker so close to them.

"No. I didn't mean to alarm you. It's just a precaution. The house has an alarm system. If he entered, it'd alert us."

"Okay. That's good. And a relief."

"Come on." He opened the truck door, then glanced over at her. "Do you want me to carry any of that to the house?"

"I've got it."

"Wait here. I want to go inside and check around, just in case, before you come inside."

"Craig, if there's trouble, I want to be with you."

"It's simply a precaution. I don't expect trouble."

"We haven't expected trouble all along, but still—"

"Fern, please wait here. I won't be long." And he was out the door and walking up the path to the house.

She locked the doors, waiting but not liking it. She didn't want to be separated from him, but she didn't want him to think she didn't trust him to take care of them either. She needed to accept that he was the experienced EMT and firefighter. He knew best about his health. He also knew best about security in his home. Still, she wanted to be with him. She clutched her purse, the EMT kit, and the oxygen bag to her chest. And waited some more.

Finally, he walked out the front door and beckoned her.

She stepped down, carrying everything, and made sure the doors were locked behind her. She went to him, feeling a little unnerved being outdoors between the pickup and the house. She quickly walked past him and into the house, breathing a sigh of relief when he shut and locked the front door.

"Okay?" He took the EMT kit and oxygen bag from her, then carried them through to the kitchen where he set them on top of the bar.

She placed her purse on the bar, too, then turned to look at him in the overhead light. He looked rough, as if he'd been on the wrong end of fighting a fire. Yet he also looked tough and determined to succeed no matter where he went or what he did. And she was with him all the way.

"Why don't you sit down and breathe more oxygen?" She tried to sound gentle, but she saw the immediate frown on his face.

"I'm okay. I want to drink a glass of water and get a shower." He grinned at her, eyes lighting up with mischief. "Want to join me?"

She smiled in return, hoping he really was that well. "How about we start with the water?"

"On second thought, there's water in the shower. Let's go straight there."

She couldn't keep from chuckling at his attempt to seduce her so quickly after the devastating fire. "Are you forgetting you just lost your barn?"

"I'm *trying* to forget it. Why don't you help me?"

"Craig, really, what do you want? I'm trying to help you. I still feel terrible about the fire...about everything."

"Why don't we help each other forget the fire, the barn, everything that's been plaguing us for so long?" He walked over to her and held out his hand. "I don't need coddling. I need loving."

And that was all he needed to say. She wrapped her fingers around his hand and went upstairs with him. He opened a door, flipped on a light inside, and motioned for her to precede him.

She couldn't keep from smiling as she stepped into a room with floral wallpaper and delicate Queen Anne furniture with crochet doilies on the chest, dresser, and nightstands. It was a very feminine room except for the king size bed with a black leather headboard and gray-and-black geometric bedspread.

"I know how it looks in here, but it works till I get time to fix it to suit me."

"If it suits you, that's all that matters. You might be able to make the styles work a little better together."

He chuckled, nodding in agreement. "I did combine two small bedrooms to make a decent bath and closet. Why don't you take a look?"

She stepped into the adjacent room and gave a happy little sigh. Lots of space and lights and a bathtub and shower and long vanity table with a padded stool in sparkling white. Lots of fluffy gray towels. Lots of scented soaps and lotions and bath salts with Morning's Glory labels.

"Let's get a shower. I want to wash away the stench of the fire." He walked up behind her and wrapped his arms around her waist and pulled her back against his chest.

"You are pretty smelly." She chuckled as she turned in his arms and placed a soft kiss against his lips, tasting soot. "Are you sure you're well enough?"

"If there's anything wrong with me, I'm sure a few kisses from you will cure it."

"How about a little more than a few kisses?" She stroked down his chest to clutch the big buckle of his belt.

"I'm feeling stronger by the moment."

"Just what I wanted to hear." She whirled away from him, walked over to the stool, and sat down. She tugged off her boots as she watched him.

He sat down on the edge of the tub. He pulled off one boot, then the other. He stopped, watching her, waiting for her.

She tugged her crimson T-shirt up over her head and tossed it on top of her boots. She wore a red, lacy bra underneath, and she saw his eyes darken as he looked at her. She smiled, knowing what he was thinking and enjoying it.

He jerked his T-shirt up over his head and dropped it on top of his boots, smiling at her, too.

They were so much in sync that she felt her heart rate

kick up in anticipation of where they were going after such a long, long day. If they ever deserved a treat, this was definitely the time. She stood up and slowly lowered her jeans till she kicked them off and sat back down.

He shucked off his jeans, too, so that he was wearing nothing more than dark blue briefs…and that smile.

She unhooked her bra, then ever so slowly let it slide down her arms to fall to the floor. Now, who would be next to strip off the final bits of fabric that barely covered them? She stood up, gave him a sultry smile, picked up two washcloths, and walked over to the shower.

She reached inside and found the showerhead by feel alone because she kept watching him watching her. When a soft rain of warm water covered her hand, she reached down, tugged off her thong, and tossed it to him.

He caught the bit of red lace in one hand while he pulled off his briefs with the other, then tossed them together on top of the vanity. He walked toward her, all hard muscle, long sinew, big bones, and a grin that said it all.

She stepped backward into the shower, letting the water cascade over her as he slipped inside, shutting the door to enclose them in their own private world. And she was happy to be there.

She tugged him close so that water covered his face, sending dark soot swirling to the drain below. She lathered a cloth, reached up, and gently washed his face, wiping the last traces of the fire that had marked him since he'd given his all to rescue a horse. She felt such an upwelling of love that for a moment she couldn't move. She just stared at him in wonder that she could ever have thought she could live without him. He was such an extraordinary man in so many ways, and she was so proud of him in so many ways. He deserved the best—always the best that she could possibly give him.

And so she gently, ever so gently, washed down his neck to his chest, across the wide expanse of hard muscle, covering every little bit of flesh as she moved lower and lower, seeing him rise to meet her, and finally, stroking, stroking the hard, hot length until he jerked the cloth out of her hands and tossed it aside.

He pressed a hot kiss to her mouth, surging deep inside as he raised her leg, positioning her so he could enter with one fierce thrust that filled her completely just as he filled her mouth with his taste, his very essence. And then he was moving fast and hard and deep, and she was riding the wave that he created inside her as water cascaded over them.

She clutched his shoulders, spiraling higher and higher with him, always with him…and then she heard music—not just a chord or two, but an entire symphony building layer upon layer of emotion until the crescendo seized her and held her and sent her over the edge into ecstasy…with the only man she could ever love.

Chapter 28

SEVERAL DAYS LATER, CRAIG WALKED THE GROUNDS OF Wildcat Park to inspect a string of cameras the Settelmeyers had installed for protection, although they were on a 24/7 physical rotation, too. He'd done all he could do for security at the ranch, but he still got mad every time he thought about the fire that cost him a barn and nearly two horses. That structure was no longer sound and would have to be bulldozed so another could be built, but it would need to wait until after Wild West Days. They were only forty-eight hours out now and in countdown mode.

It felt as if time had sped up because there was so much to do and so little time to do it. Nobody complained. Nobody shirked responsibilities. Nobody left anything undone. Everybody pitched in and got about doing their job to make it the best possible event.

Fortunately, they hadn't heard or seen any more of Fern's stalker, although they were on alert. Everybody hoped he'd been satisfied with burning down the barn and he'd disappeared back under whatever rock he'd crawled out from under. As much as Craig wished that were the truth, he didn't quite believe it. A man who went to that much trouble and put himself in that kind of precarious position to go onto a ranch and set a fire was a man on a mission. Craig feared the stalker's mission had one name and one name only: Fern Bryant. But he'd never tell her that because she didn't need any more worry. She simply needed to focus on Wild West Days, and he'd make sure she stayed safe.

He glanced around as he walked the Park's grounds. It looked beautiful, since it was manicured to perfection with roses in bloom, short green grass, trimmed hedges, and trees in full splendor. Of course, it was hot, but it looked like they were going to get the low to mid-nineties he'd been hoping for, so the heat wouldn't be unbearable. Plus, it'd cool down at night, so that'd help events at Wildcat Hall and the Lone Star Saloon. He thought it was going to be a blowout of an event.

About dusk, Craig turned toward the Hall where Fern awaited folks who were gathering to discuss last-minute details about Wild West Days. He walked the path, enjoying the peace and quiet before chaos and noise descended on the county to last three long days. But every single moment would be well worth it because the special event boosted the local economy as well as provided family entertainment in a western setting, which was available in limited places nowadays. It was not only fun, but educational as well. He was proud of Wildcat Bluff County for mustering the get-up-and-go every year to create it.

For now, he only needed to join Fern at the Hall, grab a bite to eat, and be ready to field questions. As he got closer, he was surprised to see her outside the Hall, where she stood near the side closest to the front doors and couldn't be seen from the entry. She put a fingertip to her lips, then beckoned him.

He stepped off the path, glancing around to see what was going on. He saw nothing unusual except Morning Glory stood in front of the dance hall with a tall, silver-haired man. She was dressed in her trademark full skirt and blouse with cowgirl boots. The stranger wore jeans, a shirt, and cowboy boots. They were talking intently to each other.

Once he joined Fern, he couldn't see the couple anymore, but he could hear them. He didn't think they should be eavesdropping on the conversation. Yet Fern appeared concerned for MG, so he figured that was why she wanted him there. With everything going on due to the stalker, she was right. He wasn't about to let anything happen to their friend.

"She's gone…thirteen months now," the man said in a steady voice. "I waited that long because I know your strong sense of morality."

"Mac, right is right," Morning Glory said, raising her voice.

"You never had children?"

"No. There was only ever one man…but no matter."

"You devoted yourself to this community."

"Yes."

"Did you find fulfillment?"

"I'm satisfied with my contribution to life. I help others achieve their dreams," she said matter-of-factly.

"What about your own dreams?"

"You mean *our* dreams?"

"I thought you'd go on without me. You had the talent for it."

"You have no room to talk. You didn't go on without me either."

"I had responsibilities."

"I know," she said, voice breaking slightly. "And you know I would never stand in the way of a pregnant woman who needed the father of her child to care for them."

"It was an accident. You know what Woodstock was like."

"No matter now. We did the right thing."

"She's grown…my daughter. Two grandchildren. They're fine. My wife died of cancer."

"I'm sorry to hear it. You have my sympathy."

"I stayed with her to the end."

"You loved her?"

"Yes…but not like you," he said.

"Yet you were honorable."

"You expected no less."

"And now?" She moved restlessly, bracelets jingling.

"You're more beautiful than ever."

"I'm just as I was."

"I never forgot you," he said in a voice gone deep with emotion.

"Why are you here?"

"Did you think I wouldn't seek you out when the time was right?" he asked.

"We were over long ago. There's no reason to revisit it."

"There's no love like first love."

"Was it love?" she asked.

"You know it was."

"Whatever it was, it's long over now."

"No," he said.

"You have a life. Go back to it. My life is here, and I'm happy with it."

"Are you telling me I have no chance with you?"

"I'm telling you I'm very busy. Wild West Days is almost upon us, and it will take all my time," she said.

"If I'm there, will you dance with me at the Lone Star Saloon?"

"Dance?" she asked, wonder in her voice.

"I'll never forget how you'd toss back your long hair and—"

"I don't dance anymore."

"Did you forget how persistent I can be when there's something I want as badly as I want you?" He spoke with utter conviction.

"I forgot nothing about you. It's just not relevant anymore."

"You're wrong."

"Thank you for coming. You have my deepest sympathy for the loss of your wife. Now, I have a meeting to attend and—"

"I bought Wildflower Ranch."

"You what?" she asked in a shocked voice.

"I'm a resident of Wildcat Bluff County now."

"That's not possible."

"Lorraine, I'm here to stay." He hesitated a long moment. "You're mine. You've always been mine…just like I've always been yours. Please remember." And his footsteps sounded loudly against the parking lot as he walked away.

A few moments later, the front doors of the Hall slammed shut.

Fern turned toward Craig, eyes wide in astonishment.

He felt just as surprised, but he stepped away from the building so he could make sure the stranger left. He watched the man step up into a spotless black-and-chrome pickup, so new he could almost smell the new-car scent. The guy didn't belong, but he was here, and he had history with MG. They'd need to keep an eye on him, just like the stalker. Wild West Days was shaping up to be a lot more than the usual fun event.

"Lorraine?" Fern said. "Do you suppose that's her real name? I can't even imagine calling her anything but MG."

"Morning Glory sounds about right for the sixties, doesn't it?"

"Yes, but still—"

"Let's go inside. I don't want to leave her alone after that confrontation," Craig said.

"Who knew MG had such drama in her past?"

"Somehow I'm not surprised, but it doesn't matter. We keep her safe, no matter what."

"Absolutely." Fern put her hands on her hips.

"What were you doing out here anyway?"

"I was headed inside when I saw him pull up and call to MG. He was a stranger, and I'm on alert for men that don't belong around here, so I ducked out of sight but stayed nearby in case she needed me."

"Good idea."

"How do we handle it from here?" Fern asked. "I'm not sure how she'd feel about us eavesdropping on her conversation."

"Maybe she'll want to talk about him. That way we'd know without letting her know we already heard about him," Craig said.

"Okay. But it's obviously very private, so I'd just as soon not mention it."

"Suits me. Let's don't leave MG alone too long."

He clasped Fern's hand, threaded their fingers together, and walked with her to the front, where he opened the door. He followed her inside and saw MG leaning against the bar with her back to them.

"You heard, didn't you?" Morning Glory accused as she wheeled around to face them. She clutched her necklaces in one hand, as if holding on for dear life.

"Yes," Fern said. "I'm sorry if we intruded on a private moment."

"I apologize." Craig stood still, trying to think of something else to ease the moment. "It's just the stalker has us all on edge about strangers."

"And you're our friend," Fern added. "We wouldn't let anything happen to you."

"That's right."

"Thank you." Morning Glory relaxed a little, leaning back against the bar. "You didn't have cause for concern, but I appreciate you being there for me."

"Always," Fern said.

"You're here for us," Craig added. "We're here for you. That's the way it is in Wildcat Bluff County."

"Yes." Morning Glory gave a little smile. "I know. I helped create this wonderful world where so many of us lost on the sea of life come together. And you are part of that creation."

"You brought renewed community and commitment," Fern said. "I floated up here and found your bottle with its message waiting for me."

Morning Glory chuckled, shrugging her shoulders. "We're getting poetic, aren't we?"

"Wildcat Bluff saved me…and it saved my sister." Fern squeezed Craig's hand. "Oh yes, we could've followed other paths, but love waited for us here. And there's no greater gift."

Morning Glory blinked back tears, then looked down as if to conceal her deep emotions. "Love…I haven't looked for it. And yet…"

"There's no rush," Fern said in a gentle voice.

"But it could be awkward, what with him living near now." Morning Glory shook her head, as if trying to shake away the notion.

"You can handle anything." Craig smiled at MG. "Besides, we're all here to support you. If he gives you trouble, send him to us."

Morning Glory chuckled, nodding in agreement. "His

name is Justin McKenzie. We called him Mac. But that's been so long ago. Now, I just don't know what to think or say."

"You don't need to think or say anything." Fern walked over to Morning Glory and gave her a gentle hug.

"That's right," Craig agreed. "For now, Wild West Days are coming up, and that's plenty to keep your mind busy."

"Would I look foolish…I mean, our age and all?" Morning Glory cocked her head to one side as if considering the situation.

"Did it concern Hedy and Bert?" Fern asked.

"No. But they make such a perfect couple," Morning Glory said.

"What about Wildcat Jack? He's still the heartthrob of who knows how many women." Craig chuckled at the thought of his friend's legendary exploits with the ladies of the county.

"Mac's handsome, isn't he?" Morning Glory gave a little shy smile that reflected her inner thoughts.

"He's a good-looking man. And smart, I'd guess," Craig said. "He came after you, didn't he?"

"He was always smart. Kind. Caring. Talented." Morning Glory sighed. "I just never thought I'd see him again. But now that he's here, well…I'm just not sure."

"He won't go anywhere." Fern glanced at Craig with a smile. "I can recommend giving him a chance like I gave someone here."

"Thanks. I'll think about it," Morning Glory said. "For now, Wild West Days comes first, doesn't it?"

"Right…for all of us." Craig heard pickups pulling up and parking out front. "Sound like the gang's all here."

Chapter 29

FERN STAYED BESIDE MG, FEELING AS IF SHE NEEDED TO give her friend moral or any other type of support she might want at this pivotal point. She glanced at Craig, feeling a surge of emotion that was unlike anything else she'd ever experienced in life. Love, yes…but the feeling was so much more than that single word. Music—rich and vibrant as it soared to the greatest of heights—came the closest to expressing what she felt for him. And yet, not a single one of her five senses could capture the depth of their connection.

Craig smiled at her as if he understood exactly what she was thinking… Life was so much better shared between them.

And then there was no more time for personal thoughts, as the front doors burst open and a boisterous group rushed inside, laughing and talking and gesturing to each other. Ivy and Slade. Hedy and Bert. Sydney and Dune. Misty and Trey. Lauren and Kent. Eden and Shane.

She smiled at the sight. As if a fairy godmother had passed her magic wand over Wildcat Bluff County, so many eligible bachelors had found the loves of their lives in a short space of time.

When the front door opened again, Bert Two walked inside…alone, as always. He had it all. Looks. Talent. A ranch. And a gentle heart. But he wasn't a heartbreaker. He was the one who kept getting a broken heart. Hedy had confided that he was simply unlucky in love. Everyone hoped his luck would turn around now that so many others were happily in love, but no one really thought it would happen. After all, it was Bert Two, the unluckiest cowboy in the county.

"Looks like we're all here," Morning Glory said. "Why don't we take a seat and get on with the business of Wild West Days."

"Sarsaparilla all around?" Fern asked, glancing at the group.

"You know it," Bert said as he moved a chair and wheeled Hedy in close to the table.

Fern watched them find chairs at tables, noticing that the couples didn't separate but sat side by side as if unable to be parted for any length of time. She knew how they felt because at this moment, she couldn't imagine leaving Craig again. He was her heart, and what would she be without it or him?

Morning Glory helped her pass out brown bottles of their home brew based on an original recipe used at Wildcat Hall for generations. Soon everyone contentedly sipped their drinks, chatting about mundane matters, exchanging gossip, and in general enjoying themselves.

Fern sat on a barstool with her back to the bar, sipping her own drink as she watched these people who had come to mean so much to her. She could not have picked a better place to put down roots, build a life, share a life, and create a life. She felt content in a way she never had before. Life was good, very good, in Wildcat Bluff County...and she intended to enjoy every moment of it.

Morning Glory stepped down off her stool, carrying a bottle of sarsaparilla. "Guess we ought to get our meeting underway. Anybody need help with anything? Suggestions? Last-minute glitches?"

"MG, I'm going to put this right out there because it's got to be said so everyone knows." Hedy glanced at Bert, then back at her friend.

"What?" Morning Glory grabbed her dangling necklaces and held on as if to ward off a blow. "If this is personal, please don't go there."

"It is personal, but it's already getting out there."

Morning Glory took a deep breath, then looked down, waiting for the blow to come.

"Mac's in town," Hedy said.

"I know." Morning Glory didn't raise her head.

"He bought Wildflower Ranch."

"I know." Morning Glory stayed in the same position.

"He stopped by Adelia's Delights looking for you."

"He found me." Morning Glory glanced up, tears glistening in her eyes.

"I'm sorry," Hedy said. "I didn't mean to upset you."

"It's okay. I'm a tough bird."

"You're the biggest softy I know." Hedy smiled fondly at her friend. "I showed him your store. He liked it…because it's so you."

"He's old news," Morning Glory said. "I have a new life now."

"Hedy, you're confusing everyone here." Bert patted her shoulder. "You'd better back up and clear the air."

Hedy glanced around the group, then opened her mouth to speak.

"It's my business," Morning Glory said. "And it's old business."

"He's part of the community now." Bert Two stood with his elbows resting on the bar behind him. "He'll be involved with all us ranchers. And he'll be asking about you. What do you want us to say?"

"Nothing." Morning Glory looked exasperated with the discussion. "I told you, it's my business."

"No. It's the county's business now," Hedy said. "We're looking out for you. We want to put your story out there first. Help us."

"After all this time, did he come looking for you?" Bert Two crossed one booted foot over the other. "If so, he sounds like a romantic to me. I can identify. I'm kind of a romantic myself. I wish him well, but sometimes romantics…" He shook his head and shut his mouth.

"It's just been a shock to her, I think." Fern jumped in to try and cover up Bert Two's obvious emotional regrets in life. How could any woman have ever let him go?

"Okay." Morning Glory stood up straighter. "All anybody in this county needs to know is that Mac and I have history. He bought a ranch because he wants to live here now. That's fine with me. We're still friends."

"That's good," Hedy said. "I agree. That's all anyone needs to know, but they needed to know something. We'll just put it to rest for now."

"Thanks." Morning Glory took a swig of sarsaparilla, then glared around the group. "Now, can we get back to the business at hand?"

"Suits me," Bert said, smiling and nodding.

Bert Two raised his bottle and saluted Morning Glory. "But I'm still romantic enough to wish our new cowboy gets his cowgirl."

Morning Glory laughed, shaking her head. "Bert Two, just don't tell me you're secretly writing poetry."

Bert Two looked away and took a quick drink as he eased his foot with the medical boot up on the foot rail.

Fern leaped in again to turn the attention away from Bert Two. "MG, why don't you let Craig take over since he's been on top of our schedule?" She figured it was just a matter of time before Bert Two found a cowgirl who couldn't resist a romantic, poetry-writing cowboy.

Craig walked over to the bar, picked up a printout, and scanned it. "As far as I know, we're on schedule. Out-of-town vendors will be pulling in tomorrow and setting up, so we'll get Main Street closed off by the end of the workday."

"Bert Two, what about the new bandstand for the pocket park?" Fern asked.

"I made it myself." He tapped his fingernails on the bottle in his hands. "It's not as good as I'd like, but I didn't have much time. Plus, we won't leave it up all the time. I added hinges, so it can be folded and stored till the next time we need it."

"That's a good idea," Morning Glory said.

"Yeah," Craig agreed. "Still, what if we left it up year-round or at least for the summer months? Sure-Shot is drawing their local community together with free weekend entertainment in their park."

"I like it." Ivy glanced around the group. "I know I'm pretty new in these parts, but outdoor concerts are always a big attraction in Houston. Why couldn't we do it here? That pocket park is the perfect place."

"It'd be fun for folks," Slade added, "and it'd bring more

traffic to the downtown stores. They might even stop in for barbeque or a piece of pie at the Chuckwagon."

"This is sounding better and better," Morning Glory said. "Hedy, what do you think?"

"I'm all in." Hedy nodded in agreement. "Anything to make our community stronger on every level is a plus for each and every one of us."

"I don't think I have time to take off the hinges," Bert Two said. "Anyway, if it's going to be permanent, I'll build a new one bigger, stronger, and fancier."

"Do you have time?" Bert asked. "We're so busy at the ranch."

"I'll get to it after my foot's completely healed," Bert Two said.

"Okay. That's settled." Craig glanced at Sydney. "This item is fairly new on my list. Fernando?"

Sydney chuckled, shaking her head. "Storm says Fernando is all set to welcome his followers on Fernando the Wonder Bull, his personal website."

"How do you suppose Fernando really feels about it?" Slade joined her laughter.

"If he gets his special feed, he probably doesn't care one way or another," Sydney said. "But then again, he's probably all in."

"Any news about Daisy Sue?" Fern asked.

"No." Slade shook his head in disappointment. "We're getting the runaround on all fronts. I don't understand it, but we'll settle down to pursue the matter after Wild West Days."

"Good luck," Fern said.

"How do you plan to handle Fernando's appearance?"

Craig asked. "And where would you put him? He's no lightweight."

Slade gave a big sigh. "Tell me about it. It needs to be a secure enclosure and out of foot traffic."

"We're looking at a section in the pocket park that would work for him," Fern said.

"Fernando has a large fan base, and he's a draw to Wildcat Bluff," Morning Glory said thoughtfully. "Let's don't lose this opportunity."

"Fans come to the ranch to see him, but they can't get any farther than the entry, so this is a unique opportunity for them," Sydney said.

"Ivy, what do you think?" Slade asked. "You're our social media and website guru now."

"Fernando is obviously a gift to our community marketing-wise," Ivy said. "Even so, his health and well-being should be everyone's primary concern."

"If you can keep him safe, we'd love to livestream over the Den." Eden chuckled as she looked at the group. "I bet Wildcat Jack would be happy to interview him, or at least Storm. She's popular, too."

"Let's go ahead with our plans to include Fernando," Craig said. "We can find a way to make it work."

"Okay," Slade agreed. "I'm putting together an enclosure for him. Storm's got stuff printed up. I don't think we should disappoint either of them...or their fans."

"Good." Craig set down his list. "Anything else?"

"Is the dunking booth ready?" Hedy asked.

"I rented it, and it's at the ranch." Sydney glanced around at the cowboy firefighters. "I didn't trust anybody but me to make sure we had it ready to go."

"No wonder," Slade said. "Are you sure the cowboys will show up for that event?"

"They better." Sydney gave them all a steely-eyed look. "Nathan is going to photograph them for our next cowboy firefighter calendar."

At that news, all the men groaned in unison.

"It's for a good cause, so don't complain." Sydney chuckled. "And if you're not careful, there just might be a cosmetologist from the Sure-Shot Beauty Station in your future for that photo shoot."

They groaned even louder.

Fern couldn't keep from smiling at the cowboys' reactions, but she could understand it, too.

"We do appreciate your contribution to the fire station's bottom line," Hedy said. "You know we need the funds."

"Yeah," Slade said, agreeing. "I just wish there was a better way to obtain them."

"You may as well get used to a cowboy firefighter calendar every year," Sydney said. "It's too popular to give up."

Silence met that announcement.

"Well." Fern jumped into the fray again. "If there aren't any more questions or concerns, y'all might as well get on with your days."

"You know where to find us," Craig said.

"And you've got our cell numbers, so you can contact us anytime during Wild West Days."

"If you need extra help," Bert Two said, "I'm available, if I'm not on my feet too long."

"Thanks." Fern gave him a big smile, realizing just how lonely he must be to volunteer for anything else.

"And no more talk about my love life." Morning Glory

gave each person in the room a hard stare. "My private life is just that—private."

"Right." Hedy grinned with a wink. "And if you believe that one in a community like this, then you've been asleep at the wheel."

"Well, I had to try, didn't I?" Morning Glory gave a big sigh, smiling all the while. "Bunch of busybodies, that's what."

"It's just that everybody loves you and wants you to be happy," Bert said.

"I am happy," Morning Glory insisted. "And at this late date, I don't need a man to make me happy."

Hedy glanced at Bert. "MG, there's happy and there's happy."

"Oh, go on, all of you. Just get out of my hair." But she was laughing as she said it, revealing how much she appreciated their concern.

As everyone made their way to the front door, Craig walked over, clasped Fern's hand, and leaned down to whisper, "If there's happy and there's happy, how happy are you?"

"On a scale of one to ten?"

"Yeah."

She squeezed his hand. "Ten."

Chapter 30

FERN COULDN'T PUT HER FINGER ON QUITE HOW IT HAP-
pened or how quickly it happened, but Old Town in Wildcat
Bluff went from a laid-back, tight-knit community to a bustling, arms-open community in the blink of an eye. At least so
it seemed to her, even though she'd been planning Wild West
Days almost from the moment she'd returned to the county.

She stood on the boardwalk in front of the park early
on the morning of the first day. Of course, it was no longer
called the pocket park now that it had a definite function in
the community. Bert Two, bless his generous heart, had not
only built and gotten the bandstand installed, but he'd taken
the time to create a sign. He'd burned the new name into
a piece of cedar cut in a western motif and lacquered to a
high sheen. Now it was attached to double posts embedded
in the ground near the entrance to boldly announce OLD
TOWN PARK.

He'd carried the same Old West theme to the bandstand. He'd built a natural wood structure with western
designs burned onto the pine in front. It was four feet high,
with stairs that led to the top, where folding chairs had been
set out to accommodate local musicians later in the day. A
microphone on a stand and a sound system had also been
set up, so music could be heard across town.

She was proud of their new park and glad they'd come
up with the idea to use it year round to draw folks together.

She glanced down the length of the boardwalk, where red, white, and blue bunting festooned store windows and outlined the roof of the row of brick-and-stone buildings.

On closed-off Main Street, colorful tents and white trailers also featured red, white, and blue from fluttering pennants to metallic streamers that would draw attention to each vendor. She could already smell barbeque and other delicious treats being cooked in anticipation of the big crowd to come.

She'd dressed ahead of the heat, expected to hit in force that afternoon, by wearing Wranglers, a turquoise T-shirt with the Wild West Days logo emblazoned across the front, and dark blue athletic shoes. She'd hooked the strap of an aqua handbag over one shoulder and tucked inside a bottle of water, her new cell phone, and various other necessary items. She also carried a few copies of the event's schedule printed in red, white, and blue by Nathan at Thingamajigs and available at all stores and vendor sites. To fit with the western theme and keep the sun off her face, she wore a turquoise cowgirl hat that was just perfect for the day.

Craig had been called over to Steele Trap Ranch to consult on the best way to present Fernando. She was here to walk the area, check to make sure everything was in place, and answer any last-minute questions. She had promised him to stay in sight of someone at all times and call a deputy to escort her if she needed to go off the beaten track, even though they hadn't heard from Simon and hoped he'd left the area.

She paused in front of Morning's Glory. MG saw her, hurried to the door, and opened it.

"I'm just checking to see if you have any needs or

concerns." Fern smiled at her friend as she noticed MG was wearing heart earrings and necklaces. She wondered if Mac had anything to do with MG's choice today. She hoped so.

"Thanks. I'm all set…at least for the moment. I have the artist schedules taped to the front door and available inside. Demonstrations are on the hour every hour. I'm even throwing in a free macramé class for those who'd like to learn that almost-lost art we revived in the sixties." She selected one of her long necklaces and held up a dangling brass heart.

"Is that one special?"

Morning Glory dropped it back in place. "It's just an old one I made long ago."

"Maybe about the time you knew Mac?"

Morning Glory rolled her eyes, looking a little bit guilty. "I have to admit it was one of his favorites."

"And you still have it?"

"Don't we always keep the things that are special to our hearts?"

"Yes. For me, it's musical instruments."

"Understandable."

"Is Mac coming by?"

"No idea." Morning Glory glanced outside, as if looking for him. "We haven't been in touch."

"But don't you think he'll attend Wild West Days?"

"He did say something about a dance."

"Craig and I will be playing at the Lone Star Saloon this evening. Why don't you stop by and see us…maybe even dance?"

Morning Glory smiled, looking mischievous. "Maybe I will. Somehow or other, I just feel like celebrating this year."

Fern smiled in return. "I think we all have lots to celebrate, so please come and join us."

Morning Glory nodded, then whirled around, holding out her full skirt so that it swung in a crimson arc around her. "It's new. I made it last night. Do you like?"

"Beautiful. Your style is always impeccable."

"Thanks. I've just always loved lots of movement in my clothes and jewelry."

"It certainly suits you." She took a step back. "Guess I'd better be on my way. I want to check out the dunk booth."

"I'll be happy to check it out, but not till our cowboy firefighters are in it."

Fern laughed, nodding in agreement.

"Hedy is next door. Be sure to stop in and say hey." Morning Glory hesitated, looking over Fern's shoulder. "Where's Craig?"

"He was called out to Steele Trap. He'll be back soon."

"Well, be careful now, and stay in sight of someone at all times."

"Will do." She started to leave, then stopped and turned back. "Do you know much about Sure-Shot?"

"A little bit. Why?"

"Did you ever hear of a one-room schoolhouse memorial grove near there?"

"What?" Morning Glory appeared completely confused at the news. "Where did you hear that?"

"Craig's from there and—"

"Oh, he'd know better than me. It's sounds intriguing, but more like a country legend than real. I mean, we'd all have heard about it if it was real, wouldn't we?"

"I think I'll ask around about it."

"Do that. And let me know if you learn anything, will you?"

"Yeah. And thanks."

Fern started back down the boardwalk, thinking about MG's words. Not common knowledge, then. Until she knew more, she was going to keep the grove a secret, just as it had remained for over a hundred years, because...well, you just never knew what was best left in the dark.

Adelia's Delights was next door, so she stepped inside, hearing the melodic door chime announce her presence. She smiled in delight, as she always did when she came here, because she felt as if she'd been transported back in time, particularly when she read ESTABLISHED 1883 on a sign on the wall. She admired the mellow oak floor, the high ceiling of pressed-tin tile in an intricate design, and the tall glass containers of old-fashioned hard candy on the checkout counter near the ancient black-and-gold cash register in back.

She could easily understand why Hedy loved her store. Knickknacks in all shapes, sizes, colors, and prices filled deep shelves and glass cabinets. One section contained country pickles, jams, and other edible items in canning jars. A prominent display of the Bluebird of Happiness, sky-blue glass birds in all sizes made in Arkansas, gleamed in the front window. Rosie, a pretty tortoiseshell cat, lounged in between the blue glass, soaking up early morning rays as the sun slanted through the front windows. She was known as Queen of Adelia's and everyone adored her.

"Over here," Hedy called from where she sat in the tearoom area.

Fern walked over, admiring the small, round ice cream tables with matching chairs tucked into a quiet corner near a front window.

"What can you do me for?" Hedy laughed at the old joke, then sipped from a delicate, floral china cup.

"I thought you might need some last-minute help, but if you're drinking tea, you must have everything under control."

"Don't let it fool you. You know as well as I do it's an illusion that I project to keep folks around me on their toes."

"Like cowboy firefighters?"

"You know it."

"I suppose you'll be at the dunking later."

"Wouldn't miss it." Hedy chuckled as she set her cup on its matching saucer, then cocked her head to one side. "You haven't heard any more from your stalker, have you?"

"Please don't call him *my* stalker. But no, not a peep or rose."

"Good. We can all hope he's gone, but let's still stay alert."

"I will." She moved closer, lowering her voice. "Listen, do you know much about the legends of Sure-Shot?"

"I didn't know they had any except the one about Little Miss Sure Shot herself, Annie Oakley."

"Maybe you heard about a one-room schoolhouse?"

"Schoolhouse? No, I can't say I've heard it. Why? Did Craig mention it?"

"Yeah. I just thought maybe you—"

"Not me, but it could be an interesting tale." Hedy appeared thoughtful. "You need to talk with one of the old codgers. Not Wildcat Jack. He's still a spring chicken."

"Can you recommend someone?"

Hedy tapped the edge of her cup with a fingernail. "Sure-Shot? Let's see. It'd be a horse rancher. You might try Arn of the Crazy Eight. If anybody knows a wild legend, it'll be him. The trick will be getting him to tell, but you might try to track him down after Wild West Days."

"Thanks." Fern stepped back. "Guess I'd best get on my way. I want to check out the dunk booth."

"I'll see you there later. My help will arrive soon."

"Great. Good luck with your day."

"Thanks for the wishes, but my luck is always good due to the major mojo of Rosie, the Queen of Adelia's."

"I'm with you on that one. Nothing's better than the luck of a cat."

"You know it."

"See you later."

She stopped a moment to admire Rosie, who raised her head and gave Fern a slit-eyed, sleepy look. She stroked Rosie's head for luck, then stepped back outside. She immediately noticed the day was already heating up. It was promising to be a scorcher. The cowboy firefighters were probably going to be thrilled to get a dunking in cool water.

She paused to check her surroundings, particularly for Simon, saw nothing suspicious, and walked past folks gathering on the boardwalk. She admired a pair of red cowgirl boots in Gene's Boot Hospital, which had been popular with cowboys since the cattle-drive days when they'd order their handmade boots on their way to Kansas and pick them up on the way back, after they had money in their pockets. They'd also spend some of that hard-earned cash in the Lone Star Saloon and other places that catered to them before they headed back down to South Texas.

At the end of the row of businesses rose the beautiful Wildcat Hotel with a second-floor balcony enclosed with a stone balustrade supported by five columns wrapped in red, white, and blue ribbons. Folks would have checked in the night before to get an early start on Wild West Days. She saw several couples sharing breakfast at white-linen-covered tables on their balconies. She hoped they enjoyed their stay in Wildcat Bluff.

And that's when she spotted the dunk booth. It'd been positioned at one end of the vendors, in a prime spot, with plenty of space around it. She wasn't sure if the location was to keep spectators from getting wet if water managed to splash out or to simply leave more standing room for an audience. In either case, it was sure to garner plenty of attention.

Sydney had chosen well when she rented the booth. Firefighters would sit atop a small seat above a round blue plastic enclosure with a clear section in front, to reveal the water inside the oversized tub about four feet high. A firefighter would be caged in by silver-colored metal vertical bars that rose almost five feet high above the oversized tub. To the right was what looked like an orange plastic shower curtain stretched on all sides to a frame a big white circle in the middle of a large, blue splash design. Red balls were set in a bucket in front of the shower curtain, all ready to be thrown at the white circle that would release the catch holding up the seat above the water and dunk the firefighters.

She walked around to the back of the tank to see how it functioned and saw several steps leading to the water. She walked up the stairs, glancing around from the elevated height to get a better view of the street of vendors.

Everything looked all set for fun. Folks were already beginning to mingle and walk from booth to booth, checking out food and wares. They were probably getting out ahead of the heat so they could go back to their hotel rooms in midafternoon, before they came back out for the night's activities. She figured that was a good idea.

As she stood there, she felt something hit the back of her legs. Puzzled, she turned and looked down. A single white rose lay on the ground behind the dunk booth. She felt chilled and horrified. She glanced up and saw a tall man wearing a cowboy hat pulled low disappear around the side of the hotel. Simon? If it was, he was back and bolder than ever.

She froze, not knowing whether to get down or stay there. Had that been Simon? Was he nearby, just waiting for her to move and become more vulnerable? She'd thought she'd be perfectly safe with so many people milling about. Now she wished she'd called for a deputy to escort her.

She needed to contact Sheriff Calhoun right away. He'd be somewhere in the area, but no telling how long before he could get to her. Until then, she thought she was safer staying exactly where she was because at least she was on higher ground, with a better view all around her.

She pulled out her phone to call the sheriff, but before she hit his speed dial number, she heard the jingle of bridles and clip-clop of hooves. And there, much to her relief and happiness, appeared Sheriff Calhoun at the head of his mounted patrol.

Thanks to the Queen of Adelia's Delights, she'd just gotten lucky.

Chapter 31

FERN CAUGHT HER BREATH AT THE SIGHT OF THE Wildcat Bluff Mounted Patrol—six men and women in matching navy blue uniforms with gold badges, buttons, and insignia on their jackets and the WBMP logo in the center of their cowboy hats, on their right shoulders, and on the right-back-side of their navy horse blankets. They were magnificent. Nothing said *power* like a cowboy or cowgirl on horseback. They rode strong and straight and tall with beautiful mounts in a variety of colors beneath them. They often led parades carrying the Texas Lone Star flag and the Wildcat Bluff County flag. She couldn't have been gladder to see them.

She motioned to Sheriff Calhoun and caught his attention. He left the formation and rode over to her with a concerned expression on his face.

"Fern, what are you doing up there?" he asked.

"There's been another incident."

"What!"

"I was just up here checking out the dunk tank when something hit the back of my legs. If you'll look, there's a white rose on the ground behind me."

"So he's here and he wants you to know it."

"I guess so."

"Did you see him?" Sheriff Calhoun asked.

"My back was to him, but when I looked around, there

was a man about his size wearing a beige cowboy hat disappearing around the side of the hotel."

"Not much to go on."

"No. Wish I had more information to help."

"Were you alone?"

"Yes. Craig's out at Steele Trap Ranch. I figured I'd be okay here in the open."

"You are okay. We're here. I'll send a couple of deputies to check behind the hotel, but I bet he's long gone."

"Me too."

"We'll also pick up the rose and put it in an evidence bag, but so far he's left no traces on the flowers or anywhere else."

"He seems to know what he's doing."

"Could be he's done it before."

"Craig mentioned that early on, but I hate to believe it."

"We won't draw any conclusions, but anything is possible. This guy is serious, and that means he's dangerous."

"He's certainly dangerously disturbed."

"Wait here till we secure the evidence." Sheriff Calhoun turned, motioned two of his deputies forward. "Stalker's been here. Check for a cowboy in a beige Stetson behind the hotel. I know that description fits fifty guys here, but give it a try."

"Good luck." Fern hoped some of Rosie's luck might rub off on the deputies as they rode away.

While she watched, another deputy bagged up the white rose, looked for any other evidence, then remounted and tucked the evidence in a pocket of his saddlebag.

"Fern, I'd feel more comfortable if you were indoors, in

a safe environment," Sheriff Calhoun said. "I know your job as cochair of Wild West Days is to be out and about so you can quickly respond to any issues that might arise."

"Yes, that is my job."

"Would you at least consider going someplace like the Lone Star Saloon, where you could field phone calls and be nearby if there was an emergency? You could stay there till Craig gets back."

"I hate to let this man limit my life."

"Understandable. We just don't know how far he's willing to go."

"What can he possibly think he's going to get out of this harassment?" She felt so frustrated by it.

"We don't know what's in his mind. It may be as simple as harassment to get your attention, or it could turn into... well, I don't want to alarm you, but there are cases of kidnapping involved in these incidents."

"Kidnapping! Do you mean like those cattle thieves snatched Fernando?"

"Yes." Sheriff Calhoun glanced toward his deputies riding back from the hotel. "But there is no way we will let that happen to you."

She shivered despite the heat. She wasn't as strong as Fernando. At two thousand pounds, he had the ability to fight his way free from his captors, and he had done it. She shivered harder, trying to figure out how she'd gotten into this fix and how to get out of it.

When the two deputies rode up, they simply shook their heads, then rejoined the rest of the patrol.

"That's that," Sheriff Calhoun said. "Nothing. We didn't expect anything, and that's exactly what we got."

"As much as I regret it, I guess I'd better go to the Lone Star and wait for Craig."

"Do you want a personal deputy assigned to you for the duration of Wild West Days? I'd be happy to do it."

"You need all the deputies to watch over our guests. I'd feel bad about taking someone away from their real job."

"You are our real job…and much more than that to us."

"Thank you." She finally stepped down from the dunk booth and looked up at the sheriff. "I'm sorry for the extra trouble."

"No. I'm sorry for *your* trouble. But don't worry. We'll keep you safe."

She nodded, but she didn't quite believe it anymore, not since the stalker had been close enough to touch her.

"Stay on the boardwalk, and I'll have a deputy follow you. Nobody is getting away from a fast horse."

She nodded in agreement. "That's surely the truth."

And so she turned back, feeling like a different person as she trudged past one store after another, intensely aware of the mounted patrol following her…and even more aware that there was a stalker somewhere in the crowd watching her. How one man could cast such a pall over such a fun event amazed her. She took a deep breath. What would MG do? She'd mentioned groupies in her past. She'd obviously handled them with her usual aplomb, but this was more—much more—than adoration. This guy had burned down Craig's barn and could've killed people and animals. He meant business.

She might take chances with herself, but she'd never take chances with others. There were simply too many vulnerable people everywhere around her, and that was probably precisely why he picked this day to reappear. She had no choice but to wait for Craig to return. In the meantime, she'd make the best of a bad situation and enjoy the saloon.

She waved goodbye to the officer, then pushed open the batwing doors of the Lone Star and felt as if she'd stepped back in time. Unlike Wildcat Hall, this establishment had been a fancy, popular saloon with drinking and gambling during its heyday, and the large room still retained much of the original decor and ambiance to prove it.

Crystal chandeliers hung from the high ceiling to illuminate red-flocked wallpaper with gold fleurs-de-lis on the walls and cherubs flinging arrows from bows on the ceiling. An immense mahogany bar of intricate design dominated the length of one wall. In front of it was a long brass rail for boot soles and a row of spittoons for tobacco. Behind the bar rose a huge sideboard with rows of upside-down glasses and a wide expanse of gold-flecked mirror. To each side hung an oil painting in a massive gilt frame of dusty cowboys driving longhorn cattle.

Two bartenders with handlebar mustaches and long hair, wearing white shirts, stood behind the bar ready to serve cold drinks, wine, beer, and water, unlike the old days when it would have been straight-up liquor. They also served ice cream cones, sundaes, malts, and oversize cookies for those with a sweet tooth and individually packaged nut and pretzel mixes for folks with a different taste. Faro and poker tables had been converted to regular tables with barrel chairs that hugged the walls to leave room for dancers in the center of the room.

Near the dance floor, an upright player piano tinkled out music that also evoked the era. She knew the owner had updated the vintage piano to run on electricity, because originally someone had to pump the large pedals with their feet to activate the mechanisms that created music. If the bellows inside weren't engaged, the instrument could be played using the keys like a normal piano.

She liked this place, particularly since the air-conditioning felt really good after the heat outside. People already sat at tables drinking cold drinks and eating ice cream with a few colorful packages purchased from vendors setting out on tabletops. Some folks even wore the popular Wild West Days caps, adding more color and interest to the saloon. Other than the rose incident, she'd say everything was moving along just fine. And she was happy to see it.

For now, she might as well take a break and catch her breath while she had the chance. She wanted to call Craig, but she really didn't want to update him on the stalker, because he'd drop everything and be there as quick as he could make it. He needed to finish up at Steele Trap, so he could get the situation with Fernando settled to everyone's satisfaction.

She didn't see anyone she knew in the saloon, which wasn't too surprising since she was just back in town and hadn't been in here much except to work with Hal Holston, the owner, about lining up musicians and deciding on numbers for Craig and his band, as well as what she'd sing that evening. Hal was probably in a storeroom, and she didn't want to disturb him when she really didn't need anything.

She ordered a bottle of water at the bar, then walked over to the player piano, imagining what it must have been like over a hundred years ago for a pianist to be sitting there pounding out waltz after waltz as loud as he could make it for the dancers on the floor. After months on a dirty, dusty trail drive, cowboys were eager to spend their wages on hot food and hotter baths. They'd arrive at the saloon with slicked-back hair and large mustaches to squire sweet-smelling young ladies wearing ruffled white pinafores over waists and skirts of bright colors.

She looked up at a magnificent staircase with a brass railing and burgundy carpet that swept in a wide arch upstairs, then down at a raised dais that held several green floral tapestry chairs. That was where they'd play this evening. A microphone and sound system were already in place, since the Lone Star normally had live music on weekends. It was a lovely setting and she'd enjoy being there.

For now, she just sat down in one of the empty chairs, set her purse on the dais, and opened her bottle of cold water. She looked out over the saloon and past the batwing doors to the bright sunshine, listening to the cacophony of voices outside. She'd call Craig in a bit and let him know to find her there. In the meantime, she thought about the numbers they'd perform that evening. She thought she might substitute a Dolly Parton for a Willie Nelson, but on the other hand...

Sunlight was blocked by a tall, broad-shouldered figure who thrust open both doors at once and walked into the saloon. With narrowed eyes, he looked around, obviously searching for one person and one person only. He could easily have passed for an old-time gunslinger or maybe a sheriff, hunting for somebody.

She felt her breath catch in her throat. She knew that form only too well. Craig had found her before she had a chance to alert him. Somebody, maybe the sheriff, had called him and explained the stalker situation. He didn't look happy. In fact, he looked downright mad. She sat up a little straighter, readying an explanation.

When he saw her, he stalked straight through the saloon, boots beating an angry staccato as he narrowed the gap between them.

"Why didn't you let me know?" He spoke in a voice still rough from smoke inhalation as he came to a stop in front of her.

"Sheriff Calhoun?"

"Right. Do you really think it's okay not to let me know when you're in danger?"

"I didn't want to bother you."

"Are we back to the beginning?"

"Beginning?"

"Where I'm just some guy in the band. You're the star."

"How can you say that?" She stood up, feeling shocked at where he was going with his anger.

"You didn't text. You didn't call." He leaned in closer, hands on his hips. "You just came in here where it's cool, got a bottle of water, and sat down to drink it. No thought about how worried I'd be if I knew or if I found out. In what world is that okay?"

"Well, when you put in that way, I guess—"

"Fern, we either have some kind of a relationship here or we don't. If we do, you let me know when you're in trouble, and I do the same with you. That is not something that should need to be spelled out."

She didn't know what to say. She didn't think her behavior had been that out of line. She was safe. Nothing had happened to her. Nothing had burned down. And then it hit her. He was terrified for her…and it came out as anger.

"Tell me," he said.

She set down her bottle of water, stepped in close to him, and put her arms around his neck, hugging him hard.

He resisted at first, then he grabbed her and held her so close she could hardly breathe. Finally, he eased up and looked down at her.

"I apologize. I should have called you right away. I just didn't want to worry you or interrupt you with Fernando."

He took a deep breath, nodding as he swallowed hard. "We're either in this together or we aren't. I can't go halfway with you."

She reached up and stroked his cheek, feeling such an outpouring of love that it took her breath away. "Together... always together."

Chapter 32

AFTER LUNCH AT THE CHUCKWAGON CAFÉ, CRAIG walked Fern to Old Town Park in time to hear the Red River Wranglers. He kept an eye out for the stalker, but with the big crowd filling Main Street and folks in the park listening to a wide range of local musicians, the guy could easily blend in with everybody else. Craig was still steaming that the stalker had gotten so close to Fern. He shouldn't have left her alone, knowing the dangerous situation, but he hadn't planned to be gone long, and he'd figured she'd be safe in town with a deputy watching over her. Not true. He'd been as mad at himself as he'd been with her when he'd heard the news. Now he wouldn't let her be alone until the stalker was caught. And that better be soon.

He stopped with her in the back of the crowd, feeling good about the success of the pocket park that now brought such happiness to performers as well as listeners. They'd made a good decision on use of the park, and he was glad they'd been able to facilitate its transformation.

He felt cooler here and with good reason. They stood on soft, moist grass instead of hard, reflective cement. It meant there was probably only a reduction of temperature from mid-nineties to low nineties, but that factor still helped a lot. He hoped they might hit high eighties after dark. That'd really feel cool, so he was looking forward to it.

He smiled in pleasure as Renegade stepped up to the

mic and launched into an oldie but goodie from way back in the thirties, "Under the Double Eagle" from Bill Boyd, a native Texan and one of the legends of western swing who went on to become a hero of the silver screen. Craig was glad to hear a young band paying tribute to the originators of music that had endured through so many generations. He always included a variety of standard favorites, as well as original material, too, when he performed at Wildcat Hall.

Soon, folks started clapping and singing to other down-home songs, mostly written by the Texas and Oklahoma natives who originally created western swing, as they joined together in a traditional type of community sharing of culture and heritage that was so valued in country settings.

Fern leaned close. "They're good, aren't they?"

"Yeah. And they'll get better from here on out."

"True. I'm glad they have local venues to showcase their talent and gain experience."

He squeezed her hand. "We've already made a good start on our goal of supporting other musicians, haven't we?"

"Yes. This is a wonderful start."

After several more popular songs led to more sing-alongs, he checked his watch and groaned at the time. It was now or never. If he didn't go to the cowboy firefighter dunk, he'd never hear the last of it. He just hoped he wasn't the only one to show up for the event, or he'd be sending out hunting parties for the other guys.

"It's about time, isn't it?" Fern checked her phone, then slid it back into her purse.

"Yep."

She glanced at him. "Are the others all wearing Wildcat Bluff Fire-Rescue T-shirts and Wranglers, too?"

"Sydney insisted we dress alike to promote the fire station."

"Good idea."

"She thinks so." He didn't say what he thought about dressing like all the other cowboys, because it was better to just keep that to himself or risk the wrath of Sydney. Nobody wanted get in hot water with her, particularly when she was fund-raising.

He held Fern's hand, swinging their arms together as they walked along the boardwalk, weaving in and out of the crowds that thronged every available space. From the look of things, this had to be the biggest and best ever Wild West Days. He was proud of that fact. He and Fern had worked hard to bring the event to this point.

Still, he wondered just how much Fernando had to do with the increased interest, since he was so popular. His fans wouldn't be disappointed because Slade had come up with something to use so the big bull could be featured tomorrow. He knew Slade and his family would never endanger Fernando, so Craig was satisfied all would work out for the best. For now, he just needed to focus on the next item on the list of events.

"Sydney picked a good dunk booth." Fern pointed ahead at the contraption that was already drawing a crowd.

He groaned at the sight, squeezing her fingers even as he wanted to disappear back into the crowd. "Wish me luck."

"At least you'll get cooled off."

"Good point."

"Craig! You finally made it," Sydney called, grinning when she saw him. "Get in line for the dunking. This is going to be huge."

"Fern, you'll stay with Hedy or MG or another friend while I'm involved with the dunking, won't you?" Craig didn't want to leave her, but duty called and he needed to answer now.

"Yes. I'll be careful."

"I just don't want you to be alone."

"I'll stay safe."

"Good." He gave her a quick kiss on the cheek, walked over to the end of the line of cowboy firefighters, and stopped behind Slade.

"Glad you made it." Slade rolled his broad shoulders as if preparing for rodeo. "I thought you might have used that cochair thing to get out of your sworn duty to your firefighter brethren."

"I believe I need say only two words to explain my presence, and those two words are Sydney Steele."

"I hear you."

"Don't you have any control over your sister?"

"Not so you'd notice."

"I figure about the only guy she'll listen to is Dune Barrett."

"And he's in line just like us, so what does that tell you?"

"That Sydney's a force to be reckoned with."

"Yep. And my niece Storm is coming up fast in the same mold."

Craig caught Slade's eye, and they both grinned proudly at the thought of Sydney and Storm.

And still he didn't want to be here any more than the other firefighters in line did, but they all knew their duty and were doing it to the best of their ability, as always. He nodded to his friends, who looked about as morose as he felt, particularly when Eden and Wildcat Jack showed up with Nathan to livestream on KWCB, the Den. And that was in addition to the photo op for the calendar. At least there didn't appear to be a makeup chair and cosmetologist waiting to powder their noses or some such, but he was keeping an eye out just in case.

Hedy sat in her wheelchair behind a table, selling three ball tosses to a line of women that trailed out of sight. Morning Glory was bustling around in flowing skirt and jangling necklaces, making sure there was no cutting in line. Fern joined Hedy at the table to help sell tickets, laughing and talking with her.

"Folks, step right up," Morning Glory called to the crowd. "This is your one and only opportunity to dunk a cowboy firefighter in water…and see if he looks as good wet as he does dry."

Fern and Hedy laughed at her words, rolling their eyes at the cowboy firefighters who were the objects of so much attention.

Craig felt Slade bump his arm, so he glanced at his friend, who was shaking his head as if the situation was getting worse by the moment. And he was right. Nathan had begun livestreaming Morning Glory and broadcasting to the world, catching the long line of eager women as Eden and Wildcat Jack began their clever commentary.

"We're coming to you live from Wild West Days in Wildcat Bluff in the Lone Star State of Texas, where it's hot enough to fry eggs on the road." Wildcat Jack tipped his cowboy hat as he gave his trademark twinkle-eyed, white-toothed grin for the camera. "And, folks, that's plenty hot."

"So true," Eden said in a serious, professional tone as

counterpoint to Jack's homey style. "It is in the nineties here, so that is plenty hot. And yet, all twelve of these big, strong, dedicated volunteer cowboy firefighters are about to get cooled off in a big way."

"Big way is right," Wildcat Jack replied, winking at the camera.

"We're here today to watch these firefighters get dunked for the benefit of Wildcat Bluff Fire-Rescue," Eden continued in a confidential tone. "The fire station is completely funded by donations and charity events. Our firefighters are very generous with their time and talent…and are also very brave. They protect our county day in and day out every month of every year." She turned, pointed at the dunking booth, and then continued to gesture down the line of firefighters.

"Step right up, folks," Morning Glory called again, cutting in. "This is your lucky day. Pick the cowboy firefighter of your dreams… I mean, select your choice…and dunk him to your heart's content."

Slade turned toward Craig. "That sounds like we're going to have to get up there and be dunked more than once."

"You think? You might be right. There are only twelve of us. How many women do you estimate are in line?"

"I'm afraid to count. I'm pretty much even afraid to look," Slade said with a grin. "Give me a fire to fight any day over this."

"Me, too."

"What if those cowgirls go back to the end of the line and start over after dunking us once?"

Craig groaned, braving a quick glance at the growing

line. "Do you think Sydney will limit the tosses to three balls per woman?"

"We're talking Sydney on a fire station fund-raising mission. What do you think?"

"I think we might be here all weekend."

Slade groaned this time. "I think there's a time limit, or at least I hope there is a limit, like maybe an hour."

"An hour could feel like eternity."

"What if it's more than an hour?"

"Don't even go there." Craig was wishing he were someplace else, but he reminded himself that it was a good deed for charity. Maybe next time he could just write a check... like Sydney would let him get away with something so simple.

As Craig watched, money started flowing and balls started being tossed and firefighters started falling into water while Eden and Wildcat Jack told their audience how much fun the cowboys were having as they fell into the water and got drenched.

By the time Craig climbed up the steps and sat down on the seat and waited to be dunked, he couldn't tell if the line had shortened one bit. He was surprised when Fern stepped up with three balls, smiling mischievously at him. He just nodded at her, letting her know that he'd remember this next time they were around water and then it'd be her turn to get wet all over. He didn't mind that idea at all, and an image of Fern in a wet T-shirt hugging all her curves distracted him from his present situation.

She grinned at his expression and threw her first ball. It missed the white button needed to trip the lever that'd dunk him.

He shook his head, letting her know what he thought of her lousy throwing ability.

She lost her grin on the second throw because it missed, too.

He couldn't keep from chuckling, because at this rate, she was going to lose out to another woman who would be the first to dunk him. But he lost his humor when her third ball hit home...and he splashed down into the water. It was warm from the sun, and that was a big disappointment. He climbed up and out of the tank, dripping water all the way, then returned to the end of the line.

"Guess that wasn't so bad after all," Slade said, doing his own fair share of dripping.

"Yeah. Could've been worse. Too bad the water's warm."

"Makes it hard to cool off." Slade glanced back at him, chuckling. "That Fern couldn't resist dunking you, could she?"

"She knows payback's coming."

"Maybe something in your shower?"

"I could get into that."

"Yeah," Slade said, "Ivy probably won't want to be outdone by her sister, so she may show up anytime to dunk me."

"If she didn't ask Fern to do it."

"There's always that. Once those two sisters gang up on us, we might as well throw in the towel."

"I think we already did that," Craig said with a chuckle.

Slade laughed, nodding in agreement. "And we wouldn't have it any other way, would we?"

"Not on your life."

Craig wasn't even surprised that when they were all thoroughly wet and hot and disheveled, the photo shoot began in earnest. Nathan had a new camera, and he had them pose in the water, out of the water, and beside the water. He posed them in a group, trying to get grins out of them, but finally he gave up and settled for stoic expressions that Sydney insisted were perfect machismo for the calendar.

As Craig waited with the other firefighters for Nathan to finish, Sydney hurried over to check the photos. She swiped forward on Nathan's camera as she furrowed her brows in concentration.

"What do you think?" Nathan asked, looking over her shoulder.

"Good. Thanks. But I'd also like to see that long line of women as a backdrop in a series of shots. Will that work for you?" She handed back the camera.

"Sure. We can try. I don't see why not. It'll be interesting."

Craig waited to one side as Nathan posed and clicked, posed and clicked the cowboy firefighters with the long line of women in the background. He felt a line of sweat dripping down his back as he stood in the sun. Soon he decided another dunk in the water wouldn't be a bad idea at all.

Fern walked over to him. "How are you holding up? You're not getting too hot, are you?"

"I'm hot. Everybody's hot. And the water is not cold."

She grinned at him. "Did you expect us to ice it down for you?"

"That's a good idea."

She just laughed, shaking her head.

"Anyway, it's been downhill since that throw of yours got me."

She smiled mischievously while bumping him with her shoulder. "I just wanted to make sure I was your first."

"You couldn't be anything else but my first...always."

She turned serious. "You're always my first, too."

"Hey," Sydney called. "Craig, you're holding up Nathan."

Craig stayed focused on Fern. "I'm thinking you might get dunked in the shower at home."

"As long as you're doing the dunking, I'm all in."

"It'll definitely be me."

"Craig," Sydney called again. "One more shot."

He answered her by stepping forward, but not without giving a backward glance at Fern to let her know he'd be thinking about her—and her alone—while he was in the dunking booth.

Chapter 33

THAT EVENING, FERN SAT IN A COMFORTABLE CHAIR ON the music dais at the Lone Star Saloon. She cradled her beloved guitar in her hands, taking comfort in the familiarity that always afforded her pleasure no matter what else was going on in her life. And at present, there was plenty happening to give her concern and make her feel uneasy.

No one had seen or heard from the stalker since the white rose at the dunk tank incident earlier in the day, and she was grateful for it. Still, the idea that he was out there left those who knew about him on edge, even in the midst of providing so much fun and entertainment. The sheriff and his deputies in particular were on high alert, but until Simon took another overt action and they caught him in the act, there was little they could do.

And yet, here in the saloon, she was able to focus on what she knew best, what she enjoyed most, and what she could do for others. Maybe music didn't make the world go 'round, but it did hers…and it definitely should be high on everyone's list.

Another thing that made her feel better was the fact that she had a good view of the batwing doors where everyone entered or left the saloon. If Simon was stalking her tonight, he'd come here to see her sing. Maybe he'd toss roses at her feet again…and if he did, the sheriff's deputy who stood by the bar watching everything and everyone could nab him.

She didn't expect that to happen because Simon had been too clever to get caught thus far. White roses were a give-away for him now, so surely he wouldn't employ them any-more. He'd wait to catch her alone, but he wouldn't ever get that chance again.

And so she relaxed a little bit more as she sat there with Craig and his band, waiting for their gig to start and listen-ing to the player piano. Folks stood several deep at the bar as they ordered drinks and snacks, while others sat at tables and even more stood chatting here and there in groups on the dance floor. They were dressed mostly in cowboy and cowgirl gear—boots, jeans, T-shirts or western shirts—but hats were left on tables or on hat racks or in pickups because it was the height of rudeness and socially unacceptable to wear a hat on the dance floor.

She glanced over at Craig where he sat with one leg crossed over the other and his guitar turned so the strings were against his knee to make sure they didn't accidentally make a sound if he brushed against them. He caught her looking at him and turned to smile at her. Comfortable. Happy. Love. She could list the words forever that expressed her feelings at the moment, but she could express them even better with music, and that was coming up soon.

"Are you okay?" He leaned toward her as he kept his voice low.

"Yes. I feel safe…and content here."

"Great. It's a good gig."

She smiled, tapping her toe to the piano tune. "But it's still not as good as our Wildcat Hall."

"True. But they were built to appeal to different folks at different time in different ways."

"What do you mean?"

He glanced up at the ceiling chandeliers. "Look at all the gilt and glamour here compared to our basic utilitarian dance hall."

"You're right. Wildcat Hall is mostly wood and rustic, hand-carved wood—even the furniture."

"The Hall appealed to settled farmers and ranchers as a gathering place for their families and cowboys driving cattle north or stopping on their way south to return to their ranches."

"And it's out of town on the road."

"Right. Wildcat Bluff was a pretty fancy town for its day and time. Money came through here or stayed here, so they built with brick and stone to survive the ages."

"That meant there was more cash to build a beautiful saloon."

"And it appealed to a different clientele, with drinking, gambling, and I'd guess a little extra activity upstairs with the fancy ladies."

"This place really was very different than our Hall, wasn't it?" she said thoughtfully as she looked at the splendor of the elegant staircase leading to the second floor.

"Yeah. And yet they both appealed, then and now, to lonely people wanting and needing companionship with food and drink."

"What about music?"

"And dance?"

"That's how folks come together, tossing aside their cares and troubles, even their differences." He reached over and squeezed her fingers. "Maybe we can snag a dance together later."

"I'd like that." The warmth of his hand matched the warmth in his eyes as they shared a moment of love between them.

When she looked back at the batwing doors, Bert was pushing Hedy's wheelchair inside, then bent down to whisper in her ear. She glanced up at him, smiling…and love arced between them like a zinging string of pink hearts. Fern recognized that look because it mirrored what she shared with Craig.

Morning Glory sashayed in behind them with long, crimson skirt swinging and heart necklaces swaying as she moved to the beat of a song in her own head. Right behind her came Ivy and Slade, both dressed in boots, jeans, and Wild West Days T-shirts. They all appeared happy and ready to tap a toe or swing out on the dance floor.

Fern was so glad to see this special group of people ready to enjoy the music that she, Craig, and the band would provide them. She was particularly pleased to see how happy her sister was with Slade, the love of her life. She'd felt guilty about dumping Wildcat Hall in Ivy's lap when she'd taken off for the cruise gigs, but now she knew it was the best thing she could have done for her sister. Otherwise, she'd never have met Slade and become part of his wonderful family.

She lifted a hand to acknowledge the group as the men split off to go to the bar while the women continued on toward the music dais.

"Fern, Craig, I can't tell you how proud we are of the way you took over Wild West Days and pulled off the biggest attendance we've ever had here." Morning Glory held out her arms dramatically to her sides.

"Yes, everyone is thrilled that you put us on the map big-time," Hedy said, rolling a little closer.

Ivy chuckled, shaking her head. "Better not let Storm hear you say that."

"Why not?" Fern asked.

"Fernando!" Ivy laughed harder. "Storm is absolutely convinced attendance is up because most everyone is here to see him tomorrow."

"She might not be far off," Craig said. "When I was at Steele Trap this morning, she showed me glossy one-sheets of Fernando looking handsome in his pasture."

"What's she going to do with them?" Fern asked.

Hedy chuckled, glancing from one to the other. "Sell them, of course. They're signed and everything."

"You're funning me," Fern said. "Fernando is a bull. He can't sign anything."

"Our Storm is turning out to be quite the entrepreneur." Morning Glory jingled her necklaces. "How about selling a photo that includes a hoofprint in one corner?"

"Well, okay. I agree," Fern said with a touch of humor in her voice. "Craig and I absolutely can't compete with Fernando."

"Right," Craig added. "We might as give all the credit to him."

"Might as well." Hedy chuckled as she glanced at Morning Glory. "Pretty quick, Storm will want to open a store on Main Street dedicated to all things Fernando."

"Don't be surprised if she approaches us to set aside a display case in our stores for Fernando wares," Morning Glory said. "Can't you imagine photos of Fernando on coasters, glasses, notepads, mouse pads…the list is endless."

Hedy laughed at the idea. "In my store, she'll probably want to sell items like Fernando Blackberry Jam, Fernando Pickle Relish, Fernando Clover Honey."

Fern joined the general laughter, then they all abruptly stopped and looked at each other as if the idea had taken on a life of its own.

"Storm and Fernando will probably have the last laugh," Morning Glory said. "She's my kind of girl."

"She's all our kind of girl," Hedy added as she glanced at Ivy. "Aren't you glad you're marrying into the Steele family?"

"Oh yes...if I can keep up with them," she said with a grin as Slade walked up carrying two glasses of wine.

"What about the Steele family?" Slade asked, handing a glass to Ivy. "If it's bad news, I don't want to hear it."

"It's Storm and her Fernando one-sheets." Hedy smiled up at Bert as he handed her a bottle of water.

"Oh, that." Slade just shook his head. "She discussed it all with Fernando and let him make the final photo selection."

"How did he indicate his choice?" Morning Glory asked, chuckling. "Hoof? Tongue? Moo?"

"MG, stop right there," Hedy said, a big grin on her face. "That's too funny and we must respect Storm's sensibilities."

"Hah!" Slade glanced at the group. "She'd just take you seriously and explain exactly how he communicates with her."

"Long-winded?" Craig asked.

"Another language entirely...or maybe she's an animal whisperer," Slade said. "Anyway, she's always been good with animals."

"That's a Steele family trait, isn't it?" Ivy said, tucking a hand in the crook of Slade's arm. "That and cooking."

"We're good at whatever you want us to be good at."

She chuckled as she gave him an adoring look.

Fern watched them, feeling happier than ever that she'd been responsible for bringing them together. When she glanced up, she saw Mac dressed liked an old-time gambler in black frock coat, blue satin vest, white shirt, gray pinstripe trousers, and black cowboy boots with high shine. He walked as if a dance floor was his natural element.

She was surprised to see him already attired in period costume, since most folks were saving their special clothes for Saturday afternoon's shoot-out. But she couldn't fault him—he looked as if he'd been born to wear them.

As if Mac were her magnetic north, Morning Glory slowly turned toward him with that same physical grace. He devoured her with his eyes as he drew closer and closer until they were only inches apart.

"Lorraine." He held out his hand. "Will you honor me with a dance?"

She shook her head, ignoring his hand. "No music."

"Schedule says the band is about to play."

"It's been too long."

"Never."

"Always."

He glanced at Fern. "I doubt you normally take requests, but would you do it for Lorraine…uh, Morning Glory?"

Fern glanced at Craig, who nodded in agreement. She stood up, cradling her guitar. "We'll be happy to play anything we know or can figure out."

"Thank you." Mac smiled at Morning Glory.

"No, Mac, please. It'll break my heart," Morning Glory said in a pain-filled voice.

"'Yes, Mac, please,' you should say." Mac kept smiling at her. "Maybe it'll mend your heart."

"There's nothing wrong with my heart."

"Prove it." Mac offered his hand again. "Dance with me."

Morning Glory shook her head again, stepping back from him.

Mac glanced at Fern. "Your choice of song. Jitterbug. Waltz."

Fern gave Mac a quick nod, then glanced at Craig to see if he was in agreement.

Craig grinned at her before he looked at his band. They appeared totally up for the challenge. He turned off the player piano.

When Craig stood up, putting his guitar strap over his shoulder, she knew it was time to give everyone a very special night. They'd cover Mac's choices, then move on to classic western swing that would fill the dance floor with revelers.

As the band launched Bill Haley & His Comets fast-paced "Rock Around the Clock" from the fifties and dancers started doing a spirited jitterbug, Fern watched Morning Glory hesitantly place her hand in Mac's open palm. He whirled her into his body, then twirled her back out again. She responded with a snap of her fingers, arching her back, rotating her hips, throwing back her head as he led them into the center of the dance floor as everyone else moved back to make room for what could only be…professional dancers.

Fern didn't have to hear the gasp from her friends as they watched in open-mouthed wonder as MG and Mac owned the dance floor, twirling, rotating, moving their bodies together as if they were a single, beautiful entity. He finally lifted MG up high and then slowly let her down the front of his body until she slid between his feet, then he drew her back up just as the music died away.

Craig led the band into a waltz, a slow instrumental version of Patsy Cline's romantic hit "Always," that sent Morning Glory into Mac's arms. They twined together almost as if they were one body, instead of two separate ones. Soon they whirled and dipped and spun around and around across the dance floor in sophisticated elegance that appeared as effortless as a swan gliding across a lake.

Fern was mesmerized by the sight. She realized she was seeing what would have been the usual dance in the Lone Star Saloon back in its heyday, so it looked perfectly right for Mac in his gambler attire and Morning Glory in her flowing skirts to waltz under the crystal chandeliers. They were breathtaking, and she knew everyone in the room felt the same way as they watched poetry in motion.

As she and the band let the last strains of the waltz fade away, she knew the past had caught up with the present, not only in the saloon but with Mac and MG as he dipped her low across his arm and placed a soft kiss on her lips.

Chapter 34

LATE THE NEXT AFTERNOON, ABOUT THE TIME IT STARTED to cool down, Craig stood on the boardwalk with Fern. He looked out over the noisy crowd on Main Street, where folks were eating, drinking, shopping, and in general having a grand time.

"We did it, didn't we?" Fern gave a big sigh of relief.

"So far, so good."

"I know what you're thinking. He could be out there lurking in the crowds, just waiting to strike again."

"No. I think he's smarter than that."

"What are you thinking then?" Fern asked.

"We're coming up to the biggest event of Wild West Days, and I don't want anything to go wrong."

"I don't see how it could be anything except successful. The shoot-out between the Hellions and the Ruffians is planned down to the last blank shot in front of the Lone Star Saloon."

"Yeah. But what about Fernando?"

"What does he have to do with it?"

"Let's take a walk down to Old Town Park."

She looked up at him with narrowed eyes. "This sounds like something Storm cooked up. What's going on?"

"Let's go." He chuckled as he clasped her hand and started down the boardwalk. "Let's just say nobody denies that girl anything any more than they would Granny, Sydney, Hedy, or Morning Glory."

Fern tossed him a skeptical look. "When do I get on that glorified list of 'Women Who Must Be Obeyed'?"

He laughed as he squeezed her fingers. "Not sure. There's some kind of Wildcat Bluff unwritten code about it."

She laughed, too, as she walked with him. "I guess you didn't tell me the plans y'all made yesterday just in case I might object or throw a kink in that particular rope."

"I was sworn to secrecy."

"No doubt by She Who Must Be Obeyed."

"Storm wanted to surprise you and everyone else who wasn't in on her Fernando reveal. She also planned her event to coincide with the shoot-out because that's when the big media would be here and she wanted to tie into it. Also, it'd be a cooler time of the day for the bull, so he wouldn't get too hot."

"Wow. I'll tell you something."

"What?"

"If that girl's scary now, what will she be like when she's full-grown?"

Craig tugged Fern closer. "Absolutely terrifying."

She laughed, glancing up at him.

They shared a moment when they would see a little girl they'd help nurture come into her full power as a woman in the future. He loved the idea and was glad to be part of it.

"Yeah," he finally said. "It's easy to laugh now, but wait till we get to the park. Who knows what we'll see? Storm isn't one to hide Fernando's light under a bushel. She's been working with Nathan at Thingamajigs to design and print stuff."

"Wow. Just wow. This I've got to see."

And see they did. First off, the Old Town Park sign that Bert Two had so lovingly created had been covered with a poster that read FERNANDO THE WONDER BULL. To one side of the green lawn a large, white trailer had been brought in from the alley and its back door left open. A small arena had been created by linking sturdy metal gates with horizontal bars and attaching each end to the sides of the trailer to produce a secure enclosure.

In the center of the arena stood a huge, majestic Angus bull with his sleek black coat brushed to a high sheen and a bright aqua cowboy hat perched between his long, elegant ears. He calmly watched his surroundings with big, intelligent dark eyes.

"Is Fernando safe in there?" Fern asked. "I mean, can he get out?"

"He'd be safest if he was home on the ranch, but it's not unusual to display prize animals in this type of structure. And it's perfect for his fans to get selfies with him."

"I wonder what Storm will charge for the privilege?"

Craig chuckled, shaking his head. "No telling."

"I hope they know what they're doing because that enclosure doesn't look strong enough to hold a two-thousand-pound angry bull bent on getting out."

"I figure Slade and Oscar know what they're doing. Anyway, it's not likely anything could set off Fernando with Storm around to handle him."

"Okay," Fern said, although she didn't sound completely convinced of the situation as she stepped onto the gravel path that wound up to the bandstand.

Craig followed, glancing around for Storm and finding her near the bandstand.

She wore a pink T-shirt that read *Fernando the Wonder Bull* tucked into Wranglers to reveal a big rodeo buckle and rhinestone-studded belt. She wore an aqua cowgirl hat similar to Fernando's except that hers had been hand-painted with a portrait of Fernando in vivid color. She impatiently tapped the toe of one bright pink cowgirl boot. Ginger-haired and hazel-eyed, she looked perfectly put together. In sharp style contrast, her partner in crime, Oscar Leathers—ranch foreman on the Steele Trap—wore a beat-up hat, ragged jeans, and scuffed boots. Tater, his smart and loyal cow dog, wore a faded blue bandanna around his neck.

And in even sharper contrast, Jennifer Sales, a well-known and beloved news reporter with a Dallas television station, wore a simple gray suit and heels with her big hair and big smile. She leaned toward Storm in avid interest, while a videographer wearing T-shirt and jeans and carrying a video camera on his shoulder recorded the scene.

Craig exchanged a look with Fern as if to confirm their opinion of She Who Must Be Obeyed. They moved closer to hear what was going on.

"Yes, indeed." Storm gestured toward the bandstand. "Later today, Renegade and the Red River Wranglers will be playing Fernando's theme song right up there. They'll also be giving a free concert to Fernando's fans in appreciation of their loyal support…particularly during the trying time when he was desperately making his way across dangerous territory to get home by Christmas."

"He is a very brave bull, isn't he?" Jennifer said.

"You are so right. He is the bravest of all bulls…as well as the most handsome." Storm smiled at the camera. "And if you'll come this way, I'll sign one-sheets for you and your colleagues back in Dallas to show my appreciation for your continued support of Fernando."

"He is simply a fascinating story. Whenever we feature him, our ratings always shoot up."

"You are too kind." Storm glanced down shyly, as if she were almost overcome by all the attention. She walked over to the bandstand, picked up a stack of one-sheets, scribbled her name on several of them, and handed them to Jennifer.

"Thank you so much. Everyone will just love this personal touch from Fernando."

"He is very much mindful of those who follow his story."

Craig exchanged another look with Fern, acknowledging Storm's amazing transition from spunky cowgirl to savvy entrepreneur.

Storm glanced up, saw them, and smiled. She looked back at Jennifer. "Please come this way. I'd like you to meet the cochairs of Wild West Days." She led the news team forward.

Craig took a deep breath, not knowing what to expect next. He cast a sidelong look at Fernando. He bet the bull didn't know from day to day either, but he either didn't care or completed trusted Storm.

Storm gestured toward Fern and Craig. "I'm sure you've heard of our very own internationally renowned musicians Fern Bryant, vocalist, and Craig Thorne, guitarist."

"Of course, I've heard of you both." Jennifer batted her fake eyelashes in excitement. "I'm just so pleased to meet you. And you are generous to take time out of your busy lives to support your local hometown in this special way."

Craig glanced at Fern, giving her the go-ahead to lead their response, since he reasoned woman-to-woman might work best in this situation with Storm.

"Craig and I were thrilled to be asked to help out, but most of the work was done by the talented and dedicated residents of Wildcat Bluff County."

"Everything we've seen leads us to agree that this is a very talented community," Jennifer said with a smile.

"If you have time," Storm added, "I'd like to suggest you stop by Wildcat Hall, our local historic dance hall."

"That sounds interesting."

"It is. Fern and Craig are the owners, and they support local musicians, as well as other celebrities."

The reporter looked at them with even more interest. "Perhaps we could record a segment there sometime in the future."

"Anytime. We're the North Texas version of Greune Hall in the Hill Country," Fern said.

"I'm well aware of Greune Hall. Wonderful venue. I'll definitely want to see your dance hall."

"Please stop by." Craig smiled his professional smile, feeling more impressed all the time by Storm's natural promotional talent. She was turning out to be a great asset to the community.

"In that case, I'll be in touch." Jennifer returned his professional smile.

"If you have time, please take a moment to say goodbye to Fernando." Storm gestured toward the trailer.

"Oh, I wouldn't dream of leaving without a farewell to handsomest bull I've ever met." The reporter turned toward Craig and Fern. "I'm so happy to have met you both."

"We look forward to your visit to Wildcat Hall," Fern said.

Craig stood there with Fern by his side as he watched

the news team and Storm walk away, feeling kind of out-classed by an eight-year-old. At the same time, he couldn't have been more impressed by her professionalism.

"There's a new kid on the block, isn't there?" Fern whispered. "And she's terrific."

"Let's add her to the Red River Wranglers and all our other budding talent. We're building something important here."

"And we're just getting started nurturing talent."

"Guess we'd better check on our main event."

"And change clothes."

"Yep."

As he started toward the boardwalk, Sydney, Slade, and Ivy rushed up, obviously out of breath.

"What is it?" Craig looked past them to see if he could spot the trouble.

"Everything is fine," Sydney said. "We came to check on Storm."

"We didn't mean to leave her alone during her first live television interview," Slade said. "Glad you two were here."

"Oscar and Tater are with her." Craig gestured toward them. "And I guarantee she didn't need any help at all."

"She set up an amazing event," Fern said. "Did y'all know about all of this beforehand?"

"She kept getting ideas and adding to what she wanted to do till we could hardly keep up with her, particularly since we have our own stuff going on during Wild West Days." Sydney shrugged as she shook her head.

"We finally assigned Oscar and Tater to keep an eye on her," Slade said. "They won't let her get into any trouble."

Craig chuckled as he glanced around the park. "She may

not get into trouble, but what about the rest of us after she gets done?"

"I know." Slade glanced at his niece. "She's a force to be reckoned with."

"And you just encourage her." Sydney tapped her brother on the shoulder, laughing at him.

"Last thing I ever want any of us to do is break her spirit," Slade said. "Great spirit is worth its weight in gold."

"So true," Sydney agreed. "And she's got it in abundance."

"Are y'all about ready for your roles in the shoot-out?" Fern asked. "It's coming up next."

"It's my first time," Ivy said. "And I'm excited to participate."

"You're on the Ruffians team, aren't you?" Craig asked.

"Right." Ivy appeared smug. "And y'all are on the Hellions team, so may the best outlaws win."

Craig glanced at Slade. "Didn't you explain the rules to her?"

"No point. She's decided it's a real contest, so look out."

Craig laughed, shaking his head. "At this rate, who knows what will happen when our teams square off against each other?"

"It's supposed to turn out like it did at Wildcat Falls in Indian Territory back in the day," Fern said. "I researched it. The Sun Rattlers outlaw gang tried to take over the town, so there was a shoot-out in the Desperado Dance Hall that spilled out onto the street. Townsfolk won and ran off the Rattlers."

"Right," Sydney replied. "Some of our original settlers came from Wildcat Falls and brought that story with them. We celebrate their triumph every year by reenacting the shoot-out."

"Whatever happened to Wildcat Falls?" Ivy asked, glancing around the group. "Is it still there?"

"Doubt it," Slade said. "It was an outlaw town and those either turned law abiding or got burned-out."

"That's a shame." Fern looked at Craig in disappointment. "I'd like to see it."

"There was a store there named Adella's Delights. That's where Hedy got the name for her store, only she changed the spelling to Adelia's Delights to make it her own."

"I'm more intrigued all the time," Fern said. "But I guess that past is in the past, so today we'll just dress up in period costumes and play make-believe."

"That's plenty for me." Craig glanced around the group. "We don't need that kind of reality in Wildcat Bluff."

"Isn't that the truth," Slade said. "After the shoot-out, we'll basically be done and then all we need to do is get Storm and Fernando safely home."

"Will the shoot-out scare him?" Fern asked. "Maybe she should take him home first."

"No time," Slade said. "Besides, we put him at the far end of town from the noise, so he'll be okay."

"And she's not about to miss any promotional opportunities." Sydney pointed at the folks lining up in front of the park. "She's going to get a big crowd, isn't she?"

"Looks like it," Craig replied. "I'll ask Sheriff Calhoun to send a couple of deputies over to keep an eye on things."

"They should be here soon." Slade nodded down the street where two deputies were headed their way. "We already discussed the need for security. That's a valuable bull."

"And a more valuable little girl," Craig said. "We want her kept safe."

"Absolutely," Slade agreed.

"Guess we'd better get to the saloon." Craig glanced out over the park again, but all looked calm and peaceful. He hoped it went well, but he couldn't imagine it wouldn't—not with Storm in charge.

"We'll see you up there in a bit," Sydney said. "We'll check on my daughter, make sure everything's in place, and then go change our clothes and be ready to cause trouble on the mean streets of Wildcat Bluff."

"Just be ready to hear the bark of my six-shooter." Craig made an imaginary draw from his hip.

Everyone laughed at his joke as he put an arm around Fern's shoulder, and they headed down the boardwalk for the Lone Star Saloon.

Chapter 35

FERN STOOD AT THE TOP OF THE MAGNIFICENT STAIR-case of the Lone Star Saloon. She felt decidedly decadent and as if she had stepped back in time. She wore a long-sleeve gown of emerald green with a watered silk skirt, front and back drapery, and waist of grosgrain silk, all trimmed in black lace. Soft black leather gloves covered her hands. She'd put on a corset, but it wasn't tight enough to restrict her breath as the ladies used to wear them, leading to the advent of fainting couches. With her upswept hair and rouged cheeks, she represented Belle, elegant and benevolent owner of the Lone Star Saloon.

Fern looked down the wide sweep of stairs to the ballroom below, where modern women had been transformed into their ancestors with colorful waists and skirts covered by white lace pinafores with high, black button-top boots on their small feet. They stood on the edges of the dance floor, waiting to be asked to dance, or were swirled around the room by men dressed in rough clothes like plaid shirts, blue Levi's, and cowboy boots or the fancier clothes of gamblers or gentleman who wore black jackets, white shirts, brocade vests, and Hessian boots.

As Belle, she smiled as she was supposed to do at the idea that all the men on that floor paid for the privilege of holding a sweet-smelling woman close to him for the duration of a waltz. That meant she'd become a very wealthy woman because she catered to lonely men and gave jobs to young women who might otherwise be destitute. No one knew the real name of this benefactor who had helped build and protect Wildcat Bluff. She'd only ever been known as Belle, and from the upstairs oil portrait, *beautiful* was the perfect word for her.

Craig pounded away on the piano below, providing music as he would have for dancers in the past, just as he did in the present day. He looked handsome and more like a gambler than a piano player in a white shirt, green silk vest, gray trousers, and black boots.

Inside Belle's domain on this particular day, most of her clientele were either local townsfolk or part of the Ruffians, a legendary outlaw gang believed to rob from the rich to give to the poor. Whether that fact was true or not, nobody knew for sure anymore, but Fern liked the idea as much as everyone else, so she decided to believe it.

As Belle, she also carried a double-shot, ivory-handle derringer in the pocket of her skirt. Of course, it only held blanks because loaded guns weren't allowed at the reenactment. If she'd really needed to be armed, she would have preferred her own pink pistol, an ultra-concealable Glock 43 9 mm with six-round magazine. But Belle would have carried a gun just like this one, and if necessary, she would have used it to defend her dance hall darlings.

In playing the part of Belle, she was coming to admire and appreciate this strong, capable woman who had made a difference in so many people's lives. She'd also heard that Belle sang like an angel, but she could rarely be called upon to perform for others. Perhaps she'd been shy, or perhaps she didn't want to take the limelight away from her ladies in white pinafores.

In this case, Fern had been asked to sing while Craig played the piano, completing the legend for the guests sitting at tables watching the tableau unfold inside and standing behind cordoned off areas outside. When she walked down the stairs and took her place beside Craig, the drama would begin…and unfold exactly as it had played out year after year in Old Town.

Yet she hesitated, waiting for she didn't know what. Maybe she wanted to prolong this moment that would never come again. Maybe she wanted to be the spectacular Belle a little bit longer. Maybe she felt an underlying unease that, once she put the play into motion, nothing would go as planned and life might never be the same again.

And then there was that lingering memory of the one-room schoolhouse in the memorial grove. She would forever think of the small hats tossed haphazardly across the floor in front of the fireplace where they had come to rest after being so gallantly used to save lives…at least, she hoped they'd saved lives. But now was not the time to disturb sleeping ghosts, so let them rest in peace. Now was the time to reenact a powerful moment when a town fought back to save its citizens.

She took a deep breath and took her first step downward, letting her gloved hand slide down the smooth surface of the hand-carved banister that was a work of art in its own right. Beauty. All at once she understood the original Belle had loved beauty and had built a life to support it for herself and others. And with her voice, Fern would now add to that beauty. It was her gift, small as it was, to Belle's legacy in Wildcat Bluff.

And when she reached the bottom of the stairs and

stepped onto the dance floor, Craig rose from his piano bench and held out his hand to her. She felt her earlier hesitation and angst vanish in the power of his love. She quickly walked to him and took his hand.

"You look beautiful." He smiled at her with love in his eyes.

"You look handsome." She smiled back at him with the same love in her eyes.

"Are you ready?" He looked a little concerned about her. "We practiced this number. It was popular back then and it's still popular today. Your audience will love it."

"I know. I'm ready." She took another deep breath.

And she let her voice carry Stephen Foster's "Beautiful Dreamer" to the high ceiling, where the crystal chandeliers twinkled like starry light in the heavens. She felt as if her words rode a ghost wind that crossed currents of time to bring the past into the present through a ballad that had proved so beautiful and so romantic that not even time could dim is power.

As she let the last note fade away, gunfire popped loudly outside. Even though she knew it was coming, she still jumped at the sound and looked toward the batwing doors. Smoke curled up from the boardwalk outside.

Craig leaped to his feet beside Fern. Dancers scattered to the edges of the dance floor, men going for Colt .44s on their hips while women picked up any available weapon, like whiskey bottles and candlesticks.

As Hell, leader of the Hellions, Slade—big, blond, and dangerous-looking in knee-high leather boots, leather trousers, and crimson shirt—thrust open the batwing doors, six-shooter in each hand.

Ivy pushed in beside Slade, looking about as dangerous with a dagger between her teeth. She wore a man's green plaid shirt, leather vest, leather trousers, suede boots, black Stetson, and a gun belt strapped to her waist with a six-gun in each holster.

"Belle, I'm calling you out," Hell said in a deep, gruff voice. "I'm taking over Wildcat Bluff and all that gold you're hording up there in your fancy lair."

Fern glanced at Craig. She didn't think this was part of the script. They were supposed to have the shoot-out outside, not in the saloon. Did she get the wrong storyline, or did her sister decide to up the drama by bursting into the Lone Star? The knife between her teeth looked more like it came from a pirate movie than a western film.

"Everybody's watching," Craig said quietly. "I think you have to respond like Belle would've, don't you?"

"I have no idea." She rolled her eyes. Why couldn't this have been easy? She could only figure Ivy wanted to prolong her role as an infamous outlaw. What had happened to her city-loving sister?

Ivy jerked the knife out of her mouth and made savage cutting motions in the air. "Do as Hell says, or I'll be the one to throw down on you."

Fern felt her right eye twitch. What did "throw down on you" even mean? Whatever it meant, it couldn't be good news for Belle. And in that moment, she became protective of her namesake.

"What's it to be?" Slade growled, aiming a Colt at the ceiling and firing until everyone's ears were ringing.

That did it. Fern wasn't about to let their playacting

endanger her acute hearing. She jerked her derringer out of her pocket and aimed it at them.

Ivy laughed at the sight and drew a six-gun.

Fern blinked in surprise. Her sister must have been practicing her fast draw because she was really quick with a gun. She glanced down at her derringer, realizing it was a lady's or gambler's weapon made for close action. She was outgunned and knew it. She glanced around the room. None of the men were drawing their weapons or throwing down, as that was what the term must mean. Didn't Belle have security or something?

She noticed Craig move in her peripheral vision, but she didn't look directly at him in case the two obnoxious Hellions noticed he was making a move. She realized he was opening the top of the piano and reaching inside. She'd better distract, so she aimed her tiny derringer and pulled the trigger. A pathetic amount of smoke and a soft bang was all she got out of it.

Ivy laughed and drew her other Colt .44. "Give it up, Belle. We're taking over. I'll be sleeping on your feather mattress here on out."

"She's got that right." Slade stepped up beside Fern, still brandishing both six-guns. "Hellions own this town now."

"Think again." Craig ran forward brandishing a long, black whip.

Fern just stared in shock. A whip?

Craig snapped his whip several times, sent it coiling, snakelike, so fast it looked like a blur, and jerked the guns out of the Hellions hands. He kicked the Colts so hard they skittered across the room out of reach.

"That's rich." Slade laughed so hard he bent over double. "When'd you learn to do that?"

"Not fair." Ivy put her hands on her hips and glared at Craig. "Nobody said anything about whips."

Fern simply stood there, looking back and forth between her friends. Guns? Whips? Guess she hadn't been in the country long enough to learn any useful skills. Obviously, out here, singing could only take you so far.

As if that confrontation released the other participants in the drama, the room broke out in a melee of pistol shooting, fisticuffs, and bottle brandishing with the ladies in white pinafores looking to win the battle before it ever got outside.

Finally, Fern had had enough. Belle would never have put up with outlaws breaking furniture and messing up her beautiful saloon, much less taking over the town. She'd have booted them out the swinging doors.

"Out!" she hollered using the power of her well-trained voice that could carry across a room twice the size of the saloon. "Take your fight outside."

Most folks in the saloon looked her way but didn't make a move one way or another.

"Hell, Ivy, Craig, get those people out of here before they destroy my furniture." Fern stuck her derringer in her pocket, put her hands on her hips, and glared at them.

Slade leaned toward her, eyes squinting as he looked her over. "Did you just call me 'Hell'?"

She jerked out her derringer and pointed it at his chest. "Get out of here and take your gang or pay the price."

Ivy put a hand on Slade's arm. "And I thought we'd gotten into our roles. It's okay, Belle...I mean, Fern. We'll take this shoot-out outdoors. Sorry we went off script."

As they turned away and ushered the other participants ahead of them, Fern tucked her derringer back in her pocket, feeling a deep satisfaction. Nothing had been damaged and the Hellions wouldn't be back.

"That voice of yours is quite the defense." Craig rolled up his whip.

"What?" She glanced at him, shaking her head as if coming out of a trance.

"You commanded them to go and they went."

She could hear the shoot-out continuing outside. "Aren't we supposed to be out there?"

He shrugged. "Don't you think we put on enough of a show in here?"

"Your whip was sure a show. Where'd you learn to do that? And you just happened to have it inside the piano?"

"Once Slade got the role of Hell and Ivy the one as his first lieutenant, I didn't trust them anymore."

"You didn't trust them?" She felt a laugh start to bubble up, but she quelled it because he still looked serious.

"A surprise element is always the way to go in the shoot-out."

"I had no idea this town took its reenactment so seriously."

"Well, the truth is…you just never know what'll happen at the Ruffians versus Hellions shoot-out."

"Obviously not. But a whip?"

"Saved you, didn't it?"

"Yeah, it did."

"You won't bring a puny derringer to a six-gun shootout again, will you?"

"No, I can't say I will."

"Okay. That's settled." He walked over to the piano, raised the lid, slipped his whip inside, and shut it again.

"Backup is good," she said because she could think of absolutely nothing else to say.

"Surprise is even better." And he grinned as he put an arm around her waist. "What about that feather bed upstairs?"

"Bed…any bed sounds really good about now."

"You know, this is the last of the big events. Do you think we could slip away and go to the cabin?"

"That'd be wonderful, but I think we have to see it to the end."

He cocked his head to the side, looking over the batwing doors. "How much longer do you think they'll be out there?"

"I doubt they'll stop until they've fired all the blanks."

"My thought, too."

"I'm not going out there. I had enough of the shoot-out in here."

"Me, too." He glanced toward the bar. "Tell you what, let's make ourselves great big chocolate sundaes, or caramel, if you prefer."

"I prefer both. And that's exactly what I need about now." She looked up at him. "I'll tell you something. It was disconcerting to see my sister with a dagger between her teeth."

"I thought she appeared pretty authentic."

"It was that look in her eyes."

"Remind me never to cross her." Craig headed for the bar, keeping Fern in tow.

"That goes double for me." She hopped up on a stool and looked over the top of the bar. "I want whipped cream, nuts, and a cherry on top."

"Your wish is my command." Craig walked behind the

bar. "Maybe we ought to change sides of the bar and let somebody play music while we make sundaes."

"One thing is for sure, I'm ready for a change after that whip-wielding performance from you."

"Think we should include it in our act?"

"Let me give that one some thought." She rested her elbow on top of the bar and took a deep breath. Finally, a little peace and quiet…well, except for the noise from the shoot-out.

And then everything went quiet outside.

She caught Slade's eye, knowing it couldn't be a good thing.

He stood completely still, like an animal that senses approaching danger.

Sheriff Calhoun pushed the batwing doors open and stepped inside. He looked dead serious. "The stalker's got Storm."

Fern felt chilled to the bone.

Chapter 36

FERN CLUTCHED THE EDGE OF THE BAR WITH BOTH hands, feeling as if she might faint at the news. Storm? Innocent Storm taken? How was it possible? She started to shake, trembling from head to toe so hard she felt as if she might fall off the barstool. Craig rushed around the bar and took her in his arms, pressing her close to his chest. She could hear the strong beat of his heart and feel the trembling that had somehow transferred from her to him. And yet she could think of only one thing—Simon had to be stopped before he hurt Storm.

Sheriff Calhoun walked deeper into the saloon, bootheels hitting the wood floor hard and heavy. He stopped beside them.

Fern looked up. "Is she okay?"

"For now, yes."

Fern closed her eyes in relief. At least that was something good that she could hang on to.

Sheriff Calhoun cleared his throat.

Fern looked at him again. She saw pity and sadness mixed with determination in his dark eyes. "What is it?"

"He'll trade Storm for you."

"No!" Craig crushed her to him. "I won't let that man get his hands on Fern. No way, no how."

"We sent for a top hostage negotiator. A Texas Ranger is on his way. He should be here soon."

"Good." Craig held her tighter.

Fern took as deep a breath as she could get, eased back from Craig, and gave him a slight smile. She had caused this problem and it was up to her to fix it. She just didn't know how to do it.

"Media is out in force. They're asking for you," Sheriff Calhoun said.

"She's not up to it." Craig glared at the sheriff.

"Will it help Storm for me to talk with them?" Fern asked. "I'll do whatever will help."

"You can appeal to him to let her go," Sheriff Calhoun said. "He might be watching everything on his cell phone. That's supposed to help, but I don't know if it will or not or if he's watching or not."

"Okay. If it comes to it, I'll talk to the press, but I'll only speak with Jennifer Sales and Eden Rafferty."

"She's not rushing into anything," Craig said. "She doesn't need more stress. We need to know about the situation first."

"There's not anything to find out." Fern eased away from Craig and stood up, wishing she was wearing jeans instead of a constricting ball gown. "I'm the one he wants, so I'm the one he gets."

"No!" Craig appeared horrified as he reached out to her.

She backed away, smoothing down the front of her fancy dress in an attempt to make it more manageable.

"Even if you give him what he wants, we can't be sure he'll actually go through with it," Sheriff Calhoun said.

"I think he would." Fern cleared her throat, so she could speak with more strength. "He's been after me all this time. He's frustrated and angry. I think he'll let her go if he gets me."

"We don't know that for a fact. You never do in these situations." Sheriff Calhoun appeared doubtful but hopeful.

Fern straightened her shoulders. "No, we don't. But I'm willing to take the chance, and no one can stop me."

"Don't even think it." Craig's voice shook with repressed emotion. "I won't let you do it. I'll take you back to the ranch and keep you there."

"No, you won't." She raised her chin in defiance. "If you love me, you'll help me right this wrong."

"Please don't say that." Craig shook his head with a bleak expression in his eyes. "Ask anything of me, but not this."

"I am asking it. I have to. A little girl's life is at stake." Fern turned to the sheriff. "I'm not waiting for other law enforcement to get here. They'll go by the book. And who knows how long they'll take to get here, get set up, and establish rapport or whatever they do. There's just not time. We go and we go now."

"Let the professionals handle it," Sheriff Calhoun said. "That's my honest best opinion in this situation."

"I agree," Craig said.

"If you two won't help me, I'll go alone." Fern started for the batwing doors, hesitated, and glanced back. "Are they at the park?"

"Yes, that's where she was with Fernando, so that's where he caught her," Sheriff Calhoun said. "I can't let you go in there alone. At the least, you need backup."

"I won't let you go alone either." Craig rubbed a hand across his jaw. "I love you and I'll do anything for you, but this...this is hard to do."

"Thank you." She walked back, gave Craig a quick hug, and then headed for the doors with him right beside her.

"He's got her at the bandstand." Sheriff Calhoun kept pace. "Deputies are there. Sydney's there, too. Our mounted patrol officers are keeping bystanders away, but the place is still crowded with innocent folks who want a front row seat."

"Is the boardwalk clear?" Craig asked in a strong voice, obviously taking charge now that he'd agreed to help.

"Yes. Spectators are being kept back, but that could change in a second if the crowd surges in any direction."

Fern heard all of that, and it made sense on one level, but on another it was simply noise. Only Storm was important now.

Outside, she paused on the boardwalk because everyone was focused on her with phones out snapping photographs. She felt shocked to the core. She was used to being the center of attention onstage. But this? How had she become the center of a media storm? She looked for a familiar face and saw Eden and Jack with Nathan livestreaming the event. She nodded in their direction to let them know she would talk with them when the time was right.

And then she turned and headed down the boardwalk with Craig on one side and Sheriff Calhoun on the other. Voices from the crowd called out questions, accusations, best wishes, curses, and everything in between. She didn't see how anyone out there could actually think she'd brought this on herself or caused this trouble for Storm. She supposed most people just didn't understand the stalker mentality, and she could forgive that because she didn't either.

When they reached Old Town Park, Slade and Ivy stood beside a sheriff's cruiser close to Oscar, who had a hand on Tater's head to keep the dog calm. Sydney erupted from the cruiser and hurried over with tears running down her cheeks. Dune followed, looking worried as he stayed close. Fern caught Sydney in her arms and hugged her tight, shivering despite the heat as the reality of the situation became clearer and more dangerous by the moment.

"My baby. How could he?" Sydney stepped back to look at Fern. "Thank you. You're here. I knew you'd come to Storm's rescue. They said we needed to wait for a Texas Ranger, but how can we? I don't want you in danger, but she's my baby."

"She is everyone's special little girl. I'll do anything and everything to help her." Fern wiped tears from Sydney's cheeks with her fingertips. "I'll make the trade. Storm is an innocent child, and she shouldn't be in this position in the first place."

"You're innocent, too." Craig stepped in close, nodding at Dune. "Just so you know, I'm against Fern going anywhere near that man."

"I get you. I surely do," Dune said. "But the longer this goes on, the more desperate that stalker will get and the more dangerous the situation will be for everyone. I'm all for officials doing their job, but right now I just want Storm out of there and safely back with us."

"I want the same thing." Craig squeezed his friend's shoulder. "It's a bad situation for all of us."

Oscar stepped up to join them. "I'm right sorry. Tater and me got the hankering for one of Elsie's burgers, or we'd have been here and stopped that guy from snatching Storm. She was entrusted to my care."

Sydney put a hand on his arm. "No, Oscar, you can't blame yourself any more than any of us can blame ourselves."

"That's right," Dune said. "Things had settled down

after all the folks who had come to see Fernando and listen to music had come and gone. The band left, too. You had every right to get something to eat."

"I should've stayed closer to her," Sydney said.

"Stop it," Sheriff Calhoun commanded. "You can all bicker later about rights and wrongs. A little girl needs us now."

"You're right that she needs us." Craig glanced around the group. "We can all find fault with ourselves and each other, but we're blameless. That stalker is the one to blame, and we need to put him out of action."

"I won't disagree one bit," Sheriff Calhoun said. "Fern, if you're really going in, then we need to do it right."

"I'm going." Fern gave everyone a determined stare so there would be no more disagreements or discussions.

"He's hunkered down with Storm in front of the band-stand. Once you make the exchange, he told us he plans to take you to the alley where he parked a truck. No matter what he said, you can't count on that being his real plan." Sheriff Calhoun stood straight and tall with concern in his eyes as he looked at Fern.

"I'm not getting into a vehicle with him." Fern shivered at the thought. "I'll get away from him before that."

"If you can get close enough and it's safe enough, grab Storm and run back toward us," Sheriff Calhoun said. "Don't worry about anything except getting as far away from him as you can get. My sniper isn't here yet, but we still have plenty of firepower."

"You can't take a chance with bystanders," Craig said.

"No chances," Sheriff Calhoun agreed. "We've cleared out the park, but there are still too many vulnerable people around here to chance stray bullets. But my deputies are well trained, so that shouldn't be an issue."

"What's he got?" Craig asked. "Gun? Knife?"

"Revolver," Sheriff Calhoun said. "Far as I can tell, it looks like he's using an antique Colt .44, so he could fit into the reenactment with other folks. He tried to get straight to Fern that way, but a deputy suspected something wasn't right and tried to arrest him. That man is on his way to the hospital now."

"Oh no." Fern felt worse all the time about the situation. "Will he be okay?"

"Yes," Sheriff Calhoun said. "Don't worry about him. You stay focused on Storm. Let us do the rest."

"I'll go with her," Craig said.

"No." Fern squeezed his arm. "You can't and you know it. We can't take the chance of setting him off."

"How are you communicating with him?" Craig asked.

"Nothing fancy. He used the mic on the bandstand to give us instructions, and that's it."

"I'm going in," Fern said. "We're wasting time talking, and I doubt he's a patient man."

"At least put on a vest for protection." Craig turned toward the sheriff. "You have extra ones, don't you?"

"No." Fern shook her head. "It'll look suspicious."

"We can fix you up," Sheriff Calhoun said. "It'll help, but Storm—"

"No thanks."

After that, Fern didn't say anything else because there wasn't anything else to say. She was going to do this— there had never been a question in her mind. She stepped off the boardwalk onto the soft green grass that led to the bandstand and her hearing turned acute. She heard the murmurs of the crowd, the *click-click* of a cooling engine, the squawk of an angry blue jay high in a tree, the resolute tread of her shoes, and finally the snorts of a bull.

She stopped and looked at Fernando. He lowered his head, bumped the metal fence surrounding the arena, and knocked off his hat. It rolled across the grass, and he stomped it flat with one huge hoof. He looked toward the bandstand, pawed the ground, and snorted again.

She realized he'd picked up the fear and concern of the people around him. He was worried about Storm, too. "It's okay. I'm going to free her now."

As if to deny her words, he shook his massive head and pawed the ground again, gouging out big clumps of grass to reveal the bare ground underneath.

"It'll be okay. You'll see." She spoke more to reassure herself than the worried bull, then straightened her shoulders in determination and continued on her path.

Finally, she got a good view of the bandstand, where two shapes crouched in front to make a smaller target. She stopped at what she considered a safe distance from being grabbed but not from being shot. It didn't matter. She was here to make a trade, and she'd do it no matter the consequences.

"I'm here," she said in a quiet voice.

"You look good. I like you as a dance hall darling." Simon had dressed as a formidable gunslinger in menacing all black with a leather holster strapped to his narrow hips. He appeared strong and resolute as he stared at her, holding Storm's small arm with one hand while holding his revolver to her head with the other. "I wanted to make this quick and easy, but you have too many friends around you all the time."

"Please let her go."

"Are you coming with me?"

"Yes."

"Is it because you finally recognize our love, or is it because you want this child free?"

"What do you think?"

"I want the truth." He jerked on Storm's arm, but she stayed stoically quiet.

"Both." She'd say or do anything to give Storm her chance to run.

"Good answer." He smiled at her, flashing white teeth. "I've missed you."

She nodded, trying to think how to get Storm away from him and yet stay out of his clutches herself.

"Did you enjoy the roses? I know they're your favorite." He flashed predatory teeth again. "I chose white for the purity of our love. I knew you'd appreciate the symbolism."

She froze on the spot as she realized the depths of his fantasy.

"Did you?"

"Yes, of course." She bought time with her words while she tried to fathom a way to free Storm without getting caught herself. She didn't see a way, no way at all, so she went ahead and edged closer, making sure she didn't trip by stepping on her long skirt or petticoats.

Simon rose to his feet, jerking Storm up with him while he kept the Colt .44 at her temple. "Come nearer, my love."

Fern took a step closer, letting her hands swing loose by her sides to appear as no threat. She felt the puny derringer in her pocket and wished she carried her pink pistol instead. Still, a glimmer of hope hit her. The gun was worthless for defense, but he didn't know that...not for sure anyway. If she could get his revolver pointed at her instead of Storm, then maybe they had a chance.

"Get over here," he ordered in a voice gone edgy. "Once I have you in my embrace, she can go."

Fern didn't believe him. If one hostage was good, two were better. And yet, she did move closer. She had to do it. She glanced down at Storm, who was watching her with narrowed eyes, no tears, and a determined set to her jaw. Fern tilted her head to the side, indicating for Storm to run toward the front of the park and safety as soon as she had the chance.

When Fern was in close enough range for Simon to grab her, she pulled out the derringer and pointed it at his face. Shocked, he jerked the revolver away from Storm and pointed it at Fern while he reached for the derringer.

"Storm, run!" she cried out.

Storm leaped away. "Fernando! I'm coming to keep you safe."

"You'll pay for that!" Simon twisted the derringer out of Fern's hand, put the Colt .44 to her head, and tugged her after Storm.

"Stop!" Simon commanded. "If you take another step, Fern dies right this minute."

Storm skidded to a stop in front of the arena. She looked back, hands clenching and unclenching at her sides, then she slowly turned to face Simon and dropped to her knees as Fernando looked on from the side. "Don't hurt her... please." Finally, tears slipped down her pink cheeks. "Take me. Let her go."

Fernando pawed the ground with a huge, black hoof, snorted loudly through outstretched nostrils, then raised his head toward the sky and emitted a deep, long bellow so full of outrage and challenge that it echoed across Old Town Park, down the boardwalk, across the vendor tents, and clear to Wildcat Road. In the wake of his outburst, silence reigned supreme.

Simon stopped in his tracks and turned to look at Fernando, all two thousand pounds of enraged bull. A long moment passed as they took the measure of each other… and Simon's face turned pale. He shoved Fern to the ground beside Storm, pointed his Colt .44 at Fernando, and pulled the trigger. It clicked on an empty chamber.

Fernando bellowed in outrage again, then leaped up, twisting his massive body in midair before he came down on all four feet with legs spread wide. He backed up, pawing the ground and lowering his head as he snorted and tossed clumps of grass-encrusted clods of dirt.

Fern felt her breath catch in her throat as the scene played out before her. If Fernando decided to come through the fence, nothing could stop him…and if Simon decided to shoot the bull or her and Storm, nothing could stop him. Things kept going from bad to worse.

She quietly slid her hand across the grass and gently touched Storm's arm, hoping the little girl could still move. Storm turned her head, staying quiet and still, as she acknowledged the touch. Fern put a fingertip to her lips, then pointed toward the sheriff and family waiting on the sidelines, so Storm would understand they needed to get up and run while they had the chance. Storm shook her head and crawled away from Simon and up to a section of the fence near Fernando. Fern could only follow, hoping she could keep them safe where they huddled together on the ground.

Simon raised his Colt .44 again, took aim, and fired, but the bullet went wild and hit the trailer.

Fernando gave Simon a deadly look, bunched his powerful shoulder muscles, lowered his massive head, and burst through the metal fence like it was soft ice cream on a hot day. He hit Simon in the stomach with his massive head and tossed him into the air. He hung there for a millisecond before he came back down and was caught by a massive shoulder that slung him to the ground, where he lay like a broken rag doll with arms and legs akimbo.

Fernando walked to Simon's crumpled form, sniffed him, then raised a huge hoof and placed it directly over the man's heart.

Fern felt her breath catch in her throat. Two thousand pounds of fury would send that hoof straight through Simon's body and drill his heart into the ground. She felt Storm stir beside her. She reached out to keep her away from harm, but Storm evaded her and walked over to Fernando.

She placed a hand on the bull's broad shoulder and murmured soft words of comfort. "I'm okay. I'm fine. I'm here."

Fernando turned his head, focused on her with dark eyes, and snorted a questioning sound.

She stroked down his long nose. "Thank you. You took care of the bad man. Let him go now, so the sheriff can take him to jail."

Fernando rubbed his nose against her hand, then slowly lifted his hoof from Simon's chest.

"Let's go home. Maybe we better rethink how to handle

this celebrity business." Storm turned, stepped over the downed fence, and Fernando followed her into the trailer.

Fern breathed a sigh of relief as she stood up, picked up the Colt .44, and checked on Simon. He still breathed, although she figured he'd be a long time recovering, and she'd bet he'd think twice before he ever stalked another woman, because every one of them just might have a big Angus bull as a friend.

She glanced up. Sydney, Slade, and all the family ran toward Fernando's arena. TV anchor Jennifer Sales stood on the boardwalk, speaking into a microphone. Eden, Jack, and Nathan were livestreaming everything, too. No doubt the entire episode would be on television, radio, and the internet. Fernando would become an even bigger hero. And he deserved it.

Love did indeed conquer all.

Chapter 37

FERN SAT ON A BENCH IN A DARKENED CORNER OF Wildcat Hall, nursing a sarsaparilla that had grown warm in her hands. Lots of folks from Wild West Days crowded the dance floor and nudged each other on the benches, laughing, talking, and gossiping about the legendary events of the day. They all felt special because most of them had been there to witness, or heard firsthand, Storm's kidnapping and rescue by Fernando, everyone's favorite new hero.

Lots more folks across the country saw the Wildcat Den's livestreaming of the dramatic rescue, as well as Jennifer Sale's on-air piece on her Dallas television station. Those were both being replayed constantly, so even more people would witness Fernando in action. All in all, it'd gone viral. That meant Fernando's website and Instagram page were burning up with hearts and comments and requests for him to appear at public events. It was phenomenal.

Fortunately, Storm and Fernando were now safely at Steele Trap Ranch with Sydney, Dune, Slade, and Ivy. Fern had talked briefly with Ivy, who'd said Storm appeared none the worse for wear after her experience. In fact, Storm was busy setting up online interviews and answering queries, but she'd vowed to keep Fernando close to home.

Much to her surprise, it wasn't just Storm and Fernando who were getting all the attention. She was receiving hits on her website with offers for gigs at major venues across the country. She was suddenly a name with a fascinating—and dangerous—backstory. Video of her wearing her silk-and-satin ball gown, brandishing a silver derringer, had sparked quite a bit of attention and speculation. The media had dubbed her the "Dance Hall Darlin' Chanteuse" and were clamoring for interviews and photographs.

Craig was caught up in all the drama, too, because Wildcat Hall was suddenly on the map for performers wanting new and different venues that might garner extra media interest. Lots of requests were rolling in from performers and their representatives.

She could still hardly believe it, but all that she and Craig had dreamed of doing had been jump-started by a stalker-turned-kidnapper. Simon was in the hospital, but soon Sheriff Calhoun would turn him over to federal authorities to enforce kidnaping charges and seek justice.

All in all, Fern felt grateful that such a negative situation had transformed into a positive outcome for so many people, setting into motion exciting events that would play out in their future, and that included bigger and better Wild West Days.

But for now, she was content to sit on the sidelines letting someone else take the stage and garner appreciation. She tapped her toe as she listened to the Red River Wranglers play onstage. They were already getting tighter as a band. She almost envied them the path they'd chosen because she was far from those heady days of discovery and wonder. And yet, there was also great pleasure in being this far along the road of life. She could look back and she could look forward, but for the moment, she preferred to be situated right here, right now.

After all was said and done, love made this the perfect

place at the perfect time with the perfect person. Craig had changed her, or she had changed for him, or they had changed together. Just in the short time she'd been back, they'd shared such intensity of emotion and such adversity in life that they could have been torn apart. Instead, everything they'd survived had drawn them closer, until now she couldn't imagine living a moment without him...just like she couldn't imagine leaving a place and people that nurtured her, protected her, and encouraged her to be more than she could ever be on her own out there. Wildcat Bluff County, she'd discovered, was a little slice of heaven on earth.

She had chosen it without knowing what was really here except Wildcat Hall Park, and yet she'd been driven by some inner instinct to change her life. Once here, she'd immersed herself in the lifestyle as if she'd been born to it. And then there was Craig, waiting for her to finally come home to him.

As if her thoughts conjured him, Craig walked out of the crowd and headed her way with a smile on his lips.

He sat down beside her, making sure they were so close together that heat sparked between them. "Are you hiding out?"

"After today? I'm thinking it might be a good idea."

He pressed a soft kiss to her cheek, chuckling softly. "You sound as if Wild West Days might have been a little bit more than you expected on your first time out."

"You think?"

He laughed harder. "Well, I have to admit seeing Ivy with a dagger clenched between her teeth might have set the whole thing off in the wrong direction."

She couldn't keep from smiling as he made light of a grueling day. He was right to put it in perspective. Anyway, Texans had a great love of laughing at themselves in their most ridiculous situations. Only this time, the stalking and kidnapping were a little beyond what might ordinarily be considered laughable. Still, he was right. It was over. It had a good ending. And the bad guy would soon be behind bars.

Craig slipped her bottle from her hand and took a sip of warm sarsaparilla. "You know, there were a lot of ways I'd thought of putting Wildcat Hall on the map, but I have to admit kidnapping and rescue weren't even close to being on the list."

"Please don't leave out the dramatic exploits of the Dance Hall Darlin' Chanteuse to drive social media for the Hall." She batted her eyelashes at him in a parody of a Southern belle.

"Never." He kissed her cheek again. "I think that low-cut gown with all the gewgaws was what put you over the top. I mean, who knew you could, and would, hide a fancy derringer in a pocket of that long skirt. Makes a guy wonder just what else you've got under all those petticoats."

"Wouldn't you just like to find out?"

"Yeah. I sure would." He grinned, took a sip, and let his eyes roam over the décolletage of her gown. "I've got to tell you that T-shirts and jeans won't cut it anymore."

"No?"

"There's not enough mystery."

"You like mystery?"

"I like you…and you're the biggest mystery in my life."

"I am?"

"You almost gave me a heart attack when you whipped out that gun and went for the stalker," he said.

"That's the mystery?"

"How could I not love a woman who braves everything to save a little girl from a kidnapper?"

"Well, it was sort of my fault, and—"

"Never say that again. He was at fault. He made that choice. And he'll pay the price."

"True." She leaned over and rested her head against Craig's broad shoulder. "I could stay here with you forever."

"Do you really mean it?"

"Yes." She raised her head and looked into his eyes. "I've learned a lot since I've been back."

"It has been pretty eventful. I wish I could've made it better for you."

"Without you, I wouldn't have survived it at all."

"You'd have found a way."

She shook her head. "I'm really sorry about your barn."

"Just gives me an excuse to build a new one."

"How many good spins do you think we can put on all our questionable adventures?"

"Fern," he said, turning serious. "We can make our lives the best spin of all, if you'd just…"

"What?"

He held out his hand. "Come on. They don't need us here tonight. We ought to make this our time. We've given enough to others for now."

"Our time?"

"Yeah. We don't have to carry the world on our shoulders."

"You're right. It's felt like it's been that way since I got back."

"It's time to turn it around for us."

"How?"

"Come on. I've got an idea."

She let him lead her out of the Hall, past the rocking-out

band, past the revelers in colorful clothing from two time periods, past the outer room with patrons bellied up to the bar, and into a night made for lovers with bright stars overhead, the scent of roses in the air, and the sound of cicadas.

He kept going, weaving in and out of the trees and shrubs and flower beds until he arrived at the big cabin. He stopped and looked at her.

"Are you disappointed?"

"In the cabin?"

"That I couldn't think of someplace more special to bring you?"

"With the town full up for Wild West Days, I'm not sure we have any other options."

"I wanted it to be romantic for you."

"Craig, you're romantic, so wherever you are *is* romantic." She placed a hand over his heart and felt the soft fabric of his gambler's vest, so in contrast to his usual clothes that she felt a little thrill.

"Thanks." He walked with her up the stairs, unlocked the front door, and ushered her inside.

As always, the room was neat from the Settelmeyers' gentle ministrations and cozy with the cowboy knickknacks and furniture. Soft lamplight illuminated the room.

"Will you sit on the sofa?"

"Okay." She was sincerely beginning to wonder what was going on with him. "Remember, I don't need any more surprises."

"Not even good ones?"

"Good is okay." She sat down, but she felt a little on edge with anticipation.

He walked into the kitchen, poured two glasses of wine, and came back to hand her one.

She took a small sip, feeling it heat her as it slid to her stomach. Wine was probably a good idea. She needed the warmth and relaxation. She drank a little more, then set down the glass.

He sat beside her, set his glass on the coffee table beside hers, and turned to face her. He reached into the pocket of his vest and drew out a ring of rose gold—no stone, no adornment, simply a circle representing endless love. He placed it in the palm of his hand, then closed his fingers over it.

She felt her heart beat a little faster. "Do you plan to ask me something?"

"I'm having second thoughts."

"Why?"

"It hasn't been the best of times…maybe it's even been the worst of times."

"It's been rough, yes, but I learned something important."

"What?"

She opened his hand and picked up the ring between two fingers. "Pretty."

"Like you."

"And like you."

He gave her a slow smile. "What did you learn?"

"Love. It's all about love—not fast pace, distant places, or applause. It's about being with the one you love." She held up the ring, where it gleamed in the lamplight. "Craig, will you marry me?"

"You're my love…my forever love. I'd marry you a dozen times over."

And as he placed the ring on her finger, she heard music…the beginning of a song she knew she would compose for him and him alone.

Acknowledgments

One afternoon, I sat in a comfy rocker on the wide porch of a cedar cabin overlooking the Red River, drinking sweet tea and enjoying the scent of pine trees while Joe Snow strummed his acoustic Martin guitar and Laura Romberg played her Choctaw flute. I'm grateful to them for their personal insights into making and sharing music.

Gerald Bailey of Devils River Outfitters took me on a canoe ride—deep in Texas near Del Rio where the country is hot and the river is cool—while he explained the intricacies of player pianos. Lots of thanks go to him for the fun, as well as the research.

Once more, a shout out goes to Brandon, Christina, Luke, Lank, Logan, and Laren of Gee Cattle Ranch. We shared a great trail ride around Sardis Lake on a beautiful spring day full of light and laughter. Naturally, the further adventures of Fernando came up and we made plans for my favorite Angus bull.

While sharing chocolate at a writer's conference, I brainstormed names for Fernando's ladylove with my editor, Deb Werksman. She suggested Daisy Sue, so much appreciation goes to her for this name.

Over a cozy campfire, Darmond Gee shared important information about how bulls like Fernando come to be socialized, like other animals, by gentle care and love. Once more, thanks go to him for sharing his wisdom.

Stan Briggs and Jan Briggs Montgomery were my inspiration to create Wildcat Bluff Mounted Patrol, so they deserve a big thank-you. They're always there for others, whether it's on the back of a horse, straddling a motorcycle, or at the wheel of a vehicle.

Thanks to Sabine Starr for the use of her fascinating Wildcat Falls legend from her historical novel *Belle Gone Bad*. I brought the story up-to-date in Wildcat Bluff to showcase how historical events impact present-day life.

Rachel Caine continues to inspire me…not only as an author for such notable bestselling books as *Ash and Quill*, *Still House Lake*, *Honor Among Thieves*, and the Morganville Vampire series, but also as a supportive and generous friend.

One day I ventured into the backwoods, took a canoe down the Kiamichi River, and arrived at the red rock enclave of the Williams—Buck-Saw, Hot-Rod, and Reed-the-Steed—to consult with them on the historic construction of my one-room schoolhouse and the trees appropriate for the Sure-Shot memorial grove. I appreciate their generous contributions to my book.

About the Author

Kim Redford is the bestselling author of Western romance novels. She grew up in Texas with cowboys, cowgirls, horses, cattle, and rodeos. She divides her time between homes in Texas and Oklahoma, where she's a rescue cat wrangler and horseback rider—when she takes a break from her keyboard. Visit her at kimredford.com.